W E

ON THE LEVELS

An addictive crime thriller full of twists

DAVID HODGES

Detective Kate Hamblin Mystery book 8

JOFFE BOOKS

First published 2020
Joffe Books, London
www.joffebooks.com

ISBN 978-1-78931-577-6

This book is dedicated to my wife, Elizabeth, for all her love, patience and support over so many wonderful years, and to my late mother and father, whose faith in me to one day achieve my ambition as a writer remained steadfast throughout their lifetime and whose tragic passing has left a hole in my life that will never be filled.

AUTHOR'S NOTE

Although the action of this novel takes place in the real geographical area of Avon and Somerset, the story itself and all the characters therein are fictitious. At the time of writing, there is no police station in Highbridge. This entirely fictitious setting was created from the author's imagination and there is no connection between any existing police station or personnel in the force and the content of the novel. I would also point out that I have used some poetic licence in relation to the local police structure as well as the police procedures that are followed, in order to meet the requirements of the plot. The novel is intended to be primarily a crime thriller and does not profess to be a detailed police procedural, even though the policing background depicted in the novel is broadly in accord with the national picture. I trust that these small departures from fact will not spoil the reading enjoyment of serving or retired police officers, for whom I have the utmost respect.

David Hodges, 2020

BEFORE THE FACT

Autumn 1644

They came at just after eleven at night, their torches flaring in the mist that draped the Somerset Levels, their chants of 'Witch, witch, witch' echoing through the still night air. In her lonely cottage, the old woman cowered fearfully in the corner of her tiny bedroom as she listened to them approach.

Tom Sharpe, the magistrate and self-appointed preacher, led the baying mob. His lean face set in a cruel mask, he gripped a blazing torch in one hand, and in the other held a weighty leather Bible.

Behind him, his disparate entourage, which included the blacksmith, the publican and several farmers and withy workers, kept close together as they followed the rutted track across the treacherous marshland, acutely conscious of the deep *rhynes* bordering it on each side. These man-made drainage ditches, dug by successive generations in a bid to reclaim the peat-rich soil once drowned by the sea, could swallow a man whole if he strayed too far in the wrong direction, and in the clinging mist which hid them from view, it was easy to make a fatal mistake.

Back in the warmth and relative security of the village inn, with full bellies and brains fogged by pints of Somerset's strong "scrumpy" cider, they had been only too willing to follow Sharpe out into the night. Now, enveloped in the curling skeins of marsh mist, their courage was beginning to falter, their chants becoming less confident as they peered into the gloom around them.

Their hearts jumped at every sound — the sudden squawk and splash of some marsh fowl startled at their approach, the shrill cry of a tawny owl emerging from the gloom to fly low over their heads like a ghost. They started involuntarily when a solitary willow tree materialised like the hazy silhouette of some visitant from another world, its crooked branches reaching towards them like a giant claw. In the shifting, swirling clouds, whose sepulchral chill penetrated to their very bones, they saw other things too, grotesque, unnatural shapes that were solely products of their own wild imaginings, conjured up by centuries of myth and legend.

It was said that there were strange, terrible things out here on the marsh, apparitions that no god-fearing man should see. Foremost among these were the so-called "hinky-punks," or witch fires, reputed to be the souls of unbaptised babies or omens of impending death. Like sirens, these flickering, blue will-o'-the-wisp lights bewitched the wayfarer, luring them out onto the marsh and their inevitable doom.

Two locals had disappeared in the last three weeks, one of them the comely Margaret Webber, daughter of Hal, the publican, and the other the blacksmith's idiot son, Oliver, who was much loved by the people of the village. On both occasions, they had been snatched away on a night when the witch fires had been seen, and though no bodies had ever been found, few doubted that witchery was behind it, drawing them into the clutches of the treacherous peat bogs, like John Bright's three cattle the month before.

Everyone knew who was responsible for it all — the hideous old hag who lived out here in her isolated cottage.

Had she not cursed young Oliver the day before, merely for refusing her a penny for her posy of herbs? And Sharpe's lass — had the foolish girl not mocked the creature when she had tripped and fallen over in the street, earning herself a stream of vicious imprecations?

Furthermore, was the old crone herself not also known to make mysterious potions from the plants she gathered out on the marsh, which she offered for sale in the village, promising cures for everything from the ague to high fever, and punishing drafts to be administered to those deserving of punishment? And most significant of all, had she not been seen by credible witnesses conversing with her two "familiars" — the cat and the goat — both of which were as black as the Devil's heart, and plainly communed with Satan himself on her behalf?

As Tom Sharpe had solemnly declared, the evidence was overwhelming. The only thing needed now was physical proof that Molly Clavey was indeed in league with the Devil and deserved the dreadful punishment that custom and the law decreed should be administered in cases of witchcraft.

And Sharpe was supremely confident that the "pricker" he had hired from the next village would provide that proof. The pricker carried a wooden dagger-like instrument with a long, straight blade which was commonly used to test the moles, warts and birthmarks found on the body of an accused. If the blemish, when "pricked," did not bleed or appear to cause pain, then the presence of the Devil's mark was established beyond all doubt. Prickers' tools had already sent many adepts in the black arts to the gallows, and Sharpe had little doubt of its success in this case — especially as only he knew that the device this particular pricker used had a hollow handle and a retractable blade, which guaranteed there would be no sign of injury or pain when pressed against the selected mark.

It was vital to Sharpe that Molly Clavey's guilt should be publicly proven. Sharpe was a clever, educated man who no more believed in witchcraft than he did in fairies and ghost lights. But the important thing was that the superstitious village folk did, for unbeknown to any save himself and his conscience, he nursed a terrible secret, one which he knew would surely commit him to the gallows were it ever to be discovered. Tom Sharpe knew very well how Margaret Webber and Oliver Cary had died, for he had killed them both.

It had happened in a moment of madness, though he didn't regret his action. The Webber harlot had asked for all she'd got. Having used her lustful wiles to lure him out to the marsh for a carnal assignation, she had then mocked him for his lack of sexual prowess and threatened to tell her father he had molested her unless Sharpe paid her to keep silent. In his fury, he had throttled her as she stood taunting him, consigning her body to the bog. But poor, weak-minded Oliver, hiding nearby, had witnessed the deed and, jumping up, had started to run away. He did regret killing Oliver and casting him into the bog with the scheming harlot, but it had been necessary for his own salvation. To divert suspicion from his own person, however, he'd needed a suitable scapegoat, and what better candidate than Molly Clavey?

He had no compunction about leading this ragged band of men across the stone bridge towards the old woman's cottage, his only emotion the desire to finish the whole business as quickly as possible.

He was shouting her name even before they reached her front door and he raised the Bible so all might see his righteousness. 'Molly Clavey, where be thee? Show thyself before God.'

There was no response. No lights were visible in the windows of the cottage. All was still.

'Open the door, Molly,' he shouted again, 'or we will break it down.'

Still, nothing stirred, and an angry murmur ran through his supporters. Finally, Hal Webber took matters into his own hands. 'Burn her out,' he snarled. 'See if her dark master will put out the flames and save her.'

The mob surged forward before Sharpe could stop them, the flimsy door bursting open beneath the force of a muscular shoulder. Webber was the first to toss his torch inside, with several others following suit. Within seconds, the flames had caught on the interior furnishings and the ruddy glow mushroomed into a ferocious blaze. As the mob shrank back from the cottage, the fire spread rapidly to the upper floor and ignited the thatch, burning off the mist and lighting up the night sky like a giant beacon.

Molly Clavey stood no chance, and her screams could be heard even above the roaring flames. Standing at her bedroom window, silhouetted against the blaze, her blasphemous curses fell like molten lava on the watchers beneath. She raised one bony arm to point directly at Sharpe. 'A plague on thee, Tom Sharpe,' she ranted. 'My demons will come for thee and thine this very night.' Then, with a last terrible cry, she was gone, devoured by the inferno.

Now much subdued by what they had witnessed, Sharpe and his followers made sure they found and slaughtered the black goat, casting its body into the fire, to be consumed with its mistress. But they could find no trace of the old woman's cat.

Quietly, they made their way back across the marsh.

'Ye'll have no need of me now then?' the pricker said.

'Nay,' Sharpe replied soberly. ''Tis done, fair and square, and there be an end to it.'

Yet despite his outward confidence and the sense of finality his tone conveyed, Sharpe nursed a deep sense of foreboding, which stayed with him all the way home. The old crone may have been burned to a cinder, yet her curses continued to ring in his ears, and he could still see her sinister gowned figure in his mind's eye, framed against the blaze in the window of her cottage, one arm outstretched and pointing accusingly in his direction.

Sharpe and his long-suffering wife occupied a big, isolated house a mile or so outside the village, so he soon parted company with the others. But once alone, his uneasiness mounted, and he was not content until he was bolting the door firmly behind him.

His relief was short-lived, however.

When he mounted the narrow staircase and entered his bedchamber, he saw in the flickering light of the candles on the bedside table that a black cat was crouching on his bed, its back arched and its green eyes blazing at him as it bared its teeth in a vicious snarl. With a horrified gasp, he reached for his sword. But even as he did so, the creature sprang from the bed and streaked through the partially open window, his blade scything through empty air. Striding to the window, he saw that the cat was gone, vanishing into the night from whence it had come, and he was on the point of turning back into the room and his sleeping wife when he stiffened involuntarily.

Out on the marsh, the ruddy glow of the burning cottage was still visible through the mist. Then, as he stared, other lights materialised before his gaze — tiny, blue elfin tongues that hovered in the shifting, swirling nothingness, rising and falling, as if indulging in some abominable dance.

Not much is known about Tom Sharpe's descent into madness. According to parish records, which have been preserved in the local museum to this day, he was discovered by his servants the next morning, gibbering and frothing at the mouth on the floor of his bedchamber, while lying in his bed, in place of his attractive wife, they found the hideous shrivelled corpse of an old hag . . .

CHAPTER 1

The bar at Highbridge police station was packed and, despite the no-smoking notices all around the room, a heavy bluish haze hung in the air in the suffused glow of the strip lights.

The heavy-set figure of Detective Inspector Ted Roscoe stood at the centre of it all. Whisky glass in one hand and fat Crown cigar in the other, he gesticulated to his audience in wide sweeping gestures as he recounted tales of his thirty-year prowess as the county's "greatest detective."

Detective Sergeant Kate Lewis, sitting in an alcove with her detective constable partner and husband, Hayden, watched those crowded around their ex-boss with a wry smile. It wasn't every day that an experienced detective like Roscoe retired, and it was therefore not surprising that his farewell celebration had attracted colleagues from all over the Avon and Somerset Police area. That said, she could not help wondering a little maliciously whether they had turned up to give him a good send-off or had come simply for the free booze and to satisfy themselves that he really was going.

For Ted Roscoe was not exactly the most popular DI on the force. His aggressive, bullying approach towards those under him — in particular his misogynistic attitude towards female officers — had certainly not endeared him to his colleagues. On top of this, in later years he had acquired an unenviable reputation as a senior ranker who always looked after number one, cuffing any crime likely to cause him grief and ensuring he was never short of a scapegoat to carry the can if things went wrong.

Kate and Hayden had suffered more than most during his time as departmental head. In Kate's case, it had been abundantly plain from his frequent acid jibes that his antagonism towards her stemmed not only from the fact that she was a woman, but also because he resented and felt threatened by her sharp mind and decisive style, attributes which he had not been able to match. As for Hayden, Roscoe had made no secret of the contempt in which he held her laid-back, slightly eccentric partner. With his privileged public-school background and plummy way of speaking, Hayden was the absolute antithesis of the macho, hard-drinking, hard-swearing cop Roscoe admired and modelled himself on.

Unsurprising, therefore, that neither Kate nor Hayden were sorry to see their boss go, and they had only turned up for his farewell celebrations because, having served under him for several years, it was seen as their moral duty to make the effort.

'Guv'nor seems to be having fun,' Hayden commented drily in his usual slow drawl, his gaze wandering to the buffet laid out on three trestle tables opposite where they sat.

Kate nodded, her pretty, freckled face smiling at him as she smoothed her long auburn hair back over her ears with both hands. 'Well, think of what Andy Warhol said: "*everyone will be world-famous for fifteen minutes.*" So maybe this is his moment.'

'Hardly qualifies as world-famous, though, does it?' Hayden said. 'Not even county-famous actually, and anyway, infamous would be a more accurate description where he's concerned.'

'Too right, but he got a nice farewell pressie anyway. Those expensive smartphones are only just out, I believe, *and* the case was monogrammed with his initials. That lot must have cost a pretty penny, which means his collection must have netted quite a few quid.'

'Probably because everyone was so relieved to see him finally going.' He frowned. 'But more importantly, when do we eat?'

Kate chuckled, running her sharp blue eyes over her husband in his creased yellow shirt and pink jeans with critical amusement.

'I wondered how long it would be before you thought about your stomach,' she said, focusing on his ample girth. 'But you'll have to wait a bit. He's still in full flow and we can't start until he does.'

Hayden groaned. 'Gordon Bennett. That could be hours. Chap could end up with an ulcer waiting so long.'

She shook her head in resignation, recalling the plate of egg and chips he had demolished in the staff canteen only an hour before,.

'The way you're going, you're more likely to end up with a coronary than an ulcer,' she said. 'And, incidentally, why on earth didn't you bring a change of shirt with you? As usual, you look like a bundle of shit.'

'Hey, steady on, old girl. I keep telling you that that sort of foul language doesn't befit a lady.'

She snorted, well aware of his old-fashioned antipathy towards her liberal use of expletives. 'And as I keep telling *you*, Hayd, I'm not by any stretch of the imagination a lady.' She rolled her eyes towards the ceiling. 'Bloody hell, why can't you just ditch all that pompous, public-school bollocks? You're a police detective now, not a member of the sodding aristocracy or the Bullingdon Club!'

He looked down his nose at her. 'Doesn't mean I should lower my standards, does it?'

'You already have, fat man, and we've had this conversation more times than I can remember. You're the untidiest arsehole I've ever met, and that's putting it mildly.'

Their spat was abruptly terminated as Roscoe's muscular figure materialised before them, drink in one hand and cigar in the other, smoke trailing in his wake. His slab of a face, with its bushy eyebrows and Stalin-like moustache, was flushed with alcohol and his boot-button eyes bored into Kate with undisguised hostility.

'How kind of the force's "ace detective" to come and see her nasty old boss off,' he sniped thickly, swaying a little. 'Looking to step into his shoes now, are we, Kate?'

She shrugged. 'Not at all, guv. I just wanted to make sure you didn't change your mind about leaving.'

He treated her to a wolfish grin. 'Touché, Lewis. And you can bet your bottom dollar that I won't.' He scowled. 'In fact, wild horses wouldn't keep me from leaving this shithole and all the maggots that work here. The sooner I'm out of the place the better.'

'The "maggots" would probably agree with you there, guv,' Hayden chimed in with a pleasant smile.

Roscoe studied him for a second. 'Clever prick, aren't you, Lewis? But you'll never make a proper copper as long as you've got a hole in your arse.'

'Be a pretty constipated copper if I *didn't* have one,' Hayden responded, his smile broadening.

Roscoe seemed about to say something else, then changed his mind. 'Anyway,' he continued, turning away from Hayden to stare at Kate again, 'I hear you might be about to get a leg-up.'

She frowned. 'Meaning?'

He took a swig from his whisky glass. 'Acting DI, I heard — until they find someone a lot more capable of doing the job permanently, of course.'

'Of course,' she repeated. 'After all, it would take a really *special* person to occupy the shoes of such a celebrated super-sleuth as Detective Inspector Ted Roscoe.'

His grin faded. He drew on his cigar and released a cloud of smoke in her direction. 'Be interesting to see how long it takes you to cock up the role,' he grated. 'I'll be watching from the sidelines, don't you worry.'

She shrugged. 'That's if you can keep sober long enough, guv,' she said and abruptly stood up. 'Come on, Hayd. Time for home, I think. Looks like we've already overstayed our welcome here.'

'You'll miss me, Kate,' Roscoe growled as she pushed past him, almost knocking the cigar out of his hand.

'Like a rash,' she returned, adding over her shoulder, 'Enjoy the first day of the rest of your life.'

Then, nodding to a couple of her departmental colleagues, she made for the door with as much dignity as she could manage — only to collide with a burly uniformed colleague on his way in.

'Ah, Kate,' the late-turn inspector exclaimed, stepping back to allow Hayden and herself to exit. 'I thought I'd find you up here.'

'Not for very much longer,' she replied grimly.

The inspector grinned. 'Not staying for the nosh then?'

'Hardly.' Her eyes narrowed. 'So, what's up?'

He cut in front of Hayden and followed her down the stairs. 'You wouldn't fancy a little job on your way home, would you?'

Hayden groaned, but she ignored him and turned to face the inspector. 'What sort of a job?'

'A bit of church desecration?'

'A bit of what?'

'Desecration. We've had a call from a local vicar. Says his church has been done over by vandals. One of my units is there and she has asked for CID to attend. 'Trouble is your whole department seems to be knocking it back rather heavily.'

Kate sighed. 'Okay, sir, we'll take a look. Just give us the address, will you?'

Hayden wore a scowl when they climbed into her Mazda MX5 a few minutes later. 'Why the devil did you agree to this? Gordon Bennett, we'd have been better off staying in the bar. They'll all be tucking into the food soon.'

She threw him a sideways glance as they pulled away. 'Just think of all those calories you've avoided,' she said with an innocent smile. 'And anyway, I'm sure I can rustle us up a cheese sandwich when we get home.'

* * *

The ancient parish church of St Stephen's stood on a small parcel of land in one corner of a minor crossroads just outside the village, and the hallowed building with its Norman spire was not difficult to find. Ghostly beams of light streamed out through the stained-glass windows and through the open porch doors, illuminating the gravel path from the front gate. A marked police patrol car was parked at the kerb in front of the gate.

Kate had always had a thing about churches. It was years since she had last attended a service and, far from providing the spiritual comfort and reassurance that churches were said to offer, the places gave her the creeps. She shivered involuntarily as she opened the wooden gate, and she and Hayden made their way to the porch or narthex, casting sidelong glances at the mist curling around the crooked gravestones on either side.

When they stepped in through the doorway, they saw a man dressed in a tweed jacket and creased, grey trousers talking to a uniformed woman police constable at the far end of the nave. She ushered him towards them.

'The Reverend Jacob Truly, Sarge,' she said from a few yards away, her raised voice producing faint echoes. 'He lives in the rectory next door.'

They met in the middle of the stone-flagged aisle. Briefly introducing Hayden and herself, she studied him with faint amusement.

Truly was a small, rotund man in his forties, with a twitchy expression and a completely bald head that gleamed strangely in the lights from the overhead chandeliers as if it had been recently polished. He sported old-fashioned side-whiskers, strongly reminiscent of a sketch of a Victorian gentleman. He had been wringing his hands repeatedly as he'd tripped towards them on short, quick steps, bringing to her mind the white rabbit in Disney's animated version of Lewis Carroll's *Alice In Wonderland.* So strong was the image that she'd half-expected to hear him muttering the words, "*I'm late, I'm late for a very important date*" as he'd approached.

'The Rev Truly saw lights in the churchyard from his bedroom window while he was getting ready for bed and went to investigate,' the policewoman explained. 'When he got over here, he found the church had been vandalised.'

'Disgraceful,' Truly snapped. 'Absolutely disgraceful. Come and look at this.'

Turning quickly, he led the way back along the nave to a wrought-iron rail separating the rest of the church from the chancel. Even before the detectives followed him into the chancel, they could see why he had been so affronted. The gruesome-looking head of a goat had been placed on the altar table on top of the cross, which had been laid flat on the altar cloth. The head had obviously been recently severed, its bulging eyes still registering the moment of its execution while blood had soaked through the altar cloth and formed a pool on the floor in front of the table. A few feet from the altar, a curious geometric symbol resembling a five-pointed star had been painted or sprayed in black on the flagstones.

'A pentagram,' Kate said confidently. 'Otherwise known as the "Star of David," which also has something to do with black magic, I believe.'

Hayden shook his head. 'Sorry, but that's not quite correct. You're right in calling it a pentagram because it has five points. But the pentagram has nothing to do with the "Star of David," which has six points and is the religious symbol of Zionism, as displayed on the national flag of Israel.'

'Indeed?' Kate retorted sarcastically. 'Well, thank you so much for putting me right.'

Hayden continued, unabashed. 'You're on the ball about the black magic thing, though. Although the pentagram has a different meaning to different cultures, nowadays it is very much associated with the occult and black magic.'

Truly nodded. 'Especially here,' he said, lowering his voice to a whisper and glancing nervously about the church. 'If you look, you can see that the sign is inverted, with two points of the star at the top and one at the bottom, instead of the other way around, representing evil and the overturn of order—'

'And symbolising the goat of Mendes — or the Devil — attacking the heavens with his horns,' Hayden finished for him.

Truly threw him an appreciative glance. 'Exactly. It is the mark of Lucifer, intended to desecrate this church and to defile God's holy name.'

Hayden beamed at Kate triumphantly and as the minister moved away, she threw him an old-fashioned look, murmuring sarcastically, 'Well, who's a clever boy then?'

The Reverend bent down to pick up one of two silver candlesticks that were lying in the pool of blood in front of the altar table.

'Would you leave those there, please, Reverend,' she called out, in a sharper tone than she had intended. 'I'd like to get some photographs taken before all this is disturbed. Then we'll have to have both the crosses fingerprinted by one of our Scenes of Crime officers.'

Truly frowned. 'Fingerprinted? How long will that take? I'd really like to get this mess cleared up as soon as possible.'

'It won't be tonight anyway. I'll have to ask you to you lock the church up until tomorrow morning, so our team can attend first thing.'

'Tomorrow morning?' the minister echoed. 'That's most inconvenient.' Then he released his breath in a heavy sigh of resignation. 'Well, under the circumstances, I suppose I can. There are no services or functions tomorrow. But we don't normally lock our church, as we feel it should be available to anyone who wishes to worship here — and, of course, I am next door at night anyway, which is something of a deterrent.'

Kate raised an eyebrow. 'You being there tonight didn't deter the vandals who did this, though, did it? And I'm assuming you didn't actually see anyone in the churchyard when you noticed the lights?'

He shook his head. 'Not a soul, I'm afraid.'

'I rest my case. So, maybe you should make a point of locking the place in future.'

'Point taken, Sergeant,' he replied stiffly. 'I'll talk to the church council, but they weren't agreeable to the idea after the previous incidents, so I don't think they'll change their minds this time.'

Kate's eyes narrowed. 'Previous incidents? Are you saying this sort of thing has happened before?'

The Reverend Truly nodded. 'There, er, have been other occasions, but none as bad as this. We had a decapitated black cockerel nailed to one of the entrance doors about a month ago, then some rather offensive corn dollies hung from the beam over the porch. Gravestones have also been damaged, upended or daubed with graffiti during the night.'

'Did you report any of these incidents to the police?'

'At the start, yes. Then I thought that local vandals were responsible, and they would eventually tire of their nasty fun and games, so I didn't bother after that. But this is just too much.'

'Well, this is a bit more serious than yobbish vandalism,' Kate commented. 'Have you any idea who could be responsible, other than the local yobs?'

He shook his head. 'There are any number of groups who hold virulent, anti-Christian views, Sergeant, and churches everywhere are regularly targeted. Satanists, Wiccans, atheists, I could provide you with quite a list.'

'But there's no one you can think of who has a particular axe to grind against this church?'

He hesitated. 'Not exactly. I do have a suspicion, but it's only a suspicion and I'd rather not say until I am sure.'

'Though you have a name, right?'

He looked uncomfortable. 'As I said, I don't want to accuse anyone until I am sure, Sergeant, so can we leave it at that for the moment?'

'Even if it is only a suspicion, it will assist our enquiries to know who that person is. We would be discreet, I assure you.'

His face flushed a delicate pink with obvious irritation. 'I'm sorry, Sergeant, but that is all I have to say on the matter at present — and anyway, perhaps word of your presence here this evening will get around and serve as a deterrent to whoever *is* responsible.'

Kate sighed. 'Your decision, sir,' she said, turning towards the doors, but if you change your mind, perhaps you'll let us know. In the meantime, I will arrange for police patrols to give the church passing attention.'

Truly nodded. 'Thank you, Sergeant. In any event, the culprit will be known to the Almighty through His all-seeing eye and you can be sure that the miscreant will be called to account on Judgement Day.'

'In which case, maybe we should start with interviewing "The Man Above" as a possible witness,' Kate murmured under her breath as they left the church, ignoring Hayden's tuts of disapproval at her blasphemy.

The uniformed officer caught up with them as they walked back through the gate.

'Janet Robinson, Sarge. Can I have a word?'

'Be my guest.' Kate leaned back against the driver's door of her Mazda, conscious of Hayden hovering at her elbow, plainly impatient for them to get on their way. 'What's on your mind?'

'There's something you should know that I couldn't mention in front of Truly.'

'Which is?'

'There's a bit of a feud going on between Truly and a weird, nutty woman who lives out on the Levels and claims to be a witch. I'm pretty sure she's the suspect he was referring to. I don't know much about her, but Truly is a bit of a pulpit-thumping, fire-and-brimstone priest and regularly lambasts his congregation about the Devil and his wiles. I understand he's had several run-ins with her.'

'The age-old battle between the forces of light and darkness,' Hayden quipped.

Janet threw him an uncertain look. 'I don't know about that, but he certainly wants her off his patch. He's been trying to get her evicted from the old shack she lives in, which was apparently never granted planning permission, for quite a while now. As members of the local policing team, me and another officer, Eddie West, who lives just a few doors down the road from here, have attended quite a few spats between the two of them, plus we've had several reports of alleged Satanist activity in the area since this woman came here about two years ago — you know, sheep and cattle attacked or daubed with occult symbols, cockerels stolen and later found out on the marshes, mutilated.'

Kate frowned. 'I remember reading something about this in the weekly crime bulletins.'

Janet nodded. 'The the Local Intelligence Officer has been cataloguing the incidents for us to try and spot a link. Uniform have been dealing with it all up until now, although one of your DCs, Jamie Foster, did come out to a couple of incidents.' Another little smile. 'Then your DI, Mr Roscoe, said it wasn't really a CID job but a uniformed one and wouldn't agree to greater CID involvement.'

'That figures.' Kate sighed, remembering Roscoe's policy of cuffing anything that he regarded as trivial, or which didn't offer an opportunity to push up the CID crime detection rate. 'What was this woman's name?'

Robinson shrugged. 'All I know is that she calls herself Lilith, though I don't think that's her real name. Eddie could tell you more, he's had quite a bit of contact with her.'

'Lilith, you say?' Hayden commented, raising his eyebrows. 'The "Night Monster," eh?'

Kate stared at him. 'The what?'

'In Jewish mythology, the name Lilith translates as "The Night Monster," a demon said by some to be the mother of the incubi and succubi sired by a deranged archangel called Samael.'

Janet Robinson simply gaped at him.

Kate shook her head wearily. 'Just ignore him, Janet.' She opened the car door and climbed into the driving seat. 'He's got this hang-up about witches and things that go bump in the night at present. I'll get him to see a doctor later.'

Janet grinned and bent to peer in through the window. 'Anyway, speak to Eddie about Lilith. He can give you the full SP on her.'

Kate started the engine as Hayden climbed in beside her. 'Thanks, Janet,' she said. 'We'll do that, and we'll pop across and see your sorceress as soon as we can.'

'But not before tomorrow,' Hayden qualified, his tone suggesting that there were more important things to attend to first — like filling his stomach. He beamed at her as the car pulled away. 'Do you know, a nice fish supper from the chippy might be an idea? Preferably with some mushy peas, eh?'

'*Night Monster*,' she snorted. 'I ask you! You really are a prat, fat man.'

He waggled a finger at her. 'Ah, but a clever one, you have to admit.'

'I reserve my judgement,' she said. 'Now, what is it to be, cod or hake?'

CHAPTER 2

The slender young woman was barefoot. But she ran on down the drove like someone possessed, heedless of the sharp stones cutting into her bloodied feet. Her sweater clung to her perspiring body and she felt that her heart was pounding against her ribcage. As she ran, she threw quick, terrified glances back over her shoulder, but saw only the ghostly blue tongues of fire dancing eerily among the threads of white mist that blanketed the marsh behind her.

They could not be too far behind her now. She had no way of knowing exactly how close they were, but they would be determined to try and stop her reaching the main road, where she would have the chance of stopping a passing car and getting away.

With a startled cry, a heron flapped across her path. As she swerved to avoid it, she glimpsed the gleam of water and lurched back onto the track. She had been just in time — the rhyne was only inches from her stumbling feet.

Then the road appeared, a wet, pot-holed strip of tarmac. And there, just visible through the murk, a pair of hazy, twin headlights creeping towards her from the direction of the village of Mark.

She ran towards them, waving her arms and screaming, conscious of shadows materialising in the gloom just yards behind her. They had found her. She ran faster, felt something clutch at her sweater and tore herself free. Then the car was on top of her, skidding sideways across the road, its rear end slamming into her with the force of a sledgehammer, plunging her into merciful oblivion.

* * *

'Bloody shit!' Kate gasped. 'What the hell was that?' She sat up and clutched at her forehead, the blood running through her fingers into her eye. She realised she must have cut herself when she'd headbutted the door pillar.

The car had skidded across the slippery tarmac, coming to a halt with its bonnet buried in an adjacent hedgerow. They had been lucky. If it had gone the other way, they would have ended up in the rhyne, which could have proved fatal. But right now, neither she nor Hayden was in a mood to appreciate their good fortune and for several seconds they just sat there, both of them in shock.

Then Hayden groaned and stirred beside her, mumbling something unintelligible. Throwing open the driver's door, Kate clambered down onto the road and felt her way unsteadily along the side of the car towards the boot. Through the gloom, she glimpsed the motionless shape on the other side of the road and stood for a moment, swallowing the acid vomit rising in her throat.

Seconds later she heard the car door opening, and Hayden was beside her, the beam of the torch in his hand pinpointing the body of the woman they had hit.

Kate grabbed his arm to steady herself, near panic in her voice. 'I wasn't driving fast, Hayd, you know I wasn't. She — she just seemed to run straight at the car.'

'I know, old girl,' he said, 'but we'd better check her out and call an ambulance.'

Apprehensively, they approached the motionless figure. It was a woman, dressed in blue jeans and a heavy sweater and lying on her side in a contorted position, one arm bent under her.

Kate got down on her knees beside her and felt for a pulse, in both her wrist and neck. At first, nothing, and then she detected the faint beat.

'Thank God, she's alive,' she breathed. 'Get that ambulance here pronto.'

Hayden moved a short distance away and she heard him speaking to someone on his mobile. 'Ambulance on its way, and I've also called for an inspector to attend.'

'Inspector?'

He hesitated. 'Well, it's a serious injury accident by the look of it, so police attendance is necessary, and as we're still on duty, it's a POLACC, which means the IO should be a rank above.' He cleared his throat and added wryly, 'Good job we left the nick before you finished that glass of wine. But bang goes my fish and chips.'

She retched a couple of times and Hayden touched her shoulder. 'You okay?'

She grunted. 'Banged my head, that's all, but never mind me, think about her. She could be badly injured.'

'I know, but there's nothing we can do for her right now. We just have to wait for the paramedics.'

'There should be a couple of travelling rugs in the boot. Get them, will you?'

He turned away, and she heard him open the car boot. She was on the point of getting back on her feet when she received her second shock of the night.

The hand that reached out and gripped her wrist was surprisingly strong, and although her eyes were wide open, the woman did not seem to be staring at her but over her shoulder into the mist.

'They're coming,' she gasped, struggling to raise herself up. 'Quick! Got to hide . . . Witch fire . . .'

Then with equal suddenness, she released her grip, flopped back onto the ground and lay still again.

Kate glanced behind her but saw nothing save billowing clouds of white mist, which formed indistinct shapes that broke up, disappeared and re-formed.

'*Who* is coming?' she said, bending closer to the woman. There was no reply and the other's breathing, which was now clearly audible, sounded worryingly ragged.

'Concussion, probably,' Hayden said, bending down beside her and carefully slipping a folded woollen rug under the woman's head and draping another over her upper body. 'I thought I heard you speaking to her just now.'

Kate took his arm and allowed him to help her up. For a few seconds, she stood there, trembling fitfully as the shock of the collision took hold.

'She . . . she said something about *they* are coming — whoever *they* are — and she'd got to hide.'

He glanced about him. 'No one else here but us chickens,' he said, keeping his tone light. 'She was probably suffering from some sort of delirium.'

'If she was, the whole thing seems to have been very real to her. Plainly, she was running from something when I hit her — and where are her shoes? You must have seen her feet. They're in a hell of a state, look, they're bleeding.'

He grunted. 'Well, we're hardly likely to find any answers until she recovers and can talk to us. Maybe this is a domestic thing and she was fleeing from her husband?'

'She also said something about "witch fire."'

'Witch fire?'

'That's what I thought she said.'

He chuckled and pointed over her shoulder. 'Probably referring to that, I would think.'

She turned to look and stiffened.

The strange elfin fires had chosen that moment to materialise through a break in the mist — flickering, bluish tongues, which seemed to hover above the ground, swaying as if in some sort of phantasmal dance.

'Nothing more than good old *ignis fatuus*,' he stated loftily.

'Which means what?'

'Didn't you do Latin at school?'

'No, Hayd, I didn't. My secondary modern education just about managed French and German.'

'Well, it's Latin for "foolish fire."'

'And what's "foolish fire" when it's at home?'

He looked taken aback. 'You must have seen the phenomenon before, surely? You've lived on the Levels long enough.'

'Well, yes, but I never thought much about it before.'

'Will-o'-the-wisps, old girl,' he said. 'Also called "friar's lanterns," or the "hinkypunks," as they're referred to in this part of the world. You get such phenomena in marshy areas like this. It is said to be caused by the spontaneous combustion of gas from the decomposition of decaying matter. Nothing particularly sinister about it.'

Kate glanced back down at the unconscious woman. 'She seemed to think there was. She must have been looking straight at them when she spoke to me.'

He shrugged. 'There's a lot of superstition attached to the lights, fires or whatever you want to call them. Some people believe they're the souls of unbaptised dead children or portents of death and have the power to lure unsuspecting travellers out onto the marsh to their doom in some noisome bog.'

Kate shivered again. 'How come you know all this?'

'Oh, just naturally well-read, I suppose,' he said, tongue in cheek.

There was no polite answer to that, but in any event, Kate was prevented from providing one. Suddenly, twin headlights, surmounted by a pulsing, blue light, blazed towards them through the mist. Seconds later, an ambulance pulled up just short of her crashed Mazda, disgorging two paramedics.

After explaining what had happened and irritably shaking off offers of medical attention for herself and Hayden, Kate left the ambulance crew to do what they were best at. She stood a little way off, watching as a second pair of headlights and a flashing red and blue strobe signalled the arrival of a powerful police patrol vehicle from the Roads Policing Department.

'Trying to open up a new route, were you, Sarge?' Inspector Dave Drew asked with a dry chuckle as he approached the Mazda with a woman constable in tow.

'Very funny,' Kate said, stepping out of the way as the ambulance drove off. 'Can we just get on with what you have to do?'

"Getting on with it" took another hour, involving, among other things, a breath test — which, thankfully, revealed Kate to be below the legal alcohol limit — plus measurements of the road, the sports car, and the two short skid marks Kate's wheels had left on the damp tarmac surface.

'This is a serious accident, could even turn out to be a fatal,' the inspector said helpfully, 'so I'll have to get your motor taken in for a full examination. But I can leave getting a statement off you until tomorrow if you like?' He chuckled. 'You're not going to flee the country, are you?'

His female colleague sniggered, but neither Kate nor Hayden saw anything funny in the remark.

'I'll be on duty at nine, *sir*,' she replied coldly, 'if you're up by then, of course. Now, perhaps you could call for the breakdown, so we can get home?'

The breakdown truck took nearly an hour to get to the scene, and a further half hour to pull the Mazda out of the hedge and tow it away. As a result, it was past one in the morning before Kate and Hayden were dropped off at the door of their cottage in the tiny village of Burtle.

Hayden was in bed almost immediately, and Kate could hear him snoring away as she cleaned herself up in the bathroom and downed two paracetamol with a glass of water.

But, in the process of climbing into bed beside him, she abruptly changed her mind. She padded barefoot to the window, pulled back the curtains and stared out into the night. The mist showed no signs of clearing.

At first, she saw nothing, but on the point of turning back into the room, she stiffened. The blue, elfin fires had materialised suddenly out on the marsh, seemingly hovering just off the ground, flickering like fizzing lanterns as they performed their ghostly dance. Then, they were gone, consumed once more by the mist from which they had emerged.

'Hinkypunks, my arse,' she muttered as she climbed into bed. 'What a load of old crap.'

Yet, despite herself, she was conscious of a sudden chill in the atmosphere of the room and, shivering again, she pulled the bedclothes right up to her chin.

CHAPTER 3

Kate's Mazda MX5 was not severely damaged but it had sustained a broken headlamp glass, plus an unsightly crease and deep scratches to the off-side front wing and bonnet, which would require substantial body repair work. The garage broke the news to Kate when she rang them from home the following morning. In any case, she was left with no option but to leave the car with them until the Roads Policing Department had carried out their examination, and to accept a lift to work in Hayden's treasured Mk II Jaguar.

Her day did not get any better either. Sending Hayden out to the vandalised village church to liaise with the Scenes of Crime team, she telephoned the hospital to check on the condition of the woman she had hit. The news was not good. Apparently, the "casualty" was still unconscious, evidently in some sort of coma, and wasn't allowed visitors.

Then the inspector who had attended the scene of the accident insisted on interviewing her and taking her statement while under caution, 'just to be on the safe side in case of a future decision to prosecute,' he said cheerfully. And finally, to add insult to injury, she was summoned to the superintendent's office and told that while it had been his intention to recommend her for temporary promotion to Acting DI until a replacement for Ted Roscoe had been appointed, this had been put on hold while her accident was being investigated. With an apologetic cough, he said her newly arrived departmental colleague, DS Des Percival, would fill the position instead.

She returned to her office in the foulest of moods, angry and humiliated, hardly able to hold back the tears while she struggled through an in tray piled high with paperwork.

In the end, she found herself unable to concentrate and, grabbing the ignition keys of one of the CID cars, she left the station yard with a squeal of tyres.

* * *

Ted Roscoe woke early. He had had a bad night, tossing and turning in sheets drenched in his sweat as he struggled through the familiar nightmare of whispering voices and distorted images which is often the bedfellow of the committed alcoholic.

He vaguely remembered his farewell celebrations and of vomiting into the "white telephone" before being rescued from the women's toilet, of all places, and brought home by a couple of his colleagues, totally paralytic. But nothing else. He had no memory of having undressed or getting into bed. One thing, though, was apparent. When he rolled over onto his side and tried to raise himself up, waves of nausea forced him to fall back again. He had the granddaddy of all headaches.

He lay for a while until the room stopped spinning and he was able to get up and make his way gingerly to the kitchen. Perched on a high stool at the breakfast bar, with his forehead cupped in one large hairy hand and a mug of steaming black coffee in the other, he tried to unravel his tangled thoughts and clear the fog from his addled brain.

What the hell had he done? No, not the booze. He had been there many times before and he knew that his hangover would pass — eventually. It was the retirement thing that was bugging him, surfacing through the waves of alcohol to hit him with a cold, gut-churning wrench. He had a sense of almost total loss. He was no longer part of "the firm," no longer a detective inspector in charge of his own department. Shit! No longer a bloody copper either, after nearly three decades in the job. The submission of one short report had cut him loose from practically everything he had ever known. For the first time in his life he felt alone and vulnerable.

So, why had he opted to retire in the first place? Because there was little option. He had seen the writing on the wall, heard the less than subtle hints of those above him, suggesting he was past his sell-by date. In short, he had simply jumped before he was pushed. His career should never have ended like this. After all, he had been pretty good at his job, at least in the early years anyway. A first-class thief-taker, successive bosses had told him, which had earned him three commendations, got him onto CID, Drug Squad, then Crime Squad, and ultimately promotion to DS and DI.

But somewhere along the line, it had all gone wrong. He'd sort of foundered, got stuck in a rut. Deep down, he knew that booze — the potential nemesis of every copper — had been the primary cause, though in his case it had been women too. He'd acquired quite a reputation for chasing "skirt" in fact, and as a young DI had been hauled over the coals several times for knocking off junior female officers. It had put a stop to any hope of further advancement, and he had become bitter and twisted as a result — antagonistic towards everyone, especially women, whom he had come to blame for his own shortcomings.

And one woman in particular had really got under his skin. Apart from arousing his carnal instincts every time he clapped eyes on her slim, athletic figure, he had recognised that Kate Lewis was also a first-class detective — intelligent, dynamic and intuitive. In short, everything he had once been, and he had been unable to bury his envy of the young DS, for her looks, her youth and her professional abilities. Perversely, this had given rise to feelings of resentment and blatant hostility towards her, which in turn had led to the emergence of a fractious relationship between the two of them, making teamwork almost impossible — especially in the last few months.

If only he had learned to swallow his pride and had kept his stupid mouth shut. Well, it was too late now, wasn't it? He had burned his bridges and there was no going back. Maybe he was too old for it all now anyway. Close on fifty-two — he'd used his service in the marines to stay on after fifty — he was well out of sync with the modern politically correct, equal-opportunity-focused police service, along with its state-of-the-art technology and its "be nice to the villain" approach. The rough, hard-drinking heavies he had grown up with had long gone and now he had joined them in the dinosaur club.

Washing down four paracetamol with his third cup of coffee, he reached for his cigarettes — only to find that the packet was empty. This was the last thing he needed. Launching a torrent of abuse at the unhearing wall, he hauled himself up off the stool and lumbered a little unsteadily towards the back door. Seconds later, even though he had to be well over the alcohol limit, he reversed out of his drive in his battered Honda Civic and headed towards the village a mile or so down the road.

The Black Cock had always been his favourite local. It was where he and his CID team had always got together to unwind after a heavy week, and he felt the retirement regrets surfacing again as he pulled into the car park.

For a moment or two, he just sat there, staring at the weathered side door to the bars, feeling strangely awkward and reluctant to go inside now that he was no longer one of the team.

There was only one other vehicle in the car park, a big, black Volvo XC90 with what appeared to be personal number plates. He didn't recognise the vehicle and guessed it probably belonged to a casual customer — no doubt someone after a pint and a pie to break up a long journey. He was in the process of mustering up the courage to climb out of his car and maybe get a pint himself to go with the cigarettes when he froze in his seat as if he had seen a ghost.

The door of the pub had suddenly opened, releasing a shapely young woman in her thirties with bleached blonde hair, who hobbled towards the Volvo on impossibly high stiletto heels. She was overdressed in a white fur coat and carried an expensive-looking handbag over one shoulder. For once, Roscoe wasn't interested in her. Instead, his gaze was riveted on the first of the three men who had followed her out. He was conscious of a tightness in his chest and his heart pumping fast as he studied the cadaverous, silver-haired figure in the knee-length woollen coat who sauntered past the woman to open the back door of the Volvo, allowing her to wriggle into the seat before climbing in beside her.

With his memory clawing back the years, Roscoe watched the other two men climb into the front seats before the SUV reversed towards him, then drove out of the car park, heading in the direction of Bridgwater.

'Hell's bells!' he breathed, finally recovering from his shock. 'Ronnie Coleman. Talk about bloody déjà vu!'

Starting his own car, he slammed it into gear and left the car park in a swirl of gravel, heading in the same direction as the Volvo, cigarettes and pint of beer forgotten.

* * *

Staff Nurse Jane Strong was very firm when Kate arrived to check on the woman she had struck with her car. Even her warrant card made no difference.

'Sorry, Sergeant,' the nurse said with a polite smile, 'but I cannot allow you in to see her at present. There wouldn't be much point anyway, as she is unconscious.'

Kate had expected such a refusal, but it only served to add to the downbeat mood that was already gripping her in its cold, tight claw. Her primary concern was that the woman might die on her — even though she knew that the accident was in no way her fault. But her copper's "nose" had sensed that dark issues lurked behind the woman's mysterious flight, and the detective in her urgently needed to find out what those issues were.

'You say she's unconscious,' Kate said. 'Can you give me an idea as to how serious her condition is?'

Nurse Strong shook her head. 'All I can confirm is that she is stable and that there is no immediate cause for concern. She has been seen by the casualty doctor and has undergone the usual tests to assess the extent of her injuries. I will stick my neck out and say that we don't think there's anything seriously wrong, apart from her comatose condition, but the full results are still awaited.'

'Did she say anything when she was brought in?' Kate went on. 'You know, anything about why she was running across the road miles from anywhere at that time of night?'

The staff nurse shook her head. 'As far as I know, she was unconscious when she was admitted, and her condition has not changed since.' She hesitated. 'Do you know why she was in her bare feet, or where her shoes are?'

Kate shrugged. 'I haven't a clue. I guess only she knows the answer to that. Have you any idea as to her identity?'

The nurse shook her head. ''Fraid not. She had no documents on her at all.'

'Not even a credit card?'

'Nothing, I'm afraid — just the clothes she stood up in.'

'Has anyone made any inquiries about her?'

'Not so far as I'm aware.'

'Well either that means there's no one *to* make any inquiries or, if there is, they don't yet know she's missing.'

The nurse made a face. 'Bit of a puzzle, isn't it?'

Kate grimaced. 'I never was any good at those.'

* * *

Kate's mobile rang as she was leaving the hospital and she jerked it irritably from her pocket. It was Hayden.

'Something I think you ought to see,' he said. 'Can you call by the church?'

She was there in ten minutes and parked behind his CID car and a police Scientific Support van, indicating that the SOCO team had arrived and were at work inside the building. She spotted Hayden immediately. He was talking to a tall, muscular man in his mid-forties with black, shoulder-length hair, wearing a shabby grey jumper and jeans.

'What is it?' she snapped. 'Don't tell me there's been another incident?'

Hayden coughed discreetly. 'This is Mr Ralph Trimble. He's the church sexton.'

She nodded briefly in acknowledgement. Trimble's dark eyes fastened on her, then slid away when they met hers.

'He's a sort of custodian of the church, and also helps with the digging of graves—

'I know what a sexton does,' Kate said acidly. 'What's the problem?'

'I'll show you, Sergeant,' said Trimble in a deep, rough voice, and promptly walked away from them, heading down a well-worn, flagged path at the side of the church.

Her curiosity aroused despite her ill-tempered mood, Kate threw a quick glance at Hayden and followed him.

The path ended after a few yards and Trimble turned sharp left into the graveyard, picking his way along a narrow strip of turf between a line of headstones towards the perimeter wall.

He stopped a short distance from the wall and led them along the side of it to a huge, gnarled yew tree, which must have been at least forty feet tall. In front of the tree, a broken headstone lay on its side against a mound of earth, from what was obviously an excavated grave.

'Found it this morning,' he said. 'Shocking. Must have happened when the church was done last night.'

Kate bent closer to peer into the trench. Even from where she stood, she could see some skeletal remains in the wet earth at the bottom of the trench, mixed with what looked like bits of rotted wood.

'Does the Rev Truly know about this?' she said.

Trimble nodded. 'He's at an important parochial church meeting in the village and sends his apologies. He asked me to act on his behalf. I live in one of the semis just down the road, so I'm always available.'

'Do you have any idea what the perpetrator could have been looking for here?' she asked.

'Don't know for sure, but the skull — or what was left of it — seems to be missing.'

Kate shook her head in disbelief. 'Why on earth would someone take something like that?'

'It's witchery,' burst out Trimble, as if unable to stop himself, and promptly made the sign of the cross. 'Done by the same person as desecrated the church. Calls herself Lilith and lives out on the Levels. Claims to be in the service of the Devil. I've seen her hanging about here on several occasions, and I'm quite sure she's the one responsible for all that's happened here.'

'Reverend Truly refused to say who he thought was responsible,' Kate said.

Trimble shrugged. 'He's a man of God and thinks he can solve all wickedness by forgiveness.'

'And you don't?'

He scowled. 'I think those who defame the name of the Almighty should be made to pay for their sins. Rev Truly and me went out to the witch woman's place a while back to try and turn her from her evil ways, but she just laughed at us. She showed us some rag dolls she'd made and stuck pins in. One was made to look like the Reverend and the other our local copper who'd warned her about her conduct. She said she'd put a curse on 'em both, so they would both die soon. A real nasty old woman and that's a fact.'

Kate grunted, but made no comment, instead crouching down to peer at the headstone. It was so old she couldn't make out the name or inscription.

'And what reason would this Lilith have for digging up a corpse and stealing the skull?' she snapped. 'Going by the headstone, the grave looks to be ancient. Why pick on this one as opposed to one of the others?'

Trimble sniffed. 'You don't know whose plot this is then?'

'How could I? I can't even read the name on the headstone.'

'Fella called Tom Sharpe.'

'What, a local man?'

'You could say that, but not recent. He died in 1645. You can read all about him in the local museum.'

'Apparently,' Hayden put in, 'he was a local magistrate and self-appointed witch-finder, who had a witch burned alive in a cottage out on the Levels.'

'They say he was cursed after that,' Trimble added. 'Went crazy and died in the madhouse. Local folk didn't want him brought back to be buried in the churchyard here, but they were overruled by his rich family, so he ended up in this plot in the corner — sort of out of the way.'

Kate shook her head. 'Nicking a skull, though? It doesn't make sense.'

Hayden grinned. 'I suppose it does if you're a witch.'

CHAPTER 4

With a flap of its large grey wings, a heron rose from behind the willows lining the rhyne at the side of the drove. Kate reduced her speed to a crawl as the CID car lurched and bumped along the rutted surface of the track.

Leaving Hayden to finish up at the church, she had decided to head out to the Levels to check on the place the woman had emerged from the previous night. She didn't expect to find any real answers and she had no precise idea of what she was looking for on this ancient cattle track, but she felt she needed to revisit the scene of the accident anyway. There was just a chance it might turn up something that might fill in a few of the blanks that were frustrating the hell out of her.

A man in working clothes riding an ancient bicycle passed her after a few yards, going the other way, and, glancing briefly in her rear-view mirror, she saw him half-turn in the saddle to look back at her. No doubt he was curious as to why she was driving a saloon car along a byway meant for cattle and tractors.

Otherwise, she didn't see a single soul and, reaching a crossway, where the drove was joined by three other tracks, she paused for a moment, undecided as to which one she should take. Then she saw the shoe at the mouth of the narrow track on her right. It seemed to be some sort of sandal, and, staring beyond it, she saw a second one lying just a few feet further along the same track.

Climbing out of the car, she went over and collected both of them. They were women's sandals, tan coloured and well-worn. Interestingly, the instep strap on the second of the two had parted from the stitching at one side, leaving the buckle still fastened on the other. From what Kate could see, the stitching appeared to have been wrenched apart, possibly after the wearer had tripped on something, maybe while running.

She thought of the woman who had run in front of her car and the fact that she had been barefoot. Maybe this was why. She had somehow ripped the strap off one of her sandals and, in her panic, had dumped the pair. But if that was the case, why hadn't she hung onto the sandals to get them repaired later? And why was she running in the first place, and from whom?

Frowning, she glanced around her, but saw nothing save the tall reeds and coppiced willows shielding the rhynes on either side of the track. They quivered slightly in a low breeze.

She was only vaguely aware of the sound of clanking behind her before the voice spoke.

'Your shoes?'

She turned quickly. The man she had passed a short time before was sitting on his bicycle a few feet away, having obviously pedalled back the way he had come.

The puffy, red face under the dirty cloth cap wore a big, stupid grin and one of his hands was tucked inside the strap of his dungarees.

She smiled back and shook her head. 'Nothing to do with me, but it was a funny place to leave them.'

His grin broadened. 'That's what I thought when I cycled past, so I just left 'em there.'

She studied him more closely. It was plain from the look of him and his slow, halting speech that he was not entirely all there.

'Live around here, do you?' she asked as casually as she could manage.

He nodded and, pulling some chewing gum from a pocket, offered it to her, stuffing it into his mouth when she politely shook her head.

'Hallstead Farm,' he said, waving an arm towards the main drove. 'Name's Luke.'

He held out his hand and she stepped forward and shook it. It was huge and well calloused from manual labour.

'I help me uncle,' he went on. 'Lots of work to do round the farm. I'm very strong, see?'

'I'm sure you are,' she replied, and it suddenly occurred to her how vulnerable she was on this lonely drove with this powerfully built stranger. 'Come this way a lot, do you?'

He nodded, his expression more sober. 'All the time. Not at night, though. Bad things out here at night — 'specially in the mist.'

'Oh? What sort of things?'

'Can't say. They might hear me.'

'Who might hear you?'

He glanced around him nervously. 'Hinkypunks.'

She remembered Hayden's reference to the ghostly blue fires out on the marsh and hesitated for a moment. Conscious of his apparent limited mental capability, she was anxious to avoid riling this so far genial muscleman by appearing to laugh at him.

Instead, she affected a curious expression and asked, 'Who are the hinkypunks?'

He stiffened on the saddle and scowled. 'Why you askin' me all these questions?'

She took a chance and produced her warrant card. 'Detective Sergeant Kate Lewis, Highbridge CID.'

He flinched and stopped in mid-chew. 'Police? I don't talk to no police.'

'Why's that? You're not in any trouble and we're just having a nice little chat, aren't we?'

He shook his head several times, glancing nervously around him, then resumed chewing.

'*They* might not like it.'

She continued to humour him. 'Why wouldn't they? I just want to find out who these sandals belong to and how they came to be here.'

He thought about that for a second, his face contorted in concentration. 'Dunno, but Lilith would know. Lilith knows everything. She keeps us all safe.'

'Who's Lilith?'

He nodded towards the track where the sandals had been lying. 'Lives down there. I wouldn't go there, though, if I were you. Lilith don't like strangers.'

Then, before she could ask any more questions, he had swung his bicycle around and was clanking off, back towards the main road, leaving Kate staring after him in total perplexity.

* * *

The drumming of the wheels of Roscoe's Honda Civic on the road across the Levels matched the drumming in his head. Fortunately, the Volvo he was following at a discreet distance seemed in no real hurry, so keeping it in view was relatively easy. But the road surface was pitted and uneven, and the worn suspension of his old car did little to cushion him from the frequent jolts and lurches. His head felt as if the council's road drills had already begun their excavation work.

Why the hell was he subjecting himself to all this grief anyway? He was no longer a copper. He had left all that behind him the night before. What did it matter if a "face" from his distant past had manifested itself at his local? It was a free country. People could go where they pleased. It had nothing to do with him — not anymore.

But once a copper, always a copper, and Ted Roscoe had an exceptionally long memory. The insatiable curiosity of the professional detective would never leave him, even if he wanted it to. Finding out what Ronnie Coleman was doing on his "manor" was of vital importance to him, even though that "manor" was no longer his. On top of it all, he had a big score to settle with Coleman that went back twenty years. Maybe, just maybe, he would get lucky this time after failing so many times before.

* * *

It was spitting with rain as Kate trudged along the narrow track. With a grimace, she turned up the collar of her leather coat and popped an extra-strong mint in her mouth. She was beginning to wish she had risked it with the CID car, but the track had seemed a bit too narrow at the start and there had been no way of knowing whether it would get even more restricted. Getting stuck between two ditches or having to reverse the whole way back on this wet, muddy strip was certainly not something she relished.

She had been walking for just on ten minutes, going by her watch, and had given herself a further five before turning back altogether, when the track entered a small wood.

Moments later, she spotted the outline of a roof on her left, practically buried among the trees. There was a five-bar gate on the other side of a stone bridge spanning the rhyne, and a length of wire suspended above it between two posts, hung with an assortment of grotesque, crudely carved wooden figures. Beyond the gate, which was open, a gravel path led through what appeared to be a herb garden to a single-storey habitation, which was little more than a shack, constructed of wood and corrugated iron, with a rusted corrugated iron roof from which a steel pipe protruded, no doubt serving as a chimney.

Although it was only just after midday, lights flickered eerily in the two small windows, but there was no other sign of life.

Crossing the stone bridge, she ducked under the wire supporting the wooden figures and, approaching the front door, was surprised to see that it was wide open, as if, somehow, she was expected.

With some trepidation, she knocked. 'Hello? Anyone in?' She knocked again.

A rook rose from a nearby tree with a grating cry, but nothing else stirred.

Her hair brushed a line of corn dollies suspended on a thin wire between the door posts as she ducked her head through the doorway and peered around her. She found herself in a small, square room, illuminated by an oil lamp on each windowsill. The room smelled strongly of burnt peat, and there was a rickety looking wood-burner in one corner, with a pipe extending from the back of it up to the roof. A rocking chair had been drawn up in front of the wood-burner. The only other furniture to be seen was a bare wooden dining table set against one wall, with an upright chair placed at each end, and two roughly constructed beds, made from a collection of blankets and straw, set head to head.

Shelves lined the badly patched walls, crammed with bottles of various coloured liquids and canopic-type jars containing dried plants, bearing a variety of names, including *Hemlock*, *Belladonna* and *Marsh Marigold*, and what appeared to be the mummified remains of tiny rodents, reptiles and birds. A stuffed owl stared down at her from a roof corner, while an incomplete human skull in a large glass bowl filled with some sort of greenish liquid grinned at her from a three-legged stool in another. Even the table was taken up with a gruesome collection of animal skulls and bones, carefully arranged in a geometric pattern.

There was a second door in the far wall, which was also wide open. It had been badly damaged and was hanging from the top hinge, with the bolt and part of the splintered frame lying on the floor just over the threshold. As she approached it, she felt something crunch beneath her feet. Broken glass. Closer inspection revealed a half-smashed bottle jammed behind the door in a pool of oily liquid. A shelf ran along behind the door with a single gap between the bottles it held, suggesting that the broken bottle had fallen from the shelf when the door had crashed against it.

Kate's eyes narrowed. First, a wide-open front door and now evidence that the back door had been violently forced. It looked very much like someone had broken into the place from the rear and someone else — the mysterious Lilith perhaps — had fled out the front.

She thought of the woman she had hit in her car. Was there a connection? Could *she* be Lilith and, if so, why had she fled in such a panic? Who were "they," and what had she meant when she'd blurted out the words "witch fire" at the scene of the accident?

Kate frowned, something else occurring to her as she thought about the vandalism at the church the previous night and the plundered grave just a short time before. She knew next to nothing about witchcraft, but the contents of the shack — the jars and bottles, with the preserved creatures inside, and the corn dollies — plus the other gruesome objects strung on wires over the gate and above the front door, certainly suggested that Lilith was involved in something pretty eccentric, if nothing else. Was she perhaps behind the desecration? And if that was the case, had the skull there on the stool been pillaged from the grave of Tom Sharpe?

Maybe the vicar or someone else in his congregation had found out and had come here to deal with her? It all seemed to fit — except the idea that the chubby little clergyman could be involved in anything like that, or that he could be capable of inspiring such terror in Lilith's mind as to make her bolt the way that she had.

Shaking her head ruefully, she pulled out her mobile and rang Hayden for a second opinion.

* * *

Roscoe saw the Volvo turn off the main highway around twenty minutes after leaving the pub. He had the good sense to pull over into a lay-by and wait a few seconds before going after it again. But when he turned off the main drag into a winding, tree-lined lane, heading out towards an expanse of marshland, his quarry had disappeared.

'Bugger it!' he breathed and put his foot down to try and catch up with the big limo before he lost it altogether.

But, as it turned out, he had overestimated the distance between them, and he very nearly slammed into the back of the car when, rounding a sharp left-hander, he glimpsed the double flash of brake lights just a few yards ahead.

He managed to swing the wheel at the last minute and swerve around the SUV, which had pulled over and stopped, but it was a close thing, and he glimpsed at least two faces turned towards him as he drove past, clipping the offside verge as he did so.

The Volvo had stopped a couple of yards from a gateway, and he had seen what looked like the front-seat passenger bending over a long chain suspended between two concrete posts, seemingly wrestling with a padlock.

Though burning with curiosity, he didn't stop or make any effort to turn around until he reached a T-junction a short distance further on. Then, turning in the junction mouth, he headed back the way he had come.

Unsurprisingly, the Volvo had gone by the time he got there and, pulling into the roadside just ahead of where it had stopped, he studied the gateway with its chain barrier now back in situ and secured in place by a business-like padlock.

Beyond the chain, a track cut across a large boggy field, fenced on both sides, and disappeared into a patch of woodland. This then extended like a finger to the right, running parallel to the lane, all the way across a mixture of grazing land and marsh to the main road which the lane finally joined. There was no nameplate or other identifying feature on either of the gateposts, but Roscoe glimpsed what looked like the tall chimneys of a house thrusting above the trees in front of him.

What the hell was this place, and what was Ronnie Coleman doing here? He was a city boy and hated the countryside. Okay, so it was possible he had finally decided to retire and settle down in his old age and lead a peaceful life, his past buried back in the Smoke. Roscoe smiled grimly. Yeah, and maybe the Pope wasn't a Catholic.

Ducking under the chain, he trotted, like a bloodhound on the scent, along the driveway towards the building he had glimpsed among the trees.

* * *

It was a good forty minutes before Hayden arrived and it seemed that he'd brought the new "Acting DI" with him.

Des Percival was a tall, athletic, thirty-something-year-old, with blond, shoulder-length hair, a matching, military-style moustache and a personality that exuded the sort of charisma and good humour their former boss, Ted Roscoe, could never have achieved in a month of Sundays. Kate liked Des — what was there not to like? — but she still couldn't help feeling resentful towards him for depriving her of the job she had wanted so much. Acting rank was what it said on the tin — a temporary appointment that only lasted until someone else was promoted to the position, and it didn't necessarily mean future advancement for whoever held it. But it could nevertheless result in some significant brownie points in the promotion stakes and it rankled with Kate that she had been passed over for the role simply because some stupid woman had run in front of her car.

'Thought I'd tag along for a breath of fresh air,' Percival said, his blue eyes searching Kate's expression for a reaction to his presence.

She shrugged, trying hard not to let her pique show. 'Be my guest, Des. Not much to see, though. Place is empty.'

Hayden grinned. 'So, this is the wicked witch's lair,' he quipped, glancing curiously around him. 'Looks like she's flown off on her broomstick.'

'Yeah,' Kate said, 'lots of nice bottles on the shelf over there — one with seeds in labelled "Hemlock." That's a poisonous plant, isn't it? I wonder who she's planning to poison. Looks like the skull in the bowl might be from the grave at the church too — what there is of it.'

Hayden chuckled. 'A skull in a bowl. Makes a change from a ship in a bottle.'

Wandering over to the opposite corner of the room, he pulled a pair of drab grey curtains aside to reveal a small alcove. 'And someone's certainly been at the black arts here by the look of it.'

Alerted by the change in his tone, Kate strode quickly across the room and pushed past him to stare at what he had discovered. The chill that had gripped her the previous night when she had stared at the phantom blue fires out on the marsh returned with a vengeance.

A number of wooden pegs had been driven into a length of wood attached to the wall, much like a row of coat-hooks, but there were no coats hanging from the pegs, and it was immediately obvious why the alcove had been concealed behind a curtain. Instead of coats, two crude rag dolls hung on strings from the pegs — one with a beard, a bulbous nose and fat stomach, which had been made to look like a uniformed policeman, and the other a bald clergyman, with a distinctive dog collar, sporting old-fashioned side-whiskers.

'Do you know what?' Hayden commented excitedly. 'If I were to hazard a guess, I would say that the overweight bobby with the beard and bulbous nose is meant to be poor old Eddie West, Janet Robinson's colleague from the local policing team, while the priest with the bald head and side-whiskers can only be our very own Rev Jacob Truly. These must be the nice little creations that Trimble said he and Truly were shown when they visited the charming Lilith.'

But Kate was less interested in the possible resemblance of the dolls to actual people than the fact that the torsos of both dolls had been partially wrapped in a crumpled square of white cloth spattered with what looked like dried blood, and someone had taken the trouble to force a series of long pins through both of them.

CHAPTER 5

'So, your Lilith is into witchcraft then?' Des Percival commented. They were back in the police station canteen a couple of hours later.

Kate warmed her hands on her mug of coffee. 'Someone else too by the look of it,' she said. 'I saw two beds in that shack.'

'And you reckon the skull we saw in there might have come from the church graveyard?'

'Highly probable, I should think. Maybe we should have seized it?'

He thought about that for a second, then shook his head. 'Technically, we would have needed a search warrant to enter the property and remove it as potential evidence. Hovel or not, it's still a private dwelling, and it would have been difficult to justify taking the skull anyway. After all, it's not like identifiable property. How would we have proved it belonged to the skeleton in the grave? We would have needed the expert opinion of a forensic anthropologist, maybe through a protracted and expensive DNA process, and I can't see the force agreeing to shell out for that in the case of what is in reality a very minor crime, can you?'

She shrugged. 'It is arguable, but I see your point.'

'Right then,' he said. 'What have we got? Two witches who have a penchant for sticking pins in dolls?'

She nodded. 'Possibly, and the doll thing is what witches do, isn't it? That's how they put curses on people.'

'And you think the woman you knocked down might be this Lilith, the one responsible for the attack on the church?'

'Well, it all seems to add up.'

'So, what could she have been running from?' he asked.

'That's the million-dollar question. The Devil maybe.'

Percival sat back in his chair, coffee untouched. His hands were thrust down inside the back of his trousers, a mannerism she had noticed he always seemed to adopt when perplexed about anything. 'From what you've told me, I can see why your Rev Truly may be one of Lilith's least favourite people, but I am at a loss to see what she could possibly have against poor old Eddie. He's hardly the sort to attract animosity.'

Kate thought of the big, overweight constable, whose only claim to fame was his almost legendary ability to put away huge quantities of food at a single sitting. 'My sentiments entirely,' she said, taking a sip of her coffee, 'and I've just sent Hayden to try and find out. West will be coming on duty shortly.'

Pulling his hands free, Percival leaned towards her, a worried frown on his face. 'Look, Kate, I've been wanting to talk to you about, er, this acting rank thing.'

She feigned surprise. 'Oh? Why's that then?'

He fidgeted a little in his seat and stroked his moustache with his index finger. 'Well, you know, I'm conscious of the fact that you should have been offered it instead of me.'

She smiled, reading the lie in his blue eyes. 'Don't worry about it, Des,' she said, finishing her coffee and climbing to her feet. 'Shit happens.'

Des Percival sat staring after her, open-mouthed, as she headed briskly for the door.

She heard Hayden's dulcet tones as she was passing one of the interview rooms and abruptly turned back to check.

Hayden was sitting at the interview table opposite a huge uniformed figure whose behind sagged over the edges of the plastic chair. The latter turned curiously as she walked in. The beard and bulbous nose were unmistakable.

'Hi, Eddie,' she said, propping herself on a corner of the table. 'Hayd has obviously told you about Lilith and your lookalike doll?'

Eddie West laughed, a loud, reverberating guffaw that shook his heavy frame. 'Yeah. Seems she don't like me very much.'

'Any idea why?'

'We were just coming to that,' Hayden interjected irritably.

Kate flashed him a benign smile. 'So, me being here now will save you repeating it later, won't it?'

West shrugged. 'Not much to tell anyway. Me and Janet Robinson cover that area as part of the local policing team. About a fortnight ago, I was called to a disturbance at the village hall, where they was holding one of them "bring-and-buy" things in aid of the church roof fund. Apparently, Lilith had turned up — pissed as usual — and started abusing everyone and blaspheming somethin' terrible. She'd left by the time I got there, so I went out to her shack and gave her a boll — er — rollicking. I told her that if I caught her causing trouble in the village again, I'd run her in.'

'And she took exception to that, I assume?' Kate said.

He nodded. 'Well, we'd had words before, after she gatecrashed the junior Sunday school and frit the kids by telling them she was a witch and would send the hinkypunks after them—'

'Those hinkypunks again,' Kate murmured.

'Superstitious claptrap,' West said. 'It's all to do with them will-o'-the-wisp lights you see out on the marsh some nights. Gas from the peat bogs, I've been told—'

'So I gather.'

West shifted uncomfortably on the plastic chair, which looked like a piece of dolls-house furniture beneath his bulk.

'Yeah, well, Lilith has got this idea into her head that she really is a witch. Local kids call her "Old Mother Hubbard." Whenever she turns up in the village, they dare each other to goad her into chasing them.'

'Hang on,' Hayden said. 'If I remember rightly, Old Mother Hubbard was a nice old lady who had a dog, that's all. She wasn't a witch.'

West shrugged. 'I dunno. Maybe it's because of the clothes the crazy old girl wears — you know, old-fashioned shawls and bonnets like in the Victorian era.'

'I shall never see Mother Hubbard in the same light again,' Kate said drily, but she couldn't help shivering.

West chuckled. 'You an' me both. Anyway, Lilith claims she's a reincarnation of an old crone called Molly Clavey, who was burned to death in her cottage on the same site as Lilith's shack in the sixteen 'undreds, and that she has inherited the old woman's magical powers.'

'The same site?' Hayden echoed.

'It's all in the local museum. Quite proud of it they are, an' all. Sort of makes it a must-see place for the tourists. Anyway, Clavey's cottage was burned to the ground and about two years ago this nutty woman calling herself Lilith, turns up with an old army surplus tent and lays claim to that very spot. A few weeks later, that old shack goes up there and she moves into it.'

'Just a minute,' Kate said incredulously. 'You're saying she built that place herself?'

'Nah. Somehow, she cottoned onto an impressionable lad living at Hallstead Farm nearby and convinced him that she really was a witch. Chap by the name of Luke Cobb. She got him to put it up for her.'

'Ah, I believe Luke and I have already met.'

'Right, well, he's a decent enough lad and quite good with his hands — not that his handiwork was much to rave about in this case — but he's a few sandwiches short of a picnic, if you know what I mean, and he's scared stiff of Lilith. Maybe he thinks she'll turn him into a frog or somethin'.'

'So, what do you know about this Lilith? Has she got any form?'

'A bit, yeah. I done a check on her when I took her in after she kicked up at the Village Hall. Her real name is Sara Anne Cable and she's recorded on PNC. A couple of drunk and disorderly convictions, resulting in heavy fines, near Maidenhead in Berkshire, where she used to live. Then a minor arson attempt at a church down there. Got a custodial sentence for the arson, but due to her mental state, she was sent to the funny farm — a psychiatric unit near Reading called the Gables. Spent two years in there and was released just before she came down to Somerset.'

Kate was impressed. 'You've got a good memory, Eddie. But what made her decide to come here?'

'No idea. Glastonbury is a pretty good draw for weirdos who are into so-called witchcraft and we're just down the road from there. Maybe she heard about our local witch getting burnt and thought she'd continue where the other old girl left off.'

'From what Janet Robinson told us, I gather that the local vicar isn't too pleased about having her on his doorstep.'

He chuckled. 'You could say that. Truly's been using every means possible to get rid of her. It's become a bit of a *cause célèbre* for him.'

'Which explains a lot.' She paused. 'You know him well, do you?'

'As well as anyone. I'm a member of the church and on the parochial church council, so we see each other quite a bit at council meetings and fundraising events.'

'You've heard what happened at the church?' she said.

'Yeah, Janet told me. It certainly sounds like our Lilith's work. She was no doubt getting her own back on the good Reverend, but you'd never be able to prove it.'

Kate frowned. 'You've no doubt heard about the woman who ran out in front of my car last night too?'

He looked a little uncomfortable. 'Er, yeah, picked up something about it on the grapevine.'

She gave a rueful grimace. 'I bet you did — probably the whole nick did. Could she be Lilith, do you think?'

'What does she look like?' West asked.

'Twenties, blonde—'

'Not a chance. Lilith, as she likes to call herself, is at least seventy, with long, straggly grey hair. Nose like a beak she has — typical witch, in fact. Oh, and a slight limp.'

'Then who is the woman in the hospital, why was she running down that drove and who could she have been running from?' muttered Kate, more to herself than West.

He chuckled again. 'Maybe the hinkypunks were after her?'

She gave him a scathing look, adding, 'And on top of it all, where the hell is Lilith now?'

He couldn't answer that either.

CHAPTER 6

Roscoe reached the end of the long driveway without incident. He hadn't seen any surveillance cameras on the way, so he was reasonably confident that, thus far, he had escaped detection.

In front of him, among the trees, the track blossomed out into a wide concrete hardstanding, with an old stone-built house boasting a forest of tall chimneys to his right and a large, corrugated-iron building resembling some sort of modern barn to his left. A badly patched tarmac driveway struck off sharply to the right of the house between a pair of crumbling stone statues — no doubt leading to the main entrance. The black Volvo was drawn up in front of the house and a couple of other vehicles — a maroon Land Rover Discovery and a big grey Mercedes saloon — were parked close to the barn. There was no sign of anyone, but Roscoe could hear pop music emanating, he thought, from the barn itself.

He was about to move closer when a door in the barn opened and a dark-skinned man wearing a black, knee-length leather coat emerged carrying a sizeable cardboard box. The man went straight to the Mercedes, put the box in the boot and went back to the barn. After a few seconds, he emerged again, carrying an identical looking box, which he also placed in the boot. He made three more journeys, closed the boot and was about to climb into the driving seat of the Mercedes when Ronnie Coleman appeared from the barn, smoking a cigar.

'Back roads, remember, Christos,' he called across to him. 'And watch out for Old Bill.'

The other raised a hand in acknowledgement, got into the driving seat and pulled away. Roscoe just had time to step back into the trees as the car flashed past him down the track towards the lane.

Coleman stood for a few moments, staring after him and blowing smoke rings with his cigar. Then, abruptly tossing away the stub, he turned on his heel and went back into the barn, closing the door after him.

Roscoe could feel his heart racing. What was Ronnie Coleman up to? What was in the cardboard boxes? And where was Christos going with them? Knowing the London villain as he did, he was pretty sure that the man he had pursued for so long during his time on the NCS hadn't deserted the Smoke for this isolated spot just to enjoy a healthy retirement.

But what to do about it, that was the point. It was no good contacting the nick to try and organise a raid. They wouldn't do anything without a search warrant, and there was little chance of them getting one without the grounds to justify its issue. After all, what was there in the way of evidence to back up his suspicions that Ronnie Coleman was up to no good? Okay, so "Mr Havana," as he was known from his love of expensive cigars, was a big-time London villain and a former police target criminal with a string of convictions to his name, and it was most unlikely he had chosen to settle down on the Somerset Levels to go bird-watching. But assumption was not evidence, and that was all Roscoe had — coupled with which, a pre-emptive raid that went ahead and produced nothing would be a disaster. Instead of hero of the day, he would end up looking a total prat.

No, it was clear to him that he needed to give the barn the once-over before he did anything else. That was out of the question now, in broad daylight, especially as Ronnie Coleman never travelled light. There were bound to be a bunch of his thugs there with him — and our Ronnie wasn't noted for his welcoming nature.

So, it would have to be after dark — maybe sometime in the early hours when Ronnie and his cohorts were, hopefully, away with the fairies after a few bevvies — which meant returning home in the meantime for a quick kip, something to eat and a change of clothes. Yeah, and maybe a pint or three. He tapped his pocket automatically for his packet of filter-tips as he headed briskly back to the car, then suddenly remembered he had run out. Okay, so a pint *and* a packet of fags.

* * *

It was early evening before Kate and Hayden arrived back at the shack and the light was beginning to fade. Hayden was not in the best of moods, his stomach already making those rumbling noises that let him know it had not received food for at least four hours. Kate had had to pull rank on him to get him to accompany her.

Why she had decided to return was not even clear to herself. The shack was not a crime scene, even though the old woman seemed to have disappeared. At the same time, while the trashing of the church was an offence of criminal damage, it did not amount to a major crime and, since Lilith was only a suspect and there was no evidence to connect her to the business anyway, interviewing her was not a priority in the scheme of things. But Kate's curiosity about the self-confessed "witch" and the possible link between her and the woman in the hospital had been very much aroused, and she was determined to get to the bottom of it all. She didn't like mysteries or loose ends, and this was certainly one that needed sorting if she was going to sleep at night.

Parking the CID car at the beginning of the track, as before, she led the recalcitrant Hayden to the old woman's hovel at a much brisker pace than he would have preferred, stopping for a moment by the small bridge over the rhyne to study the place and to listen for any sound emanating from inside. The front gate had been left open, the carved wooden figures suspended above it stirring gently in the breeze, but the shack itself appeared lifeless. No lights burned in the windows, and all they could hear was the tap-tapping of a woodpecker deep inside the wood and the distant, discordant cawing of a rook.

Crossing the bridge, they found that the front door was firmly shut. Kate knocked, but there was no answer and no sound of movement.

The oil lamps on the windowsills had been extinguished and the damaged back door, which they had left as they'd found it on their previous visit, had been partially jammed back into the frame. Otherwise, the place seemed to be exactly as it was before, except that the rag dolls were no longer hanging on their hooks behind the curtain.

Checking out the back, they found a gravel path leading to a lopsided wooden shed, housing a chemical toilet, which was half-buried in encroaching woodland. The path carried on beyond the shed, winding among the trees, until it opened out briefly into a clearing before continuing as a much wider track.

They made no immediate move to follow the track further, for their attention was arrested by an unexpected sight. Parked to one side of the clearing was an old, light blue VW camper van, displaying only one headlight and with almost as much rust to the bodywork as paint.

'Gordon Bennett,' Hayden exclaimed. 'A witch with a van. That must be a first. No doubt it's more comfortable than a broomstick.'

'Probably just dumped,' Kate said, walking over to it and pulling the driver's door open to peer inside.

Hayden bent down and studied the ground. 'I don't think so. There are definite tyre tracks here to suggest it is being used.'

Kate studied the interior for a moment and grunted. 'You could be right.' She reached across to pick up a pile of official looking forms in plastic sleeves, which had been left on the front passenger seat. 'She seems to be making a point of collecting fixed penalty notices. There must be a dozen here, and a couple were issued in the last few days, at Bridgwater and Cheddar.'

Hayden straightened up. 'Gets about a bit then, our wicked witch?'

Kate slammed the camper van's door shut. 'It looks like it. And, if she is using the VW, that means there must be a back entrance to this place, which we need to check out.'

Hayden groaned. 'What on earth for? We're not investigating a major crime, so why are we wasting so much time on this business? My feet are already killing me, and I reckon it's high time we knocked off and got back home to Burtle.'

Kate strode past him onto the second section of the track. 'Think how much fitter you'll feel from all this fresh air,' she threw back over her shoulder. 'It could give you a new lease of life.'

'More likely give me a coronary,' he grumbled, trudging after her.

Within a few yards, the woodland petered out in a bare field, with a hedge and a five-barred gate at the far end. A lorry drove past on the other side just as they reached it, and they found themselves staring into a narrow lane. There was another gateway opposite, but instead of a gate, it had been closed off with a length of chain suspended between two concrete posts. Beyond this, a gravel track led across another field and disappeared into some woodland, above which the tall chimney pots of what appeared to be a large house were clearly visible. Marshy fields stretched away on every side, providing a flat, gloomy vista, relieved in places only by a few coppiced willows bordering the occasional rhyne, and patches of brown-headed teasel.

'Okay, so now we know how Lilith comes and goes in her "witch-mobile,"' Hayden commented irritably. 'Satisfied?'

Kate shook her head. 'No, I'm not, for if her van's still here and she's not at home, where the hell *is* she?'

He opened his mouth to say something, but she pre-empted him. 'And don't you dare mention broomsticks!'

Dusk was already closing in on them when they returned to the clearing in the wood, and as they followed the track back towards the shack, Kate began to feel uneasy. With the approach of darkness, strange rustlings could be heard in the wood and she found herself starting at every sound and peering intently into the gathering shadows. She had a growing feeling that they were not alone.

She grabbed Hayden's arm, bringing him to an abrupt halt and whispered into his ear. 'I think we're being watched.'

'What?' He glanced around him, then stared at her. 'Watched by whom?'

She turned back to face the way they had come, scanning the trees on either side of the track. 'Is that you there, Lilith?' she called out. 'There's nothing to be afraid of. We're police officers. We just want to make sure you're okay.'

The rustling in the undergrowth ceased abruptly, but there was no response.

'Lilith?' she called again. 'Do you hear me? Please show yourself.'

Complete silence. Hayden fidgeted beside her. 'It's just your imagination, old girl. There's no one there.'

'Why are you hiding, Lilith?' she shouted. 'You're not in any trouble.'

Still nothing. Kate tutted. 'I know she's in there somewhere.'

Hayden sighed heavily. 'Forget it, Kate. Even if she *is*, she's not going to come out. Best to come back in daylight.'

He moved off again, ignoring the back door of the shack and skirting round the side of the ramshackle building to the front gate.

'So, are we agreed? It's now back to the nick to drop off this rubbish car and pick up my Jag, then home, eh? And maybe *en route* we should try that new Chinese takeaway?'

But Kate didn't respond, and he found out why when they got back to the CID car. Reversing into the drove, instead of turning left towards the main road, she swung sharp right in the opposite direction.

'Hey!' he exclaimed, 'What are you doing? You're going the wrong way.'

'No, I'm not,' she said. 'I'm making a slight detour. Someone I have to see.'

'What?' Hayden glanced at his watch. 'At this time? It's past eight o'clock.'

'I'm sure he'll still be up, Hayd, and he is the one person who might know where Lilith has gone to ground.'

Now he was visibly angry. 'Kate, you're becoming obsessed with this business. For goodness' sake, take a step back and think what you're doing. All we've got is a bit of vandalism at a church and a nutty woman who may or may not be responsible and has gone walkabout. It's hardly the crime of the century.'

She cast him a sideways glance. 'What's the matter, Hayd? Stomach juices giving you gyp, are they?'

* * *

The entrance to Hallstead Farm was about half a mile further along the drove, and its jumble of shabby buildings was approached via a long driveway, fenced on both sides.

The farmhouse, with its damp-stained, stone walls and air of abandonment, was showing lights in its front windows, and the front door stood ajar. Luke Cobb took his time answering Kate's double knock and she heard a cistern flushing before he appeared, still doing up his corduroy trousers.

He looked taken aback when he saw who it was. 'You're that police lady.'

Kate smiled. 'Right first time, Luke. And this is my partner, Hayden. Can we have a word?'

'Who is it?' a harsh male voice shouted from somewhere in the house.

Cobb turned briefly. 'Police, Uncle.'

There was a fit of coughing. 'Police? What do they want?'

Cobb winced. 'Me uncle Bob,' he said to them almost apologetically. 'He don't like police.'

'Tell him it's just a routine call,' Kate said.

Cobb frowned, obviously having difficulty comprehending what that meant.

'You'd better not come in,' he said, and pointed to a barn opposite. 'Can we talk in there?'

'Luke? What you doin'?' Uncle shouted again.

Cobb ignored the shout and pushed between them, heading for the barn. 'He's in bed, drunk,' he said. 'He's always drunk. I look after the farm for him.'

Reaching the barn, Cobb pulled back one of the double doors and reached up to pull on a cord dangling just inside. At once, the place was flooded with light. He pointed to some bales of hay dumped in a corner beside an ancient-looking, rusted tractor.

'You can sit there,' he said, crossing to the tractor and, depositing his heavy frame on the top of one of the front wheels, stared at them expectantly.

'It's about Lilith,' Kate said, propping herself beside Hayden on one of the bales. 'We want to talk to her, but she seems to have disappeared.'

He beamed. 'She does that. She's a witch, you see. She can make herself vanish just like that.' He snapped his fingers.

Kate thought about that for a second. This was obviously going to be a difficult interview.

'Her back door has been bashed in, Luke,' she went on, 'Do you know who could have done that?'

'Hinkypunks probably,' he declared solemnly. 'They are always up to mischief.' Then he added brightly, 'Tell her I will fix the door for her tomorrow.'

'We can't find her, Luke. Do you know where she might have gone?'

He shook his head. 'She's everywhere and anywhere — she told me that once — and she don't like strangers, you know. I told you before not to go to her place.'

Kate could see that she was not getting very far with this affable muscleman, but she was determined to persevere, despite Hayden's impatient fidgeting beside her.

'Does Lilith have anyone staying with her?' she asked. 'Another lady, for example? If you remember, when we first met, I'd found her shoes at the beginning of the track.'

Cobb's jaw set into a stubborn frown. 'Don't know any lady.' But it was obvious that he was not telling the truth.

'She ran in front of my car, Luke, and she's hurt. We need to find out who she is.'

He stood up quickly, a scowl on his face now. 'I said I don't know,' he replied, raising his voice aggressively and clenching and unclenching his fists by his sides. Kate felt Hayden dig her thigh sharply in warning and she forced a smile and stood up.

'Okay, Luke, that's fine, but if you think of anything later, could you let me know?'

He hesitated, then suddenly relaxed and nodded, though his gaze was anything but friendly and he took the proffered business card very reluctantly.

'Well, that went well, didn't it?' Hayden sniped as they drove off. 'You obviously made a big hit there.' Then he added, 'Anyway, now it really is time to drop this rubbish car back at the nick and collect my Jag.'

Kate ignored him. 'Consider this, Hayd. Luke Cobb built Lilith's shack for her and is obviously well under her spell, so to speak. He's a strong old lad — told me so himself when we first met — and he would do anything for her, I reckon, including maybe a bit of bodysnatching — even if it was just a skull.'

'How do you work that out?'

'I would have thought it was pretty obvious to a clever cookie like you. There's no way that a seventy-year-old woman like her would be able to excavate a grave single-handed. She must have had help, and my guess is that good old Luke provided the muscle.'

'Seems likely, but I can't see him coughing to it and we have nothing to connect him to the job.'

'No, but it's worth bearing in mind, isn't it?'

'Certainly is,' he agreed vaguely. 'So, what's it to be from the takeaway, old girl? Chicken chop suey or chow mein?'

CHAPTER 7

Kate awakened suddenly and stared around the moonlit room, her brain still befuddled from the deep sleep into which she had fallen. The clock on her bedside table indicated that it was past midnight. Hayden was completely dead to the world and snoring loudly beside her — hardly surprising after the amount of red wine he had knocked back with his extra-large Chinese takeaway.

What had woken her? A bad dream perhaps? Hayden's snoring? Or something else? Her eyes adjusted to the gloom and she pulled herself up onto one elbow, searching the shadows in the corners of the room while she listened intently for a repeat of whatever it was that had startled her into wakefulness. But there was no sound save the nasal exuberance of her husband.

Still not satisfied, she swung her feet over the edge of the bed and padded, naked, to the window. The garden below was almost as bright as day and on the other side of the low hedge bordering its perimeter, the flat, waterlogged fields stretched away from the cottage to end in the treacherous peat marshland, with its criss-cross ribbons of glittering rhynes and pools of still water. There was nothing else to be seen — no lurking intruder, no wandering fox. Not even a stray cat.

Reluctantly forced to admit that she must have been spooked by nothing more than a bad dream, she was on the point of returning to bed when she heard a more substantial sound: the groan of stiff metal hinges. The side gate between the back and front garden. Someone had just opened it!

Forgetting in the heat of the moment that she hadn't a stitch on, she left the room at a run, descending the stairs three at a time. Miraculously, she managed to get to the front door and wrench it open without breaking her neck, but she was too late. Whoever had been in the garden had made good their escape and, as she stood in the doorway breathing heavily, she heard an engine start up. Seconds later, an old VW camper van, displaying just one headlight, rattled past the cottage, heading out onto the Levels.

* * *

'So, the old witch paid us a visit, did she?' Hayden said thickly from his stool at the breakfast bar, his eyes bleary and bloodshot after he had been unceremoniously turfed out of his bed. 'And she left us a present, I see.'

Now dressed in a white bathrobe, Kate nodded, staring with revulsion at the headless cockerel which she had dumped in the kitchen sink.

'Tied to the knocker on the front door,' she said. 'No doubt meant as some sort of curse.'

'Trying to warn us off, I would think,' he added. 'Though how the devil she knew where we live is a mystery to me.'

'I've been thinking about that,' she said. 'I reckon she must have overheard us talking as we left her shack. If I remember rightly, you said something about getting a Chinese and heading home to Burtle. In a village this size it wouldn't have been that difficult for her to locate this cottage, and she may have seen my car parked at the church that first time and then spotted it tonight in our driveway.'

He looked dubious. 'Bit of a longshot for her, though, don't you think? It's more likely she followed us from Luke Cobb's place. We weren't suspecting anyone to be following us, so we wouldn't have been looking — and she has that old car, don't forget.'

'I'm sure I would have spotted that single headlight in my rear-view mirror.'

He shrugged. 'So, she drove on ahead and parked up somewhere close by until we turned up. We stopped at the Chinese, don't forget, so she would have had plenty of time.' He scowled. 'In any event, it's a bit off to have someone you're investigating turn up on your home turf like this in the middle of the night when you're not even on duty. This happened with an undesirable on one of your previous investigations, you may recall.'

Kate poured them both a black coffee. 'Two undesirables on two separate investigations actually,' she corrected, thinking back to one of them — the horrific case of Larry Wadman, alias "Twister," the psychopathic undertaker who had murdered Kate's twin sister due to mistaken identity and had then broken into her home, kidnapped her husband and had been on the verge of killing him when he was rescued.

He grunted. 'Whatever. Well it shouldn't happen. It gets too darned personal when the job intrudes on your private life like this. You should be able to leave it behind when you knock off and come home.'

'As a copper, you can never leave it behind,' she retorted. 'You ought to know that, Hayd.'

He snorted. 'Well then, maybe it's time we thought about packing it in.'

She stared at him. 'I can't believe you just said that. This job is my life, even if it isn't yours. There's no way I would quit.'

'That isn't what you've said in the past — especially where Ted Roscoe was concerned,' he retaliated. 'I can remember that at one stage — following the case of that transgender nutter, Georgina Lupin — we were *both* ready to jack it in. We even handed our warrant cards back. Pity we let Roscoe return them to us.'

Kate reached out and laid a hand on his arm, gazing at him intently, real concern registering in her eyes.

'You're tired, Hayd, I can understand that,' she said. 'We both are. Let's talk about it in the morning after a few more hours' sleep.'

'It's morning now,' he grumbled, squinting at his watch. 'In case you hadn't noticed.'

* * *

It was just after 1 a.m. when Roscoe returned to the Levels. He had managed a good few hours' sleep and a pie and chip dinner from the local chippy, but to his annoyance there had been no time for the pint at the Black Cock he had been looking forward to. He had at least got hold of a couple of packets of cigarettes from the village shop to keep him going.

Now, turning into the lane leading to Ronnie Coleman's place, he drove well past the gateway and pulled into another one a couple of hundred yards further on. He had decided to approach the property from the side this time rather than chance his luck along the track he had used previously. It turned out to be a good place to leave the car too. The gate was not secured in any way and, with a little effort, he was able to push it right back, enabling him to drive the old Honda all the way through the gap and conceal it behind the hedge.

Then, armed with a powerful torch, he followed another hedge across a boggy field towards the belt of woodland he had spotted on his previous visit. The hedge eventually ended before a three-foot-high wire fence, obviously intended to mark a boundary. Forcing himself through the hedge wasn't easy, but his bulk triumphed in the end and, keeping the wire fence on his right, he began to follow it towards the nest of tall chimneys a few hundred yards away, backlit against the face of the moon.

He was grateful for the thick, rubber-soled ankle boots he'd had the foresight to dig out of his wardrobe — old favourites that had seen plenty of service in his days as a uniformed "wooden-top" at the start of his long career — for the waterlogged ground sucked at his feet with every step, as if trying to hold him fast. At times he sank up to his shins in the small pools of water squeezed out of the peat by his weight.

Dressed all in black — jeans and hooded coat — he couldn't help but be reminded of his time in the marines, and the risky, adrenalin-pumping sorties he and the rest of his unit had undertaken deep into enemy territory, and he was under no illusions as to the danger he faced this time if Coleman and his thugs were to suss him. He was right out on a limb, with no authority to do what he was doing and no backup to call on if he got into trouble. But it was something he just had to do. Ronnie Coleman had always been a *cause célèbre* for him, and bringing Mr Havana down now would not only provide him with a sort of belated career fulfilment but would also be a smack in the eye for all those pricks at his old nick who for years had rubbished him behind his back.

His teeth were bared in a fierce grin of anticipation but, basking in the glory of his imagined success, his momentary loss of focus was almost his undoing. The bog had him in its grasp within seconds and he was up to his knees in the slimy, evil-smelling death-trap before realisation hit him. By then he was sinking fast. He managed to muster the strength and presence of mind to hurl himself backwards onto the firmer ground he had just crossed, enabling him to extricate himself from a sitting position.

His trousers were soaking and caked in mud when he finally stood up again, and he was shaking fitfully from shock at his near miss. He picked his way a lot more carefully across the remainder of the field — and the next — until the fence came to an abrupt end. On the other side, he could see the big field and the track he had earlier followed up to the house and the barn. He had arrived.

The wire fence was now all that separated him from the tangle of undergrowth and sentinel-like trees that should have concealed Coleman's house from prying eyes, though in the moonlight he could still make out part of one wall, maybe thirty feet away.

For a few minutes, he remained motionless. An owl hooted somewhere close by and creatures stirred in the scrub, but there was nothing else, just the distant cries of sheep and, briefly, the sound of a car heading along the lane where he had parked his Honda Civic, its headlights cutting a white swathe across the field behind him as it rounded a bend. Then silence once more.

Switching on his torch and shielding its bright beam with one hand, he pulled a pair of wire-cutters from his pocket and snipped through the wire strands. Then, bending them back on themselves, he pushed through the gap and into the woodland, wincing as he brushed against a flimsy trunk and received a cold shower from its sodden foliage.

He heard the loud cough just as the woodland came to an end, and he froze into immobility. Two men were standing on a small, square patio by a pair of glass doors, one of which stood wide open. He seemed to be at the side of the house. The shorter of the two was smoking a cigarette, the other a cigar. The smoke from the cigar drifted towards Roscoe on the night air, producing a strong, slightly perfumed smell. He didn't need to see the mop of silvery hair to know that the man with the cigar was Ronnie Coleman — you didn't end up with the nickname "Mr Havana" for smoking slim *panatelas*, this cigar was the real deal. Having smoked cigars all his adult life, Roscoe could tell from the smell that this was one of the expensive Cuban variety, no doubt a Montecristo at something like four hundred pounds a box. Well, if you were a successful villain like Coleman, what else would you smoke? And four hundred pounds a throw was nothing if you were making millions, was it? Who said crime didn't pay?

Moving a little closer, Roscoe tried to get a better look at the man Coleman was talking to. It was difficult to see him properly as he was standing in shadow, yet there was something familiar about him. The ex-DI was sure he had met this one before, and he was even more certain when he heard him speak.

'The woman you're looking for,' the man said in a gruff voice, 'the blonde bit. She's in the local hospital — in some sort of coma, they're saying.'

'A coma?' Coleman echoed in his familiar drawl.

'Yep. She walked in front of a car.' The other emitted a rasping smoker's laugh. 'Chose the right one too. Bloody CID car driven by one of the sergeants I work with — a woman DS by the name of Kate Lewis.'

Coleman drew on his cigar.

'Interesting,' he murmured after a long pause. 'So, there's no risk of her talking to anyone at the moment?'

'No, she's completely out of it apparently. Wired up and on a drip. Hospital won't even let the police near her.'

'Excellent. But keep me informed if she looks like coming round and any of your colleagues are likely to be interviewing her. We'd need to act fast then. Anything on the old crone I told you about?'

'Nothing. Looks like she's disappeared from that shithole she lives in out on the marsh. Obviously gone to ground somewhere.'

Coleman was silent again. 'Okay, just continue keeping me up to date on things. I don't need surprises, got that? There's a lot riding on this venture and I pay you well to keep your ear to the ground.'

There was a grunt of acknowledgement and the glowing embers from the cigarette hit the patio with a shower of sparks.

'And make sure that's out,' Coleman said harshly. 'I don't need a bloody fire.'

The other man muttered something and emerged from the shadow as he stepped forward to extinguish the cigarette with the toe of his shoe.

'Better get off,' he said. 'I'll be in touch.'

Coleman nodded and, slipping a hand inside his jacket, produced a thick envelope, which he handed over.

'Down payment,' he said. 'You'll get some more in a week — provided you keep the filth off my back.'

His visitor laughed. 'They're too busy chasing witches.'

Then he was gone, striding swiftly around the side of the house as Coleman stepped back through the open door into a lighted room and closed the door behind him.

Moments later, Roscoe heard a car start up, then drive away. He stood for a few moments, his mind racing. Now he knew why he'd thought the man with Coleman had seemed so familiar. He was one of the team he had worked with in Highbridge CID. Mr Havana had a mole in Highbridge nick. One of his ex-colleagues had been turned and was on the take.

* * *

Nurse Caroline Bates returned from her break and cast an irritable frown at the single strip light at the far end of the short corridor. It was flickering on and off, leaving much of the passage in shadow. She'd already reported the complete failure of the other strip light, which, by rights, should have been fixed by hospital maintenance hours ago. Now this one looked as if it was on the blink too. Another phone call was obviously on the cards.

It was because of the poor light that she didn't see the bent figure at first. Then she spotted her standing by the double doors of the ICU, apparently trying to tug one of them open. Her efforts had proved pointless, as entry could only be gained by punching an access code into the security keypad. As Bates reached her, she noted the visitor's shawl and ankle-length black dress, and for some reason she felt uneasy.

'Can I help you?' she asked with a frown, stepping briskly towards her. The other shrank back a few paces.

In the intermittent flashes of the strip light above her head, the nurse caught a glimpse of a wrinkled face with a prominent beak-like nose. Then the other pulled her shawl further forward over her forehead, studying her intently for a moment through gimlet eyes.

'You can start by letting me in,' she said harshly.

Bates shook her head and moved past her to stand directly in front of the doors. 'No can do, I'm afraid. The ICU is out of bounds to the general public. We have some really sick patients in here, you know.'

There was a sharp, contemptuous tutting sound. 'I do know, and I want to see one of them.'

'I'm afraid that is out of the question — especially at this time of the night. The nurse peered at her watch. 'Goodness, it's gone 2 a.m. How did you manage to get past security?'

The other ignored the question. 'Patient's a young woman,' she persisted. 'Twenties, blonde — hit by a car. Is she in your ICU or not?'

The nurse prevaricated. She didn't like the look of this weird character and, although she would never have openly admitted it, she was secretly a little frightened of her.

'I can't confirm anything without knowing who you are, and the name of the patient you want to see.'

'None of that is important.'

'It is extremely important in this situation. Are you a relative?'

The old woman gave a sly smile. 'She belongs to me.'

'Belongs? I don't understand. No one belongs to anyone.'

'She has been bequeathed to me for safekeeping by the Horned One, who is all powerful.'

Bates felt her skin crawl. Just her luck. She was dealing with a crazy woman. But how crazy, that was the point? She glanced quickly sideways to locate the red emergency button on the wall and edged towards it as she continued speaking.

'I'm sorry, but I must ask you to leave. You shouldn't be here at all.'

The old woman's face suddenly twisted into a malevolent scowl. 'You will pay for defying me, you little bitch. A curse on you and on all your kin.'

The now terrified nurse lunged for the red button.

'There,' she said, her voice shaking. 'Security will be on their way right now.'

But she was talking to empty air. The old woman had vanished as completely as if she had never existed.

CHAPTER 8

Roscoe could hardly believe what he had just discovered. One of his former colleagues on the take from a villain like Ronnie Coleman? It didn't seem possible, especially knowing the man in question, yet it was plainly a fact. In his book, the treacherous bastard deserved to be hung, drawn and quartered. What had he sold his soul for, though? What exactly was Coleman into this time? Furthermore, who was the "old crone" and the "blonde bit" they had mentioned? What had been meant by the paid-for slimeball's parting shot about the department chasing witches? And what was all that about Kate Lewis knocking down a woman in her car? It was the first he had heard of it — but there again, everything was news to him now he had packed in the job. He forced himself to calm down. He hadn't a hope of trying to piece everything together at this stage, and as for the bent scumbag he had once counted as a colleague, he would get his comeuppance, he would make sure of it. But not just at that moment. There was a more important job to do first.

Caution was the watchword. He would only get one crack at this, so rushing headlong into the thing just to get it over and done with would be a big mistake. Patience and vigilance were key if he was to succeed in what he had set out to do, and it was essential that he put everything else out of his mind — including the personal nature of his motivation to nail Mr Havana once and for all.

He stood under the trees for several minutes before making his move. He was tempted to run across the patio to the wall of the house while he had the opportunity, but he resisted and finally left cover almost on tiptoe. He reached the wall without incident and, following it along to the end, peered around the corner.

A gravel path stretched away in front of him, running parallel with the side of the building, and he saw part of the corrugated barn he had noted on his previous reconnoitre clearly visible on the other side of the hardstanding where the cars had been parked earlier. The night was eerily quiet. There wasn't the smallest sound, even from the house. Maybe Coleman and his cohorts had decided to turn in. Unlikely, and there was bound to be a guard wandering about somewhere — had to be.

He moved off again, carefully picking up his feet to avoid the telltale crunch of his boots in the loose gravel.

He stopped again when he reached the far corner of the house and studied the moonlit area in front of him. The two cars he had observed before — the Volvo XC90 and the Land Rover Discovery — were still parked on the far side of the hardstanding. The whole place appeared to be deserted. Maybe Coleman felt so secure in his new bolthole that he hadn't thought any security was necessary? Yeah, maybe . . .

Still not convinced, Roscoe stayed where he was for several long, frustrating minutes, straining his eyes and ears for anything remotely suspicious. But there was nothing, just a moth fluttering close to his ear, which he finally crushed in one fist.

Taking a deep breath, he headed out into the open, moving swiftly and relatively silently on his rubber-soled boots, to the big double doors at the front of the barn. As he had expected, they were shut and secured with a heavyweight padlock. He crept around the left side of the barn into more woodland and found a side door. It was also shut and secured, but with a much cheaper type of padlock and the hasp was rusted and coming away from the wooden doorpost it had been fitted to. Reaching into his pocket, he pulled out a clasp knife and inserted the steel blade into the gap, levering gently backwards and forwards. Seconds later there was a loud "crack." The blade snapped in half, but at the same moment the hasp itself came away completely, falling into the ankle-deep undergrowth at his feet. With a triumphant grin, he pulled the door open and stepped through.

* * *

The young police constable met the security patrol in the foyer of the hospital. The latter looked uneasy and kept glancing out into the night through the sliding entrance doors.

'An intruder, you say?' the policeman said.

The other nodded. 'An ugly old woman apparently. Like an old witch. The nurse, Caroline Bates, caught her trying to get into the ICU.'

'But she didn't?'

The security man shook his head. 'You need a code to punch into the keypad to get in. But Caroline is quite upset over it. She said the woman frightened her. Put a curse on her, she said. She thinks she might have got out from somewhere — you know, like a nuthouse.'

'And you are?'

'Tom Gratwohl. I'm the night patrol.'

'So how did she get to the ICU in the first place?'

Looking uncomfortable, Gratwhol rubbed his bleary eyes.

'Dunno. I must've been on one of my tours around the outside of the complex, an' she just slipped in. There ain't no one on reception this time of night, just a public phone if anyone wants help.'

The policeman raised an eyebrow. 'Nice and warm in the security office is it, Mr Gratwohl?'

There was an indignant snort. 'I weren't asleep, if that's what you're insinuatin'.'

'Course you weren't. So, where did this woman go afterwards then? Any idea?'

'Not the faintest. I been out lookin', but there ain't no sign of her. Caroline says she was there one minute and then . . . It was like she just disappeared.'

The policeman was grinning openly now. 'You mean like in a puff of smoke? You say she looked like a witch. Maybe she really was one?'

'This ain't a joke, you know. She could be bloody dangerous.'

'So, where's your nurse now?'

He nodded towards a door leading off Reception. 'In the waiting room. I got her a coffee from the machine 'cause she was so shook up.'

The nurse, a pretty brunette, was sitting in the corner of the room, staring out of the window, her hands cupped around a mug. She was very pale, and she was trembling slightly.

'PC Layton. Bill Layton,' he said. 'I understand you had an unwelcome visitor tonight?'

She shivered. 'A horrible old woman, yes. Scared me half to death.'

'So, what did she want?'

'She was trying to get into the ICU, but she couldn't open the door as it has keypad security. She — she told me she was here to see a young woman currently in the ICU.'

'Why?'

'I don't know. I've never seen her before.'

'What is the name of the patient?'

'I don't know that either. She's in a coma after a road accident involving one of your officers, but she fits the description the woman gave me and she's the only female patient we have at the moment.'

'I understand from Mr Gratwohl here that she left pretty smartish after the incident. Did you see where she went?'

The nurse shook her head and took a sip of her coffee. 'It was weird. She got nasty when I refused her entry and said she'd put a curse on me. Said something about the "Horned One," which I took to mean the Devil. I went to press the emergency button on the wall and when I turned back again, she was gone—'

Layton was enjoying this. 'What, you mean like "poof" — into thin air?'

Bates winced. 'I know it sounds ridiculous, but that's the way it was.'

The policeman nodded. 'I think you'd better show me where you were.'

The corridor to the ICU was deserted when the three of them entered it from the stairway, the single strip light still flickering on and off. Bates went to the ICU's double doors and stood in front of them.

'I was here,' she said, 'and she was standing there, just in front of me, before she — she vanished.'

'What did you do after that?'

'Well, I'd called security, so I just went into the ICU and stayed there until Mr Gratwohl arrived.'

Layton's gaze roved back along the corridor. 'What's that there?' he said, pointing to a small louvred door a few feet away beyond a hospital trolley laden with towels.

Bates frowned. 'It's nothing. A cupboard, I believe.'

A check revealed a small storeroom with shelves filled with cleaning equipment and roller towels. A vacuum stood in one corner, together with a large floor polisher. The room was empty.

The policeman shrugged. 'There you are, that's obviously where she went. 'Ducked in here when you turned to press the button.' He frowned. 'I don't suppose you checked this room out when you responded to the alarm call, Mr Gratwohl?'

Gratwohl said nothing, just stared at the floor.

'I thought as much. So, problem solved then. Your witch simply nipped in here and waited until you had gone before slipping out of the hospital. Have you got security cameras on the premises?'

Gratwohl nodded. 'In the car park and over the front door.'

'Okay, then let's go check them out, shall we?'

'Do you think she might come back?' Bates said nervously.

Layton's grin returned. 'I wouldn't think so, but I'll tell our control room to be on the lookout for flying broomsticks.'

The small, cramped security office was equipped with a couple of worn armchairs and a CCTV monitor on a desk. Coffee makings and a kettle occupied a shelf, together with a pile of magazines.

'Cosy,' Layton commented drily, noting the free-standing heater in the corner. Gratwohl simply scowled and dropped into a chair in front of the monitor.

Checking the recording of the camera located over the front door of the hospital, it didn't take long to pick up the elderly intruder. The old woman appeared suddenly, glanced around her furtively, then pushed through the front doors of the building. Her return was also recorded. She seemed in quite a hurry, disappearing almost as soon as she had appeared.

'So, where did she go?' Layton asked thoughtfully.

Gratwohl switched to the camera covering the car park and ran the tape back, soon picking up a bent figure scurrying across the near empty expanse of shiny blacktop to a decrepit looking VW camper van and climbing aboard. Within seconds, a single headlamp came on and the vehicle started to move across the tarmac, heading for the exit. As it pulled out onto the service road, the camera revealed that it was showing no rear lights at all and appeared also to be lacking a rear index plate. Then it became a near invisible shadow, its position marked solely by the single headlight beam forging ahead into the night, until even that was snuffed out altogether.

'Well, at least we now know how your witch got here,' Layton commented with a familiar grin, picking up his uniform cap from one of the armchairs where he had dumped it. 'Which means I no longer have to issue a general alert for a flying broomstick.'

'So, what are you going to do about her?' Gratwohl growled sullenly. 'She could come back.'

Layton donned his cap and turned for the door. 'Well, I'll carry out the usual checks to see if we have a nutter on the loose, but she hasn't really committed any offence, has she? So, apart from circulating the VW as a vehicle of interest, which one of our traffic patrols would be delighted to pull over, going by the apparent state of it, there's not a lot more I can do.'

He pulled open the door. 'If I were you, I'd get myself some rosary beads and a nice silver cross. I'm told they're just the trick for warding off witches and demons.'

And his laughter floated back to the security man on the still night air as the door closed behind him.

* * *

The VW camper stopped just before the five-barred gate. The old woman got out of the driving seat and shuffled over to it, leaving the engine running. Lilith had not had a very successful night. True, she had managed to leave her gruesome "present" tied to the door knocker of that interfering police sergeant's home, but she had been spotted by the woman copper before she could get away. Then she had failed to get into the hospital's ICU and, too late, had spotted the camera on the lamp standard in the car park as she was leaving. No doubt the details of her car had been passed to every police patrol in the area by now. Time to return home and hide the VW in the wood at the back of her shack, trusting in the Horned One to keep the police from her door.

The gate opened easily enough, and she drove through into the field and got out to close it again. Seconds later, she had parked in the clearing and slipped into the shack by the back door, closing it quietly behind her. If they came for her, she wouldn't answer the door and perhaps they would lose interest and go away again. She knew enough about the law to be confident that they couldn't force an entry without a warrant, and she had not committed a major crime to justify the issue of one anyway. So, all she had to do was sit tight and wait for the dawn, secure in the knowledge that, so long as she stayed where she was, the local constabulary could not touch her.

But, as she was about to learn to her cost, it wasn't the local constabulary she had to fear. It was the big black car that was already heading her way with deadly intent.

* * *

Roscoe shone his torch around the interior of the barn, immediately homing in on a white, long-wheel-base Ford Transit van parked just a few feet away, with the name "Silverlink Medicinal Products" on the side in green lettering, followed by the logo of a staff entwined with a snake. There were also scores of colour-coded cardboard boxes stacked in separate blocks up against the far wall, which seemed identical to the ones he had seen Coleman's man put into the boot of his car.

He was pretty sure what they would contain, and he was not disappointed. Pulling a box bearing a yellow colour code from the first block, he retrieved his trusty clasp knife, selected another slim blade, and slit the gummed tape seal. Packed inside were dozens of small plastic bottles crammed with small, coloured pills. At first sight they looked like vitamin supplements, but he knew they were nothing of the sort. These weren't the commercial health supplements, the calcium, magnesium, B12 and the rest, but undoubtedly some sort of amphetamine or psychostimulant, which would have an altogether different effect. Pills such as these provided gullible young people in particular with artificial "highs," hooking them into a downward spiral of dependence that would eventually destroy them, while filling the pockets of the suppliers to bursting.

Checking further along the stack, he selected a box from the second block, colour-coded red. This was crammed with tiny plastic bags containing some sort of white powder — possibly cocaine or heroin. A final check of the third block, colour-coded green, revealed similar tiny plastic bags, this time containing two or three light brown, sugar-like lumps, which he immediately recognised as the smoked variety of crack cocaine.

No wonder Ronnie Coleman had chosen to come to this lonely spot on the Somerset Levels. It made an excellent distribution centre for his drug-trafficking operation, far away from the heat being brought to bear by the police on the criminal gangs in the big cities. Here, in a sparsely populated rural location but close to the motorway network, he could run his narcotics business with impunity, importing his street-ready products from some illicit UK laboratory and distributing them to the main conurbations to link up with the "County Lines" network of mules and pushers via his own dedicated team of professional thugs. All without ever having to soil his own hands through direct involvement.

Coleman hadn't been the first to choose the Levels for such a despicable enterprise. Roscoe remembered the case he had investigated not that long ago, when a character they had called the "Sandman" had set up an illegal laboratory for the same purpose in the isolated village of Lowmoor during a major flooding disaster on the Levels. His operation had been smashed successfully, and now it seemed history was repeating itself.

Roscoe's mind hauled him even further back through the years, to his time on the squad and the addicts he had found dead or dying in alleyways and derelict sheds — once even on the seat of a public toilet. All had overdosed on narcotics like heroin, crystal meth and cocaine. He remembered the skeletal bodies of the ones he'd found barely alive. The white faces, drooling mouths and over-bright, staring eyes. Then there were the others, the decent, fun-loving kids out for the night in party mood to a club or a friend's house, only to abruptly exit this world after taking LSD, or ecstasy and its derivative, known as "Molly." He would never ever forget them, none of them. And just like the "Sandman," one of the sources of their misery had taken up residence here: Ronnie "Mr Havana" Coleman.

Roscoe thought about striking a match and destroying all the boxes in one delicious inferno but stayed his hand. He needed them intact for the police team to find and secure as evidence, which meant leaving the lot in situ and calling the nick before Coleman knew what was happening.

Snapping a few photographs of the boxes and their contents on his mobile, he turned his attention to the Transit van, and took several pictures of that from different angles, as well as the interior of the barn. Then he slipped one of the plastic bottles and one of the plastic bags containing what he had adjudged to be crack cocaine into his pocket and made to dial the telephone number of Highbridge police station — only to stop short, his finger still poised above the keypad.

It had suddenly dawned on him. There was no way he could risk passing the information onto some faceless control room operator or even the night turn duty inspector, when one of the team in his old department was already on Coleman's payroll and might pick up on it all. Word soon got around in the nick and a quick phone call to Mr Havana would see him and his narcotics disappear before anyone could be mobilised.

Furthermore, as he was only too aware, policing was weighed down heavily by bureaucratic protocols and any such call would be unlikely to generate immediate action anyway. At the very least, there would be all sorts of hoops to go through before anything would be approved. Not the least of these would be convincing the senior officer of his identity and the reliability of his information, obtaining the authority of a superintendent for action, obtaining a search warrant without any real evidence, apart from a few photographs on his mobile to back it up, and organising a qualified team to carry out the necessary raid, which would have to be drawn from other police areas or one of the specialist units. It would all take time, and that was one commodity he did not have at his disposal.

What was required instead was a softly, softly backdoor approach that could be managed quietly, unobtrusively, and not necessarily in line with proper procedures. To achieve this, he needed an officer to support his story, someone with status and credibility who was prepared to take risks and step over the line to obtain the proof needed. A maverick, in fact, and though it pained him to have to seek the aid of the very person he had been at loggerheads with during his time as DI, he was left with no alternative. Kate Lewis was the only one he could rely on.

Jerking his phone from his pocket, he quickly made the call. To his surprise, Kate answered almost immediately, but she was not best pleased to speak to him and he didn't get a lot of time for explanations either. In fact, he had to cut the call, for the barn suddenly flooded with light and, swinging around, he came face to face with Ronnie Coleman, flanked by two of his heavies.

'Well, if it isn't Ted. How nice of you to drop in after all these years,' Coleman drawled. 'Retirement not agreeing with you then?'

CHAPTER 9

Roscoe stood his ground as the two heavies moved in on him. He had been in worse situations before — especially in the marines — and although now getting on in years, overweight and somewhat debilitated by alcohol and cigarettes, he had retained a fair bit of his former muscle, plus the tactical ability to give a respectable account of himself.

The first thug didn't expect him to react the way he did. Roscoe turned slightly to one side as if looking for an escape route, then, before the man realised what was happening, smashed his bullet head into his face, breaking his nose. Even as he staggered backward with a wild cry, cupping his nose with both hands, Roscoe was already on the move. Instead of taking to his heels as both had obviously expected, he launched himself at the second heavy, slamming into him with his shoulder and knocking him off his feet, before stamping hard on his groin and running right over him, heading for the door.

The automatic appeared in Coleman's hand as if by magic, but he was already too late, and fourteen stone of relaxed muscle sent him spinning sideways like a weathervane before he could even release the safety catch.

Then Roscoe was gone, racing off into the night like a runaway train, out onto the immensity of the Levels.

* * *

Kate didn't go back to bed after the incident involving the nocturnal visitor. It was already after three by the time she had finished her second cup of coffee, and by then, getting her head down seemed pretty pointless. She'd be up again for work in less than three hours, and anyway, she had far too much on her mind.

Hayden had chosen not to keep her company, and she could hear him snoring again, even from downstairs in the kitchen. Nothing would wake him now. Following their argument, she had seen him swallow one of her old sleeping tablets before stomping truculently back up to bed. Not long afterwards, she had glanced into the bedroom on her way back from the bathroom and had glimpsed him spread out on the bed as if he owned it, an invisible "Do Not Disturb" sign written into his frown.

She thought again about what he had said. Perhaps he was right, maybe the job *was* intruding into their private life too much. Sometimes that intrusion went well beyond the pale and led to horrific consequences. Once again, she recalled the trauma she had suffered in the case of "Twister," the vicious psychopath who had murdered her twin sister, thinking she was the cop on his trail when in fact it was Kate. Her sister's violent death had nearly broken her and, all these years later, she still had nightmares about it.

Even in normal circumstances, she'd often felt that it would be nice to be able to shake off the detective mantle for a while. To think about something else other than crime and criminals, do all the things that normal people did, like going out for the day on a picnic or enjoying a nice meal at a classy restaurant. But life was the way it was, and she knew that, despite all the stresses and strains, she would not be happy doing anything else. She just hoped that the argument she'd had with her beloved Hayden amounted to nothing more than a minor blip, brought on by tiredness, and that he would come around to her way of thinking after a good few hours' sleep without the spat leading to an irreconcilable wedge being driven between them.

At which point, as if to rub salt in the wound and reinforce her husband's argument, her mobile phone suddenly rang.

With an oath, she slid off the bar stool she had been occupying and tugged the phone from her pocket.

'Yes?' she snapped irritably.

'It's Roscoe,' a harsh, breathless voice replied.

'Roscoe? What the hell are you doing ringing me at this hour?'

'I need your help.'

'You need what?'

'I've stumbled onto something big — a face from the past.'

She shook her head a couple of times in disbelief. 'Something big? A face? What are you talking about? You're no longer a DI. You've bloody retired.'

There was a rattling cough. 'Forget all that. Just listen, will you? I'm out on the Levels. I need you to meet me asap.'

'Meet you? Out on the Levels? At this hour? Are you mad?'

'I haven't much time. They're all around here, looking for me.'

'Who's looking for you? You're not making any sense, man. If you're in some kind of trouble, ring the nick. That's what you should have done to start with.'

'I can't. There's a guy on your team who's on the take. I can't risk the treacherous bastard picking up on what I say and passing the info back.'

'On the take? In CID? But who?'

'For Pete's sake, Kate, just meet me, will you? I've got something to show you. You won't be disappointed. Remember Yardley's?'

Kate felt as if she was in some sort of weird dream. Of course she remembered the derelict cider farm. It was where the main suspect in a previous murder inquiry had turned up dead, and where Hayden had almost ended up the same way.

'What about it?'

'It's not far from where I am now. Meet me there in an hour.'

'I still don't think—' But the phone went dead.

She rang him straight back, but the phone went to voicemail.

'Damn you, Roscoe,' she grated and bit her lip in an agony of indecision. It was no good trying to wake Hayden and seek his advice, he was still snoring loudly and, with the sleeping tablet he had taken and the amount of wine he had drunk, he would be of no help whatsoever.

So, what should she do? Was her former boss's call for help kosher, or was he simply seeking revenge for imagined past grievances by sending her off on a wild goose chase? If that was the case, she should just play him at his own game and ignore the whole damned thing. But what if he was in real trouble and she turned her back on him? She would never forgive herself if he came to harm because she had chosen to do nothing.

His revelation about the renegade in her department was another worry. She knew all her colleagues so well, and though each one had his faults, as she had hers, she couldn't for one moment believe that any of them had turned bad. But then why would Roscoe allege such a terrible thing? It seemed like a step too far even for him, unless it was true. And if it was, which of her colleagues was the renegade?

Cursing volubly, she marched up and down the kitchen before finally coming to a decision. Upstairs in the bedroom, Hayden didn't even stir as she dressed hurriedly. Throwing him a venomous look as she shut the door, she snatched the keys to his Mk II Jaguar off the telephone table, grabbed her coat from the back of the settee and stalked out of the house. She smiled to herself as she climbed behind the wheel, visualising Hayden's reaction when he found out that she had borrowed his pride and joy for a nocturnal spin. Moments later, she was speeding down the main road towards the Levels.

* * *

Roscoe took a chance after barging Coleman aside and turned right out of the side door of the barn towards the rear of the building instead of the way he had come in. He reasoned that Coleman's heavies would think he'd head for the track down to the lane, which was the obvious escape route. Hopefully, by the time they realised their mistake, he would be back to his car and away.

At the end of the barn, he was confronted by more trees and a tangled jungle of ferns and spiky bushes, but he nevertheless plunged into the undergrowth, heedless of the painful thorns. He was only just in time. Simultaneously a door slammed and boots pounded on the path behind him. He froze, teeth clenched with apprehension, but then, to his relief, the heavy footfalls quickly faded into the night. His assumptions had been right — so far.

Climbing slowly to his feet, he peered back along the path and saw the tall thin figure of Ronnie Coleman, trailing cigar smoke, emerge from the barn and walk briskly in the same direction as his cohorts. He didn't once look back.

Roscoe waited several minutes after the gang boss had disappeared to make sure this wasn't a trick, then crept back along the path to the front of the barn. The concrete hard-standing between the barn and the house was bathed in brilliant moonlight and it appeared to be deserted. Appeared to be.

He watched for a few seconds more, but the coast looked clear and he saw nothing to indicate that anyone was waiting for him. Time to find out whether he was right. Leaving cover, he crossed the few yards of open ground at a trot, expecting the sudden shout that meant he had been spotted.

But nothing happened and within seconds he was through the wood and the gap in the wire fence and hugging the shadows thrown by the line of trees, heading back the way he had come.

He managed to avoid the bog this time and, sighing with relief, got back to his car without being challenged. But his relief was short-lived. He had no idea what made him look at his tyres. Maybe it was the way the Honda was sitting so low in the grass. In any event, when he did look, he found that all four tyres were flat. Closer inspection revealed that they had been slashed. The bastards had found his car and either knew it was his or had vandalised it just in case. Now he was well and truly up shit creek without a paddle, to coin his own oft-used phrase. He peered at his watch. Twenty minutes before he was due to meet Kate at Yardley's. He was going to be late, which meant she might not wait — *if* he had managed to persuade her to come at all.

Then he got his second shock. His mobile was no longer in his pocket. A quick search of the rest of his clothes revealed it was not anywhere else either. Double shit! He must have dropped it somewhere on his way back to the car.

There was nothing for it but to walk. Fortunately, he knew the area well enough and was reasonably confident he could get there in half an hour if he put a spurt on. But he needed to make the main road linking the villages of Mark and Burtle first, then take the drove from there across country. But getting to the main road meant following the lane past Coleman's place, which could not be riskier in the present circumstances.

He took a deep breath, popped some chewing gum in his mouth and chewed furiously for a few seconds while he tried to weigh up his options, only to come to the conclusion that there was only one — he had to push on regardless.

Moving off slowly, he hugged the shadows of the hedgerow where the moonlight failed to reach, gripping his torch for use as a weapon if it were needed. The night was full of rustlings, and at one point a hawk flew out of the hedge, narrowly missing him before it veered away with a series of sharp banshee-like cries, to vanish in the star-spangled vault above. The moon dimmed as scudding clouds swept across the night sky, and he paused, standing in a peculiar half-light, which left much of the lane in front of him in darkness. He thought he heard feet scraping on the road surface, but unable to confirm whether there was someone lurking in the gloom up ahead, he stayed put, patiently waiting for the clouds to disperse. Then, abruptly, the moon reappeared in all its eerie glory and he started off again — only to freeze once more, alerted by the burning ember of a cigarette. There *was* someone there, maybe two to three yards away.

There was a cough and he saw the burning ember fly though the air and hit the ground in a tiny shower of sparks. Shit-sticks! As he had feared, they were waiting for him, and he had no idea how many there were and whether, like Coleman, they were armed.

He chewed furiously on his gum for a few seconds before making a decision. He couldn't continue along the lane, that was obvious, and going back was pointless, as he would be heading completely in the wrong direction. The only alternative was to find a way around the rather amateurish ambush ahead, which meant heading across country through the fields to his left.

He had previous for forcing his way through hedges, and he adopted the same tactic now, using his bulk to achieve it, as he had done when first setting out across the fields opposite. But the sound of his struggle with the tough foliage did not go unnoticed and, once through into the field on the other side, he ducked down behind the hedge when he heard the coarse voice call out.

'Did you hear that, Frank?'

A powerful beam traced a line through the shadows cast by the hedge onto the lane.

'Yeah,' another voice replied. 'Probably a bleedin' fox or somefing. And if it *was* Roscoe, you've just told him where we are, dickhead.'

The torch was quickly extinguished, and Roscoe heard the rasp of a match as another cigarette was lit. He remained motionless behind the hedge for a few minutes longer until he was sure neither Frank nor his pal had had second thoughts and decided to investigate further.

Turning while still in his crouched position, he scanned the field behind him and, with relief, noted the wooded area on the far side. If he could just get to it without being spotted in the moonlight, he was home and dry — well, at least temporarily.

Gritting his teeth, he finally hauled himself upright and, after a brief hesitation, took off at a lumbering run towards the wood. He picked up a track at the halfway point and stuck to it as he covered the last few yards to relative safety, expecting at any moment to hear a shout from the lane as his heavy figure was spotted by Frank or his companion and they came after him. But no one shouted or gave chase, and then he was into the gloom among the trees and completely invisible.

For several minutes he stayed right where he was, bent over and clutching his knees as he tried to slow his thumping heart and get his breath back. Then, guided by the cupped beam of his torch and the strands of moonlight filtering through the branches above his head, he started off through the trees, still following the just discernible track. His teeth were chattering now, partly from cold and partly from tension. He was scared, he had to admit it — knowing how ruthless Coleman was, he would be a fool not to be afraid — but he was also excited, excited to have got the goods on the gangland boss and be on the verge of seeing him nailed at last, after all these years. It all depended on Kate now, and whether the bottle of tablets and the suspect crack cocaine sample in his pocket would be enough to get her to take up the challenge.

* * *

Ronnie Coleman seldom got flustered. His nickname should have been "Mr Cool" rather than "Mr Havana." But behind the quiet, smooth-talking former investment banker-turned-professional criminal lurked a snake-like malevolence. It smouldered in his pale blue eyes now as he studied the big man standing awkwardly in front of him while he lounged in the swivel chair behind his desk.

'So, you lost him?' he said dispassionately. 'You let him get away?'

'Frank and Jimmy are still looking, boss,' Bruno Dodds ventured. The enforcer sounded like he had a bad cold and the plasters stuck over his fractured nose, which had only recently stopped bleeding after its run-in with Roscoe's head, gave him a clown-like look. In other circumstances Coleman might have found it amusing, but he wasn't amused now.

'So, why aren't *you* still looking?'

Dodds shuffled his size elevens. 'Thought I'd better report back.'

'With nothing to report? Rather pointless, don't you think?'

'Well, I been thinking—'

'I warned you about doing that before, you useless dipstick. I do the thinking. You do the doing. Got that?'

Dodds nodded and then winced.

He was obviously in a lot of pain, but, true to character, Coleman offered him nothing in the way of sympathy. Instead, he reached across his desk to pick up a note he had scribbled a few minutes before after a quick telephone call.

'The slimeball I have inside Highbridge nick tells me Roscoe has a beaten-up old Honda Civic. Blue,' he said. 'He didn't have the number, but the motor shouldn't be too hard to find. It's bound to be parked somewhere close by. Find it and immobilise it so that interfering bastard can't drive off in it. We can get rid of it later.'

'But what if that ex-cop has already rung the nick? Old Bill could be on his way here right now, mob-handed.'

Coleman's eyes glittered and he held up a mobile phone. 'He'd have had a job ringing anybody. He dropped this when he took off after wiping the floor with you and Frank, and my tame cop at the nick will tell me if he sees anything going on there that I should know about. So,' he hissed, 'all you dildos have got to do is find Ted bloody Roscoe. Capiche?'

'Yeah, 'course, boss,' Dodds said hastily.

'Coleman held out the mobile to him. 'And get rid of this somewhere where it won't be found.'

Dodds took the phone from him. 'Right on, boss.' He hesitated. 'But what do you want us to do with this Roscoe geezer when we find him?

Coleman studied him with a humourless smile. 'What do *you* think you should do?' he said softly.

Touching his nose tenderly, Bruno Dodds returned the smile. It wasn't a pleasant one.

CHAPTER 10

At any other time, Kate would have found it exhilarating driving Hayden's Jaguar. It was only her second time at the wheel, and even then, she had been under Hayden's direct supervision. The car was certainly old — built in 1959, it was a classic — just like the car *Inspector Morse* drove in the television crime series, although it was red instead of burgundy. It had been lovingly maintained, and the finely tuned engine was a real powerhouse. Only the poor state of the roads across the Levels, which were notorious for their uneven potholed surfaces and adverse cambers, prevented her from giving the car its head. As it was, she did reach sixty at one stage, but then had to reduce speed fast when the car began to develop an alarming bounce.

She saw the blaze when she was a couple of miles from her objective. It was further out to her left across the Levels and she didn't give it a great deal of thought, apart from wondering what there was to burn with the ground already saturated from the recent heavy rain. She never for one moment considered heading out there to investigate. She had enough on her plate as it was with Roscoe.

The derelict cider farm was much as she remembered it from her last visit — what seemed like years ago, but which was actually less than two. The moon lit up the concrete hardstanding and collection of empty buildings like a film set and, pulling into the verge by the main gate, she sat for several minutes lost in thought as she waited for Roscoe's beaten-up old Honda Civic to put in an appearance.

But after fifteen minutes had passed without any sign of him and unable to contact him on his mobile, she swore and climbed out of the car for a cursory look around.

Maybe he had parked around the back to avoid being seen from the road for some reason and hadn't heard her arrive.

She didn't bother to look in the outbuildings but made straight for what had once been the main offices, with the warehouse at the back. As she stepped through the open front doorway, the memories came flooding back. She recalled the night she and Hayden had entered the place from different ends, searching for prison escapee, Lenny Stallard, and Hayden had ended up being "clobbered with a lump of wood," as he later put it in the understatement of the century.

The offices and reception area were just as she remembered them. Broken glass crunched under her feet, the same as before. Even the splintered reception desk was still there and beyond it, the doorway leading into the warehouse. The forklift truck was also still in situ in the vast open space, silhouetted against the face of the moon, as it had been that scary night when she'd peered into the place through the open steel doors at the far end. She didn't go any further this time. It was obvious that there was no one waiting inside.

Returning to her car, she was furious to find that Roscoe had still not materialised. So, the call *had* been a hoax then, as she'd half-expected. The bastard was getting his own back on her by sending her out on a wild goose chase. Well, he would regret it when she turned up on his doorstep later.

Starting the engine, she swung the big saloon around and headed back home.

* * *

'Well?' Coleman said to the shadowy figure hovering on the edge of the light from his desk lamp. 'Found him yet?'

'No, boss,' Bruno Dodds said uneasily.

Coleman didn't even look up from his desk, but poured himself another whisky and swirled it around in his glass, before settling back in his chair to study a beetle which had had the temerity to try to cross the green leather in front of him.

'Why not?' he asked quietly.

Dodds swallowed hard. 'We looked everywhere, but it's dark out there and there's just miles of fields and woods. He could be anywhere.' Then he added in a rush, 'But we found the car.'

'Did you now?'

'Yeah, it's parked in a field behind a hedge, just down the road, and we immobilised it, like you said. It's got four flat tyres now, so he ain't going nowhere.'

'Well, that was clever, Bruno, wasn't it?'

In a sudden movement, Coleman sprang forward in his chair and slammed his fist down hard on the beetle, crushing it to a pulp.'

Dodds nearly jumped out of his skin. 'So, how do you propose getting rid of the vehicle now it can't be driven away?' Coleman spoke a little too softly for comfort.

Bruno swallowed. 'Dunno, boss.'

'Dunno, boss,' Coleman mimicked. 'Well, you'd better hope the Law don't spot it behind the hedge and start asking questions up here.'

'It's a thick hedge, boss,' Bruno added helpfully.

Coleman closed his eyes briefly. 'Not as thick as you, Bruno,' he said. 'Not as thick as you.'

* * *

Roscoe was still thinking about Kate's possible reaction to what he had to tell her when the track he was following widened into a clearing. He saw an old, dilapidated looking VW camper van parked on one side of it, and shortly afterwards a rough looking shack ahead. There were no lights showing in the windows and the place looked to be abandoned but he stopped briefly to satisfy himself that no one was lurking in the vicinity. He thought he heard something moving among the trees behind him but saw nothing when he whirled round to peer into the gloom. The sound was not repeated, so he pressed on, turning down the side of the strange looking building and through an open gateway on the other side of a small garden onto a stone bridge spanning a rhyne.

He looked cautiously both ways before stepping out onto the unmade track beyond and turning left. He knew roughly where he was and that the track would almost certainly take him back to the main road. From there, it was a sprint across an expanse of marsh to Yardley's and the rendezvous point. But he had only covered a few yards when he glimpsed the headlights of a vehicle coming very slowly towards him.

Them! It had to be. Why else would anyone be creeping along a narrow track like this at such an hour? It certainly wasn't Kate. She would be heading for Yardley's along the main road. Taking a wild leap through a convenient gap in the hedge across the rhyne that bordered the opposite side of the track, he crouched down among the trees to wait for the vehicle to pass.

It did very soon afterwards, and he saw it was some sort of big SUV. No doubt another motor from the Coleman company fleet. But, instead of carrying on along the track, the vehicle stopped right by the shack he had just left, and two doors slammed almost in unison as the occupants got out.

Climbing to his feet and adopting a half crouch, he made his way through the trees, following the track in the same direction as before. He was anxious to put as much distance as he could between him and his pursuers before they decided to extend their search. But that was made a lot more difficult when, a few yards further on, the trees petered out and the hedge that had been shielding him from view disappeared altogether, leaving him fully exposed in the moonlight, with just the rhyne between him and the track.

Instinctively dropping to the ground again, he stared up at the moon, willing the clouds to reappear, but the sky remained clear. He was on the point of deciding to risk detection and take off in a mad dash across the field, when an unexpected development took the decision out of his hands. Alerted by a sudden roaring sound, he pivoted round and saw a mass of flaming tongues leap into the sky from among the trees behind him. Shocked, he realised that the blaze had erupted right where the shack stood. As he stared, the flames rose higher and higher and began to spread out with a roar like that of some angry monster, accompanied by the sound of shattering glass and collapsing timbers. Then, the next instant, there was a massive explosion and the blaze mushroomed into something a lot more intense. He guessed the fire had reached the car parked in the wood and had found the petrol tank. Coleman's thugs must have torched the shack to prevent him using it as a refuge, which meant they knew he was in the vicinity. They might even be closer than he imagined.

Then he heard it. The stealthy movement among the trees behind him — the swish of clothing on low-level undergrowth and the squelch of a foot in a patch of wet mud. Unfortunately for him, he was a little too late turning round to investigate . . .

* * *

'You took my car?' Hayden wailed, running a hand through his mop of unruly fair hair in a gesture of despair. 'You took my Jag?'

Kate had never seen him so upset. He had been in a bad enough mood when he'd got up, but after she said she'd driven the Jag, it was as though he'd just been told a close relative had died. He didn't even seem concerned about

Roscoe's allegation of a bent colleague in their midst. It all went straight over his head.

'Sorry, Hayd,' she said, a little taken aback by his reaction. 'But I had to have wheels to get out there and my car is still in dock.'

He shook his head in disbelief. 'You know how much that car means to me. What if you'd bent or scratched it?'

'I didn't do either.'

'That's not the point. And it was a waste of time anyway. Roscoe was obviously having you on.'

'I wasn't to know that, was I?'

'But you took the car without my permission, that's what galls me.'

She stiffened. 'Without your permission? What is this? I'm your wife, you pompous shitbag. I don't need your permission to do anything.'

He stared at the floor sullenly. 'I didn't mean it like that, but that car means everything to me.'

'More than me, you mean?'

'Now you're being ridiculous. But you could have woken me, I'd have driven you myself.'

She snorted. '*You*? Bloody hell, man, you could hardly stand up last night after all that wine, and that was before you took one of my sleeping tablets.'

He winced. 'Okay, so you've got a point, but you shouldn't have gone out there on your own. Anything could have happened.'

She shook her head in disbelief. 'So, at last you're getting around to my safety — *after* your concern about that sodding heap of junk. For your information, I haven't slept at all since that old crone visited us and I'm cold and tired — not that you give a damn. Anyhow, it's great to know where your priorities lie.'

'That's not true—'

She cut him off with a wave of her hand. 'I'm not discussing the issue anymore. I'm going to work, so get your clothes on if you're taking me — unless you want to go in your PJs.'

He studied her sourly. 'And what about breakfast?'

'What about it? Either you forego it for once in your life and take me, or I drive myself in your precious Jag and you can follow on foot later.'

She dangled his ignition keys in front of him. 'Your choice, fat man. Belly or car?'

But she knew what his answer would be.

* * *

Just before leaving home, Kate received a text message from Inspector Drew, the Roads Policing officer investigating her accident, to say they had finished with her car, so she had Hayden drop her off at the garage on the way.

The Mazda certainly looked as though it had been in the wars. Apart from the smashed headlamp glass, the crease down the wing was worse than she had thought and there were several nasty dents in the bonnet, in addition to a multitude of deep scratches.

'Bit of work there, I'm afraid,' the garage hand announced with a grin, which Kate regarded as misplaced under the circumstances. 'Cost in the region of a grand, I reckon.'

'What?' Kate stared at him. 'Are you serious?'

He shrugged. 'Never more so. We've replaced the headlamp glass for you as a gesture of goodwill and it's okay to drive, but we'll need to hang onto the car for at least three to four days to do the rest.'

He scratched his nose. 'Can't do it for about a week, though. Up to our eyes.'

She took the keys from him. 'Thanks for the headlamp job anyway. I'll be in touch.'

As Kate climbed into the car, she saw that there were still dark patches on the door pillar where she had struck her head. Hayden's knee must have slammed into the facia, as part of it seemed to have come loose on the passenger side, but the car started first time and the drive from the garage was as smooth as it had always been, which was some relief at least.

Getting her car back, even in its damaged state, was a boon. Now she no longer had to rely on Hayden and his precious Jaguar, and she made the most of her recovered freedom by not immediately making for the police station.

Ted Roscoe's shabby bungalow was on the outskirts of the small village, the overgrown front garden and cracked, peeling rendering a testament to his total disinterest in anything that didn't come out of a bottle. His old Honda Civic wasn't parked in the driveway, but there was an asbestos garage with a moss-covered, corrugated iron roof down the side of the property and she thought that maybe he had found the energy to put the car away.

Parking outside, she strode purposefully up the concrete path and hammered on the front door with such force that some of the sealant around the door frame fell away onto the step. There was no reply. She hammered some more. Not even a twitch of the bay window's partially pulled curtains.

Frustrated beyond measure, she stalked around and hammered on the back door. Nothing stirred inside the bungalow. Returning down the path, she cupped her hands round her eyes and peered through the little rectangular windows at the top of the garage door. The garage contained a stack of firewood, some overturned boxes and a few rolls of carpet, but no car.

The bastard was out — and she knew just where her former boss would be.

The Black Cock had just opened when she swung into the car park, but the Honda Civic was nowhere to be seen.

Frowning, she peered through the window of the public bar, but even from where she stood, she could see it was empty.

Quitting the car park, she checked out the village shop half a mile down the road, again without success. Her "quarry" was evading her.

Returning to the pub, she parked up and went into the bar. The licensee, Mick Braithwaite, was in no hurry to answer the sound of the handbell on the counter, but he came eventually, and smiled when he saw who it was.

'Hi, Kate,' he said. 'Bit early for you, isn't it?'

'Ted Roscoe,' she snapped, unable to conceal her irritation. 'Have you seen him?'

He shook his head. 'Not since yesterday. Why, is there a problem?'

'You say he came in yesterday?' she said.

'Yeah, sort of. About lunchtime. Well, his car drove into the car park. I saw him through the window while a customer was paying his bill. But he never came in, just sat in his motor.' He shrugged. 'Then my customer and his friends left, and he drove off after them. That's the last I saw of him. He didn't come in that evening like he usually does.'

No, he was playing silly buggers with me, that's why, Kate said to herself. 'You say he drove off after your customers. What did you mean by that?'

He frowned. 'Well, he left when they left, and he churned up some gravel when he went, as if he was trying to catch up with them.'

'You mean he knew them?'

'Can't say. I just thought it was funny he didn't come in, then left like that. Maybe he suddenly remembered he'd forgotten his wallet or something.'

Roscoe's voice growled in Kate's head. 'I've stumbled on something big — a face from the past.'

'Do you know who the customers were?' she asked.

He shook his head again. 'Three men and a woman. Had a meal and then left. Punters from London, I wouldn't wonder, going by their accents, and the woman was a real dollybird, made up to the nines.' He grinned. 'Bit of all right she was too.'

'Anything unusual about them?'

'Nah, just punters, that's all. You get lots of them from the Smoke, passing through. Nice car, though. Big black Volvo 4x4. Oh, and the bloke who paid the bill stood out a bit. Immaculate, expensive suit and weird hair.'

'Weird *hair*?'

'Yeah, sort of silver colour, swept back and quite thick too. Looked like he was keen on looking good.'

'How did he pay? Didn't use a card, did he?'

'Nah. Cash on the nail.'

'What did the other two guys look like?'

'Don't remember really. Just suits. Didn't smile a lot.'

Kate nodded slowly. 'Thanks anyway. Could you give me a ring if you see any of the four again, or if Roscoe himself turns up?'

'No problem. Something going on, is there?'

'Not as far as I know. Just curious after what you said, that's all.'

Kate sat for a few minutes in the car before driving away. A face from the past? What the hell had Roscoe been on about? And if he wasn't at home or at his favourite local, where was he? For the first time, she began to feel uneasy.

CHAPTER 11

Kate finally arrived at Highbridge police station just after ten. Like most coppers who have been involved in an accident, she was majorly embarrassed by the fact, and she parked the car in the far corner of the yard with the damaged side as close to the wall as possible. She knew the state of the car would attract facetious comments from her colleagues when they saw it and she was prepared for that in due course, but after her row with Hayden and all the other worries that were weighing her down — not the least of which were the condition of the woman in the ICU and the disappearance of Roscoe — she was in no mood for their brand of humour just at that moment. She almost crept in through the back door of the station, so she wouldn't have to speak to anyone en route to her office.

But when she reached the stairs to the first floor, Dave Gort, the Local Intelligence Officer almost collided with her on the way down.

'Ah, Kate,' he said. 'Just been up to see you. Left you a note.'

She paused with one foot on the first step. 'See me? About what?'

'I understand you're following up on a complaint of an attack on a local church and, according to Eddie West, you have an old biddy calling herself Lilith, who's living out on the Levels, in the frame for it?'

'Yes, except that your "old biddy" has gone AWOL.'

'Well, it seems she's resurfaced.'

'What?'

He nodded. 'It's all in the daily bulletin I left on your desk with my note. Apparently, a woman answering her description tried to get into the ICU at the main hospital last night. Bill Layton, one of the night crew, attended, but she'd scarpered by the time he got there.' He chuckled suddenly. 'The old girl evidently put a curse on the nurse who confronted her, and the security camera picked her up driving away in a beaten-up old VW camper. No number visible on the back apparently. Anyway, Bill Layton filed a report before he went off duty and I thought you should know about it.'

'Did the woman say why she was trying to get into the ICU?'

'Yeah, according to Layton, she told the nurse she wanted to see a female patient they've got in there, but no reason was given.'

'She didn't happen to name the patient, did she?'

He frowned. 'No, but from what Layton gathered, she told the nurse the patient belonged to her.'

'Belonged to her?'

'Yeah, and something about some character she referred to as "the Horned One." He was wondering whether we'd got anyone loose from a nuthouse. Anyway, I did a PNC check and turned up this woman who calls herself Lilith and a link to Eddie West. Gave him a ring at home and he filled me in on the rest.'

Kate nodded slowly. 'Thanks, Dave. I'll get back to you if I need anything else.'

She was halfway up the stairs when she heard him chortle. 'Oh, by the way, skipper, apparently the nurse did say that the woman patient had been involved in an RTA with a police officer. Don't know who that could have been, do you?'

‘Sod off, Gort,’ she replied and, leaving him standing there shaking with suppressed laughter, she pushed through the doors at the top of the stairs and along the corridor to what the superintendent — in those grandiose moments when he received a visit from special guests such as the police authority — referred to as the CID “suite.”

But she only got as far as the doors of the department before they were opened, and she almost walked into Hayden on his way out. He was in a real hurry, which was most unlike her well-upholstered husband. His face was flushed and he was puffing with the exertion.

‘What’s up, Hayd?’ she said acidly. ‘Did you think they might sell the last lardy cake before you managed to get to the canteen?’

He stood for a moment to one side of the doorway, catching his breath. ‘On my way out,’ he blurted. ‘Dreadful shock. Can’t believe it.’

‘Can’t believe what?’

He stared at her. ‘Eddie West. He’s just dropped down dead.’

* * *

The fox was a wily old creature. He had been around a very long time for a fox. He had lost one eye and there were deep scars on his muzzle and flanks from encounters with badgers and otters, but he had always managed to survive to fight another day. He had evaded men with guns and dogs many times and managed to slip in and out of the farms on his patch with total impunity. The humans had tried to trap him, of course, but he always seemed to know instinctively when a trap had been set, circling the partially concealed steel mechanism but never suffering the vicious bite of its jaws. Once or twice he had even snatched the bait from the trap itself, maybe just to prove a point.

Reynard was wary on this particular morning too. He had smelled something interesting just before the sun came up and had crept through the brush and along the bank of the rhyne to investigate, crouching right down when he got closer and worming his way forward on his belly.

He stopped about three yards from the burned-out shell of the building, sniffing the air, his one eye on the blackened ruin. He could smell food — or what was left of it — but something else too, something that sent his hackles up and his lips curling back in a soundless snarl.

At first he couldn't see where the smell was coming from, but then he stiffened, his sharp gaze homing in on the spot. The body was lying in the adjacent rhyne, partially submerged among the reeds. If he could have sneered, he would have done so.

No, they wouldn't catch him this way. He was too clever for the men he felt sure were hidden in the undergrowth nearby with their sticks of fire. Easing back into the brush, Reynard left them to it and disappeared back into the emerging dawn light.

* * *

The amiable member of the local policing team was lying on his stomach on the kitchen floor of his small terraced cottage, dressed in his uniform tunic and trousers. He was still wearing his carpet slippers. A red-haired man in his thirties whom Kate took to be the doctor, was crouched over West's corpse.

While she waited for him to finish his examination, she threw a sympathetic glance at the white-faced policewoman standing by the door who she recognised from the scene of the vandalism at the village church. She could see that Janet Robinson was very upset and having difficulty holding back the tears, and she admired the way the young officer was coping with what must have been a particularly traumatic situation for someone who had lost such a close colleague.

'Obviously having a snack before going on duty,' Percival observed grimly, pointing to a half-full mug of what looked like tea or coffee and a plate of biscuits on the nearby kitchen table. 'Supposed to have been on for court duty at ten. Never even made it to his boots.'

Kate nodded. West was lying with his bald head in a pool of bloodied vomit and several thin lines of blood traced a web-like pattern across the fawn tiles, disappearing beneath a pair of black boots by the door.

'The likelihood is that it was a myocardial infarction — a heart attack,' the doctor said, climbing to his feet. 'Hit the floor with considerable force and his weight would not have helped matters, particularly falling, as he did, face-downwards, which would have compressed his diaphragm and lungs. Quite a nasty impact wound from the fall to his right temple too, hence the bleeding.'

'Any idea as to time of death?' Percival asked.

The doctor shrugged. 'Within the last couple of hours, I would say, but that's only a guesstimate.'

'Is — was — he one of your patients, Doctor, er . . ?' Kate began.

'Snider,' he said. 'And, yes, he was one of mine. Warned him enough times about his weight.' He frowned. 'I thought you police officers were supposed to be fit?'

Kate smiled. 'Some of us are,' she said, casting a reproving glance in the direction of Hayden who was hovering in the doorway, his face as pale as that of Janet Robinson. 'Did he have medical problems?'

Snider shook his head. 'I really can't discuss a patient's medical history with you.'

'But he's dead. I can't see that being a problem now.'

'I still can't discuss them with you.'

'Well, maybe I don't have to ask.' Kate held up a box of tablets she had found on a Welsh dresser just inside the back door, beside a big tin tea caddy. 'Losartan. Tablets to reduce high blood pressure, aren't they?'

The doctor's frown deepened. 'They can form part of the treatment, yes.'

She smiled as sweetly as she could manage. 'My late dad used to take losartan — plus aspirin,' she explained. 'Not that they did him much good in the end. So, I think it's fair to assume poor old Eddie here had a medical history we knew nothing about, eh?'

'All I can say is that from my examination and my knowledge of the patient, the likelihood is he probably suffered a sudden fatal heart attack,' he said, picking up his medical bag and snapping it shut. 'But there are some interesting aspects to his condition, including the dilation of his pupils, the fact that he seems to have vomited and the presence of excessive salivation, which might suggest an additional issue with other unofficial medication he may have been taking, such as herbal remedies, which I would never recommend to any of my patients. Because of this and the fact that I haven't seen him for a month now, I cannot issue a death certificate.

'So, there will be a post-mortem?'

'Unavoidable under the circumstances, I'm afraid.'

Kate nodded. 'But to be clear, in your professional opinion, there is nothing here to suggest that there is anything suspicious in relation to the death?'

Snider frowned again. 'Not as far as I can see. The only injury I have found is the head wound, which I am satisfied was caused when he collapsed onto the tiled floor. No, it's more likely his demise was just an unfortunate but inevitable consequence of his physical condition and lifestyle, I would say.'

'Do we know who found him? His wife?'

'Apparently, his sister,' Janet Robinson put in. 'She lives in the village. She came over to see him this morning and found the door open, and Eddie lying on the floor inside. By then he was already dead. She's an ex-nurse, so she knew what she was doing.'

'How's she taken it?'

'Quite well — on the surface anyway. I sent her home.'

'As for his wife,' Snider added, 'she's been gone these last two years. Ironically, as the result of a heart attack.'

Nodding curtly to no one in particular, he promptly departed with a brief, 'Well, my job is finished here. Good afternoon, people.'

Kate watched him go, then turned to Robinson again. 'You okay to stay on in the house to await the undertaker and sort out the formalities with Eddie's sister? We'll need to leave her with the house key so she can secure the place afterwards.'

Robinson nodded. 'My sergeant and the coroner's officer should be arriving any minute now. It's a straightforward sudden death, so we can take it from here.'

Kate thanked her and turned for the door, leaving her with just the corpse for company. How brutal life could be. What was it her tutor constable had told her when she'd first joined the job all those years ago? Oh yes, 'Life's a bitch and then you die.' Well, it had certainly been a bitch for Eddie West.

'No suspicious circumstances anyway,' Hayden murmured as they followed Percival and the doctor down the garden path to their car, ignoring a solitary female figure standing on the pavement nearby who had press written all over her.

'Not unless you count witches' curses,' Kate said.

He stopped in mid stride. 'You're not seriously suggesting that, are you? I mean, it's a bit of a coincidence after that doll with the pins in, but—'

'Joking, Hayd,' she cut in drily. 'Just joking. Okay?'

But for some reason, her words sounded hollow to her. For the second time that morning, she felt a strange sense of unease.

CHAPTER 12

'So, what are we doing here?' Hayden said half an hour later. 'I thought you didn't believe in witchcraft?'

He had been watching the route Kate was taking with little apparent interest, saying nothing. Even when they entered the village main street and pulled up outside the half-timbered building off the square carrying the sign "Museum," he simply sat, staring out of the window morosely, seemingly in a dark world of his own.

'I don't,' she retorted. 'But we've heard a lot about the woman who was burned as a witch out on the Levels, and it might be helpful to delve a little into the story to see what might be motivating Lilith.'

'Whatever,' he muttered. 'It's up to you.'

She threw open her door and glanced back at him. 'You okay?'

He shrugged, opening his own door. 'As I'll ever be, I suppose.'

She frowned. It was obvious that something was wrong. Hayden had never been what might be described as a live wire, but this "couldn't care" attitude wasn't like him at all. Maybe the tragic death of Eddie West had got to him. She had noticed how pale he was at the dead officer's house and he had hardly said a word then either. There was another possibility too. That he was still sulking after their row the previous night, coupled with the fact that she had taken his car without his say-so. Childish, yes, but that could be her Hayden at times. She determined to have it out with him one way or the other at the earliest opportunity, but this was not the right moment.

The museum proved to be open and they found themselves in a large square room with a reception desk just inside the door. The place smelled of damp and decay. A length of rope was suspended between the desk and the wall, barring further access. Beyond this, glass cases, displaying old maps and other documents, adorned the walls and there was a narrow staircase in the far left-hand corner, rising to another level. A suit of armour stood in the opposite corner and, with a start, Kate saw that the whole floor was occupied by what she now recognised as a crudely drawn pentagram.

They were greeted by a plump, middle-aged woman, who got up off the stool behind the reception desk with a smile and held out a thin brochure.

'Welcome, me ducks,' she said in a strong Somerset accent, obviously delighted to have some visitors. 'Carrie Fisher. Have you come far?'

Kate produced her warrant card and the smile instantly left the woman's face, to be replaced by a spark of alarm in her bespectacled grey eyes.

'Goodness,' she exclaimed. 'Problem, is there?'

Kate introduced Hayden and herself and shook her head. 'Just curious. We're following up some local inquiries and would like to find out about the lady who was burned as a witch just outside the village,' she gave a short laugh, 'obviously not recently.'

Fisher didn't seem to see the joke and nodded gravely. 'Aye, poor Molly Clavey. Dreadful business, that were. Display's upstairs, so why don't you come through?'

Unhooking the rope, she led them across the room towards the staircase, pointing at the floor as she went.

'Not a real pentagram,' she said with a short laugh, without explaining what a real one was. 'The museum's trustees had it painted on the floor to give the place a little more atmosphere.'

Following her up the creaking stairs, her shoulders scraping the walls on both sides, Kate stared into the lamplit gloom above and mused that the one thing this dark, musty old building did not lack was atmosphere.

The upper floor comprised another large, poorly lit room with small windows. Glass cabinets were set against the walls and in a double row down the centre, containing what looked like animal bones, broken pottery, rusty implements and weapons, and some old books laid open to reveal the spidery writing inside. There were also steel helmets and uniform insignia, plainly from the two world wars, together with a diorama depicting a major flooding scene. All added up to a hotchpotch of disparate memorabilia and historical artefacts covering the history of the area.

Even if they had wished to browse the collection for a few minutes, they were not given the opportunity. Fisher led them straight past it all to a couple of glass display cabinets in the far right-hand corner of the room beneath a banner bearing the words: "Witchcraft On The Levels."

'I al'ays think this be our most interestin' exhibition in the museum,' she gushed.

One of the cabinets contained a variety of artefacts, including crudely carved wooden dolls, fragments of glass bottles, a curved rusted knife, several rings engraved with what Kate guessed were cabalistic signs, a broomstick with just three or four inches of the blackened rush broom remaining and what looked like the similarly blackened remains of a goat's skull, with just one splintered horn attached.

'As you probably know,' Fisher went on, 'in 1644, a local woman named Molly Clavey were accused of witchcraft and burned to death in her cottage on the Levels after it were set alight by a mob led by the village magistrate, Tom Sharpe.'

'Nice touch for a magistrate,' Kate commented drily.

'Ah, but them was different times,' Fisher pointed out. 'Although the condemnin' of witches and them wicked witchcraft trials was fast coming to an end by the middle of the seventeenth century, people was still very superstitious and believed in the dark arts and the existence of witches. Poor Molly was one of the last to perish for it and it is said she put a curse on Tom Sharpe, as a result of which he lost his mind and was sent to the madhouse, where he remained till his death.'

She tapped the glass of the cabinet. 'All them artefacts is said to have been recovered from the burned-out shell of Molly Clavey's cottage shortly after the fire and were retained by the clerk of the village parish council. Fascinatin' collection, isn't it?'

Kate had her doubts about the authenticity of some of the items after over three hundred years, but she made no comment, merely nodding in acknowledgement at what she was being told. As for Hayden, he leaned against the wall beside the cabinet, hands thrust in his pockets and staring around him with what Kate knew to be a deliberately manufactured air of boredom. He was determined to be as much of a pain as possible and she could have strangled him on the spot.

'What is all this in here?' she heard herself saying, interrupting Fisher's well-practised delivery and pointing at the second cabinet, which contained an open ledger and several faded drawings.

The other looked slightly irritated at the interruption but warmed to the question.

'That book be the parish record,' she explained. 'Among other things to do with parish business, it tells what happened to Molly Clavey and the horrible fate suffered by Tom Sharpe.'

'I wouldn't think any fate could be worse than being burned alive.'

Fisher chuckled. 'Ah, but that is where you're wrong, see. At least Molly's death was quick. Accordin' to the entry in the parish records, Sharpe went home after murderin' Molly and when he climbed into bed beside his sleepin' wife, he discovered that she had vanished and in her place were a shrivelled demon hag. They say that when a servant found him, he were a babbling idiot. Poetic justice, don't you think?'

Even Hayden raised his eyebrows at that point, and there was the trace of a contemptuous smirk on his face, though he still made no comment.

Kate threw him a warning look. 'Nice happy ending then,' she said. 'No wonder Sharpe went mad.'

Fisher nodded and tapped on the glass of the cabinet again. 'The drawin' you can see here were made by Hal Webber, the local publican, who were somethin' of an amateur artist. The one on the left clearly depicts the burnin' of Molly Clavey's cottage by the mob, which Webber himself were part of, and you can see her standin' at the window, screamin' and wavin' her arms. The one next to it is a depiction of Tom Sharpe findin' the demon hag in his bed—'

'Webber plainly had a vivid imagination,' Kate interjected again, trying to divert Fisher's attention from Hayden's very deliberate bored yawn. 'Er, what's the third pic about? It seems to be just an old house.'

Fisher raised a finger. 'Tom Sharpe's place, just a short distance from Molly's cottage across the marsh. The house is still there — or at least some of it is. It were partially restored, then added to by different owners over the centuries, but it's now more or less a ruin after the last owner left around ten years ago. It's just been bought by a fella from London or somewhere, a Mr Silverman, who plans to do it up.' She laughed. 'He's got a job on his hands there — that's if the ghost of old Molly will let him finish it.'

Kate smiled. 'Haunted, is it?' she said mildly.

Fisher didn't smile back. 'They do say when them hinkypunks come out at night, then old Molly is supposed to be round about, still lookin' for Tom Sharpe at Witch-Fire House.'

Kate felt a sudden heady surge of adrenalin. Even Hayden seemed to have pricked up his ears.

'Witch-Fire House?' she echoed.

Fisher shrugged. 'That be the name one of them previous owners gave it, and it sort of stuck. Quite appropriate when you think about it. Sign's still up outside too, which helps the tourists to find it when they be ghost huntin' on the Levels.'

Kate took a deep breath as her brain processed the information, but before she could recover from the shock of the innocent disclosure, Fisher followed it up with the question that had obviously been nagging at her since the arrival of the two detectives.

'You said earlier that you was here on some sort of inquiry connected to the Molly Clavey story,' she said. 'Wouldn't be about our local witch, Lilith, would it?'

Kate was taken aback for a moment and fielded the question with one of her own. 'Why do you say that?'

Fisher shrugged. 'Pretty obvious, I'd say. She reckons she's a reincarnation of Molly, don't she? Been in here a lot, looking at that display and askin' questions. Once caught her tryin' to open one of them cabinets — the one containin' the broomstick and that. Totally crackers, of course.'

'Have you seen her recently?' Kate went on before Fisher could return to her own question.

The woman shook her head. 'Not allowed in here now. Got banned, see.' She frowned thoughtfully. 'Last time I see Lilith were about a week gone, out walkin' on the marsh near that hovel she calls a home.'

'Does she live alone, do you know, or is anyone staying with her?'

'Can't say meself. Never saw anyone with her, just a scabby lookin' cat followin' along behind her that one time.' She refocused. 'So, what's this inquiry of yours about then, Sergeant? Why you interested in Molly and Lilith?'

Kate thought quickly. She would have to say something.

'Just routine, that's all,' she said. 'Lilith has been reported missing and we just wanted a bit of background on her interest in Molly Clavey to see if it turned up anything.'

It was a lame answer, but Fisher seemed satisfied. 'Maybe she finally found Molly,' she said. 'Or Molly found her. If that's the case, she won't be comin' back from where she's gone, an' that's a fact.'

* * *

'Witch-Fire House,' Kate breathed when she and Hayden returned to the CID car. 'It was 'witch fire' that the woman blurted to me after that accident. So, it wasn't anything to do with the will-o'-the-wisp lights we saw out on the Levels. She must have been referring to that actual house.'

Hayden didn't respond. He was sitting slumped in his seat, staring out of the window.

'Didn't you hear me, Hayd?' she said. 'It could be the break we've been looking for.'

He turned his head slowly to look at her, his face pale and sullen. 'No, it's the break *you've* been looking for.'

She returned his stare with a puzzled frown. 'What are you talking about? We're in this together. We're a team, you and I.'

He gave a short unamused laugh. 'Is that what we are? Well, maybe I don't see things that way anymore.'

She shook her head in bewilderment. 'I don't understand. What's wrong with you? In there just now, you deliberately tried to undermine what I was doing.'

'Well, there was no point to it, was there? It was just a waste of time.'

'How can it have been a waste of time when we found out about Witch-Fire House?'

He snorted, suddenly more animated and a lot angrier with it.

'So, you have the name of a house which seems to link in with what some semi-comatose accident casualty came out with. What has that to do with anything? And what exactly are we chasing here? We've got a local nutter who thinks she's a witch and is the chief suspect in a case of vandalism at a village church and a woman in hospital who ran out in front of your car and may or may not be connected to her. So what? This isn't a murder case, Kate. For once in my life, I actually agree with what Roscoe apparently said about these so-called Satanist attacks. This is a straightforward criminal damage job which uniform are quite capable of dealing with. We should not have got involved in the thing to start with.' He threw his hands up in the air and hit the roof of the car. 'It's — it's a joke. You've become obsessed.'

For a moment she sat there in silence, numbed by his out of character tirade.

'Anyway,' he added, 'I'm done with it all. As I said last night, I don't want to do this anymore.'

'I thought that what you said last night was just because you were overtired,' she said quietly.

'Yes,' he said, 'I was and still am tired — tired of what you and I have been doing all these years. Tired of traipsing around the countryside on one investigation after another, tired of sleepless nights, of call-outs and bolted meals, and most especially, tired of our privacy being forever invaded by the very people we are investigating.'

She took a deep, trembling breath. She was starting to realise that this was not just a touch of pique. but something more serious. 'So, what brought all this on — Eddie West's death? I know he was a friend of yours—'

'Yes,' he interjected, 'he *was* a friend of mine, a very good friend. We were both members of the same classic car club, we shared the same love of history and politics. We often got together and talked about classic motor cars — with not even a mention of police work. And yes, his death has hit me hard because I can see that what happened to him is likely to happen to me in a few years' time. Gordon Bennett, Kate, he was just months away from retirement. Is this what he gets after twenty-nine years' loyal service — a long pine box and a miniscule obituary in the Force newsletter?'

She emitted a low whistle. 'Whew! You have got it bad today, haven't you? But you have to remember, although

Eddie's death was tragic, he obviously had serious health problems, was well overweight, and no doubt drank like a fish—'

'For your information, he didn't drink at all, not a drop. He was actually into tea and drank gallons of it. In fact, he was a bit of a connoisseur on tea and was interviewed by the local newspaper a couple of weeks ago about his passion for the stuff and the study he had made of it. If you had taken the trouble to look around his kitchen you'd have found packets of a whole load of different varieties from all over the world in one of the cupboards and there was a massive tea caddy on the Welsh dresser.'

'Okay, I did see the caddy, but the point I am making is that he would have died just the same if he had been a booking clerk for the Great Western Railway. Police work had nothing to do with it.'

'This isn't just about Eddie,' he muttered, 'though he was probably the last straw for me. I've been thinking about the job for a long time now and, as I've just said, I don't want to do it anymore.'

'And what about me? Don't I count?'

There was a tortured look on his face now. 'That's not fair. Of course you count. You're the most important thing in my life. I would probably have chucked the job in a long time ago if it hadn't been for you.'

She swallowed hard and studied him intently. 'Okay, so where does that leave us now?'

The look on his face was almost pleading. 'I thought we could try something else — another job, which would allow us to lead a normal life.'

Her mouth tightened and she shook her head. 'You know that's not an option for me. I won't jack it in. I just can't.'

'You were ready to do it once before.'

'That was because of Roscoe and his constant harassment, and he's gone now.'

There was a long pause as Hayden stared down at his knees, plainly agonising over something else he had to tell her. Then he looked up, met her gaze, and looked away again.

'There's a chance of a position at my old public school in Berkshire,' he blurted out.'

'A what?'

'It's — it's a teaching job. History. I have a chum there who says he could swing it for me.'

She emitted another hard laugh and, shaking her head in disbelief, she started the engine. 'Then you'd better take it,' she said simply, pulling away. 'You've obviously already made your choice.'

* * *

They drove back to the police station in heavy uncomfortable silence, and as soon as they pulled into the yard, Hayden was out of the car and striding quickly into the building through the back door.

He was no doubt heading to the canteen for some lunch, Kate thought, but she made no attempt to follow him. Somehow, she didn't feel at all hungry. Instead, she sat in the driving seat for several minutes with the engine still running.

She felt as though she'd been hit by a bus, so great was her shock at Hayden's revelations. She had always known he was a reluctant detective, but thought it was down to laziness and resentment towards authority. He was a rebel, a free spirit, after all, and it must have been difficult for him having to adjust to a disciplined regime like the police service. Yet he had stuck it out all these years, serving in the uniformed ranks like everyone else before becoming a detective, so why decide to throw it all over now?

And what about their marriage? Berkshire? That was miles away. It would be impossible for them to stay together if he took that job. She could always apply for a transfer to Thames Valley Police, but there was no guarantee her application would be accepted and, if it was, she would almost certainly have to start at the bottom again, forfeiting her rank and becoming a uniformed constable once more. That was unthinkable — but then so was splitting up with Hayden.

She felt the tears running down her cheeks, and quickly dried her eyes and switched off the engine. The information she had obtained from Carrie Fisher at the museum, Roscoe's apparent disappearance, the mystery attached to Lilith and the injured woman in the hospital were all temporarily buried in the tangle of personal thoughts choking her mind.

At first, she wasn't aware of the signet ring tapping against her window, and only responded when the door was unceremoniously jerked open from the outside.

'You okay in there?' Percival asked, peering at her with concern written into his expression. 'You look as though you've seen a ghost.'

Kate stared up at him and gave a rueful smile. 'Maybe I have, Des. Probably the ghost of the future.'

'You and Hayden had a row then? He stomped into the office like a bear with a sore head.'

She smiled again. 'Don't worry about it, Des,' she said, continuing with the clichés, 'storm in a teacup. What's up?'

He stepped back as she closed her door. 'I was just going out to an incident on the Levels. Thought you might like to come too.'

'Oh? What is it?'

'A fire,' he said, 'a rather curious one, which I thought we'd take a look at. It seems someone burned down Lilith's place last night and she's still nowhere to be found.'

He reached into his pocket and produced a Mars Bar. 'Here, take this. Looks like you'll be missing lunch.'

CHAPTER 13

'So, what is it with the two of you?' Percival asked, settling into the front passenger seat of the CID car beside Kate. She started to move out of the police station yard.

'I'd rather not talk about it,' she replied tersely. 'It's personal.'

He held up his hands apologetically. 'Sorry, Kate, didn't mean to tread on corns. But if there's going to be a problem between you and Hayden, I need to know about it — for the good of the department.'

'Just a minor domestic,' she lied. 'We'll get over it.'

But deep down she didn't think they would. Not this time.

Lilith's shack was now just a dismembered heap of charred wood and bits of twisted corrugated iron. The woodland and undergrowth around it — and for some distance beyond — had also taken a hit, much of it was burned to a cinder.

'Bit of a mess,' Percival commented, 'but at least they didn't find a corpse.'

He started going through the wreckage, pulling the remains of corrugated sheets aside and peering underneath them. At one stage he bent down to retrieve something, then held up what looked like part of a canvas bag.

'Someone's haversack, I would think,' he said, 'but this is all that's left of it now.'

Kate's eyes narrowed. Why was Percival so interested in the burned-out shack of a mentally disturbed old woman? What was he looking for?

Roscoe's voice cut into her brain: '*There's a guy in your team who's on the take.*' Whether her old boss had been telling the truth or simply having her on for his own malicious amusement, she was still not fully decided. But after his apparent vanishing act and what the licensee of the Black Cock had told her about the punters who had visited his pub, she was beginning to lean more towards it being genuine. But if that was the case, what had Roscoe unearthed? Surely, whatever it was, Des Percival couldn't be mixed up in it? That just didn't make any sense. As far as she knew, Des had had an unblemished career, was well liked, well trusted and earmarked for the top. So, why would he risk throwing it all away by turning on his own, and who could his paymaster be in deepest Somerset? It was not exactly the crime hotspot of the South-West.

'What are you looking for?' she said at length.

He straightened and half-turned with a shrug. 'Don't know really. Maybe something that might tell us how the fire started.'

'Didn't the fire service say?'

He picked his way back towards her. 'Arson likely, in their opinion, though they couldn't be certain, as they were unable to find the seat of the fire or any evidence pointing to exactly what was used to start it. Possibly kids with a grudge, they thought. Lilith wasn't personality of the month. Maybe they torched her place to teach her a lesson and if that was the case, it seems to have been a pretty devastating one.' He sighed. 'Still, not much we can do about it now.'

'And that's it then, is it? Just cuffed, like Roscoe used to do if it was in the "too difficult" box?'

He winced at the barb. 'That's a bit of a harsh judgment, isn't it? Let's be frank, the thing is hardly worth taking any further. After all, we're talking about the torching of nothing more than a shack thrown up without planning permission on land the old girl had no right to be on in the first place.'

'It was still someone's home.'

'If you call a shithole like this a home. Still, I take your point, but in any case, I don't intend wasting a lot of time and expensive forensic resources on it when the department has got other much more serious cases on its books.'

Kate made a face. This sounded just like Roscoe talking. But she said nothing further. Instead, she wandered away and followed the track into the partially destroyed woodland to the clearing where she and Hayden had found the old VW camper van parked. The vehicle was still there, but its days of hitting the highway were well and truly over. The fire had spread through the woodland from the shack and had obviously ignited the fuel in the petrol tank. The car was now a burned-out wreck.

'So, this was the camper van she was using? Percival said at her elbow. 'I see in PC Layton's incident report that it was picked up on the CCTV camera when she paid a visit to the hospital's ICU.'

Kate nodded. 'What's left of it. Hayden and I saw the car parked here on a previous visit.'

He grunted. 'Then she's on her toes somewhere out there on the Levels.' He waved a hand vaguely. 'I don't envy her at her age. Any idea why she wanted to see your Jane Doe?'

'Not a clue, but it's obvious there's some sort of a link between the two of them. When you were last here, I did say I noticed there were two beds in the shack. Remember? Maybe the injured woman was living with Lilith.'

'So, was she running from her when you hit her, do you think?'

Kate hesitated. 'Who knows? Until the woman comes out of her coma or we get hold of Lilith, we have no way of finding out.'

'Hmm. Then we'll just have to wait until that happens, won't we? Anything else I should know about this business?'

She shook her head. Despite feeling guilty about it, she held back the information about Lilith's visit to her home, Roscoe's phone call and disappearance, or what she had found out at the museum about Witch-Fire House.

'Not that I can think of, no.'

He studied her suspiciously for a moment, then suddenly smiled. 'Well then, nothing left for us to do but head to the nick for a coffee, is there?'

* * *

Two of the department's detectives, Jamie Foster and Danny Ferris, were at work on their computers when Kate and Percival arrived back in the office, but Hayden was nowhere to be seen.

'A guy who's on the take . . .' Roscoe's voice growled inside Kate's head and she studied the two detectives suspiciously for a moment as Percival wandered into the glass-fronted DI's office and shut the door.

She had known the slim, tousle-haired Jamie Foster for several years. He had been a loyal, hard-working DC, and had always been particularly supportive towards her. An astute, go-ahead copper, he was seen by most of his colleagues as a rising star, like his father before him, who had made chief superintendent in the Thames Valley force before his retirement.

As for Danny Ferris, the heavy-set, ex-squaddie, with his black curly hair, dark eyes and stubbled chin, he may have been a bit of a rough-house in his dealings with "uncooperative" villains, but he'd never given her any cause to doubt his integrity, and he was one of the best backup men she had ever worked with. Not particularly industrious, he had always proved to be solid and reliable and had earned two commendations for bravery.

The last remaining members of the small departmental team — apart from Hayden, of course — were Fred Alloway, who was currently off long-term sick with a back injury and

Indrani Purewal, who was on holiday, visiting her relatives in India, which put them both out of the frame.

'Where's Hayden?' she said to no one in particular.

The grey-haired office manager, Ronnie Crouch, looked up from behind his desk, 'Gone off duty with a migraine,' he said, a smirk on his lean, slightly pockmarked face. 'Said to tell you he was going to bed.'

'The hell he is,' Kate muttered and promptly about-turned, heading back through the double doors.

'Tell him he should leave himself alone,' Crouch called after her, attracting snorts of laughter from the two other detectives in the office. 'They say it can make you go blind.'

Kate never heard him, and she only got as far as the CID car when her mobile rang. Thinking it was Hayden, she answered immediately with an angry, 'What the hell are you doing?'

There was a sharp intake of breath. 'You said to ring you if I remembered anything else,' a surprised voice replied. 'It's Michael Braithwaite at the Black Cock.'

Kate winced. 'Er, sorry, Mick, I thought it was Hayden.'

There was a chuckle at the other end. 'You two had a spat or something?'

She took a deep breath. 'No, nothing like that, Mick. Has Roscoe been in?'

'No, I haven't seen him. But I was out exercising the dog just now and when I passed his place, I saw a car — a maroon Land Rover Discovery — parked outside and a big bloke peering in through one of the windows. Thought it was a bit funny.'

'Any idea who he was?'

'That's just it. It was one of the fellas who was with that silver-haired gent I was telling you about.'

Kate frowned. 'Did you get the number of the motor?'

'Sorry.'

'Thanks, Mick. Much appreciated. Let me know if you see the man or the Discovery again.'

Kate got into the car and sat there for a few moments, her fingers drumming on the steering wheel as she thought about the call she had just received.

What the hell was going on? Plainly, Roscoe was still not home if, as it sounded, the man in the Land Rover was getting no reply. But who was he, and what was he doing at Roscoe's to start with? Was he the "face" Roscoe had mentioned, or just some friend on a social visit? Her uneasiness had now developed into real apprehension. Maybe her old boss really was in trouble and not, as she had first thought, playing a perverse game with her — which meant she needed to do something, and fast.

Putting her visit home to see Hayden on hold for the time being, she drove out of the yard and headed at speed in the direction of the Levels and Roscoe's bungalow, hoping the man with the Discovery would still be there. He wasn't, but about a mile from the village, an SUV fitting that description passed her going the other way. It was just too much of a coincidence. She spun around in a gateway and went after it.

* * *

The Discovery seemed in no hurry as it made its way across country, and Kate found it easy enough to keep it in view without alerting the driver's suspicions. It made several turns onto lanes and backroads and finally Kate found herself in familiar surroundings, following the very drove from which the mystery woman had emerged in front of her car that infamous night. They passed the track leading to the burned-out site of Lilith's shack, then Hallstead Farm where Luke Cobb lived with his uncle, before turning right onto another lane, into which, unbeknown to her, Ted Roscoe had followed the black Volvo XC90 the day before.

A short distance further on, the SUV slowed before a bend, indicating left, giving her time to swing out and overtake it as it pulled into the verge in front of a wide gateway.

There was a long chain strung across it, preventing vehicular access, with a track leading across a field to a copse sprouting the tall chimneys of a house. Before losing sight of the vehicle around the next bend, she saw a short, muscular man clamber out of the Discovery and go around the front of the vehicle towards the gateway, either because he had simply been caught short and had stopped for a pee or was intending to remove the chain and drive through.

After several hundred yards the lane she was following ended in a T junction before a wider road. She was about to try turning around in the junction mouth — as Roscoe had done — so that she could go back to check on the Discovery, when a tractor and trailer laden with bales of something wrapped in black plastic appeared in her rear-view mirror a few yards behind her.

Cursing, she turned left out onto a much wider road, looking for another place in which to carry out the manoeuvre, when she spotted a pair of stone pillars on her left and pulled in just past an ungated entrance, intending to reverse back into it. As she stopped, she saw that the gateway accessed a tree-lined gravel driveway, overgrown with weeds and bordered by a strip of woodland on each side, no doubt leading to a house or farm, though, because of a sharp left-hand curve in the driveway she was unable to see anything of the property, save the tops of more trees and a tall chimney stack. Completing the first part of her manoeuvre, she edged forward onto the road, conscious of the fact that she was blind to oncoming traffic and needed to be careful about pulling out again.

Then she slammed to a stop — but not because of oncoming vehicles. Instead, she was staring rigidly at the slate sign attached to the pillar on her right. The lettering had faded over time and part of the slate had broken off at the end, but the name was still readable. "Witch-Fire Ho . . ."

'Witch-Fire House,' she breathed. 'Well, I'll be damned.'

For a few moments she just sat there, considering what to do next. This could be the place that held the key to the mystery she had been trying to unravel since her accident. She saw again the young woman lying on the roadside in the mist, heard once more the blurted words that would remain etched on her memory for a long time to come: 'They're coming. Quick. Got to hide. Witch fire.'

Who was coming and why did she feel she had to hide? Had someone been pursuing her from this very house? Was she in such a blind panic because she was terrified of what they would do if they caught her? Had they been holding her prisoner, or had she discovered something that they didn't want her to reveal to anyone else? Also, how did Lilith fit into all this, and why was she so interested in the young woman that she had tried to get to her in the hospital's ICU? It was all one huge conundrum.

She was tempted to jump straight in, mount a frontal attack, knock on the door of that house and try to get some answers, a course of action that certainly appealed to her impulsive nature. But for once, she listened to the voice of caution inside her head. What could she ask? The Jane Doe in the ICU had said nothing to justify her accusing anyone of anything. Okay, the woman had indicated that someone was chasing her and that she needed to hide, and she had come out with the words "witch fire," which now seemed more than a little coincidental. But at the same time, she might, as Hayden had suggested, have been talking about the will-o'-the-wisp lights they had both seen dancing on the marshes. It was highly possible that she was mentally unstable and had got out of somewhere but had not yet been reported as missing or was hallucinating after taking some sort of mind-bending drug, like LSD. There were many possibilities, but not one of them provided any evidence of a criminal offence. In short, Kate had nothing to question anybody about — yet.

Reluctantly accepting that she had no choice but to leave things alone for the time being, she eased the car out onto the road, resigning herself to continuing with her previous inquiry.

The lane was empty when she got back to where she had last seen the Land Rover Discovery and the chain was back in place, but she was satisfied that the SUV *had* gone through the gateway. The vehicle certainly hadn't come out of the lane behind her — she would have seen it — and it was most unlikely that the driver had taken a wrong turning and gone back the way he had come, especially as he had got out and approached the chain.

Pulling into the verge, she got out of her car and walked over to the gateway. The chain was secured by a heavy padlock, which looked to be freshly oiled. Shielding her eyes with her hand, she stared beyond the chain to study the track, which cut through a couple of acres of boggy ground to the copse at the far end. She noted with particular interest the line of trees extending from the right of the copse all the way to the main road, across a dismal mix of field and peat marsh, where patches of brown-headed teasel were clearly evident in places and coppiced willows lined a rhyne at its edge.

She could see a little more of the house, which was mostly hidden among the trees — three or four tall chimneys, part of a grey, tiled roof and, a short distance away from the building, part of what looked like the corrugated-iron roof of a barn. The SUV had disappeared and there was no other sign of life, but something else dawned on her. She was obviously standing by the back entrance to the property, the front was actually on the main road accessed via the driveway into which she had reversed the car minutes before. Witch-Fire House, with the adjacent fields and marshland, occupied the corner between the lane and the main road and it had two entrances.

And there was more. She had seen the lane and the woods sprouting the tall chimneys before. But it had been from the other side of the five-barred gate, which was right behind her on the opposite side of the lane — the gate she and a protesting Hayden had walked to previously after re-checking Lilith's shack — and the patch of woodland was clearly visible across the familiar bare field.

So, the mystery surrounding the comatose woman in the hospital, the shenanigans with Lilith, together with the torching of her shack, and the apparent disappearance of Roscoe all seemed to be linked together in some way. The problem was how and why? Kate felt more confused than ever.

CHAPTER 14

'He's what?' Des Percival said distantly when Kate found him standing rather than sitting behind the desk in his glass-panelled office. He had his coat on as if he was on the verge of going out.

She shrugged. 'Disappeared it would seem, and things don't look too good.'

He looked up briefly from the mountain of paper he was flicking through.

'And what makes you think that?' he said, returning to his scrutiny of the pile of files.

She hesitated, gnawing at her lip. She hadn't wanted to tell Percival anything, but, after visiting Roscoe's bungalow again on her way back from Witch-Fire House and finding there was still no sign of him or his car, she had decided she had no choice.

'Could you leave those files for a minute and listen, Des?' she said, irritated by his apparent lack of interest. 'I've a fair bit to tell you.'

Finally, he looked at her, his curiosity aroused.

'That sounds a bit concerning, Kate,' he replied and, dropping into the old swivel chair he had inherited from

Roscoe, leaned back with his fingertips together under his chin as if he thought he was Sherlock Holmes.

Closing the office door behind her, Kate pulled up a plastic chair and sat down facing him.

'I think Roscoe's in big trouble,' she said, and went on to relate the night's events and her follow-up inquiries, leaving out only her ex-boss's allegation that one of the detectives in the department had turned rogue.

For a few seconds, Percival just sat there staring at her in obvious astonishment. 'And you're only just telling me all this now?' he snapped, his blue eyes cold and angry. 'For Pete's sake, Kate, this could be serious. You're sure he wasn't just having you on with that phone call — I mean, there was no love lost between the two of you and getting you out of bed in the middle of the night might have seemed like a good laugh to him.'

'Don't you think I've thought of that?' she retorted. 'But if that was the case, why has he seemingly gone AWOL? I've checked his bungalow twice and there's no sign of him or his car, and he hasn't been back to the Black Cock since he left the car park in a hurry yesterday lunchtime. Also, who's the guy in the Land Rover Discovery who was at his home, peering through the bloody window?'

'And you think his disappearance is in some way connected to Lilith and everything else?'

'I can't see any other explanation. The Jane Doe in the hospital blurted the words "witch fire." She was plainly running from someone, and I followed the guy in the Volvo to a place called "Witch-Fire House," which is within spitting distance of Lilith's shack—'

'Which someone burned down.'

'Exactly.'

He emitted a low whistle, adopting his familiar habit of slipping both hands down the back of his trousers.

'We'll look pretty stupid if we send the balloon up over his disappearance and it turns out to be crap,' he said after a couple of minutes' deliberation.

'We'll look even worse if it turns out there's something seriously wrong and we've done nothing about it,' she countered.

He nodded. 'So, what do you suggest? We have insufficient grounds to apply for a warrant to search Witch-Fire House, even if the "face" he referred to is legit and is living there.'

She smiled thinly. It was plain that Percival was out of his depth. Time to realise what you've taken on, Des, she thought maliciously. As DI, this is where the buck stops. And if you're the bastard who's on the take, that will make it doubly difficult, won't it?

'Your decision, Des,' she said. 'What do *you* think we should do?'

But he simply sat there, frowning, drumming with his fingers on the desktop. In the end she reluctantly helped him out.

'I could maybe call at Witch-Fire House tomorrow on the pretext of making inquiries into the arson of Lilith's shack?' she suggested. 'After all, the incident happened just a stone's throw from there. It could turn up something and at least it will allow time for Roscoe to resurface if he's going to. And first thing in the morning, when it's fully light, you could get some of the troops out on the Levels to carry out a low-key search — maybe in an area encompassing Witch-Fire House, Yardley's Cider Farm and the site of Lilith's shack. That's where Roscoe is more likely to have been.'

His face lit up. 'Exactly what I was going to suggest,' he said, his relief patently obvious. 'We'll do that then. And let me know how you get on at Witch-Fire House as soon as you get back.'

She pursed her lips for a second, then added tentatively, 'It would be even better if we could ask for the chopper to carry out a sweep.'

He shook his head firmly. 'Out of the question on the info you've got. There's no way we could justify the cost of using the police helicopter for something like this. ACC Ops would have kittens — especially if Roscoe *is* playing silly games and suddenly reappears after a few days.'

He went to say something else, changed his mind, then suddenly began stroking his moustache, giving her his silkiest smile. 'Fancy a drink before you go home? I'm buying.'

She returned his smile with a tired one of her own. 'Sorry, Des. Other fish to fry tonight. I want to see how Hayden's migraine is.'

It was a lame excuse. He would almost certainly know that Hayden's migraine was about as genuine as her refusal. But she had no intention of socialising with a man who might turn out to be the crooked cop Roscoe had referred to and furthermore, one whose reputation for dalliance with the ladies was almost legendary.

* * *

The old woman, dressed in a black coat and shawl with a long, black dress underneath, picked her way along the bank of the rhyne, one claw-like hand gripping the carved ram's head surmounting her hazel-wood walking stick. Despite her obvious age and seeming infirmity, she was as sure-footed as anyone. Moving at a snail's pace, she was just a crooked shadow in the moonlit dusk. Even one of the sharp-eyed local fishermen, heading home with a bag full of tiny, wriggling elvers caught illegally in the nearby river, could easily have missed her. But if they had caught a glimpse of the bent figure on those lonely marshes, the superstitious among them would have quickly crossed themselves, given the old woman a wide berth, and hurried on, muttering to themselves about hinkypunks and other supernatural horrors.

The fact that, even in the twenty-first century, a belief in such things persisted among some inhabitants of the Levels had worked well for Lilith since her arrival in the area from Glastonbury two years ago. She knew very well that she inspired a supernatural dread in many of the adults in the village, even if they chose not to admit it, and that the children only taunted her out of bravado. In truth, they were all scared stiff of her and what she might do to them.

Her claim to be a witch was not just charlatanism on her part. She absolutely believed she was the reincarnation of Molly Clavey and that she had inherited her skills in the dark arts through the power of the Horned One. It was he who had sent her here from Glastonbury as his acolyte, appearing before her in a dream and instructing her to punish the descendants of those who had been responsible for his servant's destruction over three hundred years ago and, as a reward, promising her the restoration of her youth and the gift of eternal life.

She had not been surprised by his manifestation on what had been a pilgrimage to the seat of witchcraft in Glastonbury, or that he had set her such a formidable task. She had always known she belonged to him — that was why she had been committed to the asylum ten long years ago. But, with the help of the Horned One, who'd often come to her in the dark hours, she had fooled them all and, by pretending that she had been cured of the psychosis from which they said she was suffering and agreeing to take the prescribed medication, she had gained her freedom and returned to his service.

The loss of her home, such as it was, and the sacrilegious act that had been carried out on the site of Molly Clavey's last resting place had come as a shock to her, but she had always accepted that there would be privations and sacrifices along the way. Those responsible would pay in the end, the Horned One would make sure of that.

As it was, she knew she was lucky to escape the conflagration. She had heard the car stop shortly after she had got back home, then the slam of doors and the crunch of feet on the gravel. From a window, she had watched a blazing orb-like object arcing through the air before it smashed through one of her windows, sending tongues of fire racing up the curtains and across the floor, devouring everything in their path.

She had had no time to save anything. Grabbing her long coat and shawl, she had fled out the back door and into the trees to one side of the building. The action of opening the back door had produced a lethal backdraught and the shack had virtually exploded behind her, the flames reaching out into the trees like fiery serpents, as if in pursuit. Much of the wood was soon ablaze and she emerged from cover onto the marsh just as another huge explosion ripped through it, and she realised that the fire had reached her parked car. She had lost everything, but at least the Horned One had preserved her life so that she could continue serving him.

For now, though, she had to find somewhere else to live until she could persuade Luke to rebuild her shack on the same spot. There was a place not too far away that would suit her purpose well. Yes, Yardley's old cider farm would do very nicely for the present. After all, what reason would anyone else have for going there?

* * *

Hayden was sitting watching television when Kate got home. She strode across the room, turned it off and stood in front of him.

'Hey, I was watching that,' he protested.

'*Was* being the operative word,' she said, draping her coat over the back of the settee and kicking off her shoes. 'I want to talk to you.'

He looked embarrassed. 'About what?'

'About us,' she said and nodded towards the bottle of red wine on the table. 'Do I get any of that?'

He paused with his own nearly empty glass halfway to his lips and put it down on the coffee table in front of him.

'Of — of course,' he exclaimed, jumping to his feet and heading for the kitchen. 'I'll get you a glass.'

Returning with a large one, he poured her a healthy measure before slumping back into the armchair he had been occupying.

'How's the migraine?' she asked almost too casually.

He stared down at the floor. 'It's gone.'

'Well, there's a surprise,' she said. 'Now, I want you to tell me where you and I go from here.'

'What do you mean?'

'You know very well what I mean. Is it me or your old public school in Berkshire? You can't have both.'

'It isn't like that.'

'So, what is it like?'

'It — it's just an option, and I don't want to talk about it tonight.'

'So, when do we talk about this option?'

He hesitated. 'I still have an application form to fill in if I'm interested.'

'What? You mean you've had it all along?'

'It's just a form my old chum sent me, that's all. I haven't done anything about it yet.'

She gaped at him. 'And you never said anything about this to your own wife? What sort of an arsehole are you?'

Both had tears in their eyes.

'I — I wanted to be sure about things before I broached the subject,' he replied in a strangled voice. 'But it all sort of came out before I was ready.'

She took a deep breath. 'So, are you going to apply or not? Just so I know when you might be pissing off.'

'I haven't fully decided yet,' he said. 'And even if I did, there'd be an interview, which I might not pass.'

She downed half her wine, grabbed the bottle and poured more, slopping some of it onto the carpet.

'Oh, you go for it,' she said. 'But if you do, don't expect me to be here when you come back.'

Swallowing the second glass of wine, she jumped to her feet.

'Anyway, I'm going out.'

'Going out? Where?'

'I've had an offer of a drink with someone.'

He looked mortified. 'A drink? Who with?'

'That's my business.'

She slipped her shoes back on, grabbed her coat again and stalked out of the house.

For a few moments, Hayden just sat there, bewildered, and by the time he got to the front door, she was in her car and pulling out onto the road.

Des Percival answered his phone straight away.

'Kate?' he exclaimed. 'Something wrong?'

'How about that drink after all?' she said.

'But of course,' he said, sounding surprised. 'Delighted.'

'Good. I'll be at the Black Cock in twenty minutes.'

CHAPTER 15

Percival was already in the public bar of the Black Cock, waiting for Kate. He smelled of aftershave and had changed his shirt and trousers — like a man on a promise. The bar was virtually empty, just a couple of tables occupied, and he had selected one in a discreet corner. A bottle of wine and two glasses were already in evidence.

'I was thinking,' he said as he pulled a chair out for her and nodded a little sheepishly at Mick Braithwaite grinning at him from behind the bar, 'we could have gone somewhere more salubrious than here.'

She shrugged. 'What's wrong with this place? The team have always used it.'

'But that's the whole point,' he went on, 'people know our crowd in here and they might get the wrong idea if they see us, er, together.'

'Why should they get the wrong idea about a DS and her boss having a drink after work? It's only a drink — not a bloody assignation.'

He stared at her keenly, a little ruffled by her sharper than usual tone. He seemed to sense that something was not right.

'You okay?' he said as he poured her some wine. 'You look very pale.'

'Redheads always do,' she retorted, and downed half the contents of her glass. 'Something to do with melanin. It goes with the freckles.' She stared at him defiantly. 'I've got them all over — even on my tits.'

He was taken aback by the crude response. As an unashamed ladies' man, he was used to calling the shots as part of his seduction strategy, and the way she was behaving was certainly not what he had been expecting. He glanced around him nervously, concerned that one of the other customers may have heard her, but they all appeared to be engaged in their own private conversations.

'Look, would you like a meal somewhere? You look as though you haven't eaten all day.' he said, hastily changing the subject. 'There's a nice Greek restaurant just opened in Bridgwater.'

She closed her eyes for a moment, suddenly embarrassed at what she had just come out with in the bitter, irrational mood which had taken possession of her. What was she doing here with a ram like Percival in the first place? If it was an attempt to get back at Hayden by giving herself to another man, it had failed miserably because she wasn't up to it.

'Sorry, Des, but this is all wrong,' she said, rising quickly from her chair. 'It was a big mistake coming here and I have to go.'

Before he could say anything else, she was heading for the door, leaving him standing there helplessly. Seconds later, she was pulling away in a swirl of gravel.

* * *

Kate should have gone straight home after walking out on Percival, but she didn't. She guessed Hayden would worry about where she was, and she wanted him to. She wanted to punish him. He deserved every bit of it. In any case, her mind was in complete turmoil and she needed time to think things out.

Thinking was quite beyond her capabilities by then, however, and her deep sense of hurt and betrayal reduced her to a flood of tears within a few miles of leaving the Black Cock, to the extent that soon she could hardly see where she was going.

In the end, with no real idea of where she was, she pulled into a layby and simply sat there, sobbing her heart out until she had no tears left to cry. Then, totally exhausted, she fell asleep.

The cold seeping into the car off the Levels finally awoke her. Stiff and shivering, she sat there for a moment, blinking in the moonlight. In the time she had been asleep, the witch lights had returned to the Levels and she could see them dancing out on the marshes. Her skin prickling, she watched the weird, chilling display with a peculiar fascination. Then she saw the hunched figure of the old woman. She was walking slowly along the verge opposite to where Kate had parked, leaning on a stick, her shawl drawn right up over her head. There was no question. It was Lilith.

At once, Kate's worries over her threatened marriage were forgotten. She felt for the door handle, but then she froze, something holding her back. Lilith had stopped briefly at a gap in the hedge and was climbing up over what had to be a stile. As she disappeared, Kate felt for the torch in the glove compartment, gently eased the car door open and climbed out onto the road. Why she had decided to follow the old woman instead of confronting her, she had no real idea. It was just an instinctive reaction.

The stile turned out to be a low wooden bridge over a rhyne and on the other side, Kate found a partially overgrown footpath along the side of another hedge, leading across a field.

The old woman was some way ahead of her and Kate took care to maintain her distance, leaning into the hedge whenever Lilith turned round to scrutinise the path behind her.

Then there was another rhyne spanned by a wooden bridge and Kate found herself on a tarmac road in a very familiar place. Directly opposite was the derelict site of Yardley's Cider Farm.

'So that's where you've gone to ground,' Kate breathed to herself as she watched her quarry cross the road and enter the site. She went after her.

* * *

The Reverend Truly was climbing into bed after a late night writing his next sermon when he heard the scuffling sound downstairs. At first, he thought it was either mice or just the wind in the eaves of the old house, which had been the Manse for over a hundred years and was prone to numerous creaks, groans, and rattles. But then he heard the sounds again.

'What is it, dear?' a voice issued from the plump mound under the bedclothes beside him and a middle-aged woman sat up.

Deborah Truly was an attractive brunette, some five years her husband's junior. In complete contrast to him, she had a ready smile and a twinkle in her eye, which suggested an inner vibrancy that was kept firmly under control. As popular in the village as the pulpit-thumping, firebrand of a minister was unpopular, she carried out her supportive pastoral duties with a gentle calm that he could never achieve, taking all problems in her stride.

'Ssh!' her husband snapped, pulling on his dressing gown. 'There's someone prowling about downstairs.'

She giggled. 'Perhaps it's one of those naughty hinkypunks.'

'This isn't funny, Deborah,' he said pompously. 'We could be at risk here. I'm going to check.'

She fell back in bed, still laughing. 'Okay, dear. Just open your dressing gown and give them a quick flash. That would frighten anyone away.'

'Don't be so disgusting!' he admonished. 'Remember who you are.' Then he was out the door and making his way downstairs, his heart thumping and the torch in his hand shaking.

Moonlight filtered into the hallway through the glazed front door and he paused to listen. Silence. He moved on, gently pushing the door of his study open and wincing when it creaked. The room was empty, moonlight picking out his completed sermon in its red folder lying where he had left it on his desk, close to the big steel safe bolted to the wall between two heavily laden bookcases. The safe appeared to be untouched. He breathed a sigh of relief. There was a substantial amount of church money in that safe and it would be a target for any burglar.

He moved on down the hallway to the sitting room and peered in around the open door. Empty.

Perhaps the sounds he had heard were only in his imagination or had been caused by the old house easing its tired frame, as he had first thought.

He shivered. It was cold in the hallway in his bare feet. He drew his dressing gown more tightly about his plump body and headed back towards the stairs.

The kitchen was right at the front of the house and bathed in the full glare of the moonlight. It appeared to be empty, but only just. Even from where he stood, he could see the glitter of glass fragments on the floor beneath the half-glazed back door, which was wide open. Switching on the light, he saw that where the upper panel had been was now a jagged hole.

'Goodness me!' Deborah exclaimed behind him. 'Who on earth—?'

But then she broke off with a gasp, one hand to her mouth and the other pointing at the sink. A grotesque rag doll, dressed in the garb of a clergyman, was hanging on a length of twine from the curtain rail, partially wrapped in a piece of white cloth, which looked to be spattered with blood, and pierced by several long pins.

* * *

Kate paused at the open front door of the former office block, which she had previously visited in search of Roscoe. She could hear Lilith's feet shuffling along the corridor towards the reception area at the back, crunching on the broken glass, and waited for a few moments until they faded into nothing, suggesting the old woman was now in the warehouse, where her feet would make a lot less noise on the concrete floor.

Kate could see the glow of a torch ahead of her in the gloom as she entered the building, but then, quite suddenly it was extinguished and she stopped dead just inside the doorway, not quite sure what to do. Had the crafty old woman sussed that she was following her and hidden herself away somewhere, or was she lying in wait just inside the warehouse, ready with her walking stick? Old as she was, it was clear that she posed a real risk. She had once been committed to an asylum and it was plain that she was still mentally ill — possibly with a propensity for violence, going by her recent attacks on the village church.

Calling for some backup before proceeding any further was the sensible thing to do. But that was not an option. By the time the "troops" arrived, Lilith would have disappeared and she needed to talk to her face to face if she was ever going to get to the bottom of what this business was all about and be able to begin slotting the pieces of the jigsaw into place.

Taking a deep breath, she took a calculated risk and stepped through the doorway into the warehouse.

As with her earlier visit, the forklift truck, silhouetted against the face of the moon, caught her eye first. But there *was* someone here this time and, just as she had feared, they were waiting for her to one side of the doorway.

She saw the movement out of the corner of her eye just in time and instinctively lurched sideways. Because of her age and poor sense of balance, Lilith's aim was way off the mark, coupled with which, the strike lacked the necessary force to do any real harm anyway. Instead of connecting with Kate's head, the stick missed completely and slammed into the wall, tearing itself from the old woman's grasp and bouncing away from her across the floor.

Then the old woman shrank away from her would-be victim, obviously not fit enough to run, and stood there, studying her from beneath her shawl. Kate could sense the menace in her stare, and she made sure she didn't take her eyes off her as she stepped back a few paces to pick up the stick.

'That was a bit unnecessary, wasn't it?' she said, taking a chance by returning the stick to her again. 'I could have been seriously injured.'

'What do you want?' Lilith said in a harsh, gravelly voice. 'Why have you followed me here?'

'I am a police officer,' Kate said. 'My name is Kate Lewis.'

'I know who you are. A meddler in things best left alone.'

'I want to talk to you.'

There was no reply.

'Why did you defile the village church and steal the skull from the grave?' Kate said.

'Who says I did?'

'Ralph Trimble, the sexton, for starters.'

Lilith snorted. 'He's a liar and a hypocrite. Trust not the word of a snake.'

'And why did you hang the cockerel on my door?'

There was a cackle straight out of a child's fairy tale. Lilith certainly knew how to play the part.

'As a warning,' she replied. 'So, pay heed before the Horned One sends a demon to your house, as he did to the house of Tom Sharpe.'

Kate decided to play along with her. 'Did he send a demon after the woman in the hospital too? Is that why she was running across the marshes in the middle of the night with no shoes on?'

No answer.

'Why did you try to see her in the hospital's ICU?'

Still no answer.

'Do you know who she is?'

The other made a clucking noise. 'Lilith knows all there is to know of today and she has the gift of second sight for what is to follow tomorrow.'

'So, if you know so much, who *is* the woman then? What's her name? Where is she from?'

'Only the Horned One shall know that.'

'But was she staying with you?'

'The wench was lost and the Horned One sent her to me for protection.'

'Protection from whom?'

'From those who now defile these ancient marshes with their presence.'

'And are they the same people who burned down your home? The ones living in Witch-Fire House?'

There was a sharp hiss. 'You ask too many questions, police girl. The hinkypunks are listening to your foolish chatter, so have a care.'

Kate sighed in exasperation, suddenly weary of all the theatrics. 'Can we just cut out all this hocus pocus nonsense, Sara?' she snapped, deliberately using the old woman's real name.

The other stiffened. 'My name is Lilith.'

'No, it isn't. You are Sara Anne Cable, recently of the Gables Mental Institution at Reading, and unless you start talking some sense, you'll end up back there, I promise you.'

The old woman's response to this threat was immediate and singularly unpleasant. Kate was caught completely unawares. She saw her draw her head back, but before she could take evasive action, the globule of spittle hit her squarely in the face, dribbling down one cheek and into the neck of the blouse beneath her coat.

Her natural reaction was one of disgust, which Lilith had obviously foreseen. Even as Kate drew the cuff of her coat across her face to wipe the phlegm away, Lilith had stepped back into the shadows and was gone.

CHAPTER 16

After a quick scout around, Kate was able to satisfy herself that Lilith's disappearance was certainly not due to sorcery. There was another door in the far corner of the warehouse. It turned out to lead along a short passageway to the side of the building and back out onto the concrete hardstanding at the front through another external door.

Angry for allowing herself to be duped so easily by a decrepit old woman, she spent another half hour checking around the building to see if she could find her. But it was pointless and, finally seeing the futility of continuing the search, she gave up. As she trudged back the way she had come, her thoughts inevitably returned to her domestic problems and to Hayden.

She was so engrossed in her thoughts that at first, the pulsing blue light floating above the hedge on the far side of the field didn't register. But then she surfaced with a jolt and, with a muttered oath, sprinted the remaining few yards to the bridge across the rhyne.

Two uniformed police officers with torches were out of their patrol car and peering through the Mazda's windows, and they turned quickly when she stepped into view from the gap in the hedge.

A powerful beam blinded her for a second and she raised a hand to shield her eyes. The torch was quickly lowered as one of the officers came towards her.

'Your car, Miss?' he said as his colleague joined him.

Kate produced her warrant card and held it out at arm's length. The torch focused on it, then on her face again and he nodded.

'Sorry, skipper. Didn't recognise you at first. Er — what you doing out here then?'

She emitted a short humourless laugh. 'It's a long story. Let's just say I felt like a walk to clear my head.'

He hesitated, plainly still curious, but he didn't get the chance to press the point as his radio crackled suddenly. He answered, and she heard him repeat a name she immediately recognised.

'Sorry, skipper,' he said, turning to run back to his car to join his colleague who was already behind the wheel. 'Got a shout.'

'Did I hear you say St Stephen's Church?' she called after him.

'Break-in reported,' he said, slamming the front passenger door behind him.

'I'll see you there,' she shouted back, but the police car was already scorching off down the road.

* * *

The old grey house next to the village church was ablaze with light. She parked behind the police car and walked quickly up the path to the front door, passing a big black Range Rover sitting in the driveway a few feet to the right of the gate. She cast it an admiring glance. Truly was obviously not short of a bob or two.

The front door stood wide open, Ralph Trimble waiting in the hallway. He was wearing a raincoat over his clothes and his trousers were tucked into gum boots. He was holding a long rubber-encased torch in one hand and a poker in the other.

'They're in here,' he said, leading the two uniformed officers, followed by Kate, through a doorway on the right into what turned out to be a kitchen. The Reverend Truly, dressed in a white towelling dressing gown, was pacing up and down between the double sink unit and a row of built-in cupboards, plainly very agitated. A plump dark-haired woman, dressed in a similar robe, whom Kate took to be his wife, watched his irritable perambulations with a faint, amused smile from a chair at the kitchen table.

'Ah, there you are, Sergeant,' Truly exclaimed, ignoring the two uniformed officers. 'The impertinence of it. Look at the mess.'

Kate took in the scene at a glance. Someone had broken into the house by smashing one of the small square panels of the back door to reach the key, which was still in the lock. They had taped up the glass before breaking it to deaden the sound, and pieces of black tape still adhered to the jagged hole and to some of the fragments on the floor. More significantly, a blood-spattered rag doll, dressed in clerical garb and pierced with long pins now hung on a length of twine from the curtain rail — a doll that looked very much like the one she and Hayden had seen hanging in Lilith's shack.

'How did you find this, sir?' she queried.

'We heard some noises—' Truly's wife began, only to be cut off by her husband.

'You mean *I* heard some noises, Deborah,' he corrected. 'Like a crunch, then footsteps, and, of course, I came down to investigate.' He raised both his hands in a gesture of despair. 'Found this and — and *that*.' He pointed at the rag doll. 'Absolutely disgraceful.'

The two uniformed officers left the kitchen and Kate could soon hear them prowling about in the garden outside, their torches flashing periodically across the window through the gaps in the open Venetian blind. Ralph Trimble stood beside Deborah Truly, shaking his head in sympathy.

'How long ago did you hear the noises?' Kate went on.

'Must be about an hour or so now,' Truly replied, waving a hand at the window and the flashing torches. 'They won't find anything. The so-and-sos will be long gone by now.'

'The Reverend rang me,' Trimble said, 'so I came straight over.'

'Did you see anyone on the way?'

'Well, that's just it — I did.'

'Oh? Can you describe them?'

'I don't need to. It was that witch woman, Lilith, scuttling along the verge from just past the Manse like some giant spider. This must be her work — and that doll looks like the same one I told you I saw hanging up in her shack when me and the Reverend called to see her that time.'

Kate frowned, trying to calculate how long ago Lilith had given her the slip at Yardley's. The old woman would have to have moved pretty fast to have got to the Manse, broken in and disappeared before she and the other police officers arrived.

'You're sure it was her?'

'No doubt about it. The old hag has a profile that is quite distinctive, and she was dressed in that long, black coat and shawl of hers.'

Kate nodded, still not convinced, wondering whether it was a case of mistaken identity on Trimble's part or — and she smiled wryly — Lilith really was a witch and had zipped over on her broomstick!

'And another thing,' the sexton continued. 'I saw her coming out of your PC West's garden a day or so ago.''

Kate's smile vanished. 'What? Are you sure about that?'

'As sure as I am about seeing her tonight. It was around ten in the evening and I think he was at work on a late something or other. I live just across the road from him and I was on my way home from a darts match at my local. Thought it was a bit odd, as she's not exactly a fan of the police — especially him.' He smiled faintly. 'Maybe she was putting a hex on his house, and that's why he passed.'

Kate did not find this amusing. She treated him to a cold, hard stare. She had already decided she did not much like Mr Ralph Trimble, and his inappropriate remark only served to reinforce her antipathy.

Truly was plainly not amused by the remark either. 'For goodness' sake, Ralph, the man is dead,' he snapped.

'That was in very poor taste. My apologies, Sergeant.'

Kate acknowledged the apology with a curt nod and pressed on with her questions.

'Have you found anything missing, Rev Truly?' she asked.

Deborah Truly frowned. 'Now, there's a funny thing,' she said. 'We have had a look around, but nothing seems to have been touched apart from the tea caddy.

'The what?'

'Well, I'm sure my husband won't mind my saying, but he's a very precise person—'

'Everything in its proper place,' the minister interjected again.

'You could almost say he suffers from a bit of, er, OCD,' Deborah Truly continued, with a glance at her husband.

'Now, just a minute, Debs,' he protested.

'You know, pictures have to be straight on the walls, kitchen utensils and cutlery put away in their proper places, towels folded corner to corner exactly—'

Kate looked puzzled. 'Sorry, I don't understand.'

'The tea caddy, dear.' Deborah Truly stood up and crossed to the double sink and pointed. 'It has been moved to the wrong side of the toaster and is, well, skew-whiff. Jacob always checks around before he goes to bed and he would never have left things like that.'

'Quite right, my dear,' her husband agreed gruffly.

'And if you look here, some tea leaves have been spilled on the work surface.'

Kate went over to the unit and raised an eyebrow. 'You ought to be a detective, Mrs Truly,' she said, 'but are you suggesting someone broke in here and raided the tea caddy?'

'Lilith was looking for money, I reckon,' Trimble put in. 'People keep their housekeeping money in tin tea caddies like this sometimes. Maybe our self-styled witch thought there was some cash in there and decided to help herself?'

Kate nodded and stared at the rag doll hanging from the curtain rail. 'Or maybe she used a chair to climb up onto the draining board and in the process knocked over the caddy,' she suggested. 'She certainly couldn't have reached the curtain rail from floor level and I must admit, at her apparent age, I wouldn't have thought she was even capable of doing that.'

Trimble grunted. 'She's a tough old bird,' he said. 'A lot more agile than she pretends to be, I reckon. Look at how she manages to get about everywhere on foot.'

He did have a valid point. After all, Lilith must have walked several miles just to get from her burned-out home to Yardley's, so, despite her stick and shuffling walk, she was plainly a lot fitter than she appeared. She was a crafty old woman and quite capable of pulling off a convenient deception when it suited her.

Without responding to Trimble, Kate brought things to a close.

'Do you think you could leave everything the way it is for the rest of tonight?' she said to Truly. 'No tidying up, please. I'll get our Scenes of Crime team around later this morning to see if they can find anything to help identify the culprit, and someone will also be calling to take a statement off each of you if you don't mind.'

'No problem, Sergeant,' Deborah Truly said with a slightly mischievous glint in her eyes. 'I'll make sure my husband is banned from the kitchen until your people have finished.'

Kate met up with the two uniformed officers as she walked out of the front door.

'Anything?' Kate asked.

'Negative, Sarge,' one replied. 'Concrete path outside the back door, so no chance of footprints and no sign of blood anywhere either, so they obviously didn't cut themselves.'

'No burn marks from a broomstick on the path or the lawn, was there?' Kate asked drily.

The pair stared at her. 'Burn marks from a broomstick, skipper?'

She patted him on the arm. 'Don't worry about it,' she said. 'Just something I'm working on. Have a good night.'

* * *

Kate was surprised to find Hayden slumped in an armchair, fully dressed, when she got home. It was plain that he had not gone to bed at all. She closed the front door as quietly as she could behind her, but he opened his eyes as she was crossing the sitting room and he jerked bolt upright.

'Kate?' he said, his speech still slurred with sleep.

She stopped short and stared at him, tears welling up in her eyes again, but said nothing.

'What — what time is it?' he exclaimed and peered bleary eyed at his wristwatch and then at the clock on the mantelpiece. 'Gordon Bennett, it's nearly dawn. Where have you been? I was worried to death when you didn't come home.'

She kicked off her shoes and, slipping out of her coat, hung it on the hook by the front door.

'How touching,' she replied, regretting the sarcastic retort as soon as she had made it.

He stood up, swaying a little, and she gave a knowing smile when he nearly knocked over the half-full bottle of wine on the floor beside his chair.

'I — I rang Percival,' he went on, 'and he said you had walked out on him at the pub ages before. Then, when you still didn't come back, I went out looking for you in my car.'

She gaped at him. 'You did what?'

'I thought something might have happened to you,'

She emitted a hard laugh. 'And when you couldn't find me, you thought "whoopee", and came back home to drown your sorrows in a bottle of red wine. Very commendable.'

'I didn't need to find you,' he said sullenly. 'I rang the nick and the Control Room told me you had been attending a burglary at St Stephen's Church and should be on your way back.'

'Oh, I see, *then* you drowned your sorrows in a bottle of red wine? Was that through disappointment?'

'Don't be stupid. I had a couple of glasses, yes, and just fell asleep, that's all.' He scowled, his blue eyes fixed on her accusingly. 'So where were you all night, if not in Percival's bed?'

His aggressive demeanour and the brutal force of what seemed more like a demand than a question was something Kate had never seen in Hayden before. For a moment she was thrown and unable to respond.

'Well?' he blazed, fists clenched by his sides. 'What have you been up to? I won't bloody have it, do you sodding well hear me?'

Unexpectedly, Kate dissolved into fits of laughter. She fell back onto the settee, snorting and shaking.

Hayden's scowl became more pronounced. 'This is not funny, Kate,' he almost snarled. 'You're my wife, damn it!'

'Oh, Hayden,' she replied through her tears, 'for the first time since I've known you, you actually swore. Welcome to the twenty-first century at last.'

His scowl was replaced by an uncertain frown and he tossed his mop of unruly fair hair, like a child stamping its feet. 'It was your fault,' he retorted. 'You made me do it. You got me angry.'

Kate sat up again and dried her eyes. 'Just pour me a glass of wine, will you, you big lump. Then we have got to talk.'

'Tomorrow,' he snapped. 'Bed now. Talk tomorrow. I'm not in the mood to talk at present.'

CHAPTER 17

Hayden's promise was not fulfilled the following morning. After just a few hours' sleep, they both got up late. As a result, there was barely time over a snatched breakfast of toast and coffee for Kate to brief him on the night's events, and to announce her plan to visit Witch-Fire House, let alone discuss anything else. Then they were in her car and heading for Highbridge at breakneck speed.

Fortunately, Ronnie Crouch, the dour civilian office manager, was the only one in the office. Everyone else appeared to be out. But that didn't mean the telephone had been idle and Kate's desk seemed to be wallpapered in Post-its.

'Pathologist wants you to ring her asap,' Crouch said, without turning round. 'She's rung three times.'

Kate picked up the little yellow note he had left for her stuck to her phone, and she dialled the number.

Dr Lydia Summers answered after three rings, which seemed appropriate.

'Ah, Sergeant Lewis,' she said. 'Nice of you to get back to me — eventually.'

Kate smiled. She was well used to Summers's sarcasm. They had known each other a long time.

'Problem?' she queried.

'It's your dead policeman,' Summers said.

'Oh?'

'I've done his PM and I have to say I'm a little bit perturbed.'

Kate felt her stomach muscles tighten. 'Go on.'

She heard Summers release a heavy sigh. 'I'm afraid I'm not too happy with the cause of death. It is quite probable that ultimately he died of a myocardial infarction, but my examination has revealed that something else may have contributed to its incidence.'

'Meaning?'

'Poison, my dear Sergeant, poison. I have sent off some body fluids, including a blood sample, for toxicological analysis, but it is my professional opinion that he suffered a sustained ingestion of some kind of lethal substance, which triggered the myocardial infarction by initially paralysing the respiratory system. I have read the report Dr Snider emailed to me and he states that there was evidence of vomiting, excessive salivation, a dilation of the pupils and an apparent convulsion of the muscles. All this accords with the results of my own examination. As soon as I receive the toxicologist's report, I'll get back to you.'

'Shit!' Kate breathed.

'Precisely,' Summers agreed. 'That's why I felt I should ring you immediately.' There was a slight pause and then the pathologist added, 'I have dealt with two similar cases in my career and, without wishing to prejudice the findings of the toxicologist, I would mention that in both cases the culprit was a poisonous alkaloid called *coniine*, which is to be found in a rather unpleasant plant called *Conium maculatum* — poison hemlock.'

'Poison hemlock?' Kate repeated incredulously, suddenly remembering one of the bottles she had seen on the shelf in Lilith's shack. 'And it can kill?'

'Oh yes. The whole plant is toxic and ingestion of just half a dozen or so leaves, eaten or dissolved in a liquid, can be fatal unless the patient is attended to immediately. In the previous cases I dealt with, both patients survived with treatment, but sadly, your constable was one of the unlucky ones.'

Summers paused again. 'You might like to take a look in the late officer's house to see if there are any traces left there. Oh, and by the way, did you know that, once upon a time, hemlock and belladonna — or deadly nightshade — were used by witches to dispatch those who had offended them?'

'I'm learning all the time,' Kate said grimly.

* * *

'Poison hemlock?' Hayden muttered as he followed Kate out to the CID car. 'You're saying this dreadful old biddy poisoned poor old Eddie?'

Kate was pleased to see that Hayden's interest in things had returned — probably because his old pal was involved.

'No,' she said. 'I'm saying it's possible he was poisoned, but not necessarily by Lilith.'

Hayden snorted. 'Well, who else would have done it? Don't forget the dolls with the pins in them we saw in that shack. One of them was obviously made to resemble Eddie, and you yourself told me you saw a bottle on the shelf labelled "Hemlock." Furthermore, you said at breakfast that Ralph Trimble actually saw Lilith coming out of Eddie's garden a day or so ago while he was on duty. What more proof do you need?'

'Much more,' Kate said, climbing behind the wheel. 'There's a lot about this business that I don't fully understand, and in any case, we still have to wait for confirmation from the toxicologist that Eddie was poisoned.'

'So, what do we do in the meantime?'

Kate started the engine. 'We take another look at Eddie West's house. If Lilith *was* there and she left something inside, she must have been able to get in, which means we should be able to as well.'

'I take it that your visit to Witch-Fire House is off then?'

'Not at all. We can do that afterwards.' She cast him an innocent glance. 'I'm sure you won't mind missing lunch.'

* * *

Helen West was a thin, unsmiling woman in her mid-sixties, with sharp features and greying black hair bound up in a bun. She was dressed in a simple grey cardigan and plaid skirt and wore a silver crucifix attached to a long chain around her neck. The elderly widow could not have been more different to her late brother and, even though Hayden had warned Kate what to expect, she was a little taken aback when the elderly widow answered the door of her old-world cottage and fixed them with an icy stare that was about as welcoming as that of a rattlesnake.

'A fanatical Bible basher,' Hayden had said. 'She and Eddie never really got on and I can't see her being that upset by his death.'

And indeed, that seemed to be the case. There was no sign of grief on her face, or any indication of recent tears, and her manner was one of irritation rather than anything else. 'Well?' she snapped, not even bothering to look at Kate's proffered warrant card. 'What do you want?'

'We are very sorry for your loss, Miss West—' Kate began, but was immediately cut short by a disparaging snort.

'Hardly a surprise, though, was it?' the other interjected. 'He was always overindulgent, and he died because of it. Now, what is it you want?'

'We need to visit the house again,' Hayden said, 'to see what medication your brother may have been taking. It is possible that it could have contributed to his death.'

'There's a spare key under the mat at the back,' she snapped. 'But I've no intention of coming with you. I'm not setting foot in that evil place again.' She crossed herself. 'I found an — an object behind the bread bin in the kitchen when I was clearing up today, which I would thank you to remove and destroy. Such things have no place in any God-fearing Christian home.'

Then she promptly turned on her heel and slammed the door in their faces.

'Somehow, I don't think she liked us,' Kate said drily as they headed back down the garden path to their car.

'She's probably a Jehovah's Witness,' Hayden said, 'and they don't like anybody.'

The front door of Eddie West's house was tightly closed, and the curtains had been drawn across the windows, perhaps as a mark of respect.

They found a long, well-kept garden and several sheds at the back of the place and the spare key was exactly where Helen West had said it would be.

'Eddie doesn't seem to have been too concerned about security,' Kate commented.

'It's a country area,' he said. 'I don't suppose many of the locals bother to lock their doors.'

'Which means someone else could also have found the key and got in.'

'Like Lilith, you mean?'

'Like anybody.'

The kitchen had been tidied up, the floor cleaned, and the tiles were now gleaming. No indication of the horror they had come upon just a day before remained.

'Helen West did a pretty thorough clean-up in here,' Kate remarked.

'The dutiful sister,' Hayden said.

'Guv'nor won't be too pleased about it, though, if it does turn out to be a sus death,' Kate murmured. 'Nothing for SOCO to see now.'

'That's our fault,' Hayden said heavily. 'We should have got the team over to do the necessary before poor old Eddie's body was taken away.'

'True, but we didn't know about the possibility of a poisoning then, did we? The doc didn't seem to think there was anything suspicious about the death.'

He shrugged. 'Point taken. As they say, the benefit of hindsight is a wonderful thing. Now, what is this "object" that Helen West was so cut up about?'

Crossing the room to where a wooden bread bin sat on a corner worksurface, he pulled the bin away from the wall and stepped back.

'Take a look,' he said. 'Familiar to you?'

Kate drew in her breath sharply.

The so-called "object" seemed to be the same hideous rag doll resembling West that they had seen hanging up behind the curtain in Lilith's shack, and, like the doll left at the Manse, its torso was still partially wrapped in the crumpled square of white cloth affixed to it by several pins and spattered with red spots, like dried blood.

'Well, that's a dead giveaway, to coin a phrase,' he said. 'Seems our wicked old witch decided to leave her own unique calling card at the homes of her two "favourite" people.'

'And if it was her, no doubt something else a lot more lethal too,' Kate added. 'All we've got to do is find it. Leave the thing where it is for the moment.'

He shrugged and gently pushed the bread bin back in place. 'So, where do we start looking for this lethal substance then?'

'Cupboards, drawers — anywhere that might hold a clue. Pity we don't have the half-full mug that was on the kitchen table, but it appears to have been washed up when the rest of the place was cleaned.'

'And what are we looking for? I doubt it will be a bottle labelled "poison."'

'I have no idea — tablets? Powder? Who knows? All we can do is to check around and see if anything stands out.'

The search proved fruitless. Apart from the box containing the losartan tablets and other boxes of paracetamol, they found nothing of interest, either in the kitchen or anywhere else in the house. The only thing Kate stumbled upon was a high-level cupboard in the kitchen crammed with packets of every variety of tea imaginable, some of which cascaded down on her as soon as she opened the door.

'Lapsang souchong, orange pekoe, chamomile, matcha, rooibos,' she said, reading the labels on the packets as she bent down to pick some of them up and tried to stuff them back into the cupboard. 'You were right about Eddie liking his tea. I've never heard of half of these.'

He waved a hand towards the Welsh dresser. 'There's a load of books on the subject of tea up there on the top shelf too. He was a bit obsessed with the stuff. Me, I prefer a glass of red—'

He broke off in mid-sentence and snapped his fingers. 'But that could be it!'

'What could be it?'

'Socrates!'

'Who?'

'Socrates. Summers suggested Eddie might have been poisoned with hemlock. Socrates was an ancient Greek philosopher who was sentenced to death and allegedly chose to kill himself with a poisonous draught prepared from that very plant.'

'How is that relevant here?'

His eyes registered an excited gleam that Kate had not seen for quite a while.

'Socrates is said to have been executed by drinking a cup of poison hemlock,' he finished. 'And what was Eddie known to drink all the time?'

'Tea,' Kate exclaimed, but he was already wrenching open the tea caddy on the Welsh dresser and sniffing the contents.

'Anything?' she breathed at his elbow.

He shrugged. 'It has quite a pungent odour, but that could just be the tea itself, which seems to be a greenish colour. I have no idea what variety this is.'

'Well, the packets that fell out of the cupboard all looked sealed, so if Doctor Summers is right, our poison must be mixed in with the tea in the caddy.'

'And if it isn't?'

'We're right up a gum tree.'

'So, our next move is, what?'

'Get SOCO out here. It would be a good idea to have some photographs taken, including that of the straw doll in situ, just in case something does come of this. A forensic sweep of the room should be carried out too, and the caddy printed and sent off with its contents for toxicological analysis.'

He looked doubtful. 'After Helen West's mammoth cleaning job, there doesn't seem much point. And I think Percival may not be much in favour of an official crime scene examination when we don't even know whether a crime has actually been committed.'

'Better late than never, Hayd, and there's a chance they might still find something here — prints on the tea caddy or whatever. In any case, we will need to have the contents of the caddy and the apparent blood spots on the doll subjected to toxicological analysis and they can set that up for us. As for Percival, I'll use my charm to persuade him.'

'Well, that's likely to be the kiss of death,' he retorted. He stared at her keenly. 'And I've got a bad feeling about what else you've got in mind.'

'Very astute of you, Hayd. 'I want you to remain here to hold the fort until SOCO arrive.'

He scowled. 'And where will you be going?'

'To see the Rev Truly and his wife,' she said, turning for the door, 'hopefully before they decide to have any more brews!'

CHAPTER 18

The ambulance was parked half on, half off the pavement when Kate pulled up outside the Manse, its blue light flashing. With an oath, Kate ran up the garden path to the open front door, then stepped aside as the ambulance crew came out of the house, carrying a stretcher. Rev Truly had an oxygen mask over his face. Deborah Truly was just behind them, her face marble white and her eyes filled with tears.

'Oh, Sergeant,' she exclaimed, 'I'm so glad you're here. Jacob has taken a bad turn and they're rushing him to hospital.'

'When did this happen?' Kate asked, following her down the path towards the ambulance.

'About half an hour ago,' Deborah said. 'He — he's been feeling quite ill all day and he just suddenly collapsed as if he was having a fit. They've sedated him, and they say he needs urgent medical attention.'

She started to climb into the back of the ambulance behind one of the crew, while the other ran to the front of the vehicle.

'Did he drink any tea?' Kate asked urgently.

Deborah half-turned on the step of the ambulance, 'Tea? But yes. He — he drinks a lot of it when he's working on his sermon—'

'And you? Did you drink any?'

Deborah Truly looked confused. 'Me? No — no, I hate the stuff. Just coffee. But why—?'

The paramedic in the back of the vehicle tapped her on the arm. 'Hurry, madam. We need to go.'

Kate stepped back, as the rear doors were slammed shut and the ambulance pulled away with a shriek of its siren, to become a fast diminishing speck.

'Bad business.'

Kate turned quickly to find Ralph Trimble standing in the gateway behind her.

She took a deep breath. 'Ah, Mr Trimble, it's good that you're here. The house will need to be secured.'

'I'll take care of that, Sergeant,' he said. 'I always look after the Reverend and his good lady. Part of my job, so to speak.'

She walked with him back into the house and watched as he bent down in the kitchen to pick up an overturned chair.

'Fell right there,' he said, pointing to a pool of vomit on the tiles. 'Writhing he was and sort of out of his head. Deborah — Mrs Trimble — called me over and I rang 999.'

Kate nodded. 'Good work, Mr Trimble,' she said and, noting a smashed china cup and saucer lying on the floor near the chair and a teapot on the kitchen table clad in a woollen cosy, she added, 'Having a cuppa when he fell, by the look of it.'

'Yeah,' he confirmed. 'Always on the tea, he is. Proper teapot we calls him.'

She nodded briskly. 'Right, well I'm afraid I will need to get some of my colleagues over here to look at all this — just routine, you understand?'

He stared at her. 'Routine, is it? Well, in that case you'd better go ahead, hadn't you, Sergeant?'

* * *

Percival took some time to digest all that she told him on the telephone regarding the possible hemlock poisoning of Eddie

West and the collapse of Jacob Truly. She guessed that both his hands would be down the back of his trousers now and that he would be sitting at his desk, like a man suffering from shell shock, while he considered his position. The thought that Eddie West's death may not have been due to a heart attack and that a possible crime scene had not been preserved when the opportunity had been there was the stuff of nightmares for an ambitious career detective like Percival and, now facing the prospect of a second possible poisoning with the Rev Truly, he was left with a difficult resource decision.

If he authorised two expensive crime scene examinations on such flimsy evidence — one of them very much belated — and it subsequently turned out that no crime had been committed, he could end up a laughing stock. On the other hand, if he decided against calling out SOCO and it was later found that West and Truly had both been poisoned, he faced major criticism, with likely career-limiting consequences.

It was the sort of decision all senior police officers face at one time or another, a case of you're damned if you do and damned if you don't. In the end, however, with the pathologist's revelations about West at the forefront of his mind, he came down on the side of Kate's request. So, after Kate had rung off, he reluctantly made the necessary call, then sat slumped in his chair, white-faced and twitchy, with a stiff shot of something in the coffee in front of him.

* * *

The old woman was carrying a carrier bag as she made her way back along the track from the ruins of her shack. She had made another trip there to see if there was anything worth salvaging that she may have missed on her previous visit, but, like before, she had found nothing. Following the bank of the rhyne, she stopped every so often to peer at the various plants she found growing among the reeds and willows. Some she merely ignored, but others she prodded with her stick, then leaned on it to bend over and tug them out. If there was one thing Lilith did know about, it was wild plants and herbs — just like Molly Clavey before her.

She spotted the lump in the rhyne as she was nearing the end of the track. It looked like a sack of something and it was jammed between the banks, half submerged in the water. Unbeknown to her, Reynard had returned to the body again and, now that the water and damp climate had 'tenderised' it a bit more, had tried unsuccessfully to help himself to a quick snack. But all his sharp teeth had managed to do was tear the thick coat open before noises in the adjoining woods had put him to flight and he'd had to settle for a couple of fingers off the exposed hand still gripping the bank.

Lilith caught her breath when she realised her lump was actually a dead body, and she prodded it with her stick, just to make sure it didn't suddenly spring back into life.

She was so engrossed that she wasn't aware of the uniformed figure approaching along the track towards her, and when she finally heard the squelch of boots and the heavy breathing of the dog, it was too late.

'Now, what have we here?' PC George Miles exclaimed, holding back his snarling Alsatian, and peering past her into the rhyne. 'And what were you doing with that stick, me old duck?'

'Beware,' Lilith warned ominously. 'I am an acolyte of the Horned One.'

The policeman raised his eyebrows. 'And who is he when he's at home?' he said, fumbling for his personal radio.

'You know him as Lucifer, or Beelzebub, the Dark One,' she retorted, shrinking away from the slavering jaws of the dog. 'Let me pass before I summon him here.'

'Why don't you do that, my love?' Miles said. 'He'd be in very good company. The dog is called Satan.'

* * *

Hayden had lapsed into his previous apathy by the time Kate finally picked him up from West's home, much later than she'd anticipated after the SOCO team had attended both addresses and completed their forensic work. But she'd had the foresight to sweeten his mood with a visit to the canteen before leaving the station, and his eyes nearly popped when she handed him the thick ham sandwich and the extra-large lardy cake in the greasy paper bag.

'Thanks,' he said a little grudgingly. 'Very thoughtful of you.'

'I didn't want you to fade away before I got back,' she said and watched out of the corner of her eye as he stuffed the sandwich into his mouth as if he had never seen food before.

'Did you get to the Manse?' he said through a mouthful of lardy cake.

She nodded and told him about Truly's collapse. He glanced at her. 'First Eddie West and now the vicar. Death seems to be following us around.'

She nodded, remembering that others had said the same thing to her on previous murder inquiries. 'Maybe Lilith's rag doll curses really do work,' she commented with a shiver.

He finished his lardy cake and wiped his hands on his trousers. Kate winced.

'So, with all that's been happening, I don't suppose you've had time to eat,' he said. 'Sorry, you could have had some of my lardy cake.'

She screwed up her face in disgust. 'You needn't feel bad about *that*, I assure you. Anyway, I managed to squeeze in a coffee and a sandwich in between things.'

'In between what things?'

'Well, actually, I went for a walk,' she said. 'Quite invigorating it was too.'

'A walk?'

'Yes, Hayd, that thing you do where you put one foot in front of the other.' She patted his stomach. 'You should try it one day.'

He ignored the dig. 'So, where was this walk?'

'From Yardley's Cider Farm to the Manse.'

'Whatever did you do that for?'

'I wanted to see how long it would have taken Lilith to cover that distance on foot, since she'd lost her car in the fire.'

'And how long did it take?'

'For me, twenty-eight minutes.'

'So, what did that achieve?'

'Well, I'm young and fit, but Lilith is old and not in the best of health. I think it would have taken her a lot longer, which means that maybe it wasn't Lilith Trimble saw after the break-in at the Manse.'

'Who else could it have been?'

She shrugged. 'I'll let you know if anyone springs to mind.'

'Look forward to it,' he said unenthusiastically.

* * *

The driveway of Witch-Fire House was badly pitted and overgrown with briars and other rampant vegetation. Kate winced at the scraping sounds coming from both sides of the CID car as she forced it through.

'Workshops will love you when they do the next service,' Hayden sniped. 'That's if the guv'nor doesn't spot the scratches first.'

'I'll tell him you were driving,' she retorted. 'Who do you think they'll believe?'

'Me,' he said. 'They know how cack-handed you are.'

At which point the driveway veered sharply to the left and they emerged from the tunnel of greenery onto a concrete hardstanding outside a gloomy, stone house with dirty windows, behind which lights glowed faintly. As she switched off the engine, Kate glimpsed a large, corrugated iron barn just around the corner. She parked end on to the encircling woodland, a few feet from the black Volvo XC90 she had followed there earlier, and a maroon Land Rover Discovery.

'Make a note of the index numbers,' Kate said out of the corner of her mouth as she spotted a short, muscular figure, dressed in a grubby, grey T-shirt and jeans, striding towards them from the direction of the barn. She climbed out of the car.

'So, what's your game then?' the ape-man snarled.

His bullet head was thrust forward on a thick, veined neck and his fists were clenched at his sides, as if he was intending giving her a pasting. She saw that he had a large tape stuck across his nose, which looked as though it had been recently broken, and his piggy eyes were bloodshot at the corners. Not exactly a welcoming sort. She stepped forward, thrusting her warrant card practically up his injured nose.

'Police,' she snapped. 'And I'm not here to play games, arsehole.'

Whether he would have taken any notice of the card or not was debatable — maybe he couldn't read — but the cold, hard voice from the front doorstep settled matters.

'You must be more polite to visitors, Bruno. I've told you that before. Now back to work if you please.'

A tall, thin man with a head of thick, silvery hair, wearing a dark grey suit and tie, stood on the front doorstep, a cigar in one slender hand.

'Good afternoon, Officers,' he drawled, as Bruno threw Kate a nasty scowl and strode off. 'John Silverman. Do come in.'

Standing to one side, he ushered them both through the front door into a square hallway with a threadbare carpet and a wide staircase at the far end. A number of doors opened off on both sides and he showed them into a room immediately on their left. It turned out to be a study, furnished with a large, old-fashioned desk and a bosun's chair under the window, and a couple of other shabby, upholstered chairs against one wall. There was a laptop and printer on the desk and a wire tray filled with documents. A cocktail cabinet in the form of a globe stood to one side of the desk, its lid open to reveal a variety of bottles inside, and there was a glass of what looked like whisky on the corner of the desk.

An air of neglect pervaded the room, but Kate judged this to be superficial. Mr Silverman was plainly a man of means, going by his exceptionally well-groomed appearance and the gold Rolex watch winking at her from one slender white wrist. Roscoe's words echoed in her head. 'I've stumbled onto something big — a face from the past.' Could this be the "face" he had been referring to and if so, what exactly had her ex-boss stumbled onto?

'Please, have a seat,' Silverman said through a cloud of cigar smoke, and waved a hand towards the two chairs. 'Sorry the furnishings are a bit spartan, but I haven't been here long and most of the stuff has been obtained from local charity shops until I can furnish the place properly.'

He treated them to a brief smile that failed to reach his pale blue eyes. 'Now, can I offer you a drink? Whisky, gin, vodka, it's all available.'

Kate shook her head. 'Thank you, sir, but not while we're on duty.'

Silverman deposited himself in his bosun's chair as they sat down and swivelled around to face them.

'Then what can I do for you? Happy to see that the police are out and about, but I must admit, I'm intrigued by your visit.'

Kate smiled back. 'Nothing serious, sir. Just routine. We're investigating a fire that occurred just across the lane from the rear of your property during the early hours of yesterday morning. It was the home of an elderly lady, and it was unfortunately burned to the ground. We just wondered whether you may have seen or heard anything that could help us with our investigation.'

Silverman balanced his cigar in an ashtray on his desk and shook his head, frowning. 'Not that I can think of. I saw the flames from the house, of course, and heard the fire engines arriving, but nothing else comes to mind, I'm afraid. Arson, was it?'

'What makes you say that?'

He shrugged. 'Well, I hardly think the police would come all the way out here to make inquiries if it was an accidental fire. No one was hurt, were they?'

'Fortunately, no, but the person who started the fire wouldn't have known whether the woman was at home at the time or not.' Kate stared at Silverman fixedly for a moment. 'They may have torched the place hoping she was inside.'

Silverman plainly got the message, but he didn't turn a hair.

'I do hope not,' he practically purred, a mocking glint in his eyes. 'But there are some nasty people about nowadays, aren't there? Even the police have to be careful, don't they?'

Ostensibly, it was just a casual comment, but the threat was there, thinly veiled, and Kate was not slow in picking it up.

'Oh, we're always very careful, sir,' she parried. 'And, like the Mounties, we always get our man.'

Silverman stood up. 'Well, if there's nothing else, Sergeant . . .'

Kate nodded. 'No, sir, we'll leave you in peace. Thank you for your time.'

On the way to the door, she half-turned and said, 'What is it you actually do here?'

Another cold smile. 'Silverlink Medicinal Products eventually. But we're still doing the place up, so it will be a long time before we can get the business running properly.'

He opened the door for her and held out a slender white hand. 'Nice meeting you, Sergeant Lewis. Best of luck with your investigation.'

Then the door closed gently behind them.

'Smooth bastard,' Kate said as they drove off. 'Did you get the numbers of the two motors?'

Hayden nodded and patted the breast pocket of his coat.

'Good. Get them checked out on PNC when we get back, will you? Did you notice something, though?'

Hayden shrugged. 'What?'

'Silverman called me Sergeant Lewis, but I never actually introduced us, and he wasn't close enough to have been able to read my warrant card.'

He frowned. 'Good point.'

'Which means he must already have known who I was.'

'From Roscoe's bent detective?'

'Exactly.'

'So, there was obviously something in what Roscoe said to you on the phone.'

She nodded. 'And it also means that our Mr Silverman is more than likely the "face" Roscoe said he had seen, and that somehow Silverman's presence at Witch-Fire House, the disappearance of Roscoe, the panic-stricken flight of the girl in the ICU and Lilith's involvement with her are all pieces in the same damned jigsaw.'

'So, all we have to do is fit the pieces together,' he said drily. 'Piece of cake, I don't think.'

'Talking of cake,' she said, 'I think a large piece of it and a cup of strong coffee would be just the job to get the brain cells working.'

'I wouldn't argue with that,' he said, with more enthusiasm than he had displayed in the last twenty-four hours. 'Or better still, seeing as we have missed out on lunch again, maybe a nice hot dinner.'

* * *

But dinner was not to be. Hayden had passed the vehicle numbers to Dave Gort, the Local Intelligence Officer, and he and Kate were just starting their meal in the police canteen when Percival burst in on them.

'You'd better get that down you toot sweet,' he snapped, staring at the plates of steaming curry. 'The lads have found a stiff out on the Levels, near the site of Lilith's shack. I'm off to the scene now. You can join me there.'

'What sort of a stiff?' Hayden queried through a mouthful of curry.

'A dead one,' Percival replied sarcastically. 'And the worst part about it is that we think it might be Roscoe.'

CHAPTER 19

Kate and Hayden joined Percival at the scene twenty minutes later, parking behind Percival's car and a marked police patrol car. The lane had been cordoned off by two uniformed officers. Percival was up on the bank a few yards away, and quickly confirmed their worst fears.

'It *is* Ted Roscoe,' he said grimly, jumping down off the bank to meet them. He jerked his head towards the corpse, which had been pulled from the rhyne and was lying on its back on a tarpaulin.

'Nasty business by the look of it. At least the press haven't found out about it yet, so we haven't got to keep them at bay.'

Kate felt her legs about to give way and her head started to spin.

'You okay?'

Hayden's voice seemed to boom at her as if from the end of a long, echoing tunnel and he gripped her arm tightly.

She swallowed the acid vomit forming in her throat.

'Do you want to sit in the car for a moment?' Percival said, studying her white face with some concern.

She shook her head impatiently and took a deep breath. The damp marshland air seemed to revive her.

'I'm fine,' she snapped, pulling herself free of Hayden's grip.

She had seen death many times before, in all its horrible guises, and should be well used to it by now. But this time the corpse was that of someone who, just days before, had been a close colleague. The boss she had worked with for so many eventful years and had got to know so well. A real, living, breathing human being, with a unique personality, likes and dislikes, and individual character traits. This wasn't just another anonymous stiff to be labelled and packed off to the morgue for dissection like some inanimate object. She now appreciated why Eddie West's death had affected Hayden so badly. The fact that Ted Roscoe had been one of her least favourite people made no difference. His death, and where he had ended up, was personal and it had come as a terrible shock, especially as she felt partially responsible for not getting to him before this had happened.

'Seems he was found by a dog-handler, lying face down in the rhyne and wedged between the two banks,' Percival said. 'Looks to me like he drowned and has been here for a fair time, going by his condition.' He frowned. 'He has a nasty wound on the back of his head, which suggests he was struck from behind, and he has also lost two fingers, though how and why that could have happened is a bit of a bit of mystery. They don't appear to have been severed cleanly but chewed off, maybe by an animal — a dog or a fox.'

Kate shuddered. 'Poor old Roscoe. He didn't deserve to end up like this.'

Percival frowned. 'No, he didn't, but we may have been given a lucky break in that respect. The dog-handler who discovered the body found an old woman standing over it, prodding it with her walking stick.'

Kate's eyes widened. 'Lilith!'

'Spot on. She is now in custody at the nick, and I suggest you get back there to see what's what. Hayden and I will wait here for the forensic pathologist and SOCO.'

* * *

Ronnie Coleman received the call on his mobile just as Kate was driving away from the scene of Roscoe's death. The caller was his tame detective and the excitement in the other's tone was palpable.

'They've found Roscoe.'

Unconcerned, Coleman said, 'And who are "they?"'

'The plods. My DI and DS Lewis are out at the scene now.'

Coleman sighed. 'Bully for them.'

'They found him in a ditch.'

Coleman smirked. 'Oh dear. Poor old Roscoe. I wonder how that could have happened? Perhaps he tripped over something — like his inquisitive nose?'

But the grin was suddenly wiped from his face.

'They've nicked that old witch woman on sus for his murder.'

Coleman's expression darkened. 'They've what?'

'She's in the nick here right now, due for interview.'

Coleman released a sharp hiss. 'That can't happen.'

'What do you mean? I thought you'd be pleased that they've got someone in the frame.'

'Don't be a fool! If that blonde bitch in the ICU managed to blab to the old bag about what she found here, the so-called witch could pass that on to Old Bill.'

'So, what do we do?'

'What do *you* do, you mean. You're in exactly the right place, and no one will think anything of it if you're seen down the pokey or wherever else they've got her.'

'You're not seriously suggesting I—?'

'I'm not suggesting anything. Just shut the old cow up for good.'

'I can't do that. I've never topped anyone in my life.'

'Then now's the time to start.'

'But — but I can't just walk in. Getting into the custody suite isn't as easy as that. There's a custody sergeant and you have to have a reason for being there.'

Coleman's voice was suddenly menacing. 'Listen, you slimy toad, I don't care how you do the business. Just do it. Remember, if I go down, you go with me, and I've got lots of friends in stir who'll be only too pleased to gut you in the shower.'

Coleman cut the call. Then, selecting a fresh cigar from the wooden box on his desk, he sat for several minutes, eyes hooded, lost in thought.

'Problem, boss?' Bruno asked, lumbering into the office shortly afterwards.

'Could be. The Law have found Roscoe. That means they'll be looking for his car. So, you'd better get the lads to load all the stuff from the barn into the Trannie, just in case they find it and we need to leave PDQ.'

* * *

Lilith was being held in a women's cell at the end of a short corridor. Kate found her squatting on the bed, with her shawl, coat and shoes off and her long grey hair streaming down over her shoulders. Her ankle-length black dress was badly stained and, even from the cell doorway, Kate could see that her talon-like nails were filthy. For someone who imagined herself to be a witch, she certainly looked the part — a grotesque image from a child's nightmare.

'Hello, Lilith,' Kate said quietly. 'I think you and I should have a little talk, don't you?'

There was no answer. The old woman simply stared at the floor, as if in a trance.

Leaving her there to stew for a while, Kate headed to the CID office. Ronnie Crouch, the thin, grey-haired office manager, looked up as she pushed through the double doors, and Detective Constable Danny Ferris swivelled round in his chair.

'Is it true they've found Roscoe's body out on the Levels?' Ferris said.

'Sadly, yes,' Kate replied. 'News certainly travels fast around here.'

Crouch scratched his long nose and shook his head. 'Bloody shame,' he muttered. 'He wasn't perfect, but he was a good bloke underneath it all. I worked with him in CID for quite a few years and when I retired, it was his recommendation that got me this job.'

Kate nodded. 'Yes, it's a bad business. Where's Jamie?'

'Dunno,' Ferris said. 'Down the bog probably. He spends half his life in there.'

Kate frowned. She wanted the sharp, accomplished interrogator to partner her when she interviewed Lilith. Foster had all the necessary skills and, although Ferris was a good thief-taker, he wasn't in the same league. This particular case called for a delicate, probing strategy.

'Thanks a lot, Danny. I really wanted to know that. I'll come back in a jiff.'

He shrugged, apparently missing the sarcasm. 'You're welcome, Sarge, adding quickly as she turned to leave, 'Poor old Roscoe, though. What a way to go. Thirty years' graft in the job, only to finish up brown bread in a bleedin' ditch.'

She thought of what Hayden had said about Eddie West's death and nodded. 'Bit of an ignominious end for him, isn't it, but you know what they say.'

'Yeah, life's a bitch and all that. The old witch cow stiff him, did she?'

'What makes you say that?'

'In the pokey, isn't she? George Miles, the dog-handler, says he caught her red-handed, prodding the corpse with her stick. She obviously caught Roscoe unawares and clocked him over the head with it, then dumped him in the rhyne. She was just making sure he had snuffed it when George caught her at it. Open-and-shut case, I reckon.'

'With such a razor-sharp mind, Danny, you're wasted in Somerset. You should be at the Yard.'

He scowled at the rebuke. 'Yeah, well, maybe I'll be proven right in the end. Then you'll be laughin' out of your arse.'

She smiled at the retort and, winking at a grinning Ronnie Crouch, she left them both to it.

The LIO was sitting at his desk studying his computer screen when she walked into his office.

'Ah, Kate,' he said and, swivelling round in his chair, rubbed his eyes and yawned.

'Anything yet on the two cars or the name Silverman, Dave?' she asked, perching on the edge of his desk.

He reached into a wire tray behind him and handed her a sheaf of papers.

'Checked PNC,' he said. 'Both motors registered to a company called Silverlink Medicinal Products at an address in Slough. Nothing about them on any of the main indexes, so they seem to be clean.'

'Damn it!'

He held up a hand. 'So, I did a bit more digging. The company itself has a managing director called Barney Johnson.'

'And?'

'Barney Johnson is on PNC as an associate of Danny Beldon, who is well CRO — a nasty bastard with cons for protection, GBH, arson and the supply of class A narcotics — who is himself the bosom pal of one Ronnie Coleman.'

'So, where does this get us?'

He grinned mysteriously. 'Quite a long way actually. You see, based on the info you gave me, I delved a little deeper and PNC threw up a twenty-year-old crime squad file on Coleman, who, going by the date of birth recorded, would be about sixty-two now. He was apparently nicked after an armed raid on a post office in the Smoke resulted in the death of a young copper, who was run down by the getaway car when he tried to stop it. Coleman's prints were in the car, which was later found abandoned in Chiswick, but at his trial Coleman claimed that the month before, he'd sold the car to a man in a pub called Bill Smith, and the jury believed him. He was done for failing to notify change of ownership and acquitted of any involvement in the raid.'

Kate looked confused. 'Obviously you're going to tell me in a moment what all this has to do with Silverman but, firstly, why is there still a file on Coleman after all this time? If he was acquitted, it would have been destroyed with his prints.'

'Yes, but as a young man, Coleman had already acquired a string of convictions for a variety of criminal offences, including theft, assault occasioning actual bodily harm, and taking and driving away, so he had a nice fat record which the jury were not allowed to know about until after his acquittal. Much later, as he rose up the criminal chain to become a top London mobster, he earned himself a special place in criminal intelligence records as a "target criminal," and numerous police surveillance operations were mounted to try to bring him to book, all without success.'

'And I deduce from all this that Coleman is Silverman?'

'Well, the name Silverman is an alias he was known to use in the past, though among the criminal fraternity he is actually known as "Mr Havana" because of his liking for Havana cigars. His updated d/f describes him as sixty-two years of age, six foot two in height, thin build, with a shock of unusual silvery hair.

Kate slid off the desk. 'That's Silverman, for sure,' she exclaimed, her eyes shining. 'Excellent work, Dave. At least now we know who we're dealing with.'

He held up his hand again. 'I'm not finished yet.'

'What, you mean there's more?'

'The most interesting thing is that throughout the years the crime squad strove to catch Coleman, nailing him for a serious crime became a *cause célèbre* for the young DS who had been the case investigating officer in the raid on the post office. He never gave up, it seems, but Coleman always managed to slip through his fingers.'

Kate gaped at him. 'Bloody hell! You're not telling me—?'

Gort nodded. 'That young officer was a Detective Sergeant Ted Roscoe.'

CHAPTER 20

Kate was heading back to her office, bursting with excitement over the information the LIO had given her, when she heard shouting coming from the direction of the front foyer. Swinging around, she went to the door of the station duty office, which served the public reception area, and stared past the civilian station duty officer at the man shouting at him through the glass partition. She recognised Luke Cobb immediately. He was dressed in a cloth cap, the usual corduroy trousers and a baggy sweater, his puffy, red face even redder than usual.

'I don't give a shit what you say,' Cobb blazed, slamming one balled fist against the glass screen. 'Lilith's in here. I saw her being taken away.'

Groaning inwardly, Kate pulled the door open.

'Come on, Luke,' she said sternly. 'What's all this?'

He spun round, his raised fist still bunched.

She glared at him. 'If you don't calm down now, you'll end up inside too.'

His contorted features relaxed as recognition dawned. He lowered his fist. 'You're that police lady, the detective. You came to the farm.'

'Right on the nail,' she said. 'Now, what's all this nonsense about?'

His hand dropped to his side. 'They — they took Lilith away. An old lady who wasn't hurting no one.'

Kate held the door open, ignoring the furious buzz issuing from the security box on the wall.

'Okay, why don't we have a chat about it?' she said.

He hesitated, frowning suspiciously. 'You going to lock me up?'

She shook her head. 'No, Luke, not if you behave yourself.'

He thought about that for a second, then nodded. 'Do you have Coca-Cola?'

She forced a smile. With everything that was whirling around inside her head, she could really have done without this unwelcome distraction. 'I can get you some from the machine if you like?'

He nodded and she showed him into the public waiting room just inside the door. The drinks dispenser was outside the canteen at the far end of the corridor.

'Make yourself comfortable,' she said. 'I'll get you that Coke.'

'When she returned with a can and a plastic cup, she found him standing in the middle of the room, his eyes darting everywhere, clearly nervous. She handed him the can and his eyes lit up. Refusing the cup with a shake of his head, he snapped open the tab and took a gulp.

'Is this where you question prisoners?' he asked.

'No, the interview rooms are further along the corridor,' she said. 'This is where we talk to people who need our help.' She waved a hand towards one of several shabby easy chairs. 'Please, have a seat.'

Drawing up a chair beside his, she smiled encouragingly. 'You have nothing to fear from me, Luke. We're just having a little chat to straighten things out, aren't we? After all, you've cycled a long way over here just to help Lilith, so sitting down to chat with you is the least I can do.'

His eyes were watchful over the rim of the can, which he had raised to his lips again. 'It isn't so far,' he muttered after taking a gulp. 'I can't drive, see, so I've always had to use my bike.'

'And cycling keeps you fit, doesn't it?' she said.

'Yes, I'm very fit,' he said, 'strong too.'

'I can see you are,' she said. 'Is that why you were able to build such a fine house for Lilith?'

'Wasn't all that fine — just a shack — but she liked it. Then someone burned it down.'

'That wasn't very nice, was it?'

He scowled again and took another drink. 'No, and it weren't very nice that she was locked up here neither.'

'So, how did you know she'd been locked up?' she went on carefully. 'Were you there when the police took her away then?'

He didn't answer immediately but drained his can of Coke noisily and shook his head. 'I went to her house to see if she wanted me to build her another one and I saw her being put into a police car stopped in the lane. I was going to ask why they were putting her in the car but there was this policeman with a big dog. I don't like dogs, 'specially fierce ones like that one. So, I hid in the woods till they'd gone. Then — then I got on my bike and rode over here.'

'Oh, why did you do that?'

'Cause I was worried about her. See, she's a witch and she told me once that the police don't like witches.'

'That's not true, Luke. The police don't mind witches. They just don't like people who try to hurt other people.'

'Is that why Lilith was taken away — 'cause you think she hurt someone?'

'That's what we're trying to find out.'

'Did she put a spell on someone then?'

'We don't know yet, Luke. We're hoping she'll tell us.'

He took off his cloth cap and wrung it between his meathooks for a few seconds, like a small child confessing mischief to his teacher, before putting it back on his head and blurting, 'There was a body in the rhyne near where Lilith was. I saw it. But Lilith wouldn't have had nothing to do with that. She wouldn't put a spell on no one unless they tried to hurt her first. I think it was the bad men who put the body there.'

She tensed. 'What bad men, Luke?'

He hesitated. 'I mustn't say. I could get into trouble.'

'You can tell me. After all, we're friends, aren't we? Friends don't let each other get into trouble, do they?'

He thought about that for several seconds, frowning again, then picked up the now empty can he'd dumped in his lap and crushed it into virtually nothing with one muscular hand.

'The bad men who came to the farm. Me and Uncle heard them, and I got out of bed to look.'

'So, who were these bad men?'

'Dunno, but they were in a big black car. They went all around the farmyard, looking in the barns and sheds. Then they drove off. Uncle told me to keep quiet and not to go out to them. He said they might hurt us.'

'When was this?'

'The night Lilith's place was burned down. I — I saw the fire from my bedroom window about half an hour after the men had gone.'

'Did you know it was Lilith's house?'

He nodded. 'I guessed it was and went to have a look. I thought Lilith might have been hurt, but she weren't there. The men in the black car drove off as I got there, but they didn't see me.'

'And you don't know who these men were?'

He hesitated. 'If I say, will you tell them I told you?'

'Of course not. Friends don't do that, do they?'

'I think they live up at the spook house.'

'Spook house? Where's that?'

'It's where the man lived who burned Lilith's cottage down lots of years ago.'

Kate was confused now. 'You're saying Lilith lived here before?'

He nodded. 'She told me she was a witch then too and she was called Molly something or other.'

'Ah, Molly Clavey?'

He brightened. 'Yes, that was Lilith before, but she's come back as Lilith.'

Kate took a deep breath. Luke had certainly swallowed Lilith's story of reincarnation, which was hardly surprising in view of his limited mental competence.

'So, why has she come back?'

'To punish everyone in the village for what was done to her before.'

'Does that include the Rev Truly, Luke?'

He looked down at his feet.

'Rev Truly says some not very nice things were done at his church, like messing up the altar and digging up a grave. Did Lilith make you help her do those things to frighten him?'

He shook his head emphatically. 'I never done nothing like that, and Lilith wouldn't neither or she would have told me. She just uses spells, that's all. She told me she had put one on Mr Truly and also on Constable West to punish them. She said they deserved it for picking on her all the time, and she was going to do the same to the man at the spook house too because he shouldn't have opened up that house again when it was cursed.'

'Have you ever been to the spook house, Luke?'

He shook his head and shivered. 'Not me, but Lilith's new friend went there, and Lilith told me they tried to hurt her, so she ran away.'

Kate could feel the tiny gold hairs on her arms tingling. 'Was that the night before I first met you on the drove?'

He gaped for a moment, realising he had said too much, then nodded sheepishly. 'Lilith told me not to say nothing about it to no one.'

'So, the sandals I found, they belonged to Lilith's friend?'

He shrugged. 'Dunno.'

'Was she a young, blonde lady?'

He nodded. 'I only saw her once. Lilith was letting her stay at her house.'

'Do you know her name?'

'She said it was Ela — spelt E L A. I think she's foreign, 'cause she talks funny.'

'Do you know Ela's other name or where she came from?'

'No, but she was nice to me. She gave me some chocolate.'

Kate guessed she would get no more out of him on the mystery woman and changed the subject, leaning forward and placing a reassuring hand on his arm.

'Luke,' she said, 'I have a very important question to ask you and you must tell me the truth. It could help Lilith.'

He frowned. 'I always tell the truth. Uncle says it's the measure of a man, though I don't much know what that means.'

'It means someone who is a proper man that people can trust, Luke.'

'Oh,' he said. 'Then that's me. I can always be trusted, and I work hard.'

'Right then, tell me, did you hit or push the man who was found in the rhyne? You might have been angry because you thought he had set fire to Lilith's house, which I can understand.'

He looked horrified and shook his head furiously. 'No, I didn't touch him. Honest. I wouldn't do nothing like that. Uncle would be very angry with me.'

He gripped the arms of the chair, staring wildly about him, and began to breathe rapidly. Afraid he was about to hyperventilate Kate squeezed his arm. But he started to get up.

'I believe you, Luke,' she said quickly. 'It was just something I had to ask you, all right?'

'I never touched him,' he repeated, stumbling to his feet, and shaking himself free. 'You're trying to trick me. You said we was just going to have a chat.'

'Steady, steady,' Kate soothed. 'Would you like another Coke or maybe a cake?'

He shook his head and moved towards the door. 'I just want to go home.'

‘Okay, Luke, I’m sorry. I didn’t mean to upset you. I won’t ask you anything else. Let me show you out.’

She followed the big man out of the police station and saw him climb onto a rusty looking bicycle leaning against the wall. Then, casting her an angry, resentful glance, he rode away with a familiar clanking of pedals.

‘I thought you’d made a pal there,’ the station duty officer said with a grin as she made her way back inside.

‘Not anymore,’ she grunted, heading for the stairs.

And it was at that precise moment that pandemonium broke loose as the custody suite alarm blasted through the station.

CHAPTER 21

Kate met Jamie Foster as she ran through the open door of the custody suite. He appeared to be on his way out and looked badly shaken.

'What is it?' she shouted above the din.

He screwed up his face, then relaxed as the alarm suddenly went off. 'Real bummer, skipper,' he said. 'Someone's in for the high jump over this.'

The corridor to the cells seemed to be full of people. Phil Manning, the custody sergeant and Faith Wexford, the detention officer, had been joined by Jim Graham, the uniformed shift inspector. Also present was a very sour-faced, blond man in civvies, whose manicured fingers were nervously toying with a luxuriant blond moustache. Kate recognised him as Toby Ricketts, the seldom seen DCI.

Kate saw that they were all crowding around an open cell door, and with a sinking feeling in her stomach, she realised it was the very cell in which Lilith was being held.

Pushing past Manning, she peered around Graham into the cell, and her worst fears were realised.

Lilith's diminutive figure was lying on the floor in a contorted position, close to the door, both eyes wide open and staring sightlessly at the onlookers, her mouth gaping wide in an obscene rictus grin. That she was dead was obvious, though the young woman police officer working on her seemed oblivious to the fact as she knelt beside the corpse, gamely trying to resuscitate her.

'Shit! Shit! Shit!' Graham muttered. 'How the hell could this have happened?'

Both Manning and Wexford threw each other uneasy glances, obviously fully appreciating the vulnerability of their position. They seemed too shocked to say anything.

The woman police officer kneeling in the cell finally stood up. Kate recognised Janet Robinson, Eddie West's colleague. 'I'm no doctor, sir,' she said to Graham, 'but it looks like she had a heart attack—'

'I don't care what it was,' Graham cut in savagely. 'She's still dead, isn't she? There'll be hell to pay over this.'

He wheeled on Manning, his eyes blazing. 'She should have been checked every half hour.'

'She was,' Wexford put in, her voice trembling and tears streaming down her face. 'I only looked in at her before I went for my ten-minute break, and the sergeant was there when I left.'

Graham rounded on Manning. 'So, how come it wasn't until Wexford here came back that she was found? Where the hell were you?'

Manning swallowed hard, obviously seeing where all this was heading.

'I had to go to the toilet, sir, but I checked on her before I went, and she was fine. I was only gone a couple of minutes.'

Graham shook his head. 'Death of a prisoner on my watch. Of all the rotten luck.'

'Even more unlucky for her, guv,' Kate put in grimly, thinking, *And a real bugger of a turn-up for our investigation.*

'This will mean a full IPCC investigation,' Ricketts said abruptly, a noticeable tic starting in his left cheek. 'Anyone bothered to call for a medic yet?'

'En route, sir,' Manning said.

Ricketts grunted. 'Bit too late now, I know,' he said, 'but we must follow the proper protocols.'

Kate smiled without humour. Oh yes, she thought to herself, and you're just the man for protocols, aren't you? A graduate entry candidate and, at thirty, already fast-tracked for accelerated promotion, the blue-eyed whizz-kid was in the same category as Percival, but not nearly as likeable. A company "yes" man, he was, as Roscoe had once put it, as reliable as a broken wristwatch. Somewhere along the line, he had lost his glow in the eyes of the hierarchy, which was why he was still just a DCI after a good two years in the post. Kate was very wary of him and when he turned to her, her defences automatically went up.

'I gather your DI is still down at the Roscoe incident scene?'

She nodded. 'As far as I know, yes, sir.'

'Well, you'll have to do then,' he said dismissively. 'Get the forensic pathologist out and arrange for a SOCO team to be deployed here. I'll have to brief the superintendent so that the IPCC may be alerted, and an outside senior officer appointed to investigate.'

* * *

Complying with Ronnie Coleman's instructions had been a lot easier than the mobster's tame detective had expected. In fact, matters seemed to have fallen right into his lap. He'd had a brainwave as to how to stiff the witch bitch and make it look like an ordinary sudden death after remembering seeing some villain do it in a TV crime drama a few weeks before. All he'd needed was a large plastic bag and pinching it from the Scenes of Crime office had been a doddle. The team were still out at Roscoe's death scene and their office was empty.

The biggest problem he'd thought he would have to face was getting past the custody sergeant to the old girl's cell, but luck was on his side. He'd just gone to the canteen to grab a quick cup of coffee to help him summon up the

Dutch courage to get the job done, when on his way out he'd almost collided with Faith Wexford, the custody suite's late-turn detention officer, on her way in for a tea break. Then, approaching the custody suite itself, armed with a cock-and-bull story about needing to check some filed custody records, he had spotted Phil Manning, the custody sergeant, heading away from him down the corridor towards the toilet.

There was no knowing how long Manning would be away from his desk, but it would have been stupid to have passed up the opportunity. The bunch of cell keys was actually lying on the custody sergeant's desk instead of attached to his belt, as was usually the case, which to the mole's twisted mind smacked of some sort of divine providence, and he'd soon unlocked the cell gate and sprinted down the passage to Lilith's cell.

She hadn't even looked up as he'd entered the cell, and he'd pulled the plastic bag tight over her head before she knew what was happening. She'd struggled then, frantically clawing at his wrists as she gasped for air, but she was no match for him, and he'd stared at the wrinkled, white face and glassy eyes with a kind of peculiar fascination for several seconds after she had suffocated.

The only hitch had been removing the bag, part of which had been sucked into her mouth and caught on the stumps of her rotten teeth, but he'd managed to pull it free with a little bit of effort and stuff it into his pocket.

Then he had locked the cell again and returned to a still empty custody office, locked the gate to the cell passage and dumped Manning's keys exactly where he thought he had found them before heading back to CID, with no one being the wiser.

Seated at his desk afterwards, he could hardly believe the way everything had worked out so brilliantly for him. He must have been in the custody suite a full six minutes and yet Manning had still not returned by the time he'd left. Six minutes amounted to a hell of a long pee, so he could only assume that the good sergeant had gone for a number two — and, incredibly, right on cue. The gods had certainly smiled down on him on this occasion and no mistake.

All he had to do now was wait for the balloon to go up, secure in the knowledge that, without any evidence to the contrary, the old witch's death was bound to be put down to a heart attack — and, even if foul play *was* later suspected, there was absolutely nothing to connect him to the crime. After all, no one knew that Coleman had settled in the wilds of Somerset, or that organised crime had a mole in Highbridge CID, so he was home and dry.

* * *

Kate's excitement, following the revelations of the LIO and Luke Cobb about Ronnie Coleman and the implications attached to them, had been severely tempered by the death of Lilith. The old woman could have been her ace card in nailing the London mobster, for Kate was convinced she had been somehow mixed up in what was going on. Now that was all out the window.

Percival indirectly echoed her thoughts when he returned to his office from the Roscoe incident scene late in the evening and dumped himself in his chair, glancing up briefly when Kate walked in and closed the door.

'What a mess!' he said, having just learned of Lilith's death. 'As if we haven't enough on our plates at present. Press turned up at the Roscoe crime scene an hour after you left and they're camped outside the nick now, clamouring for info. Bloody parasites. Won't be long before they find out about our cell death too.'

Sitting across from him, Kate nodded, but she deliberately held back on revealing the information she had uncovered. She knew that keeping things to herself was completely out of order and part of her desperately wanted to unload on him, but she was still unsure as to who she could trust, and she wanted to mull things over and get her head straight first before telling anyone anything.

'This will be a full IPCC inquiry,' Percival went on. 'The Home Office forensic pathologist is carrying out an examination as we speak, and another SOCO team are waiting in the wings to do their stuff—'

'At least you won't have to be involved in this one,' she interjected quickly. 'The DCI seems to be handling the situation at the moment.'

He shrugged. 'I wouldn't be allowed to, as it's happened at this nick. And he won't be able to have much more involvement either, once the IPCC have been alerted and a senior officer is appointed from Headquarters to investigate the circumstances.'

'So, what's the latest SP on Roscoe?' she queried.

His frown deepened. 'Been dead about two days. Nasty bang on the back of the head, which Dr Summers reckoned would have put him out and possibly caused him to tumble into the rhyne, where he drowned. SOCO couldn't find any trace of a weapon, and the ground on both sides of the rhyne was very soft and had been churned up by so many feet — the dog plod who found him, as well as ourselves — that any footprint evidence had been totally obliterated.'

'But his death is being been treated as murder, right?'

'Can hardly be anything else, can it? Incident room's being set up here in the club tomorrow, but an SIO is yet to be appointed. Did you get anywhere with Lilith before she snuffed it?'

Kate paused. For a moment she was thrown. If only she hadn't allowed herself to be sidetracked, first by the LIO and then by Luke Cobb, she might have got something out of the old woman with a second visit.

''Fraid not,' she said. 'She refused even to acknowledge my presence when I went to see her in her cell, and before I was able to set up a formal interview, she was dead.'

'And now we'll never know whether she did for poor old Roscoe or not.'

'Hardly likely, is it? She was an old lady. I wouldn't have thought she was capable of knocking a powerful man like him senseless.'

'Probably not, but SOCO are sending her stick off to forensics anyway, just in case.' He hesitated. 'What about this Luke guy you mentioned? He was in pretty great with her, wasn't he? Even built her that hovel she lived in. "Big strong lad", was how you described him to me, I believe. He could easily be our perp.'

She shook her head. 'I wouldn't think he was capable of killing a wasp. He's a sandwich short of a picnic, certainly — but no way is he a murderer. And why would he kill Roscoe? He didn't even know him.'

He grunted. 'Point taken, but as it's now after nine and I'll want you back here early tomorrow, I suggest you clutter off home and get a good night's sleep. There's nothing more you can do here tonight.'

She nodded and stood up, not sorry to be calling it a day, and went to collect Hayden from the general office on her way out, knowing that a good night's sleep was the last thing she could look forward to after all that had happened.

* * *

Hayden said nothing on the way home, apart from muttering something derogatory about the reporters gathered around the back entrance as they drove away. He seemed to have reverted to his morose mood. She could only guess at where his thoughts were and she was not surprised when, the moment they were inside their cottage, he broached the subject that was obviously weighing him down.

'I promised we'd have a talk about things,' he said in a hesitant voice as she threw herself onto the settee. 'About us and the — the job at my old school.'

She nodded and, kicking off her shoes, rested her head against the back of the settee.

She closed her eyes for a moment. 'Pour me a drink, will you, Hayd,' she said wearily. 'Then we'll talk — but not about us yet. I have some other things I want to chew over with you.'

He was scowling so much his face resembled a gargoyle. 'Police work again, is it?' he growled and when she didn't answer, he snapped, 'See what I mean? Even at home we can't escape the nick. Can't you see why I'm so browned off with it all? It's now nearly half past nine at night, we've been on duty for over twelve hours and still we can't get away from it.'

'Please, Hayden,' she said, opening her eyes and staring at him. 'I need to run some things past you. Just open a bottle, will you?'

His mouth a hard line and anger burning in his blue eyes, he stalked off into the kitchen and seconds later she heard the pop of a cork.

When he returned with two large glasses of red and put one on the coffee table in front of her, his anger seemed to have largely evaporated. He sighed heavily and dropped into the chair opposite, splashing some red wine on his trousers and the floor.

'Right,' he said, 'let's get it over with. 'But then I really *do* want to talk about us.'

'Deal.' She sat up, took a big gulp of her wine and launched straight into a verbal outpouring of all that she had discovered.

For once he listened without interrupting, and even when she had finished, slumping back against the cushions, he said nothing for at least a full minute.

'So, Coleman was Roscoe's "face?"' he said thoughtfully. 'That explains a lot.'

'And it looks like his thugs were searching for Roscoe the night he died,' Kate added. 'Why else would they turn up at Luke Cobb's farm?'

'And it also looks like they might have torched Lilith's shack.'

'Exactly. Which suggests they wanted her out of the way too. It is almost certain that the woman I hit in my car was connected to Lilith — possibly staying with her — and was running away, not from so-called hinkypunk*s*, but from Coleman's men. Which is obviously what she was trying to tell me when she blurted the words, "witch fire."'

He frowned. 'And it also puts a whole new complexion on the sudden death of Lilith, doesn't it? It may not actually have been due to natural causes at all. And if her death *wasn't* a natural one, that would mean . . .'

Kate studied him eagerly. 'Precisely. Coleman's paid-for insider is also a cold-blooded killer. The only thing we don't know is how he did it.'

'Have you told Percival about all this?'

'How the hell could I? He might be the bent cop in question. I can't trust anyone at present.'

He grunted. 'What if Dave Gort happens to tell him? If he *is* the villain, that means Coleman will be forewarned and you'll have lost your advantage, but if he isn't, you'll be in the hottest water imaginable. Withholding information on a criminal investigation is a serious matter.'

'I've asked Gort to keep the results of my enquiry to himself and I trust him.'

He threw her a dubious glance. 'I hope you're right. So, what are you asking me to do?'

'I'm not asking you to do anything, just put that clever brain of yours to work and let me know if you come up with anything.'

He gave her an old-fashioned look. 'Well, one thing my "clever brain" tells me right now is that if Lilith *was* murdered and our corrupt copper did the business, Percival can't have been responsible, for he was down at the Roscoe scene with me when she was found.'

She frowned. 'Okay, I take your point. Which means we're left with just Danny Ferris or Jamie Foster as suspects, and—'

She broke off, her eyes widening. 'Just a minute. I remember now. When I went down to the cells after the alarm went off, Jamie was already down there, and on the way out.'

Their gazes locked. Then he shook his head dismissively. 'I can't believe Jamie would . . . I mean, I've known him ever since we joined the department.'

'I agree, but would you suspect Danny any the more? He's rough and ready, but bent? No way.'

He sucked on his teeth. 'Then we're back to square one, old girl, aren't we? Which means you should confide in our acting DI without further delay. After all, if you want to move on Coleman, you will have to have a legitimate reason for doing so and get a proper operation set up. You can't do it alone.'

'Yes, but that's my dilemma. The more people who know about what I've uncovered, the more likely it is that Coleman will hear about it before we can get that operation underway.'

'It's a gamble, I agree, but you really have no choice. First thing tomorrow, tell Percival, okay? Now, I think it's time for you and me to have that chat about us that we promised ourselves.'

'Fine,' she agreed wearily and held out her glass. 'Get me a refill first, though, will you?'

But when he returned from the kitchen with another glass of red, she was slumped over with her eyes closed, dead to the world. With a resigned shake of his head, he gently lifted her legs up onto the settee and slipped a cushion under her head. Then, stoking up the fire, he left her there and went upstairs to bed.

CHAPTER 22

Highbridge police station was a hive of activity when Kate and Hayden arrived the following morning. This had resulted in swelling the ranks of the press outside, so much so that the back entrance was now guarded by a couple of PCSOs to prevent any unauthorised access.

The car park itself was jam-packed with vehicles and Kate's reserved bay was occupied by a sleek black Volvo, which she recognised as one of the Headquarters staff cars, used by chief officers and other very senior ranks. Ordinarily, she would have instructed whoever had parked a vehicle in her reserved space to move it, but since she had no wish to commit career suicide, she found another spot instead.

The main corridor and staircase of the station itself were full of bodies moving in opposite directions, most of them heading for the lift, carrying box files and electronic equipment up to the club on the top floor, which served as the incident room on major investigations. Both Kate and Hayden had seen it all before and were unsurprised by the seeming chaos, which in reality, was quite an organised operation. They made their way straight to the CID general office, leaving all the hustle, bustle and commotion on the other side of the department's double doors.

Percival was in his own glass-panelled inner sanctum, apparently on the phone. Kate parted company with Hayden to join him, picking up on his twitchy stressed demeanour as soon as she closed the door behind her. If he was in that sort of mood, she mused, what she had to tell him was certainly not going to be a walk in the park.

But, as it turned out, she had a while to wait before she could tell him anything.

Replacing his phone, he sat back in his chair and ran a weary hand through his blond hair.

'Been up most of the night,' he explained with a long yawn, adding, 'I know we need to talk, Kate, but there's a lot going on and I've got a meeting in an hour with the DCI the SIO Headquarters have appointed to head our investigation — a Detective Superintendent Raymond Ansell.' He raised his eyebrows. 'You know him, I believe.'

'You could say that,' she replied tightly.

'What's he like?'

She made a face as she remembered the slightly effeminate man with the build of a whippet whom she had crossed swords with on two previous major crime inquiries — the dark eyes like gimlets, the lean, saturnine face, the slightly lopsided mop of jet black hair reminiscent of photographs she had seen of Adolf Hitler and the aura of cold, ruthless efficiency that emanated from him like an invisible force. Oh yes, she remembered Raymond Ansell. He was not easily forgotten.

'Honestly?' she asked. 'Well, in a nutshell, you could say he is ruthless, analytical, efficient, and has all the charisma of a stone statue.'

He grimaced, 'Great. That's all we need right now. He'll have plenty to bite on when he gets here anyway. You've heard the latest, I expect?'

She looked at him, puzzled. 'What latest?'

'Obviously not then. Well, the forensic pathologist found a thin piece of transparent plastic, like off a supermarket food bag, stuck between Lilith's teeth and pressure marks and some scratches that she felt were fingernails around the old woman's neck. She believes she was asphyxiated, most likely by someone placing a plastic bag over her head.'

Kate gaped. 'Plastic bag — in *our* cells?'

'Exactly, which makes three possible homicides we've got at present, if we count Eddie West, and that's not all that's come up either.'

'There's more?'

He nodded. 'SOCO found a spare battery in Roscoe's pocket, but no mobile. He must have dropped it somewhere and there's a search on for it as we speak.'

'What about doing a GPS track?'

'Already tried. We got his private number from our records, but there was no response. The phone, wherever it is, appears to be dead.'

He half-turned in the doorway. 'Oh yes, and guess what they also found in one of Roscoe's pockets? A bottle of about a dozen tablets, which they believe to be some form of amphetamine, plus some sugar-like lumps in a bag that look suspiciously like crack cocaine!'

'Drugs? On Roscoe?'

'Yep. Looks like our ex-DI was nursing a deep secret.'

She shook her head firmly. 'Sorry, but I don't buy that. Roscoe may have been many things, God rest his soul, but an addict or a pusher? No way.'

'Then how would you explain it?'

'I can't yet, but there is a possibility we shouldn't overlook.'

'Which is?'

'That Roscoe found some sort of evidence — maybe the drugs in question — at Witch-Fire House. That was perhaps why he wanted to meet me at Yardley's Cider Farm — to produce the goods — but was caught by Coleman's men and stiffed before he could get there.'

He emitted a low whistle. 'That's one hell of a conclusion to draw from the little info we've got. Which reminds me, did you manage to visit Witch-Fire House? So much has been happening in the last twenty-four hours that I could understand if—'

'Hayden and I both went,' she cut in and told him quickly about the visit.

He sat back down, his hands characteristically sliding down inside the back of his trousers.

'Not a lot there to justify further action, is there?' he said after a long pause. 'Silverman may be a villain and up to something at Witch-Fire House, but we still haven't got enough to make a move on him, whatever we may suspect. After all, we're talking about a murder here, not just a potential drugs bust.'

She hesitated for a moment, biting her lip, then with a heavy sigh, took the plunge. 'Silverman *is* a villain,' she said quietly, 'and his name isn't Silverman — it's Coleman, Ronnie Coleman.'

He frowned, his eyes narrowing. 'Coleman? And how do you know that?'

'I've got something else to tell you,' she said. 'Quite a lot in fact.'

It took her some time to tell him everything. He listened in silence, the expression on his lean face growing darker and darker, and when she had finished, he sat there in silence for quite a while longer. Finally, he leaned forward, removed his hands from the back of his trousers and treated her to a cold, hard stare.

'And, like Roscoe's initial disappearance, you're only telling me all this now?' he rasped. 'Am I missing something here? About teamwork and trust in your colleagues?'

She looked down at her lap.

'I mean', he went on, 'if you hadn't caught me just now, when would you have told me about your little chats with the LIO and Luke Cobb — bearing in mind that I have to attend a major briefing with the SIO in,' he looked at his watch, 'half an hour? You've been sitting on information which could be crucial, not only to what is a serious crime investigation, but one which concerns the murder of one of our own former colleagues. This is inexcusable. Furthermore, had you not spoken to me I could have delivered a major investigative briefing with half of that brief missing. Can you even imagine how much of a prat I would have looked?'

Kate nodded. She fully accepted his castigation, but secretly thought that him looking a prat was probably the main issue as far as he was concerned.

He relaxed a little and shook his head. 'I just can't understand what's got into you. Why on earth didn't you tell me about all this yesterday?'

She shrugged. 'I couldn't, not until I was sure.'

He frowned. '*Sure*? I don't understand. 'Sure, about what?'

She told him and waited for another outburst, but to her surprise, it never came. Instead, he simply gaped at her with a look of absolute incredulity.

'You thought I was *bent*?' he exclaimed. 'You actually thought I was in hock to someone like Ronnie Coleman?'

'I didn't know what to think,' she said. 'I didn't know who I could trust, so I had to tread warily.'

He looked more disappointed than angry now. 'And what made you decide the slimeball wasn't me in the end?'

'I realised that if Lilith had been murdered, the culprit couldn't be you, as you were down at the Roscoe incident scene the whole time she was in custody here.'

He emitted a disparaging snort. 'Well, thanks for the vote of confidence. So, if not me, who have you got your eye on now?'

'If Roscoe was right, it can only be Jamie Foster or Danny Ferris — and Jamie was coming out of the cell complex when I went down there after the alarm went off.'

He grunted. 'The DCI was down there pretty damned quick too, I gather.'

She nodded. 'So was the duty inspector, Constable Janet Robinson and both the custody officers, but Roscoe said it was — and I quote — "a guy on your team," and that only leaves Jamie and Danny.'

'And Hayden, of course,' he sniped.

She gave him a tight smile. 'He was with you at the Roscoe incident.'

'Oh, so he was. Then Jamie is our chief suspect?'

She shook her head. 'I'm only saying I saw Jamie there, but it was when everyone else was down there too. It could still be Danny as much as him.'

'And what do you think we should do about it? Haul them both in for a chat?'

'That's the last thing we should do. It will only alert the culprit to the fact they're under suspicion, even if we don't name it, and they're not likely to admit it, are they?'

He glanced at his watch and stood up, tugging his jacket off the back of the chair and slipping it on.

'So, we keep schtum and maintain a watching brief, as they say?'

'Something like that, yes — and avoid giving out too much information at the incident room briefing — especially the fact that we suspect Lilith didn't die of natural causes but was actually murdered.'

'Keep it all to ourselves, you mean? Just like you did with me?'

She ignored the barb. 'We need to make sure Coleman's mole is kept in the dark about what we've discovered, otherwise he'll be on the QT to his paymaster like a shot. That could put paid to any chance we might have of feeling Mr Havana's collar.'

'Catch you later,' was all he said, and then he was gone, striding across the general office towards the exit doors.

* * *

'How'd it go?' Hayden queried when she joined him in the canteen afterwards. 'I could see him giving you a hard time and couldn't bear to watch, so I came down here.'

''Course you did,' she said drily, looking at the sausage sandwich and slice of fruit cake on his plate. 'You must have been so stressed that you just had to eat something. I feel for you.'

He scowled. 'I *was* stressed actually and I still am. I just want us to grab some time together for that chat. You were all for it at the start and now the shoe is on the other foot, you seem to be avoiding any discussion.'

'When this is all over. I promise.'

She took a sip of her coffee. 'You heard about Lilith?'

'What about her?'

'Percival just confirmed it to me. The likelihood is that she was murdered. The pathologist thinks someone put a plastic bag over her head and asphyxiated her. She found marks round her neck apparently and a sliver of plastic, probably torn from a plastic bag, stuck between her teeth.'

He whistled. 'The plot thickens, as they say.'

'But we have to keep all this info to ourselves, so our mole doesn't get wind of it. I shouldn't really be confiding in you either.'

'Well, thanks a lot.'

'Nothing personal, but we need our killer to think he's got away with Lilith's killing. Then he might get careless and give himself away.'

He shrugged. 'And I'm going to spill the beans to him, am I? Nice to be trusted.'

'Don't be daft. If I thought that, I wouldn't have told you. Do you also know about Roscoe?'

'I know he's dead, if that's what you mean. People who've been lying face downwards in water for any length of time usually are.'

'I assumed you knew because you stayed down at the scene with Percival after I'd left.'

He shook his head. 'I was there until Doc Summers had finished examining the body, then left Percival and SOCO to do the bus and came back here with a plod mobile.'

'Well, apparently SOCO found a spare battery in Roscoe's pocket, but no mobile, so he must have dropped it somewhere. Also, they found a bottle of tablets they think might be amphetamines and a plastic bag containing what appears to be crack cocaine in his pockets.'

'Phew! You reckon he was using or pushing?'

'Hardly. Most likely he found the stuff at Witch-Fire House and grabbed it for evidence.'

'So, what's Percival going to do about it? We need to move fast if we're to catch Coleman with his knickers down.'

She shrugged, suddenly weary of the whole thing. 'That's the DI's call and, thankfully, I'm not privy to his decision-making processes.'

Hayden slapped his hand against his forehead. 'Oh, nearly forgot to tell you. You had a call while you were in with Percival.'

'A call? From whom?'

'The hospital,' he said. 'Apparently Jacob Truly died half an hour ago. They confirmed that there'll be a PM, probably tomorrow morning.'

She closed her eyes tightly. 'Four,' she breathed.

'Four what?'

'Four dead people, Hayd,' she snapped, angry that he hadn't passed on the information before. 'Eddie West, Ted Roscoe, Lilith and now Jacob Truly. Four bloody murders. There's rarely been so many in such a short time. They *must* all be linked somehow, it stands to reason.'

'I agree and everything certainly seems to point to Lilith as being the key figure in it all. She is the most likely suspect for Eddie West's murder. There's her antipathy towards him. The rag dolls with the pins in we saw at her shack, which were later left at the homes of both victims. The suspicion that hemlock poisoning was the cause of Eddie's death. The fact that one of the jars you saw in Lilith's shack was labelled "Hemlock." And now the death of Truly, whom Lilith hated just as much as Eddie, and who looks to have died from some sort of poisoning too.'

'Though Truly collapsed after Lilith had been murdered, don't forget.'

'I know, but you told me she was allegedly seen by Trimble in the area of the Manse after the burglary yesterday, and she could have put the poison in Truly's tea caddy then, which he drank in a cuppa just before he collapsed. There is every reason to believe she was responsible for the break-in, as well as all that earlier vandalism at the church. After all, who else could it have been?'

'Maybe, but I can't see an old woman like her being able to dig a skull out of a deep, three-hundred-year-old grave — and where would she have got the spade, even if that was possible?'

'Don't forget, she had her car at that time, she could have brought the spade with her. Maybe she had help too — Luke Cobb, for example. He could have dug it out for her without even working up a sweat.'

'I asked him about that when I interviewed him at the nick earlier, and he categorically denied it.'

'Well, he would, wouldn't he?'

She shook her head. 'I can't see him coming out with a barefaced lie. He's got a child's mentality, and I feel sure he would have felt bound to admit it if he had been responsible.'

'Okay, so, if not him, you're right, she would certainly have needed help from someone, but what I'm saying is that being old doesn't mean she couldn't have been ultimately responsible for the vandalism, desecration — call it what you like. And remember, we did see that damaged skull in her shack afterwards, which could have come from the grave, it looked old enough.'

She was still far from convinced. 'I don't know. There are certain aspects to the business that still bother me.'

He shook his head irritably. 'Well, just put them to one side for the moment, will you? We are detracting from the point I was trying to make. Whatever you say, Lilith *has* to be our main suspect for the murders of Eddie West and Jacob Truly. We can't get away from that fact. The pity is that we can no longer ask her about it — unless we find a medium to go through.'

Kate ignored this. 'But, if Lilith murdered both West and Truly, and our bent cop then murdered Lilith on the orders of Coleman, who the hell stiffed Ted Roscoe? Not Lilith herself or the same bent cop, surely?'

He shook his head. 'More likely one of Coleman's thugs because poor old Ted saw or heard too much.'

She sighed. 'So, three killers possibly, including Lilith. I suppose it's the most plausible explanation.'

'Can't think of any alternatives at this stage, but we'll never get even part way to the bottom of it all until we actually pull Coleman in.'

'You're remarkably enthusiastic for a change.'

He snorted again. 'I just want to get this business over and done with, so we can move on.'

'Move on, Hayd? Where to? A nice little public school in Berkshire?'

CHAPTER 23

It was after lunch and Kate was back at her desk when the entourage arrived. Percival looked subdued as he walked in, stopping briefly and holding one of the double doors open for the two men who were following him through.

The first was Toby Ricketts, the DCI, who only gave Kate and the other detectives a cursory glance as he followed Percival to his office. However, the second man paused by Kate's chair.

The mop of lopsided black hair was greying now, but the cold, hard face was the same and the dark eyes held the welcome of an undertaker. Immaculate in his expensive looking blue suit and perfectly polished black shoes, Detective Superintendent Raymond Ansell had changed very little since Kate had last clapped eyes on him. The same powerful aura emanated from him and enveloped her in an invisible cloud.

'Sergeant Lewis, I believe,' he said softly, treating her to an icy smile. 'It's been a while, hasn't it? Still a sergeant, I see.'

Kate climbed to her feet. 'Yes, sir,' she said as pleasantly as she was able. 'Quite a while. It was the Sandman case if I remember correctly.'

He nodded, the dark eyes seeming to penetrate her skull and read her thoughts.

'Ah yes, the Sandman. And I am led to believe we may have a similar criminal enterprise ongoing here on the Levels?'

'Yes, sir,' she said in a low voice, seeing from the corner of her eye the other members of the team trying to look as if they weren't listening in on the conversation.

He seemed to pick up on her unease and cast a glance of his own around the room. 'Ah,' he said, obviously cottoning on to her reticence. 'Why don't you join the three of us in the other office?'

The DI's glass-panelled "inner sanctum," as the team called it, was little more than a large cupboard. Percival was obliged to occupy the windowsill overlooking the police station's rear yard, while the DCI sat behind the DI's desk after Ansell had waved away the privilege. Kate found herself on a plastic chair on the other side of the desk, feeling a bit like a prisoner under interrogation.

Ansell closed the door, giving the team in the general office a cold "none of your business" stare through the glass partition, before perching on the corner of the desk.

'Well now,' he began, 'isn't this cosy?'

He stared directly at Kate, that familiar intimidating, humourless smile hovering on his thin lips. 'I've asked Sergeant Lewis here to join us, as I feel she has a perspective to offer regarding the rather complicated situation we find ourselves in. So, let us start by summarising what I have gleaned from Acting Detective Inspector Percival's excellent briefing. Correct me if I am wrong, but we appear to be dealing with three homicide investigations here—'

'Possibly four now, sir,' Kate cut in. 'I presume you were told about the suspected poisoning of the Rev Jacob Truly?'

Ansell nodded, so she carried on.

'Well, tragically, he has now died.'

Ansell grimaced, though it was difficult to determine whether this was due to the fact that he now had an additional potential homicide on his hands, or because of the interruption.

'Four then,' he said. 'And from what Mr Percival has told us, there is a possible link between them, but that is not conclusive?'

He raised an inquiring eyebrow which Kate took as her cue.

'It is possible,' she said, 'that Lilith — real name Sara Anne Cable — murdered both deceased after breaking into their houses and lacing the loose-leaf tea in the tea caddies with poison hemlock. I am currently awaiting a response from the lab on the samples that have been sent to them. But I don't believe she had anything to do with the death of our ex-colleague, Ted Roscoe. However, there does seem to have been some sort of connection between her and the activities of a target criminal who has taken up residence in an isolated property called Witch-Fire House on the Levels — someone Roscoe seems to have taken an interest in.'

'Ronnie Coleman?'

She nodded.

'And you believe this Coleman — whom I have heard a great deal about from Mr Percival — probably murdered Ted Roscoe after the latter uncovered evidence of a criminal enterprise he was running from Witch-Fire House?'

'Yes, and I think he ordered the execution of Lilith for the same reason.'

His dark eyes bored into hers. 'As, I'm told, you also believe he would by now have disposed of the mystery woman in the ICU if you had not conveniently run her over and put her in a coma, which is certainly a novel way of guaranteeing witness protection.'

Kate coloured up but said nothing, and he carried on speaking in a more sombre tone.

'It certainly seems that our Mr Coleman is someone who likes to clean up after himself, and I understand you support the late Mr Roscoe's allegation that our target villain has a mole inside this police station — in your own department, in fact — who actually carried out the murder of the Lilith woman on his behalf, which has appalling implications.'

'Yes, I am convinced of it, and I feel we need to move on Coleman as a matter of urgency before this same mole tips him off about our interest in his activities.'

Another cold smile. 'Very eloquently put, Sergeant, but you see, there is a problem here, in that there is a dearth of real evidence to substantiate what you are alleging, which would make it very difficult to obtain the necessary authority for a search warrant.'

Kate had expected this, and she reacted a lot more forcefully than she probably would have done had she thought about it.

'Sir, this man is a known, big-time London villain, operating in our manor under an alias. There is documented history between him and Ted Roscoe, which is obviously why Roscoe went after him in the first place. Furthermore, Roscoe rang me just before he disappeared, saying he'd seen "a face from the past" — plainly referring to Coleman. And Roscoe's body was actually found just a stone's throw from Witch-Fire House where Coleman is living. I think, all in all, that is substantial enough.'

'Do you, Sergeant?' Ansell purred. 'But where is the *evidence*?'

Kate stared at the DCI and then at Percival, but her silent plea for support met with no response.

'For goodness' sake,' Kate ejaculated, 'I've been to Witch-Fire House, I have met this so-called Silverman *and* one of his thugs. I have never been so sure of anything in my life before. And— and there is also the torching of Lilith's shack and the visit by Coleman's thugs to Luke Cobb's farm. I assume you do know about all of that, sir?'

Ansell nodded, then released a sigh. 'I commend your zeal, Sergeant, but I must repeat that we need evidence, circumstantial or otherwise, before we can apply for a warrant or at least be able to make a strong enough case to a judge for one. So far, all you have given me is opinion, conjecture, assumptions, suspicion and gut feelings. We have nothing positive, not only about Coleman's criminal activities, but also as to what we would be looking for in respect of a search.'

'You know very well that we must have a specific reason for searching premises,' the DCI added unhelpfully. 'We can't just go in on a fishing expedition.'

'It has to be drugs,' Kate said. 'Roscoe evidently had some amphetamine-like tablets and a plastic bag containing what looked like nuggets of crack cocaine in his pocket. I am sure these will prove to be class A or B drugs when they are analysed. He clearly took them from Witch-Fire House to provide us with just the sort of evidence we need.'

'Hypothetically, they could have been for his own use, or he could have been involved in supplying them,' the DCI said.

'Oh, come on, guv'nor . . .'

Ansell smiled patiently. 'The point we are making, Sergeant, is that, while we in this room are quite clear as to Coleman's culpability, there are insufficient grounds to justify the issue of a search warrant — not a single witness, no forensic material, nothing physical to connect him to Roscoe or the suspected drugs our ex-colleague had in his pocket. Again, we come back to the lack of evidence.'

'And by the time we get that *evidence*, sir,' she snapped in disgust, 'Coleman will have shut his operation down, got rid of any merchandise he has on the premises and disappeared back to the Smoke. Can't we at the very least, set up some surveillance on Witch-Fire House to monitor his movements and prevent everything turning to rat-shit?'

Ansell slowly eased himself off the corner of the desk and fixed her with a cold stare.

'That is not going to happen, Sergeant,' he said softly and without a trace of emotion. 'To set up round the clock surveillance would require a substantial manpower commitment for an indeterminate period. The force is already severely under strength, and I understand that in two days, racial discrimination protests are to be held in several major towns in Somerset, including Bristol, Taunton and

Bridgwater. As a result, a huge operation is being mounted, pulling in all available personnel throughout the force area as well as from adjacent forces on a mutual aid basis. On the strength of the intelligence we have on Coleman, the sort of open-ended, "pie in the sky" surveillance operation that you suggest cannot be justified, any more than the application for the search warrant. I'm afraid you will just have to swallow your frustration, accept the reality of the situation and hope that something we can actually act upon materialises.'

He half-turned on his way to the door. 'Incident room briefing at 1800 hours. Good afternoon, lady and gentlemen.'

Then he was gone, withdrawing like a departing cold North wind.

* * *

'It's done.' The voice at the end of the phone sounded very pleased with themselves.

Ronnie Coleman allowed the smoke from his cigar to drift lazily towards the ceiling.

'I hope you're using a burner?'

'Of course.'

'So, what is it that's done?' he asked quietly, knowing full well what his mole was referring to, but wanting him to confirm it.

'The witch bitch. She's done her last broomstick ride. I smothered her with a plastic bag, so they all think she died of a coronary. Couldn't be more perfect.'

'Good, then you should find the next job a lot easier.'

There was silence for a couple of seconds. 'Next job? What do you mean?'

Coleman smiled thinly and leaned back in his swivel chair, staring through the window, watching Bruno ushering Frank out of the barn and closing and locking the heavy door behind him. Excellent. They must have finished loading up the Transit. If Old Bill forced them to get out fast, the merchandise could be on the road and heading back to the

Smoke almost immediately. The little lock-up in Chiswick would accommodate them for a while until somewhere else could be found for the business, but at least the Law would have nothing on him.

'What's this other job?' the voice asked again, its self-satisfied tone gone. 'You never said anything about that before.'

Coleman drew on his cigar. 'Oh, didn't I? I must be getting forgetful in my old age. There's the unfortunate lady who's currently lying in the local ICU in a coma. I think it's about time we put her out of her misery.'

There was a sharp intake of breath. 'What? No way. I'm not doing anything like that again.'

'Oh, but you must. She could wake up any day and, like Lilith, she has seen much too much for the good of her health.'

'You can forget it, and that's final.'

'Oh, I don't think so. As I told Bruno only today, it's either her or your little wifey, and you wouldn't want Bruno paying a visit to Maureen, would you, especially as she already has so many problems?'

'Leave her out of this. She's not well.'

'All the more reason not to risk her relapsing.'

'But — but I can't do another hit. The ICU will have a security coded entry door and cameras too probably.'

'But you've shown yourself to be such a resourceful chap, so where's the problem? Pretend to be a doctor. Borrow a white coat or something. Use your imagination. Anyway, I'll leave it with you, okay?'

He put the phone down and sat watching the smoke from his cigar curling up towards the ceiling.

* * *

'Done up like a kipper,' Kate said mournfully as she walked with Hayden to the CID car in the yard. 'And Percival didn't even say a word.'

'Where are we going?' Hayden said.

'Did you hear what I said?'

'Every word, but I still want to know where we're going.'

He opened the door for her, and they climbed in.

'Just a quick trip out. Come on, what do you think about what I've just said?'

'What did you expect? They have to go by the rule book and, when you think about it, we *haven't* got anything positive on Coleman, just suspicion.'

'If this was China or Russia, they wouldn't bother,' she grated, starting the engine. 'They would just march in.'

He stared at her. 'I can't believe you just said that. We do have rules in this country, and it's a good job too.'

She shrugged. 'Yes, but I don't have to go by them, do I? They want evidence, then I'll bloody well get it for them.'

He looked horrified. 'Oh no, you're not going off at half-cock again. Don't you ever learn?'

'No, I'm not going off at half-cock.' She grinned. 'We both are. I'll tell you about it after we've been to the Manse.'

'The Manse? Why are we going there?

'I thought it was the least we could do after Jacob Truly's tragic death. I'm sure Deborah Truly will really appreciate some support right now. We'll just have time before the incident room briefing.'

'But she'll still be at the hospital.'

'I'll take a chance.'

He stared at her suspiciously. 'What are you up to?'

She smiled sweetly. 'Whatever do you mean? Just don't take the tea if it's offered.'

CHAPTER 24

He sat for a long time in the office, his head reeling. Stiff another one? He wasn't a hit man for frig's sake. This wasn't right and it wasn't fair. He had done what he'd been asked to. It should have ended there. But what was the alternative? He pictured Bruno and shivered. He'd seen enough of him to know he was an animal who loved inflicting pain. And Coleman never made idle threats. Mr bloody Havana would do what he had threatened, even though he knew full well that Maureen was disabled and in a wheelchair. No, like it or not, this second job had to be done, if only for her.

He looked at his watch. He could slip away when everyone was at the six o'clock incident room briefing, that was the best idea. He could always leave a note to say Maureen had been taken ill and he'd needed to leave early. That would give him enough time to get to the hospital, do the job, and be home again afterwards before his colleagues all trooped back out of the incident room and one of them decided to ring him to see how his wife was.

He'd been to the ICU as a visitor several times — twice in the course of his job a couple of years back and more recently when Maureen had been admitted after a tablet overdose, so he knew the layout, but how the hell he was going to get into the place he hadn't a clue. He would have to give it some thought. Careful thought.

* * *

There was a solitary light showing upstairs at the Manse, but otherwise the house was caught up in the misty mid-afternoon gloom, with leaves fluttering across the path to the front door and rooks cawing from the trees in the adjacent churchyard.

'Told you she'd be at the hospital,' Hayden muttered when there was no immediate response to Kate's knock, and she caught him studying the black Range Rover that was still parked in the driveway with the curious eye of a committed petrolhead.

Kate shrugged and turned back from the door. 'It doesn't matter anyway,' she said. 'It was just a sympathy visit to say how sorry I was to hear about the minister—'

At which point, she broke off as the door opened a crack, then widened.

Ralph Trimble stood there staring out at them curiously. 'She's still at the hospital,' he said. 'What do you want? I was having a kip.'

He was dressed in an open-necked striped shirt without a collar, and brown corduroy trousers, the braces hanging down over his thighs. He looked strained and half-asleep.

'We just called to give our condolences to Mrs Truly,' Kate said with a smile.

He seemed to perk up. 'Thanks, Sergeant. I'll tell her when she gets back from the hospital. She — she asked me to stay here in the house while she was away, see. Worried about things after Lilith broke in, I s'pose, and didn't want to come back to an empty place.' He gave a rueful grin. 'I fell asleep on the sofa, I'm afraid. Not much of a security guard, am I?'

Kate smiled again. 'No problem, Mr Trimble. So, you're still convinced it was Lilith who broke in then?'

He nodded. 'Positive. Who else could it have been? She certainly did for poor old Jacob Truly with that poison hemlock of hers, same as she did for your PC West. What kind of a wicked creature does things like that, eh? And he was such a decent God-fearing man too. Deborah — Mrs Truly — is in a terrible state.'

He scowled. 'Wouldn't surprise me if old Lilith hadn't also done for that ex-copper they found face-down in the rhyne.'

'Oh? Why do you say that?' Kate said.

'Well, he was found pretty darned close to her hovel, wasn't he? Maybe the old crone thought he'd had something to do with burning her place down. I reckon she was pretty lethal with that stick of hers. That's probably how it happened — you know, she crept up behind him in the dark and gave him a belt, knocking him into the rhyne. That's probably how he got that bang on the back of the head. Easy to drown in them ditches it is, 'specially if you're unconscious.'

Kate nodded politely, thinking it was much more likely that Ronnie Coleman and his thugs had been responsible for Roscoe's untimely end. But Trimble obviously had a bee in his bonnet about Lilith, so she didn't bother to discuss the issue any further, and she didn't tell him that Lilith was dead either.

Instead, she smiled and turned back towards the gate. 'Anyway, Mr Trimble, I didn't want to disturb you at this difficult time. Give Mrs Truly our condolences, won't you? Tell her that if we can be of any help, to please contact us at the station.'

Then abruptly she swung around again. 'Oh, just as a matter of interest, do you keep your tools for your work as sexton — you know, spade, fork and so forth — at the church?'

He shook his head, looking puzzled. 'No, I only live just down the road there, so I bring me own when I need them.'

'Oh, and just one more thing. When you spotted Lilith, after the Manse had been broken into, I think you said she was hurrying along the road. Can you remember which way she was going — towards or away from the village?'

He waved an arm. 'Away from here, towards the marsh. She was fairly moving for an old 'un too.'

'Did you see anyone else lurking about in the vicinity, someone who might have been with her?'

He shook his head. 'No, she was on her own.'

'She owned an old VW camper van at one time. You didn't see one of those parked nearby, did you?'

'No, and anyway, I believe that wagon was destroyed in the fire at her place.'

'Oh yes, I forgot, so it was. What about a bicycle?'

'Didn't see one of those neither, though I know she did have an old rusty thing.' He stared at her curiously. 'But why all these questions?'

Kate gave a short laugh. 'Nothing really. I just wanted to be sure it was Lilith you saw, that's all, and not someone else from the village.'

'Who else could it have been?'

'I don't know. Dark night, no street lamps. You could easily have made a mistake, couldn't you?'

He stiffened. 'It was definitely Lilith, Sergeant. One hundred per cent.'

She nodded. 'Great. Part of my job to ask questions.'

''Course. Anything else?'

'No, Mr Trimble, that's about it, thanks. Once again, give our deepest sympathy to Mrs Truly.'

'So, what was all that about?' Hayden said as they climbed back into the car. 'Do you still think the person he saw wasn't Lilith at all? Maybe it was the weird woman at the museum, dressed up to look like her?'

She glanced back at the house and switched on the ignition with a satisfied smile. 'I'm not sure,' she said thoughtfully, and, pulling out her pocketbook, scribbled some notes.

Hayden peered over her arm. 'What are you scribbling?'

She closed the notebook and returned it to her pocket. 'Just a few bits of info for future reference.'

He shrugged. 'Seemed to me that visit was a complete waste of time.'

'Is that what you think?' she replied mysteriously as they pulled away. 'Oh, I'm rather glad we came.'

Despite himself, his curiosity was aroused. 'Okay, what's going on in that head of yours?'

'Quite a lot actually. In the light of what Mr Trimble told us, I think I need to do a little research.'

'Research?'

'Yes, I think it's about time I checked the incident room press cuttings file to see what the newspapers are saying about this investigation. It could answer a lot of the questions that desperately need answering.'

He shook his head. 'I don't understand.'

'You will,' she assured him. 'Just be patient. Soon, all will be revealed.'

* * *

The incident room briefing was, as Kate had anticipated, a long tiresome affair, with Ansell and Percival answering the multitude of questions from the large gathering of uniformed and plainclothes officers sent from all over the force to contribute to the inquiry. Nothing was held back, except the allegation of the mole in the camp, and she looked for Jamie Foster and Danny Ferris, so as to see if she could spot any visible reaction when Coleman's name came up and it was also revealed — against Kate's pre-briefing advice — that Lilith's death was now a potential murder inquiry. But to her surprise, both were conspicuous by their absence.

Where the hell were they? It was a three-line whip for all personnel to be present for the initial briefing, not a matter of individual choice. Surely, it would have been imperative for Coleman's inside man to be there, in order to keep his paymaster in the loop as to what was going on. Alarm bells jangled in her head. Something was wrong. Had the mole discovered he had been sussed and bailed out already? She determined to find out at the earliest opportunity but was forced to sit there for the duration of the briefing and rein in her impatience.

A thin, forty-something woman in a neat, blue trouser suit arrived just after the briefing had started, striding confidently to the front to join Ansell and Percival. Her short, blonde hair gleamed in the strip lights and her keen blue eyes swept around the room, as if seeking to memorise all the faces.

Kate recognised her immediately. So, this was to be Ansell's number two, was it? DCI Deirdre Hennessey hadn't changed since Kate had last worked with her, and she acknowledged the wink the senior detective directed towards her with a returning smile. She was relieved to see that Hennessey appeared to have been appointed second in command, as she had always got on well with her, and, with a caustic, oddball like Ansell at the helm, this shrewd, no-nonsense ranker would provide the sort of balance the investigative team needed.

At the end of what was a real endurance test, not the least of it having to sit on a hard, plastic chair for something like an hour and a half, a smiling Hennessey came over to Kate and Hayden, putting paid to the quick exit Kate had hoped to make.

'It's a wee while since we last worked together, Kate, so it is,' she said, her Northern Ireland accent as strong as ever.

Kate nodded. 'It takes a murder to bring us all back together again, it seems, ma'am.'

'Aye,' Hennessey agreed, 'and I'm so sorry to hear about Ted Roscoe. Not the sort of end he should have come to. He and I never really saw eye to eye, but he was a decent enough fella with strong convictions, and I respected him for that, so I did.'

Kate responded with a tight, knowing smile. Hennessey was certainly right about the fractious working relationship that had existed between her and Roscoe. She had witnessed it first-hand. There had been several occasions when it had been daggers drawn between the two of them, so Hennessey's admission was something of an understatement.

The DCI seemed not to notice her reaction, but her expression abruptly changed to a frown. 'From what I gather, this particular inquiry looks like being a holy terror,' she went on, 'with four suspected homicides on the books.'

Kate nodded again. 'And the involvement of a resident London mobster on top of it all.'

Hennessey nodded. 'I hear from Mr Ansell that there's an added complication too.'

Kate glanced about her cautiously, watching the bulk of the other personnel filing out of the room on their way to the canteen.

'Can we talk somewhere else, ma'am?' she said.

Hennessey nodded. 'Of course. 'One of the interview rooms perhaps.'

Hayden made a tactful withdrawal and the DCI followed Kate downstairs.

The interview room was empty and, closing the door, Kate told her what she needed to know.

'And you think one of the two DCs you've named is the mole, which means they almost certainly killed this Lilith as well?' Hennessey said.

Kate shrugged. 'I can hardly believe it, knowing both officers as I do, but after Roscoe's allegation, it's difficult to see what other explanation there could be.'

'Maybe,' Hennessy acknowledged, 'But sometimes you have to unscramble your thoughts and look at things from a different perspective.'

'I don't understand.'

'I have been here all day nosing around, so I have, and I've already had a long hard look at the cells and the custody suite — that's why I was a wee bit late for the briefing. When I did my recce, it struck me just how difficult it would have been for someone to waltz down the stairs to the basement, get through the custody office and the cell gate door, open Lilith's cell, kill her and get out again without being spotted. So, I walked the walk meself, so to speak, and timed it. Then I spoke to the custody sergeant and the detention officer, both of whom I've had to suspend unfortunately.'

She paused. 'Know what I found out? The custody sergeant wasn't gone for just a couple of minutes, as he said originally. He was away at least five or six, leaving the cells completely unprotected while the detention officer was on her break. Know why he did that and told the initial fib that he was away for just a couple of minutes? Because the poor wee man was embarrassed, it seems. You see, he has haemorrhoids — piles — which are a cause of great distress and inconvenience to him. When he has to go, he has to go, and, without going into the gory details, setting himself right afterwards takes quite a bit of time and effort.'

Kate grunted. 'So, he was caught short,' she said, 'but how could anyone have known that would happen? And how did they get through the gate and into the cell? He would have had his keys with him, attached to his belt.'

Hennessey shook her head. 'He left the keys on his desk, it turns out, and my guess is that whoever stiffed Lilith just got lucky and found the custody suite empty at exactly the right moment, with the keys there waiting for them. From my calculations I would suggest our killer had about five or six minutes at his disposal before the detention officer returned, and he must have known Faith Wexford was in the canteen on her break when he made his move.'

'Even so, he would have been taking one hell of a risk. What if he'd been caught in the custody suite before he could get out? He would have had no justification for being there. It's off limits to virtually everyone in the nick without a specific reason.'

'Quite right, which is why I think he must have been equipped with a legitimate excuse for being there — some plausible story, which would have carried weight because of the nature of his duties.'

Kate nodded. 'Exactly, which supports my contention that the culprit must be one of the two DCs I have mentioned. The thing is, I actually saw Jamie Foster coming out of the cell area when I responded to the alarm call.'

'Aye, but, according to my initial inquiries, that would have been *after* everyone else had arrived and the detention officer and custody officer were already back in situ. When I spoke to Sergeant Manning, he maintained that on his return from the loo, the custody office was empty, and the cell gate was locked. It wasn't until Faith Wexford came back and opened up to check on the prisoner that her death was discovered. The killer was long gone by then.'

Kate was confused. 'But then, who . . . ?'

'Who indeed? Someone officially entitled to visit the custody suite in the normal course of events.'

'But Roscoe actually said it was one of my team.'

'One of your *team*?' Hennessey repeated slowly, with emphasis on the word 'team', and stood up, her gaze sharp and penetrating. 'Maybe you should widen your horizons, Kate. You see, in my book a team can incorporate a variety of different people, depending on the task it is required to perform at any given time. For example, it can mean a particular group of people working in a department on a specific job or alternatively, everyone in that department. Maybe you have fallen into the trap of tying yourself down by preconceived notions of who Roscoe was referring to, which has skewed your judgement? Think about it.'

Then she was gone, her high heels tapping away along the corridor outside in the direction of the stairs.

* * *

The hospital was quiet at this time of the day. All the clinics were shut, together with the outpatients department and most of the other technical units, such as X-ray and physiotherapy.

Avoiding the main car park because of the CCTV camera, he donned the white coat he had purloined from an empty SOCO office before leaving the nick. He slipped around the back of the main building carrying a clipboard with dummy folders attached to it, trying to look like a man on a mission. He was looking for the fire escape that connected all the upper floors. He remembered that when he had visited Maureen in the ICU, the nurses had wedged the fire-escape door beside the ward entrance open with a towel so that they could nip out onto the fire escape for a smoke. He only hoped the practice was still in vogue.

To his relief, he found it was and, after a hard tug, the door creaked open. The white-painted double doors to the ICU were clearly visible at the far end of the corridor and he marched towards them with a confidence he did not feel. He could see the keypad on the door well before he reached it and peered through the oblong windows above the small grey box, looking for movement beyond the tinted panes.

He had no idea what he was going to say if anyone appeared, but then he hit on another idea. Hearing the sharp tap of high heels on stone stairs, while his back was towards the corridor he stretched his arm out, leaning against the wall by the doors with one hand while holding his mobile phone to his ear with the other, as if he were holding a conversation. The tap of heels grew louder as the approaching woman turned into the corridor towards him from the stairs and out of the corner of his eye, he saw that it was a nurse, carrying a bundle of files.

'Excuse me,' a breezy voice said a second or two later and, uttering a quick, 'Hold on a minute, Michael,' he stepped back with a mouthed 'sorry,' to let the nurse pass. Smiling at him, she tapped in the security number, the door buzzed and she went through.

What a little darling. She'd certainly done him a massive favour, her polished nails — he thought nurses weren't supposed to have polished nails — had tapped out the access code right in front of his gaze. He thanked his lucky stars that he had good eyesight.

The corridor was now deserted. He tapped in the same number, heard the buzz, hauled the door open and let it close gently behind him.

Another corridor lay beyond, with rooms opening off it. There was no one else in sight. He moved along slowly, checking each room in turn. They all appeared to be empty. Surely the casualty hadn't woken up and been moved somewhere else? Coleman wouldn't be at all happy about that.

He heard the faint sound of laughter, followed by a soft thud coming from the end of the corridor. Must be the nurses' station. Then silence — like the grave, he mused. He shivered. Two more rooms and he was getting perilously close to where he thought the nurses' station was situated. Then he saw her. She was in a bed in a room on his left, wired up with drips, monitors and an oxygen mask, her blonde hair spread out on her pillow, soft and silky. He felt sudden regret and hesitated at the door. She was very pretty and so young. His late daughter, Miranda, had been young and pretty when she had been killed in the car crash that had also crippled Maureen. He couldn't do this. He'd killed the witch, but she had been different — old, ugly and smelly. This girl was quite the reverse. Then Coleman's voice echoed in his brain. 'You wouldn't want Bruno paying a visit to Maureen, would you?'

Taking a deep breath, he stepped into the room and stopped by the bed. Which tubes or wires should he pull out? Maybe it would be better to shut off the machine by the bed.

He was still trying to make up his mind when the young woman in the bed opened her eyes and stared up at him.

CHAPTER 25

The first thing Kate noticed was that the CID general office was empty. Her face set into a hard mask, she picked up the telephone on her desk and rang the Control Room.

'DS Lewis,' she snapped. 'Location of DCs Foster and Ferris?'

There was a pause and then the operator said, 'Foster is out at Bason Bridge on a witness inquiry, skipper.'

'What witness?'

'Dunno. Some crime inquiry he's been dealing with, I understand.'

'And Ferris?'

'Wife ill apparently. Had to rush home.'

Wife ill? That was convenient. So, had he gone home or was he at that moment blabbing everything to Coleman? Maybe she had been wrong about Jamie Foster. Maybe the culprit was Ferris. He was a big powerful man. Lilith wouldn't have stood a chance against him, whereas Foster had Ansell's whippet build. She put the phone down and perched on the corner of her desk, chewing her lip. 'There's a guy on your team who's on the take.' Roscoe's voice growled at her. 'Look at things from a different perspective,' Hennessey's voice chimed in. 'Unscramble your thoughts.'

Unscramble them to what end? The only members of the team who could be in the frame were Foster and Ferris. Then she remembered Hayden saying he had returned from the Roscoe murder scene before SOCO had completed their job. Had Percival come back then too? That would mean he could have been in the nick a lot earlier — early enough perhaps to have stiffed Lilith and innocently returned to his office a decent interval afterwards. Had she been daft confiding in him after all? He knew everything now, including the information about the mole. He could already have phoned Coleman and given him the full SP.

She closed her eyes and squeezed the bridge of her nose between her finger and thumb. Bloody Nora, she mused. Talk about a conundrum. So, where did she go from here?

And then she got the answer. Opening her eyes and gazing absent-mindedly around the room, the glint of something flickering beside the adjacent desk caught her eye. It turned out to be a shiny piece of plastic protruding above the rim of a wastepaper bin that had been brought to life by a draught from an open window. At first, she took no notice of it, her mind returning instead to wrestle with her dilemma over the likely identity of Coleman's mole. But for some reason her gaze kept being drawn back to the bin as if it were trying to tell her something. Finally, with a snort of exasperation, she eased herself off the corner of the desk and crossed over to it. What was it about that scrap of plastic that refused to leave her alone? Maybe it was the beginnings of OCD and the compulsion to tidy things up?

The bin was overflowing with pieces of torn and screwed-up paper — handwritten messages, dumped printouts and several newspapers — and the piece of plastic turned out to be a bag of some sort, which at first sight she assumed to have previously held a colleague's sandwiches. She was on the point of pushing it down further into the bin, out of sight, when she recognised it for what it was — the distinctive type of bag used by SOCO for evidence found at crime scenes. Peering more closely at it, she was just able to make out a stationery order number on the edge.

With alarm bells jangling in her head, she bent down and very carefully used a biro to prise the bag free of the rest of the detritus. It was as she opened it out on the desktop with the aid of two biros that she saw the small, ragged hole in the bag.

Now it was Percival's voice she could hear in her brain: 'a thin piece of transparent plastic . . . stuck between Lilith's teeth.'

Her head swam. It was most likely just a discarded evidence bag from an old crime case that had been filed, but what was it doing here, in a bin in the CID office instead of in SOCO? And even if it had been used for another purpose, like someone's packed lunch, which was highly unlikely, the small, yellowish deposit on the inside to which two long straggly grey hairs had stubbornly adhered appeared recent and didn't look at all like sandwich piccalilli.

For a few moments she simply stared at the bag in disbelief as it dawned on her what she must have inadvertently stumbled upon. 'A ruthless killer you may be,' she breathed, 'but a master of artifice you certainly are not!'

'Talking to yourself then?' Hayden commented as he strode into the office. 'Whatever have you got there? Looks disgusting.'

'That's because it is,' she said. 'And if you sit down quietly for a moment, I'll tell you all about it.'

But she never got the chance, for at that precise moment the station Tannoy blasted its dramatic message, 'Any unit to attend general hospital? Intruder disturbed in ICU.'

The message was repeated, as it was on the police radio in the harness attached to Kate's belt, but she didn't need to hear it again, for she was already racing for the stairs, with Hayden puffing along indignantly in her wake.

* * *

He'd expected the girl in the bed to try and scream when she saw him bending over her, but she was obviously still not fully conscious and she just stared up at him, a bewildered look on the face behind the mask as she struggled feebly to pull it off. His shock at her sudden awakening had thrown him, however, and for a few seconds he just froze where he stood.

He didn't hear the nurse approaching on her rubber-soled, white shoes and her sharp voice shook him out of his daze and made him swing around.

'Who are you and what are you doing in here?'

He snapped out of his temporary lethargy then all right and, completely losing his nerve, lurched for the door in a panic.

She tried to stop him, but she was only a little thing and he shouldered her out of the way without difficulty. Then he was running for the exit, his white coat flapping.

He heard the security alarm go off even before he reached the fire escape and, glancing back up the metal staircase as he got to the bottom, he saw the knot of figures staring down at him from the top, gesticulating wildly.

He got to his car without being challenged and was streaking away down the service road even as the first flashing blue light appeared in the dusk, undoubtedly some way off, but almost certainly heading for the hospital.

His plan was to head home, construct some sort of story about Maureen's condition and wait to see if the nurse's description of him was accurate enough to result in a visit from his colleagues. As he began to slowly calm down and think a little more rationally, he was imbued with more confidence. There had to be dozens of people who fitted his general description, so why would his colleagues necessarily home in on him? He was actually *in* the police, for heaven's sake and no one had a clue about his involvement with Ronnie Coleman, so why would they suspect him? Suddenly he took a deep breath and grinned. You're in the clear, old son, he told himself, just carry on as normal.

Maureen was pleased and surprised to see him come home so early, and she had unwittingly done the best thing she could have done by falling out of bed after her nurse had left and ending up on the floor. Good old Maureen, she had provided him with a perfect reason to be at home. Not actually an alibi, but the next best thing since, being more than a little vague with Alzheimer's, she wouldn't know exactly what time he'd arrived home in the first place, or if she had called him. Someone above certainly seemed to be looking after him, though after everything he had done, it was more likely to be an entity with a forked tail and horns than a halo.

* * *

'She's still not fully recovered,' the sister said to Percival, who had arrived at the hospital just seconds before Kate and Hayden. 'We cannot allow you to see her until the doctor is satisfied that she is well enough to be interviewed. There is a danger she could relapse.'

Standing beside the DI in the corridor of the ICU, Kate glanced through a gap in the partially closed door opposite and glimpsed the doctor bending over the blonde woman in the bed.

'Was she hurt in any way?' Percival asked.

The sister shook her head. 'Not as far as we can ascertain at present. The man was discovered bending over her, with one hand on the apparatus beside her bed. But he was challenged before he could do anything, if, of course, that was his intention.'

'I very much fear it was,' Percival said. 'And if you agree, we would like to have a police officer stationed outside the room from now on as a precaution.'

The sister didn't look too happy about it and, knowing how opposed most hospitals were to having police officers on duty in their critical units, he expected a firm refusal. But, after a brief hesitation, she nodded. 'I'm sure the hospital administrator won't object, given the special circumstances.'

'Can we also speak to the nurse who disturbed the intruder?' Kate asked.

'Certainly. Nurse Bates. She's sitting in the rest room — a bit shaken, I might add.'

Kate recognised the name of the nurse from PC Layton's report on the incident at the ICU involving Lilith, and she smiled at her as she sat beside her on a battered settee.

'Caroline isn't it?' she asked as Percival hovered impatiently in the background, and Hayden chose that moment to disappear in the direction of the toilet. 'Caroline Bates? I believe you suffered a similar shock a couple of days ago involving a rather unpleasant old lady?'

The nurse smiled. 'You have a good memory.'

'I just hope *you* have, Caroline. Can you tell us what this man looked like and how he got in here?'

Bates nodded a little uncertainly. 'I'll try. I first saw him when I came back from my break. He was dressed in a white coat like the doctors wear, and was standing by the doors to the ICU, apparently speaking to someone on his mobile. He must have seen the numbers I punched into the security keypad, then used them after I'd gone inside.'

She paused, her brows puckered in thought. 'I only saw him briefly and he was turned away from me for the most part, so I only got a partial glimpse of him.'

'But you must have got a much better look at him when you disturbed him in the ICU?'

She made a face. 'Yes, but I'm afraid that in the shock of the moment, I was more concerned about the welfare of my patient and myself than anything else, and I didn't pay much attention to what he looked like. All I can recollect is that he was a white man in his fifties, I would say, tall and thin and, I think, clean-shaven.'

'Hair colour?'

'I really couldn't say.'

'Anything distinctive about him?'

She shook her head. 'Sorry, I really can't remember.'

Kate sighed. 'Would you know him again?'

'I'm not sure.'

'Do you know how he got into the building?'

'He must have made use of an insecure fire door at the end of the corridor because when he ran away, he used the fire escape and me and my other colleagues saw him run across the grassed area at the bottom.'

'Did you see him drive off?'

She shook her head again. 'Sorry. He must have had his car parked around the corner. But I did hear a car race away shortly after he disappeared. Do you think you'll catch him?'

Kate glanced at Hayden who was lounging against the wall. 'We'll do our best,' she said without much conviction. 'We'll do our best.'

* * *

'It's our mole, trying for a second hit,' Kate said to Percival when they were out of anyone's earshot and walking back to their cars. 'Absolutely no doubt about it.'

Percival came to a stop in the service road. 'Not much of a description to go on, though, is there?' he commented. 'What the nurse gave us could probably fit half the men living in this area and on her own admission, she doesn't know whether she would recognise him again.'

Kate's eyes gleamed. 'True, but I think I might just have sussed who he is.'

'What? You're joking!'

'Far from it,' she replied and told him about the torn plastic bag she had found in the office wastepaper bin.

His eyes lit up. 'Where's this bag now?'

'Locked in my drawer,' she said. 'When the shout went up, I didn't have time to do anything with it. I'll get it to SOCO and then forensics as soon as we get back. Hopefully, they'll be able to turn things around quickly for us.'

Suddenly he looked doubtful. 'I don't know. Let's be honest, I can't see a man with police experience dumping evidence like that in his own wastepaper bin. More than likely, that bag has nothing to do with Lilith's death.'

'Fair comment,' she said. 'But remember, at the time he probably thought he had got away with murdering her and that everyone would assume she had died from natural causes, so why not get rid of it in his bin? Why would anyone want to go through the thing in the first place? And don't forget, he has no reason to believe he is under suspicion for passing information to Coleman and, since he wasn't at the incident room briefing, he may not even be aware that Lilith's death, like Roscoe's, is now being treated as murder.'

He grunted. 'Nevertheless, dumping the evidence in his own wastepaper bin wouldn't have been a very bright thing for an experienced copper to do, would it?'

'With hindsight, you're probably right. But maybe he wanted to get rid of it PDQ and was short on time,' she suggested, 'possibly because he needed to get to the hospital to stiff the woman in the ICU while we were all still tied up at the briefing. Anyone can make a mistake, no matter how sharp they think they are. And certainly, if the bag *is* the murder instrument, it could be the biggest mistake this character has ever made.'

'So, what do you suggest we do now?'

'Well, there's no point in nicking him on sus. We would only get one crack at a cough and if he kept shtum and our nurse was unable to pick him out in an ID parade, we'd be snookered. Coupled with which, we would almost certainly lose our chance with Coleman, who would just disappear.'

He nodded. 'Then our only hope is that your bag turns up trumps.'

'Or that our Jane Doe in the ICU is able to give us something on Coleman when we are eventually allowed to interview her,' she added.

'The waiting game continues then,' he said bitterly, 'and while it does, we're going to have to let a suspected killer, who has also been feeding operational police information to a London mobster, carry on working with us as if nothing has happened.'

'It's all part of life's rich tapestry,' she said drily. 'Be honest, you'd be lost without the buzz it gives you.'

CHAPTER 26

Hayden was back in the doldrums by the time he and Kate got home at well after ten, and she guessed what was dragging him down. She had seen the signs reasserting themselves the moment he'd strolled off to the toilet while she was interviewing Nurse Bates in the ICU, and he had shown little interest in her revelation about the plastic bag she had discovered, and her inevitable conclusion as to the identity of the mole.

It was always the same with Hayden. He was either full of the joys of spring or morose and uncommunicative — the latter mood usually because he hadn't been able to get his own way over something.

'What's the problem, hon?' she asked brightly as she tipped his share of the cod and chips they had purchased on the way home onto the plate in front of him.

'You know very well what it is,' he said, ramming his plastic fork into the batter-coated fish as if he wanted to murder it. 'We still haven't resolved the issue of my potential new career.'

She nodded. 'I realise that, but in case it has escaped your notice, I've had rather a lot on my mind lately.'

'It's always the same,' he complained. 'Job first, our life when it can be fitted in. It's exactly why I want out of it.'

She pushed her fish and chips away from her, suddenly no longer hungry.

'Okay, Hayd,' she said, settling back on the settee, 'you want to talk, let's talk, though I'm not sure there is really much left to talk about.'

He frowned. 'What do you mean by that?'

'Just this,' she said, leaning forward again. 'You want out of the force, I don't. You want to move to Berkshire for that teaching job, I don't. I think I've made my views clear already. So, it's your decision now. Berkshire or me. Make your choice and let me know what you decide, eh?'

She climbed to her feet and carried her plate out into the kitchen, dumping her half-eaten meal in the waste bin. Then she headed straight for the stairs, emerging from their bedroom minutes later, dressed in a heavy sweater, knee-high boots and a woollen hat.

He looked up as she lifted her black leather coat off the back of the settee. 'Where the devil are you going at this time of night?'

She crossed to the table and picked up a heavy-duty torch. 'Out.'

He jumped to his feet, spilling chips all over the floor, as it dawned on him what she was up to. 'You're not doing that maverick thing at Witch-Fire House, are you? I won't hear of it.'

She shrugged. 'I had thought we'd do it together. If you remember, I suggested as much earlier. But since you'd rather be a teacher, I'll do it on my own.'

'But — but they'll kill you if they catch you in there. Look what happened to Roscoe.'

'I have to find the evidence we need, Hayden,' she snapped, 'or Roscoe will have thrown his life away for nothing. If Ansell and the others want to play safe and sit on their bloody hands, that's up to them. I'm not prepared to.' She turned for the door. 'See you later.'

For a moment he just stood there, gaping. She was out of the door before he sprang to life. 'Wait! he shouted, grabbing his own coat, 'You can't go alone. I'm coming with you.'

Her face reappeared in the doorway, wearing a wry smile. 'Don't you think you should put your shoes back on first?' she said.

* * *

Mist, rolling across the marshland like advancing smoke, cold, clingy tendrils populated by grotesque evanescent shapes which appeared then disappeared at the whim of the vast, creeping tide. The car's wipers scraped the windscreen like a metronome and its headlamps burrowed into the gloom, half-blind like moles searching for the end of a tunnel. The road seemed to change direction as if it were moving, trying to shake the vehicle off its back and into one of the rhynes on either side.

Hayden had hardly spoken since they had left home, sitting bolt upright in the front passenger seat like a shop mannequin, remote and withdrawn. He had the collar of his coat turned up and a cloth cap pulled down low over his tangled mop of blond hair.

Smiling to herself, Kate cast the occasional sidelong glance at his sullen face. His anger and resentment seethed like a dragon's breath in the space between them, yet she found reassurance in the presence of that big, ponderous shape at her side. A naturally mild-mannered man with an intense aversion to violence, Hayden was nevertheless powerfully built, and she knew from past experience that he was a formidable opponent if the situation warranted it. She had no illusions as to the risks involved in this particular venture. She just hoped that she hadn't bitten off more than she — both of them — could chew.

'I think we're here,' she said, her voice sounding too loud. Out of the mist arose the main entrance to Witch-Fire House and, driving slowly past, she swung the wheel and turned into the lane running along the back of the property.

Seconds later she spotted the gateway and brought the car to a halt in front of it. The gate had been pushed right back and, had it been daylight, she would have thought twice about parking there for fear of obstructing the entrance. But in the middle of the night, it was highly unlikely a farmer would be looking to use the field, so she took a chance.

Hayden stared across at her. 'Now what? I don't know what you hope to see in this white-out.'

'At least it'll mean they won't see me coming,' she said, 'and anyway, they're unlikely to be expecting company on a night like this.' She switched off the engine.

'You stay here,' she said, releasing her seatbelt. 'The rear entrance is a few hundred yards further along the lane. Be ready if I come running.'

He released his own seatbelt. 'No way. You're not going in there on your own.'

She reached out and placed a restraining hand on his arm. 'Don't, Hayd. I need you to be waiting for me here, just in case something goes wrong. There's no sense in both of us recceing the place.'

He slumped back in his seat. 'Thirty minutes. That's all I'm giving you. If you're not back by then, I'm belling the nick for the heavy mob.'

'Agreed, but I *will* be back as soon as I've found what I'm looking for.'

She opened the door, and the mist enveloped her in its cold embrace. She shivered and was about to move off when she stopped dead, turning suddenly to knock on the window. 'Quick, Hayd! Look at this,' she called hoarsely, pointing into the field beyond the open gateway. Then she promptly disappeared behind the hedge.

Frowning, he climbed out.

The car had been driven into the field and parked close behind the hedge. With her hand cupping the beam of her torch, Kate played it over the vehicle. Only parts of it were visible in the feeble light, but they both recognised it immediately.

'Roscoe's old Honda Civic,' Kate said in a low voice, switching the torch off. 'I'd know it anywhere.'

Hayden took the torch from her and, bending down, directed the beam at each of the wheels in turn. 'All four tyres flat. Someone made sure the car didn't hit the road again.'

Kate whistled through her teeth. 'He must have parked it here out of sight while he went to check the house.'

He grunted. 'Surprised our search teams never came across it, though. 'I know it's hidden from view, but even so . . .'

She shrugged. 'They probably stopped looking when they discovered his body.'

'Well, Coleman's thugs obviously found it.'

She stared at him fixedly. 'And found Roscoe, it would seem.'

He was silent for a moment, then nodded soberly. 'Which means we can forget this madcap plan of yours. The evidence we were looking for is right in front of us. It proves that Roscoe was definitely here, just a stone's throw from Witch-Fire House. It gives Ansell grounds for paying Coleman a visit.'

She shook her head. 'I hate to agree with Ansell, Hayd, but it's still not enough. There's nothing to connect Coleman to the vehicle. If a team were to be sent in, it could only be for a routine inquiry, which would get us nowhere. There still wouldn't be sufficient grounds to search the place or to nick Coleman on sus. All this does is confirm our suspicions, nothing more. I still have to get the goods.'

'Well, I think it's madness,' he snapped.

But she had already made her way back through the gateway and disappeared into the mist.

'Thirty minutes, Hayd,' her voice floated back. 'See you then.'

* * *

In his silk kimono, its sleeves like wings, Ronnie Coleman hovered above the naked young woman like a predatory hawk. He stroked her bare thigh.

'How old are you, Linda?' he asked quietly.

She looked up at him from the bed, smiling seductively, arched her body towards him and said, 'Old enough, Ronnie.'

His eyes narrowed and, drawing on his cigar, he bent over and pressed the glowing tip to her navel.

Her agonised scream rang through the house, and he smiled at the loud knock on the door. 'You okay, boss?' called someone in a rough voice.

'Fine, Frank,' he drawled, his cold eyes on the weeping, writhing young woman. 'Linda likes to make a fuss.'

Lifting a jug of water from the bedside cabinet, Coleman poured it over the hands clutching at her belly.

'You really must learn to be more respectful, my dear,' he said. 'You know I like a straight answer to a straight question.'

In response, she jumped off the bed and, still sobbing, ran across the room to the bedroom door, and he heard her bare feet smacking the floorboards on her way to the toilet.

He had found Linda in one of his strip joints, doing a nice erotic version of the Salome dance, complete with extras. It had turned him on like nothing else. He'd dumped Irena, his previous acquisition — or at least Bruno had — in the Thames, after learning of her covert "business" liaison with an undercover Met copper. 'Very disloyal,' he'd told Bruno. 'And after everything I've given her.' He had hoped Linda would make a good replacement, but he was beginning to have his doubts. She was young — maybe only twenty — and a blonde beauty who was very inventive where sex was concerned. She had, however, what he called "limited horizons," and he couldn't see her lasting much longer. He now regretted bringing her to Somerset and thought he might have to leave her behind when he left — possibly in a bog somewhere.

His phone rang just as she returned, a large sticking plaster over her navel and clearly still in pain. Glancing at the caller display, he gave her a curt nod. 'Get out.'

'What is it?' he snapped at the caller, as she flounced out of the room. 'Do you know what time it is?'

'S . . . sorry, Ronnie,' a small, nervous voice came back, 'but I needed to tell you I couldn't complete the job.'

Coleman stiffened. 'What do you mean "couldn't complete" it?'

'I got in okay, but — but the bitch bloody woke up, didn't she? Then I was rumbled by this nurse. I only got away by the skin of my teeth.'

Coleman stubbed out his cigar on one of the posts of the four-poster bed and slipped it into his top pocket.

'You're telling me she's conscious? Able to talk?' he said softly.

'I couldn't help it. One minute she was just lying there and the next she opened her eyes and stared up at me. It was really creepy. But I thought I'd better warn you in case my colleagues get to interview her and she spills the beans.'

Eyes half-closed, Coleman tapped the phone against his teeth. 'Then you'd better make sure she doesn't, hadn't you? You'll just have to try again.

'I — I can't. I hear they've put a police guard on her. I won't be able to get near her.'

Coleman released a heavy sigh. 'So, that's it then. Time to clear out.' Then he added in a voice filled with menace, 'Just remember, Bruno takes two sugars in his coffee.'

Abruptly ending the call, he shouted for Frank.

'Yes, boss?'

'Get ready to roll. We're moving the stuff out — like now.'

CHAPTER 27

The mist seemed to get heavier as Kate felt her way along the hedgerow, as if it was trying to hold her back, and twice she almost collided with tree branches overhanging the path.

The back entrance to the house appeared suddenly beside her, the chain across it glistening in the damp air. She thought she saw something else too, a bent shape, like that of a woman dressed in a long coat and shawl, leaning on a walking stick, which materialised maybe three or four yards in front of her. For several seconds she simply stood there, as if frozen to the spot, the beam of the torch shaking fitfully in her hand. Then, with equal suddenness, the shape seemed to disintegrate and fade back into the swirling clouds of white.

'Fool!' she breathed to herself. 'Lilith's dead — gone. It's your imagination playing tricks on you.' Nevertheless, it was several minutes before she was able to pluck up the courage to climb over the chain and head along the barely discernible track towards the house. As she did so, imagination or not, she couldn't help feeling that someone — something? — was close behind her, and she repeatedly glanced behind her as she crept through the gloom, her smarting eyes searching for that same bent figure. But there was nothing, only the swirling clouds of vapour.

She knew she was heading into danger, yet she couldn't help feeling relieved when the house emerged slowly from the mist. She paused by the trees at the entrance, as, unbeknown to her, Roscoe had done before.

Nothing moved. The only sound was the steady "drip, drip, drip" of moisture from the branches above. She stepped out onto the concrete hardstanding. To her right, the house showed only a single light in a downstairs window — a fuzzy stain in the fog. She saw the barn at the same time and approached it cautiously. The double doors at the front were ajar, with a padlock hanging loosely on the projecting hasp, and a bar of light showing in the opening. She took a chance and peered through the gap, her heart racing.

A big, long wheel-base Ford Transit van was parked nose in at the far end. The vehicle was painted white, with the words "Silverlink Medicinal Products" in green lettering across both back doors above a logo depicting a staff entwined with a snake. Otherwise, the barn appeared to be empty.

Very carefully she pulled one of the barn doors a little further open, slipped through, and pulled it to behind her. The fact that the door had been left unlocked and the strip lights inside were still on gave her an uneasy feeling. It suggested someone had been in there just before her arrival and planned to return. She wouldn't have much time.

She snapped a quick photograph of the Transit with her mobile phone, including the all-important registration number, then went across to the vehicle, wondering if she would be lucky enough to find that whoever had left the barn unlocked had also failed to lock the rear doors of the van. She tried the handle and felt it give. Bingo! She was in business. Gritting her teeth in case the mechanism made a noise, she turned the handle fully and one of the doors opened without a sound on well-oiled hinges. The van was stacked to roof height with cardboard boxes, leaving only a small space between them and the rear doors. She put one foot on the step, ducked her head and climbed up inside.

The boxes all seemed to bear colour-coded markings but no other indication of the contents. With her torch jammed between her neck and shoulder, she felt for her clasp knife and slit one of them open. Inside, plastic bags of white powder. Kate's mouth went dry. She had been right all along. Roscoe had stumbled upon a store of illegal narcotics, masquerading as medical supplies under the banner of Medicinal Products, and it looked as though Coleman was just about to move the lot out.

She reached for her mobile to call Hayden, but then froze as she heard the barn doors being opened on creaking hinges, then the bang as they came to a stop against the walls of the building.

'I'll drive,' a rough voice said. 'Better check the back of the motor.'

Kate felt her insides tighten. If they opened the doors, they wouldn't fail to see her. There was hardly anywhere to stand, let alone hide.

She heard a loud cough and a hand began to pull one door open. She closed her eyes and waited for the yell.

'Just lock the bleedin' thing, will you, Jimmy? We got to get to the Smoke before it's light.'

The door banged shut and Kate heard it lock. Seconds later the two front doors slammed, the Transit's engine started up and she felt the vehicle begin to reverse out of the barn.

She was trapped inside, heading heaven alone knew where.

* * *

Hayden watched twin fuzzy headlights plough through the mist. A vehicle, driving across one of the fields that lay between him and the back of Witch-Fire House. The vehicle was apparently heading towards the lane, and he had to crouch down in his seat when the white Transit rumbled slowly past.

He glanced at his watch. Kate had been gone thirty-five minutes. She should have been back by now. He picked up his mobile from the seat beside him, but hesitated. She had said to give her half an hour and it was only just over that time. Maybe he should wait a bit longer?

He wondered where the Transit had been going at this time of the night. Could it be, as Kate had feared, that Coleman was clearing out, getting rid of the evidence just in case the police decided to make a move on him? Though if that was the case, why hadn't Kate called to tell him to contact the nick? He didn't like it. What if she couldn't ring because she'd been rumbled?

He looked at his watch again. It was now forty minutes since she had left him. 'Come on, Kate', he muttered. 'What the devil are you playing at?' Should he ring her? But no, that would be plain stupid. If she was hunkered down somewhere, hiding from Coleman and his thugs, the last thing she would want was for her mobile to ring and give her position away, and he couldn't be sure she had the thing on mute.

Forty-five minutes. He took a deep breath and picked up the phone again. This was ridiculous. There was no way he could wait any longer. He had to get help, even if that meant blowing the whole thing. He was actually about to dial the number when his mobile alerted him that he had a message. At this time of night? Probably one of those darned online sales promotions from a supermarket or internet company. He was about to ignore it and make his call instead when a warning voice in his brain made him open his message log.

The text message was from Kate and it was brief:

'*Goods in white Transit just leaving.*'

There was an attachment to the message and, opening it up, he found himself staring at a photograph of a white Ford Transit, bearing the name "Silverlink Medicinal Products" in green writing on the back. With a start, he realised it had to be the same vehicle that had passed him minutes before. He began stabbing frantically at the keypad of his phone.

* * *

Ronnie Coleman felt a lot happier now that his illicit merchandise was safely on its way to London. If Old Bill *did* decide to put in an appearance, he was clean, and there was no way they could connect him with it. Yet he was still strangely uneasy.

Watching from his study window as the Transit drove off, he had caught sight of those weird bloody lights again. He'd seen them several times since moving into Witch-Fire House, but this time they had seemed a lot closer than before.

The locals apparently called them the hinkypunks, believing them to be some kind of malevolent fairies or whatever, and he had laughingly dismissed it as superstitious rubbish, like the nonsense he had heard about Witch-Fire House being haunted. Ronnie Coleman prided himself on being an intelligent, educated man and he had researched the phenomenon on the internet. The bluish lights that seemed to dance across the marshes like tiny elfin fires were nothing more than the sudden combustion of gas from decaying vegetation, which often occurred in boggy, peaty countryside like the Levels. Yet for some reason the lights continued to bother him, as if, despite his outward contempt for local superstition, he nursed a secret fear of the peculiar will-o'-the-wisps.

Now, as he stared through the mist at the lights, he caught sight of something close to the open barn doors. It resembled the bent figure of an old woman, dressed in a long, black coat and some sort of shawl. But when he looked again, the figure had vanished. At first, he dismissed it as nothing more than a trick of the mist. But that was before he heard the noises — slow footfalls upstairs in the empty rooms he had never bothered to occupy, accompanied by the 'tap, tap, tap' of a walking stick.

'Bruno!' he called.

'Yeah, boss?' the other replied, stepping into the room.

'Check out the upper floor,' he snapped. 'I keep hearing bloody noises up there.'

Bruno frowned. 'Noises, boss?'

'Like someone walking.'

'Walking?'

'You a sodding parrot or something? Just check it out, you savvy?'

'Right away, boss.'

Coleman heard Bruno's heavy footsteps lumbering across the floorboards above his head, and then he was back in the room. 'No one up there, boss. Creepy place though. Smells like a bleedin' grave.'

'Yeah, okay, I don't need a bloody description. Just go out and shut the barn doors.'

'On my way, boss.'

But Bruno had only just left when, turning back to the window, Coleman saw that the bluish lights flickering in the gloom beyond the house seemed not only to have multiplied, but increased in intensity, and the next moment the police cars were sweeping in through the back entrance, flooding the room with their flashing strobes.

CHAPTER 28

Ronnie Coleman, the very picture of "Mr Cool," drew calmly on his cigar while the half-dozen uniformed police officers carried out a thorough search of the house and barn.

'A woman detective?' he echoed in response to the young night-turn inspector's question. 'I have no idea what you're talking about. There's just my man, Bruno, who's somewhere outside locking up, my girlfriend and my good self here, no one else.'

'We know she was at the house, sir,' the inspector said, 'and she hasn't been seen since.'

Coleman shook his head slowly, releasing a stream of cigar smoke from between his teeth and smiling as the policeman took a step back. 'Sorry to hear that, but what would this detective of yours be doing on my property anyway? Did she have a warrant? As a matter of fact, do you have a warrant, Inspector? If not, then what legal right do you have to be here at all?'

'What have you done with her, Coleman?' another voice snapped, and Coleman turned his head to study the dishevelled looking plainclothes man with the mop of untidy blond hair who had just entered the study.

'Done with her?' he echoed. 'I've never seen the lady. And for your information, my name is Silverman, not Coleman.'

'We know exactly who you are,' Hayden retorted, 'so let's stop playing games, shall we?'

Coleman manufactured a sigh. 'Games? At this hour of the night? I'm afraid I'm not in the mood for games, Officer. So, unless you have a warrant, I suggest you get off my property.'

The inspector threw Hayden an uneasy glance, knowing full well that Coleman was right and that they had no authority to be there. But as he was about to buckle and order everyone back to their cars, there was the sound of a scuffle. Two more officers, one a well-built woman sergeant, appeared through the doorway, dragging a struggling Bruno between them.

'Found *him* in the barn, sir,' the sergeant said, her face set in a scowl.

'So?' Coleman sneered. 'Bruno happens to live here. He works for me. He has every right to be in the barn or anywhere else for that matter. I'd advise you to release him immediately.'

But the woman sergeant maintained her grip. 'He was trying to hide this.' She held up a silver mobile phone in a black flip-case.

Hayden snatched it from her hand.

'Where the devil did you get this?' he said softly.

Bruno scowled defiantly at him. 'Found it out on the marsh. Was going to 'and it in.'

'What's with the phone?' the inspector interjected, looking at Hayden.

Hayden pointed grimly at the clearly visible monogram inscribed in the top right-hand corner of the case.

'Initials "TR,"' he said. 'Ted Roscoe. It was the phone we gave him as a parting gift at his farewell do.'

Coleman's pale face was even paler. For the first time, he forgot himself and, glaring at Bruno, almost choked, 'You bloody idiot!'

'Oh? And why is he an idiot?' Hayden said softly. 'Didn't dump the phone as he was told to do, eh? Too cool to be chucked away, was it?'

Coleman only partially succeeded in regaining his composure. 'I don't know what you're talking about. I've never seen the thing before. As he said, he found it and was going to hand it in.'

'Only a halfwit would believe that,' Hayden said.

'Well, you have no means of proving otherwise.'

'Stiff Roscoe, did you?' Hayden continued, staring at Bruno, 'then nick his phone?'

'I ain't stiffed no one. Never met the bloke.'

'Funny that his car is parked in a gateway just down the road then, isn't it?'

'So what?' Coleman cut in before Bruno could answer. 'The fact that someone chooses to park a car near my property doesn't mean anything. Lots of people park their cars in the lane, for many different reasons.'

'Was it you who slashed his tyres, Bruno? Hayden persisted. 'So he couldn't drive away?'

'That's enough!' Coleman snapped, determined to regain control of the situation. 'This is scandalous. You burst in here without a warrant, carry out an illegal search for heaven knows what, accuse myself and Bruno here of a vicious crime without the slightest strand of evidence to back it up, and then suggest we had something to do with the disappearance of some detective sergeant of yours—'

'How did you know she was a sergeant?' Hayden grated. 'We just said a female detective.'

Coleman said nothing, apparently tongue-tied.

'A detective sergeant who just happens to be my wife,' Hayden added.

Coleman swallowed hard and tried to gloss over his faux pas. 'So what? It has nothing to do with me, any more than the death of this man Roscoe. You'd be better employed out looking for your wife instead of harassing me.'

'You're a liar!' a shrill voice accused. Hayden and the others spun round to see a pretty, blonde woman, dressed only in a flimsy bathrobe, standing in the doorway, her face puffy and red, tears streaming from her eyes. 'Look what he did to me.'

To the astonishment of everyone, she pulled open her bathrobe, to reveal that she was completely naked underneath. Unabashed, she pulled a large sticking plaster off her belly. They saw that her navel was swollen and badly inflamed. 'It isn't the first time either,' she said. 'He likes hurting people. Well, I've had enough of him.'

'Shut it!' Coleman snarled, but she was now unstoppable, in full vengeful flow.

'You sent the boys out on the marsh after that man when he broke into your barn. I heard you telling Bruno to find him.' In a dramatic gesture, she waved an arm towards the desk. 'And — and he's got a gun in the drawer there.'

'You bitch!' Coleman rasped. 'You crazy bitch!'

The sergeant released Bruno and strode across to the desk. With a flourish, she produced an automatic pistol.

'Glock 17,' she said. 'And it seems to be fully loaded.'

'Well, Mr Coleman,' Hayden said triumphantly, 'what have you got to say about that?'

'I want my solicitor,' he muttered, suddenly looking smaller, deflated.

Hayden nodded. 'Very wise. Because you're going to need one. I'm arresting you on suspicion of murder and unlawful possession of a prohibited firearm — and that's just for starters.'

* * *

'What was that?' Little ferret-faced Jimmy Snell turned pointlessly in his seat to look at the solid metal partition which separated the cab of the Ford Transit from the cargo area.

Frank Dobson grinned, exposing a row of broken, decayed teeth set like tombstones in his ugly slab-like face. Not the best of drivers, he had almost piled into the back of the artic in front of him when it had braked suddenly.

'What was what?' he said. 'Probably some of the boxes falling over.'

Snell grunted. 'Didn't sound like no boxes to me. They're all pretty light and that was a loud bang, like somefing 'eavy hittin' the side of the van.'

Dobson's grin faded. 'Yeah, all right, s'pose we'd better check it out. Boss won't be too happy if any of the stuff's been spilled. We'll pull off at the next stopover.'

Even as he spoke, the headlights lit up the blue motorway sign that indicated "services" two miles ahead.

In the back of the van, Kate sat on the floor, having wedged herself between a box and a corner of the vehicle, her arm pressed tightly to her side and trying not to cry out in pain. Dobson's sudden braking had thrown her forward into the boxes and then back against the rear doors. It was a miracle the doors hadn't burst open, pitching her out onto the carriageway, and, although they had held fast, her shoulder had suffered the consequences of slamming into an unyielding steel frame. She could hardly move her right arm and the initial pain that had scorched through her muscles had been replaced by a numbness that had spread right through the limb to her fingertips.

Things had certainly gone sour for her since her initial success in uncovering the evidence of Coleman's drug-trafficking operation. Trapped in the van, although she had initially managed to get a brief text message off to Hayden with the photo of the vehicle, that had been it. For some reason, maybe because of the weather, the lie of the land or simply all the metal around her, her mobile signal had dropped out and now, even if it came back on, the numbness to her fingers meant it would be virtually impossible in a moving vehicle for her to try and send another message.

But the next moment she had a lot more to worry about than her injury. The Transit suddenly braked again and pulled sharply to the left. They were leaving the motorway, but where? They couldn't have got too far in the relatively short time they had been on the road and, if they were heading for London, the M5 and M4 motorways provided the only direct route available.

Then it dawned on her. They must have heard her fall over and were pulling off to check on their load. Incapacitated and with nowhere to hide, there was nothing she could do but wait for those back doors to open. She felt sick.

* * *

Hayden too felt sick. Where was Kate? She had sent him the text message nearly two hours ago and there had been nothing since. He had sent her three text messages, but they had gone unanswered. He knew she had a GPS enabled phone and the control room had already obtained her IMEI number and were trying to locate her through the satellite triangulation process. But for some reason, the mobile signal had died and the last location that had come up was bang in the middle of the Somerset Levels, in the area of Witch-Fire House. A full search of the house and its wooded grounds had been carried out, but no trace of her had been found and he was terrified that she could be lying somewhere hurt — or worse — and he felt totally helpless.

Coleman and Bruno were in the cells, both refusing to answer questions, and Ansell, who had been called out after the arrests, had stated that they were not to be interviewed until Coleman's lawyer could attend — which would almost certainly not be until well into the following day, since he was coming all the way from London. That only added to Hayden's frustration. It was doubtful that either of the two villains would be inclined to help the police find Kate — especially if they were responsible for her disappearance. Now, in contrast to his normally mild, conciliatory nature, it was all he could do to stop himself marching down to the cells and beating the information out of one of them.

He had already been told by a newly arrived DCI Hennessey to go home, as there was nothing he could do, but he'd refused point-blank, insisting on remaining at the station until Kate was found, one way or the other.

It was a good job that he had, for the Control Room tannoyed him just half an hour later. 'Picked up the mobile signal again,' the operator told him. 'She seems to be in a moving vehicle. They've tracked her to the M4, heading east.'

'Bloody hell!' Hayden shouted, forgetting himself for the second time in so many days. 'She must actually be in that Transit I circulated. Why hasn't anyone pulled it over yet?'

'No idea. But the details went out force-wide.'

'Well, send them out again and tell those motorway muppets to get their fingers out. It's my wife we're talking about!'

* * *

The motorway services looked to be practically empty, which was hardly surprising considering it was well into the early hours of the morning. Dobson followed the signs to the car park and drove to a quiet corner in a shadowy area, away from the main building.

'I need a piss,' Snell announced, throwing open his door.

'Yeah, and I need some fags,' Dobson said. 'Back here in ten, okay? We'll check the boxes then but watch out for Old Bill. Cop cars are always in and out of these places and the M4 seems to attract 'em like flies round a corpse.'

Nice analogy, Kate thought drily, crouched in the darkness listening to the muffled conversation. So, how do we get out of this one, Miss? she asked herself. She had no idea where she was, except that it was almost certainly in one of the service areas along the M4. Wrenching her mobile from her pocket, she saw that the signal was a lot better. There were text messages waiting for her, but she had no time to read them. She could, however, send a message herself now that the vehicle was stationary, maybe to Hayden. But what would she tell him? That she was locked in the back of a Transit van with a load of illegal narcotics? But he must already have worked that out after seeing the photograph of the van she had sent him, including the registration number. The police must be out looking for it, surely. She could only hope her colleagues had had the good sense to activate the GPS tracker system and would home in on the signal from her phone to pinpoint her location.

But the technology, sophisticated as it was, depended for its success on the mobile signal and, more often than not, only provided an approximate indication of position. So, maybe a text message would be a good backup.

She was actually in the process of keying it in when she heard the voices. The next moment the door rattled.

Shit! They were back. Stuffing the mobile back in her pocket, she felt for the little cylinder she had been carrying. She had slipped the police issue CS gas spray into her pocket as an afterthought when she and Hayden had left the station earlier, remembering from previous experience the pain she could have saved herself if she hadn't neglected to take it with her. At least she had the element of surprise and she was confident that the lethal spray directed at face level could temporarily immobilise one of the thugs and enable her to make a break for it. It all depended on the reaction of the other one.

Hauling herself upright with the aid of her uninjured arm, she leaned against the boxes with the spray held out in front of her, waiting for the key to turn in the lock and the doors to open. But nothing happened and everything went strangely quiet. What the hell was going on?

Lowering her arm, she relaxed a little. Maybe her unwitting captors had been making sure the doors were securely locked before going back for something to eat. Or maybe the door had been tried by a couple of "tea-leaves" looking for insecure vehicles to steal from.

She was not long kept in suspense. The sudden loud, splintering crack sent a violent tremor through the body of the Transit, and the next instant the rear doors flew open and the back of the vehicle was flooded with pulsing blue light.

Several uniformed police officers stood there in the headlights of a powerful patrol car parked behind the Transit with its engine running, roof strobe lighting up the night sky and staining the tarmac blue.

* * *

'What's the verdict then?'

Hayden jumped to his feet as Kate walked slowly down the hospital corridor from the casualty department. She looked very pale and had her left arm in a sling.

'Badly bruised and a possible torn ligament, the doc thinks,' she said. 'Nothing broken, according to the X-ray. He says it should heal in a few days. Let's go home.'

'You gave me the fright of my life,' he said as they walked to her car.

'I gave *you* a fright?' she exclaimed. 'What do you think it did to me? Have they picked up Coleman's two heavies yet? They must have scarpered when they saw the police around the Transit.'

'Not yet, but they'll be caught eventually and anyway, they're small fry. The main thing is we've got the van with the dope.'

He opened the passenger door of her MX5 and helped her to climb inside.

'Does Coleman know we've got the van?' she asked as he got into the driver's seat.

He grinned. 'Not yet. Ansell's saving that and a few other choice items for his interview later today when the brief arrives.'

'What other items?'

'Well, to start with, when we searched Coleman's drum, we found a nice Glock 17 automatic in a drawer in his desk — fully loaded. It's with SOCO for printing as we speak.

Then it will go to Ballistics to see if it can be married up with any previous crimes.'

She whistled. 'Unauthorised possession of a prohibited Section 1 firearm. That should wipe any smug smile off his face.'

'And that's not all.'

'Go on, you're really cheering me up.'

'I've already told you about Roscoe's mobile turning up in Bruno's pocket. Well, the phone has been interrogated and guess what? There are some lovely pictures on it of your Transit van parked in Coleman's barn—'

'I have some on mine too.'

'Great, and they will obviously provide further valuable evidence. But Roscoe seems to have really gone to town. He has a nice, comprehensive selection of pics, not only of the Transit and the interior of the building, but of the stacked boxes and, more importantly, the contents of two or three of them.'

'Brilliant! So, we can now link Coleman and Witch-Fire House to the drugs, in addition to his possession of an illegal firearm. That will earn him a nice dose of porridge.'

'He started the engine. 'Maybe, though according to Percival, we could have a problem on our hands at Crown Court, as the search was technically illegal since we didn't have a warrant. I can see his brief trying to secure a ruling that our evidence is inadmissible because it was obtained illegally.'

She snorted. 'It would be a very brave judge who would exclude a lethal firearm and a van full of narcotics on that basis.'

He shrugged and pulled away. 'Nevertheless, it's a funny old world and the justice system is about as funny as it gets. Coleman is unlikely to admit to murdering Roscoe and, with juries as naive as they are at the moment, there's a very real chance that Bruno's ridiculous claim that he found Roscoe's mobile out on the Levels will be accepted.'

‘We’ll have to work on Bruno then. He’s the weak link and he may be open to a deal if he thinks he could be railroaded for Roscoe’s murder.’

‘*You* won’t be working on anyone for a while.’

She stiffened. ‘Oh? Why’s that?’

‘You’ll have to go off sick until your injury is healed.’

‘Is that so? Well, we’ll see about that, Gunga Din!’

CHAPTER 29

Kate wasn't wearing her sling when she got up after just a few hours' restless sleep. Hayden didn't believe her for one moment when she claimed that she didn't need it anymore as her shoulder was much improved after her lie down. He could see from the way she was holding her arm by her side that she was still in pain, but he also knew it was pointless trying to dissuade her from doing what she had made up her mind to do, so he merely shrugged and let her get on with it.

Even Percival got nowhere, and she nearly bit his head off when he tried to insist that she go home again to rest.

Ansell proved to be less concerned about her welfare, but then Ansell was of a kind that paid less attention to the well-being of his personnel and more to the business of bringing an investigation to a successful conclusion. When she had finished briefing him in his office on the night's events, he said nothing about the undoubted courage she had displayed, nor did he compliment her on securing the evidence that was so badly needed. Instead, coldly making reference to the illegality of her actions, he warned her that she could face a discipline inquiry as a result.

Still in pain and bitterly resenting Ansell's attitude after all she had been through, she made her way to the canteen for a strong dose of caffeine. She was on her second cup of coffee when Hayden joined her, having just undergone a similar grilling by Ansell.

'That man is about as useful to human endeavour as a clockwork orange!' he complained.

Kate smiled faintly in spite of herself. 'The term is "queer as a clockwork orange," Hayd.'

He grunted. 'And that as well probably. But see now why I want shot of this job with cretins like him at the top?'

She waved a weary hand. 'Not that again, Hayd, please. Can we just concentrate on what we do next?'

He scowled. 'There's nothing *to* do. Ansell and Hennessey will apparently be interviewing both Coleman and his sidekick in the presence of their bent QC at three. So, it's all down to them. We're out of the picture.'

She shook her head, stretching her injured arm out in front of her for a second to relieve some of the pain and popping her fourth couple of paracetamol into her mouth.

'Don't you be so sure,' she said, washing them down with some coffee.

He groaned. 'What scheme are you hatching now? Haven't we created enough hassle for ourselves without adding more?'

'No scheme,' she said. 'But we still have work to do.'

'What work?

'Stick around and you'll find out.'

* * *

Coleman's inside man had just got the shock of his life. He'd been on his way down to the basement to get a couple of paracetamol for his raging headache from the bottle he kept in his locker, when he had been confronted by a man being escorted in handcuffs up the stairs by two uniformed policemen, no doubt on his way from the cells to one of the interview rooms on the next floor. For a moment they stared at each other before Ronnie Coleman was pushed on past him. But he'd had enough time to see the mobster's lips curl in a thin, humourless smile. A smile that held a malevolent promise.

Heading unsteadily to the canteen, he got himself a black coffee and dropped into a chair at a corner table to try and think things out. Coleman in the nick? Despite the hot coffee, a ball of ice was developing in the pit of his stomach. If Coleman was in custody, that meant Percival and his team must have cracked the mobster's drugs operation and probably had him in the frame for Roscoe's murder too. The net was closing in, and he could be next if Coleman carried out his threat to take him down with him. The prospect of incarceration for life in a tiny prison cell, with the risk of a knife in the back at any moment, was terrifying. He had to get out, clear off somewhere remote where he couldn't be found. Ireland maybe, or somewhere further afield? He had quite a bit of cash stashed away, so it was a feasible option. All it needed was the balls to do it. But what about Maureen? It wouldn't be possible to take her with him. She needed constant medical attention and her Alzheimer's was getting worse every day. He couldn't just abandon her, yet if he stayed and ended up inside, she would be left just as alone.

Why the hell had he ever got involved with Coleman in the first place? He had run into him at that backstreet gambling joint in Bristol. He'd overstepped the mark yet again and had ended up owing the greasy Greek proprietor a bundle. The suave, silver-haired man in the neat blue suit had taken him to one side, bought him a drink and offered to settle everything — for a price.

He'd had no way of knowing that Ronnie Silverman, as the man called himself, owned the place, or that he was a mobster from the Smoke, and it was certainly a mystery to him as to how his new "friend" had known he was with Old Bill. But at the time he had been so far up his own arse that he hadn't much cared. All he'd wanted was to have his debt to the Greek wiped out and avoid ending up in the river with his throat slit. At first, keeping Ronnie informed about what was going on at the nick hadn't seemed too bad and it had paid well, but then the demands had increased and before he knew it, he was in too deep to pull out.

Now, with Ronnie in the nick, he faced the stark choice — run and start a new life somewhere else while he had the chance or stay where he was in the hope that everything would turn out all right. But he was too long in the tooth to believe in fairy tales.

* * *

Unbeknown to Coleman's mole, he was not the only one in a hole at that precise moment. His former boss was no longer wearing his confident smirk, and the grey-haired man in the expensive Saville Row suit sitting beside him looked distinctly uneasy as the two of them stared at the photographs Ansell had pushed towards them across the table.

The interview had started late, after Coleman's lawyer, Malcolm Sneed QC, had been delayed by traffic holdups on the motorway. To begin with, it had looked promising for Coleman. Sneed had immediately gone on the attack, taking Ansell and the hard-faced woman seated beside him — who had been introduced as a Detective Chief Inspector Hennessey — to task over what he described as the illegal search that had been carried out at Witch-Fire House without a warrant.

The eminent QC was used to bamboozling police officers, but this time, he was dealing with a different class of detective to the rough, predictable crime squad cops he usually ran rings around.

He realised a bit too late that Ansell was a dangerous adversary, a man with a cold, clinical mind, who cut through bluster and got to the crux of the issue in a focused, totally unemotional way that was difficult to counter.

The Glock 17 had already been produced and Coleman's lame explanation that he had obtained the weapon for his own protection because his life had been threatened dropped him straight in the mire because it meant he faced prosecution for the illegal possession of a deadly Section 1 firearm. However, he was prepared to swear that in the expectation that Sneed could swing a light sentence for him with the judge. But after that, his fortunes had rapidly taken a turn for the worse, beginning with the incriminating photographs.

'Pictures printed off the late Detective Inspector Roscoe's mobile phone, which your man Bruno had in his possession,' Ansell drawled. 'I think it is clear that they show the interior of your barn and the Transit van in which you conveyed a large quantity of illegal class A and class B drugs to Witch-Fire House.'

'Those photos could have been taken anywhere,' Coleman retorted, though he was obviously rattled.

Ansell sighed. 'But they weren't taken anywhere, Mr Coleman, they were taken on your property, and the boxes pictured contained a large quantity of illegal class A and class B drugs, as two of the opened boxes reveal.'

'As my client has just said, they are just photographs,' Sneed butted in. 'They prove nothing, Superintendent. You are clutching at straws.'

Ansell treated him to one of his thin, humourless smiles. 'Am I, Mr Sneed?' he said softly. 'Am I really? But what you don't know is that this same Transit van, with the same registration number, has now been seized by the police on the M4 motorway, with its cargo intact. So, you see, we can categorically link your client to the van and the narcotics, and I'm sure our Scenes of Crime department will find a fingerprint or two of Mr Coleman's somewhere on the vehicle. Trafficking prohibited drugs is a very serious offence, as I'm sure you'll agree, and it carries a particularly heavy sentence.'

Coleman's face was the colour of the interview room's pale grey walls by now and it seemed to have shrunk, exposing his cheekbones, as he stared over Ansell's shoulder at the winking red light of the recording machine. His thoughts were racing. He was well in the cacky, despite his lawyer's earlier assurances. He was facing at least ten to fifteen years for the trafficking offence and, if the police managed to tie his shooter into other serious crimes it may have been used for, he could be looking at life.

But Ansell was not about to give him time to think things out.

'Then there's the matter of the late ex-Detective Inspector Roscoe's mobile phone itself,' the senior detective continued. 'For him to have taken those photographs, he must have been in the barn at the time, so how come his phone has now turned up in Bruno's pocket, and Mr Roscoe has been found dead on the marsh?'

'Mr Dodds has already told you he found the phone,' Sneed answered for Coleman. 'Your Mr Roscoe must have accidentally dropped it before his unfortunate accident.'

'No accident,' Hennessey cut in for the first time. 'We are talking cold-blooded murder here. We think it is far more likely the phone was taken off his body after he was killed by Dodds — on your orders, Mr Coleman — and we have your young lady, Linda Coates, who is willing to testify that you sent Bruno and the others out onto the marsh after him.'

Coleman's legendary cool was shot to pieces. He began to show real signs of panic.

'I didn't order Bruno to kill anyone,' he blurted, sweat gathering on his forehead and upper lip. 'No way was Roscoe stiffed by us. This is a stitch-up. The girl's lying to get back at me.'

'Well,' Ansell said, rising to his feet, 'maybe Mr Dodds will have something different to say when we interview him, especially if it looks like he is likely to take the rap for the murder he committed on your orders. We'll leave you to think about that for a while, Mr Coleman. We'll talk again later.'

Then, after announcing to the recording machine that the interview was terminated, he switched it off and walked out of the room, leaving a once omnipotent gang boss to face the bleak prospect that his second night in police cells would be just the taster for the very much longer term behind bars that awaited him.

CHAPTER 30

When Kate returned to the general office, Percival was pulling his coat on, and he beckoned to her.

'Hospital rang,' he said. 'Our Jane Doe is asking to see us. Be a good idea if you came with me.'

At the hospital, Percival parked in one of the ambulance bays. The ICU staff nurse was waiting for them.

'She's still very weak,' she said, 'but she's anxious to talk to the police, and the doctor has agreed to it, provided you don't stay too long.'

'Ten minutes,' Kate said.

'Not a minute longer,' the nurse warned.

The young woman, no longer connected to the support apparatus, was propped up on several pillows. Her face had a lot more colour than before and her blonde hair — dyed, Kate noted — had been freshly combed. She looked to be well on the mend. She smiled at them as they sat down beside the bed on a couple of chairs the staff nurse had provided.

'They move me to ordinary ward tomorrow,' she said in halting English. 'They say I leave hospital soon, now I am awake because I have no injuries, just lot of bruises.'

'Delighted to see you back with us anyway, Miss . . . ?' Percival began.

'Petrović,' she replied. She sounded resigned, as if she didn't really want to say but was past caring. 'Ela Petrović.'

'And where *is* home?' he said.

She hesitated, then shrugged. 'Croatia.'

Percival frowned. 'Croatia? So, what brought you all the way to Somerset?'

She sighed. 'It is long story.'

'We have as much time as you need,' Kate said. 'But first, do you remember being hit by my car?'

Petrović made a face. 'I am remembering there is mist and I am running along path. There is a road and lights of car, but I am remembering nothing after that.'

'But why were you running and who from? Before you lost consciousness, you said something to me about "witch fire,"' Kate said.

The other nodded excitedly. 'Witch-Fire House is place I am coming from.'

She reached for a glass of water on her bedside table and Kate handed it to her. 'Why don't you tell us everything that happened, starting with how you got here?'

Petrović said nothing for a few seconds and then took a deep breath. 'I come to UK with my twin sister, Irena, three year ago. Both our parents die in car crash year before and there is no future for us in Croatia.'

'So, you paid some people to get you to the UK by the back door?'

The young woman paused, apparently struggling with her emotions.

'We are promised bar work in London club and place to stay as well. But when we arrive, we are told we have to pay money to man who own club for bed and food, which is most of wages. He say we can make more money if we dance for customers, so we do this. But then we find that dancing is taking all our clothes off and being specially nice to customers.'

'Prostitution,' Kate said grimly.

Petrović brushed away tears.

'We are told that if we leave, we will be arrested by police and go to prison for what we do, so we stay. Then one night, after Irena dance, a man with silver hair come over to her and offer job as exotic dancer at club in Soho. Irena not listen to me. She go with him and I hear later she is living at his big house. I never see her again. One day I see her picture in paper, and they say her body found, drowned in river.'

She paused again obviously struggling to hold back her tears.

'Take your time,' Kate said. Petrović gave her a weak smile of thanks and stared down at the sheets on her bed for a few moments, absently smoothing out the creases.

'They say she has cocaine inside her, but Irena never take drugs,' she went on bitterly. 'So I know she is killed — maybe by silver-haired man she go with. But I cannot go to police because I am illegal.'

She took a deep breath and sank back onto the pillows. 'I decide to find man myself and say to him about Irena's death and I spend many months with inquiries. Soon I find man's name is Silverman and that he is very bad. I also hear from customer I give special favour to that he leave London to start other business here in Somerset.'

'So, I steal money from bar where I work, take train to Bristol, and Highbridge, and get taxi out to place called Shapwick. I stay at farm for one night, then steal bicycle and ride out onto these Levels.'

'So, how did the old woman Lilith become involved?' Percival asked.

Another faint smile. 'Ah, Lilith, yes. She see me looking at Witch-Fire House when she is picking flowers. She tell me house is cursed and Devil live there. I am lonely and scared and she is friendly, so I tell her why I come, and she say she will help me if I help her. She tell me she has bed for night if I want. I am cold and tired, so I say "yes" and stay for two days while I watch house—'

'To see the lie of the land?' Percival cut in.

She nodded a little uncertainly, plainly unsure of his meaning.

'Presumably you got into the house, though?' Percival went on.

She nodded again. 'Lilith show me way through some woods, but before she leave me, she give me ugly doll with silver hair, stuck with lots of pins, and ask me to hang it on front door. I thought this silly, but she help me, so I have to help her.' She frowned. 'But doll big mistake.

'While I am hanging it on door, two men see me and I run away. They chase me and I think I have left them behind, but later they come to Lilith's house and smash in back door. Lilith is out somewhere, but I have to run away again as fast as I can—'

'And as you did so, you broke one of your sandals,' Kate said.

Petrović nodded. 'Yes. I trip and strap breaks, so I have to be in bare feet.' She frowned. 'I leave my rucksack behind when I run and all my things inside. I hope Lilith still keep it for me.'

Kate winced, remembering the remains of the canvas bag Percival had found in the wreckage of the shack after the fire.

Choosing her words very carefully, she told Ela Petrović about the fire and explained that Lilith wasn't there anymore, which was true in a literal sense, but she didn't say the old woman was dead. Seeing from the shocked look on her face that Petrović was about to ask more questions, she quickly went off on another tack, much to Percival's puzzlement.

'You met Luke Cobb while you were staying at Lilith's, didn't you?'

'Luke? Yes, nice young man. A bit — how you say it — slow? But he kind and friendly. Lilith like him a lot. He bring her some wild flowers, so I give him bar of chocolate I have in my pocket.'

'Yes, he told me about that,' Kate said. 'Did you ever see him go anywhere with Lilith?'

'No, he just come to see her once before we go to Witch-Fire House, and he leave after giving her flowers.'

'While you were staying at Lilith's shack, did you see any tools there or in the car she had parked out the back — you know, a garden spade, fork — anything of that sort?'

Petrović frowned and shook her head again. 'I not see anything like that or any car.'

Percival coughed discreetly, plainly concerned at what he saw as a drift away from the issue at hand. 'The man who came into your room here last night,' he said. 'Can you describe him?'

Petrović shook her head.

'I am remembering waking up after long sleep and seeing face, but then I hear nurse shout and it is gone.' She paused for a second. 'You think Mr Silverman send man to kill me?'

Percival glanced at Kate, then nodded. 'We think it highly likely, yes, but you needn't worry anymore. Your Mr Silverman — whose real name, by the way, is Coleman — has been arrested and will soon be going to prison for a very long time, and we hope to have the man he sent here to hurt you in custody as well before long.'

'This Coleman, he will be punished for what happen to Irena?'

Percival hesitated, obviously not wishing to destroy her hopes, so Kate put in instead, 'I'm afraid we don't have enough evidence to prove he was responsible for Irena's death, Ela, but he will be locked away for other things he has done, which will be just as bad for him, so he won't be able to hurt anyone else.'

Petrović sighed, smoothing her sheet again, with her gaze fixed on her slim hands. 'And me? What happen to me?'

It was Kate's turn to throw a glance in Percival's direction. 'I'm afraid you are here illegally, Ela,' she said gently. 'The authorities are almost certain to want to send you back to Croatia, but I will do my best to see that you get proper legal representation.'

To the surprise of both her interviewers, she looked up again with a big, beaming smile. 'Then I go home again? But that is good. This time I find husband and have family.'

Kate laughed. 'Well, that is something I cannot arrange for you. But yes, finding a husband would be a very good plan.'

And all three of them were still laughing when the staff nurse reappeared to call an end to the interview.

'That was a long ten minutes,' she commented as she showed them out.

Kate smiled at her. 'According to Albert Einstein, time is an illusion,' she said philosophically, leaving the nurse staring after her with a puzzled frown.

* * *

'So, what was all that about Luke Cobb and garden spades?' Percival said as they were driving back to the police station. 'I must admit, you had me confused there.'

'Just something else I'm working on,' she replied mysteriously.

He cast her an irritable glance. 'What "something" is that?'

'I'll level with you when I'm sure.'

He shook his head in resignation. 'You are a real pain in the arse, you know.'

She nodded. 'But not as much of a pain as that lot,' she said as they approached the knot of reporters and camera crews gathered around the rear entrance to the police station.

Scowling, Percival edged through the press of bodies, blinking under the repeated flashing of camera bulbs. He winced when a young red-haired reporter holding a microphone, darted forward and shouted through his half-open window, 'Is it true a woman has died in your cells? Can you confirm you are you investigating a murder?'

'Bloody hell. They know about it!' he breathed.

'Which means our mole knows that we know too,' Kate replied grimly.

* * *

They returned to find Hayden waiting for them. As soon as he saw them, he grabbed a file off his desk and followed them into Percival's office, closing the door behind him.

Kate stared curiously at the orange file in his hand. 'SOCO?'

He nodded, dropping it onto Percival's desk.

'Prints from the plastic bag you found in the bin,' he said. For once, he had a glint of excitement in his blue eyes. 'They've been able to match them to Lilith.'

Percival whistled. 'So, it *was* the bag used to suffocate her,' he said. 'I'd better let Ansell and Hennessey know.'

'They've found some other prints on it too,' Hayden said. 'Nothing on PNC, but they could belong to our killer.'

'What about the yellowish substance that was stuck to the inside of the bag?' Kate asked.

'Sent for DNA analysis but it's not back yet,' he said. 'Could take a while apparently as there's a backlog at the lab. SOCO evidently found blood traces under Lilith's long nails too, suggesting she may have scratched her attacker.'

'All good stuff,' Kate murmured, glancing at Percival. 'And if we nail the perp, the blood traces could be the conclusive factor.'

Percival looked unconvinced. 'A lot of ifs there, though, aren't there? Think about it. We're relying solely on possible forensic evidence to come. All we have is the plastic bag found in his wastepaper bin with Lilith's prints on it and possibly some other DNA evidence yet to be provided. The other prints on the bag may turn out to be someone else's, perhaps even a member of SOCO who was handling the bag in the department before the perp stole it. We can't say at this stage. As for the blood traces, they may end up having nothing to do with the crime at all. Furthermore, we have no witnesses who can positively ID him, either in connection with Lilith's death or the attempt on Ela Petrović, and Coleman is unlikely to finger him as his mole, since that would mean dropping himself in the cart. Finally, we have nothing, other than those unidentified prints on the bag, to physically link him to the bag itself. Without them, he could easily claim that someone else dumped it in his bin.' He spread his hands. 'I rest my case.'

Hayden frowned, the glint in his eyes beginning to fade. 'So how do we end this?' he said irritably. 'What more can we do to bring this beggar to justice?'

Percival glanced through the glass partition at the other members of the team, all sitting at their desks, heads down. 'It's going to be hard carrying on working with the bastard, knowing what we know.'

'Then we need to draw him out,' Kate said suddenly. 'He'll know by now that we have his paymaster in the nick, and he'll be stewing over the possibility that Coleman or Bruno might grass him up. So, we have to add to his fears and panic him into giving himself away.'

'And how do we do that?' Percival said.

Kate peered through the partition. 'Well, I see the cleaner hasn't emptied his wastepaper bin yet, so he'll think the incriminating plastic bag is still where he dumped it. We slip another similar bag in the basket and encourage him to try to get rid of it to save his skin. All he needs is a little push.'

'Then what?'

'We cross our fingers.'

And she told them what she had in mind.

* * *

Surprisingly, Ansell appeared to like what Kate proposed — he even seemed to find it amusing.

Hennessey glanced at him and winked at Kate. 'Just be careful,' she warned. 'This character will be desperate, and he has nothing to lose.'

The impromptu briefing took place twenty minutes later.

'What gives, guv?' Danny Ferris growled, sitting back down, clearly annoyed at being asked to hang fire. 'I was told we could all have an early off tonight, since Roscoe's killer is in the pokey and there's nothing else for us to do.'

‘Something to tell you all,’ Percival said. ‘It won’t take more than a few minutes.’

Jamie Foster shrugged, winking at Hayden, who was back in his chair. ‘Sounds mysterious,’ he laughed, also sitting down.

Kate played her part, giving a show of surprise. She propped herself on the corner of her desk.

‘Any reason for me to stay?’ Ronnie Crouch, the office manager asked, rising from his chair with his coat already on.

Percival shook his head. ‘Not really, Ron. You can clutter off if you like.’ He gave a short laugh. ‘*Secret Squirrel* stuff anyway.’

‘Just for that, guv, I’ll stay,’ Crouch grunted, his usual truculence surfacing. He sat down again.

Percival’s gaze roved around the room, taking in each face in turn. He cleared his throat.

‘You may not all be aware that inquiries have revealed that the recent death in the cells was not from natural causes. It is the subject of a murder investigation—’

‘What?’ Ferris ejaculated. ‘I didn’t know that.’

‘Maybe if you and Jamie had turned up at the last incident room briefing, you would have known about it,’ Kate said icily.

Percival cleared his throat again. He was plainly a little nervous. Clenching her hands tightly together, Kate willed him on.

‘Further to that,’ he said, ‘we now know that the deceased woman, Lilith, died from asphyxiation caused by a plastic bag being placed over her head.’

There was an almost unanimous gasp.

‘But that means it must have been an inside job,’ Ferris blurted.

Percival nodded. ‘Precisely. Someone in this police station committed the crime. We don’t know why, but we believe the bag that was used may have been hastily dumped after the murder, so it could be anywhere in the nick. A team of senior officers from outside the area is to carry out a search of the whole station tonight. It will start on the ground floor promptly at 2000 hours. I must ask you all not to remove anything from this department until the search has been completed. That includes briefcases and bags and other similar items. They'll be quite safe here, and you can pick them up when you come in tomorrow morning.'

'Seems a bit daft to me,' Foster commented. 'Whoever did the job is unlikely to have been stupid enough to leave the evidence on site for anyone to find. It's probably long gone by now.'

'And it's a bloody liberty anyway,' Ferris growled.

'Sorry, lady and gents,' Percival said. 'But we have to go through the motions.' He gave a short laugh. 'I'm in the same boat as you, and after you lot have gone, I too shall be leaving here by seven. Enjoy your evening off.'

CHAPTER 31

Crouched on the floor beneath her desk, a cushion supporting her back, Kate felt utterly ridiculous. What would her colleagues say if they could see her now, or some uniform plod who happened to nip into the office for something? Even worse was the thought that her suspect might see her before he gave himself away. Perhaps he wouldn't turn up at all, and she'd be a laughing stock for Ansell and Hennessey.

As it was, it was only half an hour or so before she heard the double doors of the office open and footsteps cross the room. She hunched, trying to make herself smaller, and held her breath. Then she frowned. Something wasn't right. Then she heard voices and knew why. There was not just one person in the office, but two.

'What the hell are you looking for anyway?' a female voice exclaimed, her voice trembling slightly. 'You know we shouldn't be up here.'

'Balls to that,' her male companion said. 'That shitbag Danny owes me some dosh, and I know it's up here somewhere.'

'Dosh for what? You said you were coming up here to check on a file.'

'Well, I lied, didn't I? Listen, Danny runs this pyramid thing in the nick. You pay into this fund and get one other person to join it. Then they do the same. The more people who join, the more money is divvied out. Danny's the banker and he owes me fifty smackers.'

'Sounds like a real con to me.'

'Yeah, I'm beginning to think it is.'

'Well, I'm not staying up here any longer. I shouldn't have come in the first place. I only did it for you.'

'Okay, okay,' came grudgingly 'I'm coming. I'll see the bastard tomorrow.'

Kate heard the door bang behind them and breathed a sigh of relief, vowing to have a few words with DC Danny Ferris at the earliest opportunity.

She sank back against her cushion and listened to the rain hammering against the windows. Somewhere in the building someone shouted, and she heard running feet, followed by the sound of a car churning out of the yard at speed. Situation normal.

The evening dragged on and the cramp in her back and legs got worse, while her injured arm began to send shooting pains from her shoulder into her fingers. She stretched it out in front of her for a few seconds, then delved in her pocket for her paracetamol. Maybe she'd made a big mistake and her suspect hadn't fallen for her con. Could be he was sitting at home, oblivious to the discomfort she was suffering, or had gone, flown off to obscurity.

She stuffed two paracetamol in her mouth and then she froze. Someone had opened the office doors very cautiously with hardly a sound. Once again, she pressed herself further back under the desk. She held her breath.

Footsteps approaching, soft, sticking slightly to the floor. Trainers? Heavy breathing close to her desk, then silence for a few moments. She held herself still.

A rustling sound, an oath and the telltale crackling of plastic. She took a deep breath and erupted from under the desk, slamming her swivel chair back against the wall.

He stood there, gaping, the dummy bag she'd planted in the bin falling from his nerveless fingers.

'Hello, Ron,' she said to Crouch. 'You've dropped yourself right in it now, haven't you? And that isn't the right bag anyway.'

Seeming to shake himself, he reached behind him and grabbed a paperknife off his desk, extending it towards her as he backed away.

'Don't be a fool, Ron,' Kate said, advancing towards him. 'Put it down.'

He jerked his head back towards the fire door. At the same moment, the main office doors crashed back against the wall. Hayden and Percival stood in the entrance.

'Saw him come up,' Hayden said, panting. 'Thought we'd better join you.'

'Forget the fire door, Ron,' Kate said. 'We chained it up, just in case. Now, *put the knife down*.'

In response, Crouch just seemed to fold, dropping the knife on the floor and sinking onto a nearby chair, his head in his hands.

'It's finished, Ron,' Kate said firmly, picking up the knife and setting it back on the desk. 'You're well and truly nicked.'

She started to issue the standard caution.

'Do me a favour,' he interrupted in a broken voice. 'I don't need that.'

He raised his head slowly, tears running down his face and a haunted expression in his eyes.

'How did you sus me?' he whispered.

Kate shrugged. 'That really doesn't matter now, does it? I just can't understand why an ex-copper like you ended up working for a scumbag like Ronnie Coleman. How could you, in cold blood, suffocate a vulnerable old lady with a plastic bag?'

'I didn't want to do it,' he said. 'Ronnie made me.'

'No one can make you do something like that.'

'He could. I was in hock to him, see,' Crouch said bitterly. 'It was the gambling that started it all. I was into it big time and I just couldn't stop. It was like a drug and I ended up in real shtook, with debts I could never repay. Then I met Coleman and he sorted it all for me. But he kept demanding favours in return, and before long, I was in much too deep to get out.'

'A pact with the Devil,' Hayden murmured.

He nodded. 'He made me kill the old girl because she knew too much.'

'And got you to try and kill the young woman in the ICU too?' Percival cut in harshly.

Crouch looked down at his feet. 'Yeah, but then she woke up and I had to scarper.' He broke off, his eyes widening in sudden realisation. 'Look, I know I'm looking at life for what I've done, but what will happen to Maureen? She's ill and she's got Alzheimer's. She won't be able to look after herself when they put me away.'

'We'll see what we can do for her,' Kate said bleakly. 'But right now, you have an appointment with the custody sergeant.'

* * *

'So, Crouch has coughed nicely, has he?' Ansell drawled when the top team met in his office later that night.

Percival nodded. 'Caught red-handed and admitted everything.'

'All thanks to Kate,' Hennessey put in quietly from the windowsill in the corner of the room.

Ansell gave one of his thin, humourless smiles and inclined his head briefly towards Kate. No word of praise was forthcoming, and she didn't expect him to offer any.

'But she was somewhat off beam with her initial suspicions, wasn't she?' he said instead, as if she wasn't in the room.

Hennessey came to her rescue. 'Roscoe alleged that the mole was one of the departmental team, I believe, and most people would have assumed from that that he meant one of the detectives. After all, who would ever have thought that someone like the civilian office manager could have been the culprit?'

Ansell threw her a hostile glance. 'Then that should teach us all the danger of making assumptions. Had we been more open-minded, we might have got to the truth a lot quicker.'

Kate bit back the caustic retort that had risen to her lips.

Percival fidgeted in the chair behind the desk where he'd been told to sit. True to form, he made no comment in support of her.

'Well then,' Ansell continued breezily, 'most issues appear to have been resolved.' He ticked them off on his fingers. 'We've got the culprit for the witch woman's murder. We've got a target criminal in custody, shortly to be charged with illegal possession of a Section 1 firearm and drugs trafficking — maybe even complicity in her murder too if we can get Crouch or Dodds to make an allegation in a written statement under caution, as Coleman's girlfriend already has with regard to Roscoe's demise. We have also smashed a major criminal drugs operation and seized a van load of class A and B narcotics into the bargain. Not a bad result in just a few days, is it? The chief constable will be pleased.'

'We still haven't got sufficient evidence to charge anyone with Roscoe's murder, though, sir,' Kate quietly reminded him. 'I know Coleman's girlfriend has said he sent his thugs out after Roscoe, but that on its own won't be enough for a jury to convict Coleman or Bruno Dodds.'

A tic developed in Ansell's cheek. 'I am well aware of that, Sergeant. But if Dodds thinks he's going to take the rap for the murder, he might decide to be a lot more willing to implicate his master.'

'That's if the murder was actually committed by either of them in the first place,' Kate persisted.

'You think there's some doubt about that, do you?'

Kate shrugged. 'I'm not persuaded they had anything to do with it, sir.'

'Oh,' he sneered, 'the sergeant is not persuaded, is she? Well now, I'm sure we would all be most interested to hear who you would be persuaded to believe the perpetrator might be?'

Kate's face reddened. Why did she always have to open her mouth?

'I am keeping an open mind at present, sir,' she said, conscious of how weak her response must have sounded. Nevertheless, she was reluctant to share her suspicions with him.

Out of the corner of her eye she saw Hennessey wince.

Ansell's eyes gleamed like a hunter in for the kill.

'Well now, Sergeant, while you are keeping your mind open, I'm sure you won't mind if DCI Hennessey and I crack on with our closed ones. We may even get somewhere.'

He snapped his fingers. 'Oh yes, I almost forgot. As regards the other deaths in this multi-victim case, I omitted to mention that the forensics laboratory confirmed earlier today that the tea in the caddies taken from the homes of PC West and the Rev Truly do contain lethal quantities of poison hemlock. Furthermore, the forensic pathologist, Dr Summers, has also confirmed that both deceased died from ingestion of an identical poison. On the grounds of probability, supported by the additional circumstantial and witness evidence we have to hand, I think it is safe to conclude that the so-called witch woman was our killer. Consequently, both homicides can now be recorded as detected, with the offender herself also shown as deceased. All nice and tidy.'

'I think it's too early to say that, sir.' Kate hadn't been able to stop the words from coming out of her mouth.

Ansell's face darkened. 'What do you mean?' he snapped.

'I have serious doubts as to whether Lilith was the culprit.'

He studied her for a moment, but she met his cold, reptilian stare without flinching.

'Serious doubts about that as well, Sergeant?' he sneered. 'My my, you are a Doubting Thomas, aren't you? Well, to set your mind at rest, apart from the forensic evidence and the post-mortem results we have received, we have motive, in that she had an axe to grind against both deceased, which was widely known locally. Furthermore, you yourself saw a jar labelled "Hemlock" on a shelf in what we may euphemistically call her home before it was destroyed by fire, while rag dolls similar to the ones you also saw there were later left at the two crime scenes. Finally, we know that a witness actually observed her leaving both premises prior to the deaths of West and Truly. All pretty conclusive evidence in my view. So, precisely what more do you need in order to be convinced?'

Kate bit her lip but said nothing.

He stood up. 'Exactly as I thought, so let's press on, shall we? People to see, confessions to hear and so forth. Is that okay with you, Sergeant, or do you have another outlandish hypothesis to put forward?'

* * *

Kate sat for a long time staring into the crackling flames of the open fire.

'Penny for them?' Hayden said, using one of his favourite expressions, and pouring her another cup of coffee from the percolator.

She looked up quickly and gave him a rueful smile. 'Sorry, I was away with the fairies.'

He grunted, using his last bit of bread to mop up the remains of the egg and bacon fry-up Kate had cooked for them when they'd got home. 'You've been gone a while, so you were obviously enjoying their company.'

She stretched and yawned, pushing her empty plate away and bringing her legs up onto the settee.

'Very tired,' she said. 'You must be too. Neither of us has had much sleep over the last few days because of this complicated case.'

He sat back, staring at her fixedly. 'Well, from what you told me, Ansell was pretty clear. The investigation is practically over, subject to securing a confession from Coleman or Dodds.'

'Which he won't get.'

'Why?'

'Because they didn't kill Roscoe any more than Lilith poisoned West and Truly.'

'How can you say that?'

'Because it is a fact. We know Roscoe must have got into Witch-Fire House, taken his pictures in the barn and called me. We know he must have been caught but somehow got away, and that at some stage — either in the barn or as he was fleeing — he dropped his mobile.'

'The way Coleman reacted when he learned that Dodds was in possession of the mobile, suggests to me that he had expected his underling to have already disposed of it, which means he himself must have had it in his possession before he gave it to Dodds, obviously because it was taken off Roscoe after he had been murdered.'

Kate shook her head. 'I don't think so. Why take the phone off Roscoe's body, yet leave incriminating drugs still in his pockets? And why dump his body in the rhyne for someone to find, almost within spitting distance of Witch-Fire House, when they could quite easily have got rid of it in a bog somewhere? It doesn't make any sense. My feeling is that it was either taken off Roscoe or was dropped by him when he fled from the barn, which indicates he was belted over the head by someone else and only left there afterwards because that same someone panicked.'

'So why would someone belt him over the head?'

She frowned. 'There was the fire which gutted Lilith's shack during the same twenty-four-hour period that Roscoe went missing. My belief is that he was stiffed because he saw something he wasn't supposed to see — maybe who started the fire.'

'But we know who started the fire — Coleman's men. Luke Cobb saw the men get out of the car when he went to investigate the blaze and he told you they were the same men who searched the outbuildings on his uncle's farm.'

She shook her head. 'No, Luke told me there were two men in a big car, that's all. He's not the brightest of people and he naturally assumed the men were from Witch-Fire House, but I don't think they were. Plainly, they were looking for Lilith and they probably burned down her shack, either hoping she was in it or to make sure she had nothing to come back to. But what would be the point in Coleman having the shack destroyed — especially as, once again, it was so close to his house and would have been inviting unwelcome police interest in him? He wanted Lilith dead, yes, and I am quite certain Crouch was speaking the truth when he said Coleman ordered the hits on Lilith and Ela Petrović, but the murder of Roscoe and the burning of Lilith's home had to be the work of someone else.'

She shifted on the settee, settling herself more comfortably. 'As for Sara Anne Cable, to give Lilith her proper name, it's true she was a nasty, vindictive old lady, but she also had a mental condition. She had spent some time in a psychiatric hospital and, from what I've heard, was probably an alcoholic. She wasn't physically or mentally capable of doing half the things that were laid at her door, especially the desecration of Tom Sharpe's grave.'

'We did see a skull at her place, though, if you remember, and it looked old enough to have come from that grave.'

'It could have come from anywhere or been planted there by someone else. It still doesn't explain how an old woman like her could do all the things that have been alleged.'

He still looked dubious. 'I know we've gone over much of this before, but I still think it's possible she could have had help.'

'And as I told you before, the only person she could have called on was Luke Cobb, but he strenuously denies being involved in any of it and I believe him.'

'And as *I* pointed out before, he could have been lying.'

She shook her head. 'He has the mentality of a child. He doesn't have the brain power to engage in lies and subterfuge.'

'I don't think you could say the same about Lilith.'

'Probably not, but, though she may have had a kind of primitive cunning and been a public pain in the arse, I don't see her as a dangerous psychopath. Okay, so she was suffering from some sort of paranoia and really believed she was a witch, but that doesn't make her a murderer.'

'So, what does it make her?'

'Delusional — and a patsy for someone else.'

'A patsy for whom?'

'I'm hoping we can finally establish that for certain tomorrow.'

'Tomorrow?' He sighed. 'I think you'd better fill me in.'

So, she did, and at surprising length.

For several seconds after she had finished, Hayden just sat there, sipping his coffee and staring into the fire.

'You intend doing this without Ansell's knowledge or say-so?' he asked.

She shook her head. 'No, I intend for *us* to do it and now you are *au fait* with everything, you'll be able to follow my lead.''

He grimaced. 'He'll do his crust.'

She gave a tight smile. 'As Clark Gable said to Vivien Leigh in *Gone With The Wind*, "Frankly, my dear, I don't give a damn!"'

CHAPTER 32

'Up, you lazy sod!'

Kate shook Hayden repeatedly. There was no response, which didn't surprise her, Hayden could sleep through a volcanic eruption. Finally, there was a grunt, a choking gulp and he opened his eyes.

'Whassat?' he muttered.

'We've got this job to do,' she said, 'so stir yourself.'

With a groan, he struggled onto one elbow and peered at the clock. 'It's six o'clock for goodness' sake. It's still the middle of the night.'

Kate was already pulling on her trousers, and she grabbed a pile of clothes from a chair and tossed them onto the bed.

'I've got everything there for you,' she snapped, 'so get in the shower and then get dressed.'

She pulled on her sweater and turned for the door. 'Toast and coffee in ten, so buck up.'

As usual, Hayden took a lot longer than that, but she had allowed for it, so when he came downstairs half an hour later, muttering and mumbling, breakfast was already on the table.

'Darned imposition,' he mumbled through a mouthful of toast and marmalade. 'I need my sleep, you know.'

‘You need a kick up the arse,’ she said, ‘and when you’ve got all that down you, that’s exactly what we’re going to do to someone else.’

‘But why at this diabolical hour? They won’t be up.’

She smiled grimly. ‘That’s exactly what I’m hoping.’

There was a penetrating drizzle sweeping across the Levels as they drove away from their cottage in Kate’s Mazda and headed out across the patchwork of waterlogged fields and marshes.

Almost immediately the car began moving, Hayden began to doze again, but a sharp jab in the ribs from Kate’s elbow soon roused him with a loud snort.

Several turns later they pulled into the side of the road opposite a big grey house.

Hayden pointed. ‘I told you. Look, the curtains are still drawn upstairs, so they’re obviously still in bed. I told you they would be.’

She turned off the engine and studied the house for a moment. ‘That’s what I wanted,’ she replied and settled back in her seat.

He threw her a puzzled glance. ‘Aren’t you going to call then?’

She shrugged. ‘What, at this ungodly hour? Patience, my dear, Just a few more minutes.’

The upstairs curtain twitched about twenty minutes later, but she waited a little while longer before throwing open her door and climbing out of the car, with Hayden following at her heels like a reluctant spaniel.

Hunched forward against squalls of rain, they made their way to the front door. A black cat ran across the narrow concrete path in front of them and Kate chuckled.

‘How appropriate,’ she said. ‘Maybe Lilith’s ghost is out here somewhere, watching us.’

The smell of frying bacon issued from behind the door as she raised the heavy iron knocker. She waited and was just about to knock again when the door opened, and a woman peered out. She was barefoot with a knee-length, blue and yellow patterned dressing gown wrapped around her.

'Good heavens, Sergeant Lewis,' the woman exclaimed. 'Why on earth are you calling at this hour?'

'Hello, Mrs Truly,' Kate said. 'Can we come in?'

The door opened wider and Kate glimpsed the bare feet of a figure standing at the top of the stairs.

'Tell Mr Trimble there's no need to be shy,' Kate said. 'He can come down now.'

Deborah Truly seemed too taken aback to object as Kate, followed by Hayden, stepped into the hallway.

'Mr Trimble?' Kate called up the stairs. 'I do believe your bacon is burning.'

Deborah Truly emitted a gasp and ran back towards the kitchen as a familiar figure began a slow descent of the stairs.

Ralph Trimble was dressed in nothing but a pair of shorts. His muscular torso was covered in tattoos.

'This is totally out of order,' he said. 'We were—'

'Just about to have breakfast,' Kate cut in. 'Yes, I know, but I'm afraid this won't wait. Mind if we, er, adjourn to somewhere where we can talk?'

He shrugged. 'Can I get some clothes on first?'

'Might be a good idea,' she said, adding mischievously, 'though I was just admiring your tattoos.'

'Army,' he muttered with a scowl. 'Long time ago.' He turned and clomped heavily back up the stairs.

Ten minutes later, with the bacon going cold on the grill, they were all seated around a small kitchen table.

'What is all this about?' Deborah Truly asked sharply in a tone of righteous indignation. 'I've just lost my husband, and this is just too much while I'm still grieving.'

'Grieving?' Kate echoed. 'Is that what you call it? And with poor old Jacob not yet in his grave.'

'How dare you!'

'Oh, come on, Mrs Truly, don't play the affronted innocent with me. Tell me, how long you two have been having an affair?'

Truly swallowed hard.

'We — we aren't,' she replied, a tremble in her voice now. 'Mr Trimble was sleeping in the spare room. He — he offered to stay the night because I was nervous here on my own.'

'That's right, Sergeant,' he snapped. 'So, you're out of order.'

'Am I?' Kate murmured. 'Funny that when I was last here you were doing your Good Samaritan act then too — looking after the house I believe you said, while Mrs Truly was at the hospital with her late husband.'

'He was,' Deborah Truly exclaimed.

'No, he wasn't, my love. He answered the door with his trousers undone, claiming he had fallen asleep on the settee.'

'Which I had,' Trimble cut in.

'No you hadn't, Mr Trimble, and Mrs Truly really should have avoided the temptation of lifting a corner of the curtain to see who was calling, because I saw her face appear at the window as I was getting into my car. That's what aroused my suspicions, which I came here this morning to confirm.'

'Suspicions about what?' Trimble demanded, abandoning all attempt at denial. 'That we were having it off? So what? There's no law against it, is there?'

'My husband was a difficult man to live with, Sergeant,' Deborah Truly put in quickly. 'He could be quite nasty at times and we had grown apart. Ralph and I—'

'We're not here to question you about your love life,' Kate cut in, 'unsavoury as it might be, but it does show motive.'

'Motive? Whatever do you mean?'

'For your husband's murder, Mrs Truly.'

'Murder?' she gasped. 'I didn't murder him!'

'No,' Hayden said quietly, 'Mr Trimble did — as he also murdered PC West.'

Trimble snorted derisively, apparently unshaken. 'What absolute rubbish. That old witch woman did for both of them. Everyone knows that.'

Kate shook her head. 'That's what you tried to make it look like. It was all part of your poorly conceived plan to get rid of Jacob, so that Deborah was free to marry you.'

Trimble sprang to his feet, his face contorted with anger and his fists clenched. 'That's a lie and you know it. I looked after the Rev Truly because I believed in him, and I did my best to help him.'

'Oh, you helped him all right,' Kate said. 'Helped him to believe that the attacks on the church and the break-in here were the work of a vulnerable old lady with a mental problem. You must have been delighted when Lilith first turned up in the village claiming to be a witch, and then put her roots down in that shack of hers out on the Levels. It was just what the doctor — or the sexton in this case — ordered.

'Lilith played right into your hands with her drunken antics in the village, didn't she? So, then your tiny brain came up with the plan of carrying out a few attacks on the church, so she would get the blame. You told me yourself that you went with Jacob Truly to see Lilith and remonstrate with her over her anti-Christian behaviour, but that she had laughed at you, showing you the rag dolls and saying PC West and the Rev Truly were cursed and would die soon. What you didn't say was what you did after that visit. You see, when Hayden here and myself checked out the shack a second time, I heard someone in the undergrowth and thought it was Lilith watching us. But it wasn't, was it? It was you. You had just been back there to steal the dolls and some of the poison hemlock you had seen in a jar on the shelf, intending to mix it with the loose tea leaves in both your victims' tea caddies. You got out of the place just in the nick of time as we arrived.'

'I did nothing of the sort.'

She ignored his denial. 'And right at the start, after you had trashed the church the night we were first called to the scene, you were also responsible for digging up poor Tom Sharpe's body, stealing his skull and planting it in Lilith's shack, in the hope that we would find it when we went to see her.'

'You've got a vivid imagination, Sergeant,' Trimble sneered, his face still flushed and angry. 'The whole thing's a pack of lies.'

'Is it? Well, not long after that last job, I started thinking about the likelihood of Lilith being responsible for the vandalism. You see, in my book, it just wasn't feasible for an old woman in her seventies, an alcoholic who needed a stick for support, to be able to do all the things she was supposed to have done. For example, carting a tin of black paint into the nave and crouching down to paint a hexagram on the floor, as well as desecrating the altar by sticking a large goat's head on it and splashing blood everywhere — presumably from another receptacle, which she would have had to carry in with the goat's head and the tin of paint.'

Trimble opened his mouth to speak, but she gave him no opportunity. 'And then, after all that, to have the strength and energy to dig up a three-hundred-year-old grave and steal a skull from it. And where would she have got the tools from for that — the spade, the fork or whatever? There was no trace of any tools at her shack, and you yourself told me there are none kept at the church, only at your house.'

'None of this suggests Ralph had anything to do with the vandalism, and it certainly doesn't prove he murdered anyone,' Deborah Truly said, a note of desperation creeping into her voice.

'No, it doesn't,' Trimble said. 'And why would I want to kill PC West? He'd done me no harm.'

'Because you wanted to test the strength of the hemlock,' Hayden said, 'and ensure that Truly's death would be seen in the light of a vendetta by Lilith against the people who had given her grief. You were particularly conscious of the fact that awkward questions might be asked of you when it emerged from the post-mortems that both the deceased were the victims of poisoning, and you wanted to lessen the risk of ending up as the prime suspect.'

'Rubbish. If that were the case, how could I have been sure that either West or Jacob would actually drink the poisoned tea in the first place?'

'Easy,' Kate continued. 'You regularly associated with West at parochial church council meetings, and probably visited his home, which is how you were aware he kept his back door key under the mat — and you knew that he had a passion for loose-leaf tea and didn't drink anything else. Furthermore, you also knew that Jacob Truly liked his tea too, but that Deborah hated the stuff and drank only coffee, so there was no risk of Jacob expecting her to join him in a cuppa.

'In fact, you thought your plan was foolproof, but it was actually full of holes. It was conceivable — just — that Lilith could have found PC West's key under the rear door mat and slipped into the house to poison the tea caddy and leave the incriminating rag doll behind, but it was a different kettle of fish where the Manse was concerned.

'Okay, so the break-in itself was plausible, though how a so-called "crazy old woman" would have known to tape up the glass in the door to deaden the sound of it breaking is a little curious. But there is no way Lilith could have reached the curtain rail to hang up the doll and there is no indication that she used a chair for the purpose. And how is it, Mr Trimble, that, according to you, she was "scuttling," I believe you called it, along the lane outside when you arrived in response to the vicar's telephone call?

'Presumably, it would have taken the Rev Truly at least five to ten minutes to come downstairs after hearing the noises, assess the situation and phone you. Then you would have had to pull on some clothes and rush from your house to the Manse. Though you live quite close, all this must have taken you ten to fifteen minutes at least, on top of the time Rev Truly took before he rang you. Yet, according to you, Lilith was still there, in the lane. That just doesn't ring true. Why would someone who has just committed a burglary remain on the scene afterwards for, at the very least, a further fifteen to twenty minutes instead of making off immediately afterwards?'

'Maybe the daft old cow wanted us to know it was her?' Trimble retorted, his respectable Christian persona forgotten.

'Perhaps,' Kate agreed, 'but what you don't know, Mr Trimble, is that on the night of the break-in at the Manse, I followed Lilith to the old, derelict Yardley's Cider Farm just an hour or so before the report of the break-in at the Manse was reported to the police. She was on foot and would therefore have had to walk over two and a half miles to the Manse after giving me the slip, carry out the burglary and leave the property, all within that time. Now, I have walked that route myself and it even took a young, fit person like me twenty-eight minutes. But Lilith was far from fit and it would have taken her considerably longer, which means there is no way she could have carried out the burglary within the time frame in question.'

'You calling me a liar?'

'Yes, Mr Trimble, I am. A liar and a murderer. You see, you rather gave yourself away when we spoke at the front door here after Jacob Truly's death. You made the point that poisoning someone with hemlock was a wicked thing to do. The thing is, I never told you that PC West and Jacob Truly had died from hemlock poisoning. There was only one person, apart from the investigation team, who would have known poison hemlock was involved, and that was the murderer.'

Trimble swallowed, his Adam's apple moving up and down. 'I must have read it in the newspapers.'

Kate shook her head. 'That information was never given out — I made a point of checking. No mention was made of hemlock at all, merely that the police regarded the two deaths as suspicious.'

'You're talking a load of bollocks,' Trimble said. 'You'll never get a conviction on what you've got.'

Kate sighed. 'Oh, I think we will, Mr Trimble. '*And* for the murder of ex-Detective Inspector Ted Roscoe.'

'Roscoe? I don't even know any Ted Roscoe.'

'Oh, you wouldn't know his name, as it has not yet been released to the news media. When you hit him over the head and left him in the rhyne to drown, he was just one of two witnesses,' Kate neglected to mention the fact that Luke Cobb would be unable to confirm anything, 'who saw you and the Rev Truly arrive in the vicar's black Range Rover, which is now parked in the driveway here, then burn down Lilith's home in the hope that she was inside.'

'What?' Deborah Truly blurted out. 'Good grief, Ralph, you didn't tell me you did that as well.'

'Shut it, you silly bitch,' he snarled and her hand shot to her mouth as she realised, too late, the implication of her outburst.

Kate smiled. 'Yes, Mrs Truly, I'm afraid he did. You see, Ralph here wound your husband up about Lilith to such an extent that he decided he would have to wreak God's vengeance on her, and Mr Trimble had no choice but to go along with the good vicar, having unintentionally set the ball rolling with his staged attacks on the church. I think your husband was a religious fanatic. He wouldn't have viewed it as a criminal act but God's just retribution. Unfortunately for the pair of them, however, Ted Roscoe was following up on an entirely unrelated investigation in the area that night and, as I've already said, he witnessed the whole thing. So, he too had to go.'

Deborah Truly buried her face in her hands, sobbing.

Kate studied Trimble fixedly. 'What did you use to smack Roscoe over the head with, Mr Trimble, a rock?'

'I didn't do anything. I only know about him from the papers and there was a big story about this guy's body being found, so it was common knowledge to most of the village.'

'There was quite extensive coverage, I agree, but very few details were released, and I'm afraid you gave yourself away there too.'

Kate pulled out her pocketbook and flicked through it until she found what she was looking for.

'If you remember, you mentioned Mr Roscoe being found face-down in a rhyne, close to where Lilith lived, and that Lilith probably — and I quote, "crept up behind him in the dark and gave him a belt, knocking him into the rhyne . . . that's how he got that bang on the head." The thing is, none of that information was released to the media, except the fact that he was found drowned in a rhyne. For that reason, the story the media reported made no mention of where he was found, that he was face-down or that he had been struck on the head. As with the poison hemlock, only the murderer could have known the details you provided.'

He snorted. 'Your word against mine that I said anything like that, and I'll deny it anyway.'

'You forget, I was there too,' Hayden said.

Trimble shrugged and gave a brief smirk, apparently having recovered from his earlier dismay. 'Okay, two against one, but it still doesn't prove anything. You've only got a few written notes taken from memory to rely on and they can be disputed.'

'Oh, I don't know,' she replied. 'Maybe you have a point, but I don't think Mrs Truly will be happy about being jointly charged with you for three murders.'

Kate's remark produced the expected reaction from Deborah Truly. She raised her head quickly, her crocodile tears almost dry on her cheeks and a harder expression on her face now.

'I'm not going down for what you did,' she said coldly, glaring at Trimble.

'Quiet!' he snarled.

'It — it was all your idea to kill PC West,' she said, 'and — and poor Jacob. I didn't know anything about it until you'd done it.'

'You were in on it from the start,' Trimble shouted, the veins on his temples standing out. 'You wanted Jacob dead as much as me.'

'That's enough!' Kate rapped, jumping to her feet. 'I must caution both of you, that—'

But Deborah Truly was now hysterical and wouldn't be silenced. 'It was all your idea,' she shrieked. 'I knew nothing about it until afterwards.' She stared desperately at Kate. 'Listen to me! He only told me what he'd done after Jacob had died — that he'd been to the museum and found out all about witchcraft and the woman who was burned to death in the old days, and that he had vandalised the church and stolen some hemlock from the witch woman's shack to poison Jacob's tea and make it look like she'd done it. I didn't know about any of this until Jacob was dead, I swear it—'

'Liar!' Trimble was on his feet now, his face almost unrecognisable in his rage. He made a lurch for Deborah.

Hayden reacted immediately. His fist hit Trimble squarely in the face, sending him crumbling to the floor just as Kate pulled Deborah back out of harm's way.

Then Kate was on her personal radio, and within seconds the front door could be heard, crashing back against the wall, and heavy boots thumping along the hallway.

The two burly policemen she had earlier detailed to be within call had Trimble flat on his face even as he was trying to climb back on his feet, and there followed the distinctive "snap" of handcuffs being applied.

Kate took hold of Deborah Truly firmly by the arm, her face grim.

'You are both under arrest for the murders of Edward West, Jacob Truly and Edward Roscoe,' she said, as Trimble was hauled back onto his feet, and this time she was able to issue the full caution, without interruption.

'But I had nothing to do with it,' Deborah Truly pleaded. 'It was all his idea.'

Kate threw her a contemptuous glance. 'Tell that to the jury,' she said, 'and pray that they are more naive than me.'

AFTER THE FACT

'So, it's all over?' Hayden remarked later that evening. 'Game, set and match.'

Kate kicked off her shoes and smiled wearily. She settled into a corner of the settee as he stoked up the fire.

'Seems that way — finally,' she said. 'Percival told me Crouch made a deal with Ansell that may earn him brownie points at his trial, with the privilege of vulnerable status in stir, which should prevent Coleman's thugs getting to him. He has made a full statement, admitting to Lilith's murder and fully implicating Coleman in the hit. This has been supported by Coleman's girlfriend, the lovely, venomous Linda, who really has it in for him after what he did to her. It appears she was pretty good at eavesdropping and knows enough about the criminal activities of our Mr Havana to have him put away for life, even without a conviction for Lilith's murder.'

'The chances of Trimble being convicted for the other two murders is a bit iffy, though, don't you think?' Hayden said. 'After all, there was no conclusive evidence, just your hypothesis, the inadvertent admission of Trimble himself and the allegations of Deborah Truly, which they could easily contest in court.'

Kate smiled. 'Except that I understand from SOCO that they have matched two of Trimble's prints to the inside of Eddie West's tea caddy, which was a funny place for them to be, especially as they were right near the bottom, and a search of his address has produced a nice tin full of what I have every reason to believe will turn out to be poison hemlock. Trimble will have a job explaining those things away, so I think that under the circumstances we are home and dry with a prosecution.'

There was the pop of a cork as Hayden opened a fresh bottle of red wine.

'Excellent news,' he acknowledged. 'But how did Ansell take your "go it alone" initiative with Truly and Trimble?'

She shook her head in puzzlement. 'Do you know, he never even commented on it at the briefing, just stared at me with that icy gaze of his and smiled.'

Hayden poured some wine into two large glasses and grunted. 'Don't like the sound of that. He's not the forgiving type.'

'I suppose he couldn't really have had a go at me, since you and I delivered the goods. No doubt he'll take the credit for it with the Chief, as usual.'

'Maybe, but I should watch your back in future. You've made a dangerous enemy there, and that man never forgives or forgets.'

She raised both eyebrows as she took the glass from him. 'In future? Does that mean you agree I still have a future with the police? You don't expect me to come with you to jolly old Berkshire?'

He looked embarrassed and handed her a crumpled piece of paper. 'An email I got this morning on my phone,' he said. 'It seems my old school chum has been pipped at the post. Another former pupil has been appointed to the position I was interested in.'

Kate nodded slowly, making a point of not crowing. 'I can't say I'm sorry, Hayd,' she said quietly. 'But where does that leave us?'

'Leave us?' he echoed.

'Yes, you're plainly unhappy about the job and want to move on, so what are you going to do now?'

He frowned and sipped some wine while she waited anxiously for him to say something. Then suddenly his face split into a big, good-natured grin. 'I'm afraid you're stuck with me now, old girl,' he replied, 'warts and all.'

There was a mischievous glint in her eyes as she set her wine glass down on the table.

'Then maybe we should celebrate,' she said.

'Celebrate? I thought we were already doing that. This special bottle of wine cost me a fortune, I'll have you know.'

'The wine can wait,' she said, pulling her sweater up over her head. 'I have a different sort of celebration in mind — and it doesn't cost a thing.'

Crossing the room, she threw her arms around his neck in a passionate embrace and soon they were totally engrossed in each other as the fire crackled and spat in the big iron grate just feet away.

And as they lost themselves in each other, out on the marsh, the tendrils of white mist curled upwards from the waterlogged ground and the phantasmal, elfin fires began their strange, ethereal dance.

THE END

ALSO BY DAVID HODGES

DETECTIVE KATE HAMBLIN MYSTERY SERIES

Book 1: MURDER ON THE LEVELS
Book 2: REVENGE ON THE LEVELS
Book 3: FEAR ON THE LEVELS
Book 4: KILLER ON THE LEVELS
Book 5: SECRETS ON THE LEVELS
Book 6: DEATH ON THE LEVELS
Book 7: POISON ON THE LEVELS
Book 8: WITCH FIRE ON THE LEVELS

FREE KINDLE BOOKS

Please join our mailing list for free Kindle books and new releases, including crime thrillers, mysteries, romance and more.

www.joffebooks.com

Thank you for reading this book. If you enjoyed it please leave feedback on Amazon or Goodreads, and if there is anything we missed or you have a question about then please get in touch. The author and publishing team appreciate your feedback and time reading this book.

We hate typos too but sometimes they slip through. Please send any errors you find to corrections@joffebooks.com. We'll get them fixed ASAP. We're very grateful to eagle-eyed readers who take the time to contact us.

Printed in Great Britain
by Amazon

48829939R00182